Mary Ann Chulick

All Creatures Great and... Dead

Cerridwen Press

To Eddie,
Remembering the fun time we had at at RT 2008.
Love you!
Mary Ann Chulick

What the critics are saying...

5 Lips "A fascinating and convoluted read, *All Creatures Great and…Dead* provides one of the finest essentials in suspense fiction: a mystery plot and subplots that no reader will be able to piece out before the final astonishing denouement. […] The characters are delineated in depth, and their emotional involvements and entanglements will have the reader "ooh-ing" and "aah-ing" right along through the pages to the end, and then wishing the book hadn't finished. *All Creatures Great and…Dead* is one for the Keeper Shelf, folks."

~ *Two Lips Reviews*

4 Stars "This book truly is a murder mystery with everyone of its characters suspect. I loved how this story was penned, it throws in plenty of red herrings. […] Ms. Chulick has written an enjoyable story that encompasses mystery and romance, one that will leave readers cheering at finally solving the crime and a happily ever after for its hero and heroine."

~ *ECataRomance Reviews*

3 Angels "Ms. Chulick kept me on the edge of my seat trying to guess who the murder was, will JayBee and her sister be able to stop Angel's ex-husband before he hurts one or both of them, and will JayBee and Travis overcome all the obstacles in the way of their relationship developing further? I enjoyed *All Creatures Great and...Dead* and look forward to reading more by this author." ~ *Fallen Angel Reviews*

A Cerridwen Press Publication

www.cerridwenpress.com

All Creatures Great and…Dead

ISBN 9781419957338

Edited by Helen Woodall.
Cover art by Elphaba.

This book printed in the U.S.A. by Jasmine-Jade Enterprises, LLC.

Electronic book Publication May 2007
Trade paperback Publication March 2008

Cerridwen Press is an imprint of Ellora's Cave Publishing, Inc.®

Also by Mary Ann Chulick

Game Time

About the Author

My first serious attempt at creative writing occurred in eighth grade, when my best friend and I tried to write a sequel to Gone with the Wind. We soon moved on to original historicals, fantasies, and science fiction novels, and I realized I had found an all-consuming interest.

Joining RWA and my local chapter, NEORWA, has been a wonderful experience. Five of my novels have finaled in or won RWA chapter contests. The support from my critique group has been very important to me.

Many years of working at a law publishing company, where I index the Laws of Ohio, Kentucky and Indiana, gave me an interest in legal matters pertaining to children--an interest which has found its way into several of my novels. I enjoy fixing up my 1920s house, playing with my two black lab-type dogs, and drawing my characters. Although my husband died in 2005, he enjoyed my novels and always encouraged my writing.

Mary Ann welcomes comments from readers. You can find her website and email address on her author bio page at www.cerridwenpress.com.

Tell Us What You Think

We appreciate hearing reader opinions about our books. You can email us at Comments@EllorasCave.com.

ALL CREATURES GREAT AND...DEAD

Dedication

Dedicated to my husband, Joseph Walter Chulick (1966-2005), who listened to me read the book aloud, made several great suggestions and always encouraged my writing.

Trademarks Acknowledgement

The author acknowledges the trademarked status and trademark owners of the following wordmarks mentioned in this work of fiction:

Bacitracin: UnitedHealth Group Incorporated

Beck's: Brauerei Beck GmbH & Co.

Big Mac: McDonald's Corporation

BMW: Bayerische Motoren Werke

Brooks Brothers: Retail Brand Alliance, Inc.

Carrie: Copyright held by Stephen King

Cat Fancy: Fancy Publications, Inc.

Children's Tylenol: Tylenol Company

Civic: American Honda Motor Co., Inc.

Coach: Coach, Inc.

Corvette: General Motors Corporation

Crown Royal: The Crown Royal Company

Denny's: DFO, Inc.

Disney World: Disney Enterprises, Inc.

Dockers: Levi Strauss & Co.

Earthlink: Earthlink, Inc.

Elmo: Sesame Workshop Corporation

Embassy Suites: G & S Hotel Services

ER: NBC

Federal Express: Federal Express Corporation

Ford Explorer: Ford Motor Company

Ford Focus: Ford Motor Company

Ford: Ford Motor Company

Ford Mustang: Ford Motor Company

G.I. Joe: Hasbro, Inc.

Happy Meal: McDonald's Corporation

Harley Davidson: H-D Michigan, Inc

Chapter One

Between the ages of seven and twelve, Travis Kellman had a favorite daydream, the murder of his stepmother. Sometimes he shot her with his grandfather's deer rifle. Occasionally he shut her in the "punishment closet" until she starved to death. Most often he left her screaming, her room in flames, while he ran safely from the burning house.

Although she usually spoke to him in honeyed tones, Travis had quickly taken her measure. She adored his father, liked his older brother Pete and hated him.

Her antipathy was returned.

Now that he was close to thirty years old, if anyone had reminded him of those forgotten childish fantasies, he would have been startled and upset. As a veterinarian, he was all about saving lives. He'd been known to give clients the sharp side of his tongue if they brought in a healthy pet for a "convenience" euthanization. Just today, he'd had an argument with the Sullivans about their three-legged dog and had wound up taking Queenie home with him rather than putting her to death.

Queenie was a good dog, less high-strung than many Golden Retrievers. He'd spent two days at the clinic after she'd been hit by the car, setting an alarm to check on her every three hours. He fondled her ears as he drove slowly around Priam Town Square. The crisp scent of fall leaves wafted through on the breeze. The maple trees on the square, turning a beautiful flame color, shaded the slate sidewalks. People talked about New England falls, but in Travis' opinion, nothing compared to autumn in southern Ohio.

Taking the turn for Crocker Road, he headed out of town, driving a few minutes until he reached the welcome sight of his own fields. He slowed the pickup as he came to the gravel drive of Creekside Farm. "You're out of your mind," his stepmother had told him when he bought the place. "Why in the world would you want a run-down country farm? For heaven's sake, Travis, it'll cost you a fortune to heat that house all winter!" She had been right about the heating bills, but nothing he had bought had ever made him happier. His spirits lifted as he came in sight of his newly painted yellow farmhouse. An old black milk can stood on the low front stoop. Today it was filled with ornamental grasses and dried seedpods. A new touch by Katie, no doubt.

He drove around to the back and opened Queenie's door. She hesitated, intimidated by the jump to the ground. He stood back. "Come on, girl! Come on, Queenie!" She finally got up her courage and jumped down, awkward on three legs. "Good girl!" She frisked around him and followed him in the back door.

Travis glanced around the old-fashioned country kitchen. Worn linoleum and faded wallpaper notwithstanding, it was still good to be home. He took a deep breath, detecting garlic and onions. It always smelled great in the kitchen when Katie did the cooking.

His half sister Katie stood at the kitchen sink, washing chicken. She turned when she heard him, smiling. "Hi, Travis. Maman is here already. We were fighting, so she went out to the parlor."

"Great," he muttered. "I thought she was coming with Dad."

"No, he's going to be late. Why did you bring that dog with you?"

"Tell you later. Are you going to fry that chicken?"

"You bet. I know it's your favorite."

"Thanks for arranging this dinner, Katie."

She gave him a quick grin. "I thought it was about time you and Dad made up."

The kitchen door swung open and Travis' stepmother came into the room. She was her usual perfect self, dressed in a British-style tweed suit. Her love of all things French had recently been replaced by a fascination with English Country style. "Good afternoon, Travis," she said, offering her cheek, which he dutifully kissed. "Did you really wear that outfit to work?"

He looked down at his jeans and flannel shirt. "I wear a lab coat in the office, Alicia." At least he no longer had to call her by that ridiculous Frenchified version of "Mama" now that he was a grown man.

She sniffed. "Your father was always impeccably dressed at work. A starched white shirt and a tie, always. I'm sure he hoped you would keep up the Kellman standards when he helped you buy the practice."

"He never explained there was a dress code," said Travis. Katie giggled.

Alicia treated the remark as she did any conversation of which she disapproved—she ignored it. "You need a haircut, too," she told him.

Katie rolled her eyes. "Maman, stop fussing." She gazed at him for a long moment, then nodded. "Travis, you look fine."

He patted Katie's shoulder. "You do, too." In fact, she looked exceptionally pretty today, her cheeks pink in the warmth of the kitchen, a half-smile lingering on her face as though she were thinking of some pleasant secret. Katie often lamented that she wasn't beautiful like Alicia, with her porcelain-angel beauty. "I'm just so boring," Katie often complained. "Brown hair, brown eyes—so blah."

"Brown freckles, too," Travis would tease her, but privately, he thought his little sister had nothing to complain about. Thank God she wasn't like her mother, either in looks or personality.

Queenie took a long, noisy drink from the cats' water bowl and then turned to their food bowl. Travis let her eat a few mouthfuls before he took it away and put it on the kitchen table.

"Isn't that a lot of chicken for the four of us?" he asked.

Katie glanced guiltily at her mother, who tried to change the subject by saying, "I don't know what's going on with your father lately. He knows we always go away in December, but he refuses to make any plans this year."

Travis had a suspicion of what was up, but let himself be distracted. "Maybe he's thinking he won't want to leave town if he gets elected to the school board."

"When he gets elected, he won't take office until January," said Alicia.

"There'll be plenty to do before then," said Travis. "You should see my list of things to do, if they vote me in."

Alicia gave him the look, the expression that had had the power to stop bad behavior cold when he had been a child. "Travis, this is so unnecessary. How can you run your practice and be on the school board? And what makes you think you know anything about running a school district, anyway? You have no children in the school here, you have no experience—"

"You forget, I've had some vitally important experience."

"What are you talking about?"

"I was a pupil in the Priam schools myself. That's experience Dad never had."

Katie grinned as she began to dip chicken into batter, but Alicia looked angry. "Travis, I want to speak to you in private."

He followed his stepmother into the parlor, where she chased away two cats and ostentatiously brushed off the antique velvet sofa before seating herself. "Honestly, I don't know how you can stand these animals in the house, getting their hair all over everything."

Used to this type of little pinprick, he didn't answer that, just settled into the big easy chair across from her, stretching his legs out. It always felt good to sit after standing most of the day.

"What did you want?"

She leaned forward, clasping her hands together and looking at him intently. "Travis Jeffrey, I want you to withdraw your candidacy."

"Alicia—"

She raised a hand for silence. "No, hear me out. I know why you're doing this and it's not a good reason. I think you'll admit that if you think about it."

"Oh? What's my reason, according to you?"

She looked impatient. "You're trying to show your father you're just as good as he is, that you can beat him at his own game."

"I'm not running just to beat Dad. That's ridiculous."

"I happen to know Ralph Peterson talked to you about it months ago and you didn't do anything until after your father made his announcement."

Travis shifted uncomfortably. "I wasn't sure I'd have enough time to do a good job." He thought of all the long dull evenings at home with nothing to do after he prepared supper and read a few professional articles. Getting involved with the local school board would give him something new to think about, as well as doing some good for the community.

Better to do that than sit alone in the parlor, brooding about Georgia.

"This is something your father wants very much. You should respect that and not ruin things for him."

"Why do you care so much whether Dad gets elected?" he asked. "Usually you hate things that take him away from you.

Didn't you convince him to retire ten years before he was ready?"

"Well..." Alicia looked away, sounding uncertain for the first time. "He needs something to do, something to interest him and keep him busy. Men need to keep busy or they just get into mischief."

"You make him sound like he's six years old," Travis said.

"Believe me, I know what I'm talking about. That's why I'm asking you to reconsider your decision to run for the school board."

"Now, look here, Alicia." Travis straightened and looked her in the eye. "I don't know why you're making this your business, but I'd advise you to stay out of it. Dad hasn't asked me to withdraw."

She glared at him, her gray eyes narrowing. "And I'd advise you not to let that be your final decision. I know something about you that would ruin your chances. And I will reveal it if you don't agree to withdraw."

Travis stared back at her, hardly able to believe he'd heard her correctly. "Are you trying to blackmail me?"

She pursed her lips, looking down for a long moment. "Blackmail—such an ugly word. I think 'persuade' is much nicer."

"I can't believe what you're doing! Good Lord, I'm your own stepson!"

"You're getting in the way of what your father wants."

"How about what I want?" He could tell by her forbidding expression that she was unmoved. "Anyway, what the hell is this big secret you know about me?"

"I'm not going to say anything else."

Travis frowned. "It's not much of a threat if you won't tell me what it is. You're bluffing."

"Do I bluff? Did I bluff when I told you to settle down or you wouldn't go to Disney World with the rest of the family?"

His hands clenched into fists. One of his clearest childhood memories was watching from his grandfather's window while the car pulled out of the driveway.

"Know something, Alicia? You were a real bitch of a stepmother."

"Wait'll you see what a bitch I can be, if you don't withdraw from the election. You think about it and think hard." She stood up, turning to go, then took a step closer to him. Lowering her voice, she said, "If I tell what I know, your whole life will change."

Angry words sprang to mind, but he clamped his lips tightly. He stared after her, fighting to regain control as she returned to the kitchen. Twenty-eight years old and he still felt frustrated and miserable when he had to be around her for any length of time. He was an adult. She no longer had the power to punish him. Why did he always let her get to him?

Fancy came creeping out from behind the sofa and jumped into his lap. She was a tiny white cat with a loud purr. Stroking her silky fur absently, he thought about his past, wondering what the hell Alicia thought she knew about him.

Like everyone else in the world, he had done things he was ashamed of…

His reverie was interrupted by a knock on the front door. Probably his father had arrived—he always insisted on coming to the front door even though he knew it stuck. Travis put the cat down gently and went to the door, struggling with it until he finally wrenched it open.

He had had a hint before, because of his sister's guilty look, but still it was a shock to see his brother Peter. And worse than a shock to see that Peter's wife, Georgia, was there too, hanging back behind his brother.

"Jesus, you still haven't had that door fixed?" Peter demanded.

An apology would have been nice, but Travis knew his brother well enough not to expect it. "I planed it, but it swelled again this summer." He couldn't believe he was standing here talking to his brother about the damned door, after a whole year of silence. He'd imagined a face-to-face meeting many times, sometimes longing for a reconciliation, sometimes fantasizing about punching him out.

"So, are you going to let us in?" Peter asked, a hint of challenge in his voice.

Travis stared into his brother's blue eyes, trying to reconcile his lingering anger with the love he had always felt for Peter, his best buddy throughout his childhood. Memories flashed through his brain—Peter teaching him how to swim, building a fort with him by the creek, helping him dissect a pig for anatomy class.

"Oh, hell." Travis put his hand out. Peter grabbed it and they shook. Then in another moment, they embraced, pounding each other's backs.

"I still can't believe you got taller than me, little brother," Peter said with a grin. Travis, at six foot one, had a good four inches over Peter in height and weighed about sixty pounds more. Peter was their slender, dapper father all over again, while Travis resembled the grandfather he was named for.

"Yes, you're taller and broader than Peter," Georgia said, her eyes flickering over his big frame. "You look like you've been working out, Travis."

"I try to keep in shape," he answered, trying not to show that her comment had pleased him. It'll never be this tough again, he thought and took her hand for as brief a moment as courtesy would allow.

"Father here yet?" Peter asked as he and his wife followed Travis into the house.

"He's running late."

Alicia and Katie came out of the kitchen, Katie looking anxiously from Peter to Travis. Peter kissed his half sister's cheek. "You were right, he let us in."

"You could have warned me," Travis murmured to Katie.

"You're not mad, are you?"

He shook his head. "Let's go ahead and eat. That fried chicken smells terrific."

"I think we ought to wait for your father," Alicia said.

"He said to start without him," Katie answered.

Alicia looked displeased, but led the way to the dining room. Travis followed his sister into the kitchen and took a bottle of white Zinfandel out of the refrigerator. He opened it with a corkscrew as Queenie watched with interest. "There's nothing here for a dog," he told her, but she trailed behind him as he came back into the dining room.

Katie came out a few seconds later, a platter of fried chicken in one hand and a big bowl of mashed potatoes in the other. Travis hastened to take the heavy platter away from her and set it on the table in front of Peter. But his brother's attention was on Queenie.

"Isn't that Bob Sullivan's dog?"

"Yes. The Sullivans left her with me today. They wanted her euthanized." Travis took more serving plates from Katie.

"Then why isn't she dead?" Peter asked.

"I can kill things in a minute, but once they're dead I can't bring 'em back." Travis sat down. Queenie, pressing close, leaned against his knee.

"What's that supposed to mean?"

"Well, I hope they might change their minds. Queenie's a great dog." Her tail waved a few times as Travis said her name.

"Jesus, Travis! I know damned well what that means—it means you've adopted another animal. Aren't five cats enough?"

"Seven cats," Travis corrected him quietly.

"Honestly, Peter's absolutely right," said Alicia. "If you take in everyone's unwanted animals, people are going to think you're a patsy. Are you running a veterinary clinic or a no-kill shelter?"

"Not that it's any of your business, but I've euthanized plenty of animals for this town. If there's a few I want to save, that's my privilege." Defiantly, Travis patted Queenie's head.

"If you didn't want to kill things, you should have become a real doctor, like Father wanted," said Peter. He didn't add, "Like me," but everyone caught his implication.

"Isn't one Peter Perfect in the family enough?" Travis snapped, dredging up an old childhood taunt. The brothers glared at each other.

"Guys!" said Katie. "This is supposed to be a reconciliation dinner. Let's not fight, okay?"

Alicia jumped in and began to tell a long, dull story about her garden club. Travis eyed Georgia across the table, wondering if she felt as uncomfortable in his presence as he did in hers. It was impossible to tell by looking at her, she was calmly taking dainty bites of her chicken, her features composed. It seemed to him she was even more beautiful than a year ago. It was almost a physical pain to see her at his dining room table, where he had once hoped to see her every evening.

The front door opened with a bang, causing everyone to jump and Queenie to stand up and bark excitedly.

"It's me!" Robert Kellman called from the parlor. He appeared in the doorway, beaming. "Hello, hello! Alicia, my beauty, you're looking radiant!" He swept to his wife's side and gave her a quick kiss on the lips. "Princess!" He kissed Katie's forehead. "Peter, my boy!" He shook hands with Peter, kissed Georgia's cheek and clapped Travis on the shoulder. "I'm so sorry to be late for our reconciliation dinner. Thank you for hosting it, son," he added to Travis. "Maybe we'll need another one after the election, do you think?" He winked.

"Maybe so," Travis answered with a smile, relieved that his father seemed to have gotten over his anger about the election. "When I win, I'll invite you to my victory party, Dad."

"Keep dreaming, son," his father said, filling a plate with food. "Excellent job, Princess," he told his daughter.

"I was trying to convince Travis to withdraw his candidacy," Alicia said to her husband as he sat down and started eating, "but he's being very stubborn, like always."

"No reason for him to withdraw," said Robert. "He doesn't have a snowball's chance in hell, anyway. Tecumseh County voters are conservative."

"That's true," said Peter. "And you've done a lot for your party, Father."

"Of course I have. I believe in the party that upholds traditional family values. Morals and decency."

"And the Ten Commandments, right?" Travis asked dryly.

"Most people around here support my position," said Robert. "What harm would it do to hang the Ten Commandments in the schools? They're valued by both Jews and Christians."

"Judaism and Christianity aren't the only two religions," said Travis. "Anyway, public schools should be free of religion."

"Oh, but it's fine to teach young people how to have sex and to have gay-lesbian clubs?" Robert demanded.

"Well, whether it is or not, I thought we were talking about the Commandments."

"Just which Commandment do you object to, Travis?" Alicia asked. "The one that goes 'Honor thy father and mother'?"

Travis gave her a dirty look. "Notice the wording. It's 'mother', not 'stepmother'."

Alicia pursed her lips and Robert sighed. Travis got up and began to clear the dirty dishes.

In the kitchen, he took a Sara Lee cake out of the refrigerator, then filled a dishpan with hot water and soap and began washing the dishes. Not the way to be a good host, but right now he didn't think he could take one more minute of his family. It was soothing to carefully wash each plate, rinsing it clean in hot water. It was only when the family came over that he used the china. It had been his mother's—his real mother's. His memories of her were dim—she had died of cancer when he was five years old—but he could recall her setting that china out for some special meal. Alicia had never used it once she took possession of his childhood home. A few years ago, she had dragged it out of a cupboard, intending to donate it to a rummage sale and he had claimed it.

The kitchen door swung open and Katie and Peter came through. "I'm going to show Pete my latest painting," Katie announced. The two of them went out the back door. Katie's apartment and studio were in Travis' barn, thirty feet behind the house. Katie had come to him when she left art college, announcing, "I can't live with Maman one day longer. Do you have room for me at your place?" They had tried to share the house for awhile, but her messiness had driven him crazy. So together they'd remodeled part of the barn, opening out one whole wall and putting in a huge picture window so she could have a light-filled art studio.

Travis heard his father's voice, raised now in anger and an occasional murmur as his stepmother answered. It was time to serve dessert, but he had no desire to go back into that dining room.

The door swung open again and this time Georgia came in. She stood and looked at him for a long moment. "It's not exactly the most comfortable situation in the world, to be left alone out there while those two fight."

"You should have gone out to the barn to see Katie's painting." He held up the glass he was washing, gazing at it intently.

"I wasn't invited. Your sister never had any use for me, you know. I'm surprised she didn't invite Petey over and tell me to stay home."

"She liked you just fine until you jilted me."

"Oh, is that what you call it?" She came a few steps closer, her arms folded under her breasts. "Is that what you tell people, that you were jilted? Do you know how many times I tried to call you?"

"What would have been the use of talking? I caught you in bed with my brother. To me, that was a pretty clear indication you wanted to break our engagement."

"You shouldn't have assumed that." She put her hand on his forearm. "I was trying to get back at you for—for something I'd heard."

"Something you heard? What are you talking about?"

"Oh, it's no good bringing it up now. I'm married to Petey, what's the use of dredging up the past?" Her gold bracelets jangled as she ran a hand through her sun-streaked hair. "Everyone in this family is against me." Her voice sounded as though she were fighting back tears. "Alicia is so cold. Your father never liked me."

Travis recognized the signs. Georgia was working herself into one of her states. Hoping to forestall it, he put his arm around her shoulders. "Now, just calm down." He couldn't help it—he had to ask the question that had been on his mind for months. "You're happy with Pete, aren't you? He's good to you?"

"Yes…I suppose so. When he's around…"

"Is something wrong?"

The words seem to burst out of her. "Travis, I need your help. Please. Don't say no. Promise you'll help me."

He drew back slightly. "You want my help?"

Tears welled in her eyes as she gazed up at him. "Yes—yes—but I can't tell you now. Would you meet me tomorrow after the school board meeting?"

"Why can't Pete help you?"

She shook her head. "I can't tell him about it. Would you at least talk to me? Even if you can't help, maybe you could give me some advice."

He had the feeling he was being maneuvered into something that would be better avoided, but found himself unable to refuse her. "All right."

She smiled. "Oh, Travis, I knew I could count on you." She put her arms around his neck and kissed him, just as the back door opened and Peter stepped in.

"I knew it was a mistake to come over here!" Peter glared at them.

"Petey, don't be silly. I was just thanking Travis for agreeing to help with the Hospital Charity Auction."

Travis blinked at the swift, smooth lie.

Peter's angry expression didn't change. He said to his brother, "Now we know which Commandment it is you disagree with—the one about not coveting another man's wife!"

"Now, look here, Georgie and I were just talking—"

"I don't want to hear your excuses. And don't call her by that ridiculous nickname!" He grabbed his wife's hand. "Come on, we're leaving." They exited through the back door. Georgia looked back once, giving him an apologetic little wave.

Katie looked puzzled as she stepped in. "What happened?"

"You don't want to know," said Travis, handing Katie the cake. "Come on, let's have dessert and get this thing over with." He picked up some small plates and forks and walked into the dining room.

"Where's Dad?" he asked his stepmother, who was sitting by herself, chin in hand.

"We had a tiny little disagreement. He can't bear to lose an argument, so he went storming out." She looked at the Sara Lee box. "Pound cake, Travis? Really, you should know by now, I only like chocolate desserts."

"I meant to go to the bakery in Remus, but I didn't have time, so I had to get what Pooley's had in the freezer case." He wondered why he was apologizing to this woman who had been trying to blackmail him a short time ago. "Besides, this is my favorite."

She looked offended. "Well, perhaps you ought to think about your guests next time, rather than yourself." She tossed her hair back. "I'm going home."

Travis made no attempt to stop her. Katie walked her mother to the door and then returned to the table.

"We should have called this the Irreconcilable Differences Dinner," Katie said, dropping into a chair.

Silently Travis handed her a piece of cake.

Chapter Two

JayBee Hauser yawned and opened the window of the treehouse, scattering birdseed in the tray below. Taking a deep breath of the crisp morning air, she looked up into the maple tree. Some of the leaves had started to turn a lovely bright yellow. She couldn't wait to see the tree in a few weeks, when all the leaves had changed.

She closed the window and stepped back, waiting for the birds to come. It never took them long to find the seed.

She was glad now that she'd let Angel persuade her to move away from Dayton. Priam was a quiet country village, just what the two of them needed after the upsetting events of eighteen months ago. She felt comfortable here. People were friendly without being nosy. There was very little crime and she wasn't afraid to go for a long walk, even at night.

If only poor Angel would settle down and get over her fears.

She smiled as the cardinal, her favorite, alighted on the food tray and pecked at the seed.

"JayBee!" Angel called up the stairs. "Will you get up already? You're going to be late!"

"I'm up!" JayBee yelled back.

"What?"

It was no wonder Angel couldn't hear her. JayBee crawled through the treehouse window, walked the branch and jumped down to the back porch of the house. "I'm up!" JayBee yelled again, coming through the door and into her bedroom.

"Move your butt! It's already eight o'clock!"

JayBee washed her face, brushed her teeth and came down the stairs at breakneck speed.

"What were you doing all that time?" Angel asked. "I heard your alarm go off an hour ago."

"Feeding the birds." JayBee shrugged her arms into the straps of her knapsack and smiled at the other woman. Although Angel was only a year older than JayBee, she wore a perpetually worried expression that made her look ten years older.

Angel sighed, flipping her long blonde hair over her shoulders. "So now you're going to be late over a bunch of dirty sparrows? That's a great example to set for your students."

"I won't be late." JayBee looked around for her purse. "Are you going to go grocery shopping today? I've got the list all ready."

"I'm not sure." Angel's eyes avoided hers. "I may not have time."

It was no use nagging her, JayBee knew that. "Forget it. I'll take care of it after work."

"Good." Angel handed her a hot Poptart wrapped in a paper towel. "Here, don't go on an empty stomach."

JayBee kissed her on the cheek. "Thanks, you're a real sweetheart." She went flying out the front door and quickly down the street, taking large, enthusiastic bites as she went along. Was there anything better than a juicy cherry Poptart in the morning?

The homeroom bell would ring at 8:25. If she walked fast she would make it just in time.

She was just two blocks away from the high school when she heard the meow of a terrified kitten.

*****

Travis stopped by the barn before starting on his morning run. Katie had already been painting for over an hour, but she wasn't happy with the way the work was going and refused to show it to her brother. "I really need to go to Paris," she said. "I think it would give my work a whole new perspective."

Travis had heard her talk about Paris since she was a teenager, so he changed the subject. "I called Bob Sullivan last night. He said it was fine for me to keep Queenie. I think he was relieved she was still alive."

"Do you want to leave her with me today? She'll be good company."

Travis smiled at his sister. "Sure. Thanks." Taking a blue bandanna out of his sweatpants pocket, he folded it into a long rectangle and tied it around his forehead. "Coming to the school board meeting tonight?"

"Yes, I'm coming straight from the restaurant. Maman called to remind me this morning."

"What a great way to wake up."

Katie grinned. "I couldn't believe it when the phone rang at six-thirty. I think she's trying to catch me in bed with a man. But so far she hasn't succeeded."

Travis made no comment. "Don't ask, don't tell" might have been a dubious policy in the armed forces, but he thought it a wise choice between brother and sister, where their love lives were concerned. He was always uncomfortable when she tried to confide in him about various boyfriends, so he refrained from mentioning he had heard a car coming stealthily down the driveway that morning around two a.m. The lights in Katie's studio had gone on for about five minutes, then had gone off.

Travis did some stretches in the yard, then took off down the driveway, turning right onto Crocker Road. If Katie was seeing someone new, perhaps she was finally getting over her last unhappy love affair. She had seen a lot of different fellows in art school, each succeeding one stranger than the last. There had been the one who worked exclusively in unbaked clay and sequins, the one who came for Thanksgiving and fell for Alicia, the tattooed jewelry maker who never spoke…the list went on.

"But none of them really mattered," Katie had once confessed, when they'd been out drinking together. "Only Grayson." And Grayson was a married professor. He and Katie had spent a wonderful month together one summer. Then he had reconciled with his wife. "I don't think I'll ever get over him," she had concluded.

"Best keep away from married men," Travis had told her.

"But they're the most attractive ones."

Travis slowed his pace as he saw something odd up ahead. A neon green knapsack, sitting upright like an alert puppy under a maple tree…

"Damn it, hold still!"

Travis stopped, searching for the source of the voice.

"Come here, you silly little thing!" It was an extremely frustrated feminine voice.

He drew nearer to the big tree and looked up.

"Oh, you startled me!" she said.

Travis drew a deep breath. He had never seen such an enchanting sight in his life—a pointed chin, a little tilted nose and big brown eyes peering down at him through the leaves.

"As long as you're here, do you think you could give me a hand?" she asked.

"Are you stuck?"

"Of course not!" She added, after a moment, "But the kitten might be. I'm not sure. Go over toward the street and clap your hands. Maybe that will scare it toward me."

"That's what this is all about? A kitten?"

"Well, I'm not climbing a tree at this hour of the morning for fun!"

"I thought maybe you were a wood nymph."

She giggled. "A dryad in Dockers? What a concept!"

The kitten meowed loudly. Travis backed off a little and finally spotted it clinging to a thin branch. Its blue eyes were wide and scared.

As she had suggested, he raised his arms and clapped his hands together. But the kitten didn't move.

She sighed impatiently. "You little brat, you just don't know what's good for you!"

Travis heard a lot of rustling. Several brown leaves wafted down on him as the woman tried to climb higher. "Careful!" he said. "I don't think that branch is going to support you—"

He was just quick enough to get under her and brace himself as the branch broke. She tumbled out of the tree and landed against his chest and right arm. Travis managed to stay on his feet and help her steady herself. The kitten, galvanized into movement at last, skittered down the tree trunk and ran off.

She gazed at Travis, concern shining in her big eyes. She was a tall woman, perhaps in her early twenties. "Sorry about falling on you like that. Are you okay?"

"I enjoyed it," was what first came to mind. "I'm fine," he answered. "Good thing I happened along." Absently, he rubbed his upper arm where she'd landed against him.

"Oh, I'm afraid I hurt your arm!" Reaching up, she laid her hand against his biceps. At her soft touch, all his senses sharpened. He was aware of her faint, flowery cologne and the tingle in his arm where her fingers brushed. She could have recited the alphabet in that charming, breathy voice and he would have stood there listening, mesmerized.

"I'm so sorry. I'm not usually that clumsy," she said.

"It's nothing. Don't worry about it." Nothing? It seemed like the nicest thing that had happened to him in weeks.

A twig was caught in her hair. As he disentangled it, he was suddenly aware of her lips, red and slightly parted. He imagined just how he would press a kiss on them, softly and how they would open under his. She leaned a little closer, trustingly.

He drew back, wondering what the hell was wrong with him. He wasn't the kind of man who stole kisses from pretty strangers, however enticing they were. She blinked and brushed her hair behind her ears in a quick gesture. "Did you see what happened to the kitten?" she asked, looking around.

"It came down by itself. They usually do. You find very few kitten skeletons in trees."

"And now I'm going to be late to school over nothing!" She picked up her knapsack. The thought didn't seem to bother her very much, her tone was cheerful. "Well, thanks for catching me!" She hurried off with a jaunty wave.

Late for school! Good Lord, is she a high-school student? Travis stood and watched her rush toward Priam High School. Then he turned and headed back to Crocker Road. He had gone only about a mile, but he didn't want to run any farther today.

Early senility? he asked himself caustically as he pounded along the pavement. Didn't a man have to hit middle age before he found himself lusting after high-school girls? Even if she were a senior, that meant she wasn't more than seventeen years old. Much too young for a man of twenty-eight.

Ever since Georgia had jilted him a year ago, he had tried to put all that out of his life. He had mostly succeeded, except during that one trip to Cincinnati… Well, he wasn't going to think about that now. Seeing Georgia again had awakened feelings he thought he had vanquished. Her arms around his neck, her kiss on his mouth, had brought old appetites to the surface, appetites he had been trying to suppress for a year.

He thought of that pretty face, framed in green leaves and set his mouth.

Not for you, Kellman.

* * * * *

Alicia exited her Lexus just as Travis pulled into a parking space. So, she had been waiting for him. Her glance was coldly critical as he stepped down from the truck. "Is that what you're wearing tonight, Travis Jeffrey?" she asked.

He shrugged his big shoulders out of his lab coat and changed into a corduroy jacket. "I thought I'd let Dad be the suit guy." It was no use competing with his father on the basis of sartorial elegance, he had decided earlier. Robert Kellman always looked like he had just stepped out of a Brooks Brothers catalog, even on informal occasions. Better to wear an everyday shirt and jeans, slightly dressed up with the jacket, a look that might appeal to the farming community more than his father's tailored suit. "Did you want something?"

"I wanted to give you one more chance. Are you planning to make your speech, or are you going to withdraw from the election?"

He waved a sheaf of notes under her nose. "Here's my speech. Hope you enjoy it."

To his surprise, she smiled. "You still think I'm bluffing, don't you?"

"I don't know and I don't care. I guess I wouldn't put it past you to make up some evil gossip about me."

Her sly smile widened. "Oh, I don't have any need to do that—this time." And she turned and walked toward the school, her high heels crunching against the gravel.

Travis didn't move. This time? What the hell did she mean? For a few moments, all he wanted to do was get his hands around her scrawny neck and squeeze. He wasn't a little kid anymore, terrified of her rages and her punishments. He hated her and he could hate like an adult and not like a child.

He'd better calm down if he wanted to go in there, talk to people like a normal person, make a good impression. Taking deep breaths, he let his head drop toward his chest and tried to relax.

The roar of a motorcycle made him look up again. A Yamaha Virago swooped by him and screeched to a stop at the end of the row of vehicles. Sweet machine, Travis thought. He hadn't seen anyone in town with a bike like that. Maybe it was one of this year's new professors from the college. Had to be a young guy, with such a slim back…

Travis watched as the rider dismounted. *Good Lord, it's a woman!* She walked quickly up to the school, pausing on the steps to lift off her helmet. Her red hair spilled out and he realized it was the woman from the tree. He hurried after her.

Ralph Peterson must have been keeping watch for him inside, because he grabbed Travis by the elbow as he came into the gymnasium. "Travis! Thank goodness you're here. Come this way. I've got some people I want you to meet before this thing starts."

Travis had seen a good deal of Ralph in the past two years. Ever since Ralph's wife died, he had been taking in cats. He had four of them right now, all elderly cats who needed much care. Travis estimated he saw Ralph at the clinic at least once a month.

Ralph's cheerful, red-cheeked face, curly white hair and neat goatee had always reminded him of Santa Claus, a slimmed-down Santa with lots of off-season interests, gardening, grandchildren and politics.

"It's such a shame your father's running against you," said Ralph. That drew Travis' attention away from looking for the red-haired woman.

"Why do you say that?"

"He'll be hard to beat. I really expected that old fossil Davis to run again. I know you could have beaten him. The voters are still mad about that business with the typing teacher. But your father," Ralph shook his head, "folks around here think the sun rises and sets on Dr. Kellman."

"We'll have to see how it goes. I know a lot of the farmers since I take some of Doc Henderson's calls. And I think my ideas may appeal more to the college community than my dad's."

Ralph tilted his head, thinking about this. "Yes, I've been trying to think about what you could do to get some attention from the college faculty. The farmers like you, I know that, but they're more in tune with your father's conservative philosophy. When you give your speech, try to tone down the bleeding-heart-liberal stuff, okay?"

Travis nodded. Ralph had made that comment to him at least six times over the last two weeks. He had stuck to practicalities for his talk. But he wasn't planning to hedge his answers if people asked him about his political beliefs. He hated weasel words from politicians.

It was a tough balance, because he wanted to win the election. He wanted to achieve a resounding victory over his father. Sometimes it seemed like his whole life had been a struggle to be remembered, to be noticed. The world had centered around vibrant, brilliant Robert Kellman, the famous surgeon who had saved so many lives. Dr. Kellman, with his beautiful, popular young wife and his older son, the intelligent young man who had so much in common with his father. The son he always introduced with that unmistakable ring of pride in his voice, "This is my oldest child—he's a surgeon, just like I was." Travis wished that sort of pride could be directed his way, even once.

He was sure that winning this election would show his family and everyone else that he was more than a dull, small-town vet.

Ralph led him from group to group, introducing him to the principal of the high school, the current members of the school board and some of the teachers. Tonight's board meeting was open to the public and almost a hundred people had shown up. Travis shook hands and smiled. When he met his clients, he asked about their pets, which went over very well.

It wasn't until he took his seat at the front table that he spotted the redheaded motorcycle rider. She was standing at the back of the room with several other young women, gesturing animatedly. She was even prettier than he remembered, tall and long-legged in blue jeans and motorcycle boots.

Seventeen or eighteen years old was not really such a distance from twenty-eight. Of course he wouldn't date a high-school girl, but if she were a senior, she would be out of school in a mere nine months.

Well, it was a nice fantasy. A woman like that probably already had someone in her life. And even if she didn't, he doubted he could go through that whole thing again. Fall for someone, expect a whole life with them and then get shot down. Once was hard enough, but it had happened to him twice. He wasn't sure he could take it a third time.

The president of the school board leaned over. "Have you met our new phys ed teacher? She's an unusual sort. I think she'll be a breath of fresh air for our students."

"I don't think I know her."

"You're looking right at her—black leather jacket, red hair."

She's a teacher. Not a high-school student. A teacher.

Travis watched with heightened interest as she took a seat near the back.

* * * * *

JayBee hoped she was doing the right thing. The three students had come to her between fourth and fifth period and stated their case eloquently.

"But what made you think of me?" she asked.

That had seemed to be a hard question to answer, judging from the way they looked at each other. "We thought Mr. Souter was going to do it, but then he changed his mind," Miranda volunteered at last. She was in JayBee's first period gym class. JayBee liked her because she was a fierce competitor at every game.

"We figured maybe you'd be open to something new," said Donna. "You know, 'cause you're from the big city."

Dayton's the big city? JayBee wondered.

"Besides," said Miranda, "our gym teacher last year told us all about her phys ed courses in college. She said all the other women were lesbians."

"And we know you live with another woman," Donna chimed in.

Geez, Angel was going to love this.

Their friend, a tall young man, gazed at JayBee imploringly. His ears were pierced multiple times and his hair was red. Not naturally red, like her own, but a gorgeous crimson, about the color of a red M&M. JayBee found it oddly attractive.

"Help us, Ms. Hauser. You're our only hope."

That sounded vaguely familiar.

Donna said, "Terry, we don't have time for *Star Wars* right now." Turning to JayBee, she asked, "So are you willing?"

"I'll give it a shot," said JayBee. It seemed perfectly natural to her that some of the students would want such a club—they had certainly had one at her high school in Dayton, ten years ago—so she wasn't prepared for the reaction at the board meeting when the principal made the announcement.

"Some of you who attended the last meeting remember that we had a…a discussion about the formation of a new club that was requested by a group of students. As I explained at the time, the school must not discriminate against a club that is formed for a lawful purpose, so long as at least ten students petition for its formation and a faculty advisor can be found. Since Ms. Hauser has agreed to act as advisor, I am permitting the formation of—" he consulted his notes, "—the Spartan Queer Folks and Friends Lavender Collective."

Whispers and murmurs broke out among the audience and a small group of students applauded. Other students whistled derisively. The head of the school board, acting as the chairman of the meeting, rapped his gavel for order.

A young woman in the back stood up and asked, "How can this be a lawful purpose? This club is all about having underage sex!"

JayBee sprang to her feet. "The club is not about 'having sex.' It's about helping students and their friends deal with issues of gender identity, sexual roles and discrimination."

Supporters of the club clapped loudly. JayBee, looking straight toward the front of the room, caught the eye of a man seated at the table. It took her a second to recognize him as the man who had helped her that morning. He looked different in street clothes, with his light-brown hair around his face instead of tied back with a bandanna. Different…better. He was nodding as though he approved of her words.

A stern-looking woman stood up and announced she would consult her attorney to determine whether there was any way to stop the club. Some members of the audience murmured support. The chairman closed his eyes briefly, looking pained. The meeting moved on to new business, which included speeches from the two candidates for school board. JayBee sat back in the uncomfortable steel folding chair, preparing to be bored.

Then she sat up straight again as she realized the nice-looking man, introduced as Dr. Travis Kellman, was one of the candidates. JayBee wondered what kind of doctor he was. He spoke briefly, only occasionally looking down at his notes. He said that although the Priam-Remus school district was small, it had as much to offer as one of the larger, richer districts up north. If elected, he would work to raise funds for a better computer lab and an updated library for the high school.

"I'm well aware that the rival candidate is a fine person and a good father," he ended with a wry grin. Most of the people in the audience chuckled, although JayBee didn't see anything humorous in the remark. "However, I feel that as a fairly recent pupil of the Priam schools, I am a better judge than my opponent of what the schools need."

He nodded to the audience and sat down as they gave him a brief round of polite applause. The chairman said, "We were expecting to hear from the other candidate tonight, but unfortunately, he seems to have been delayed."

At that moment, the door at the back swung open and a handsome older gentleman strode in. JayBee thought he was perhaps in his early sixties, with a thick head of well-cut gray hair and lively dark eyes. He would have looked quite at home in a New York board room in his beautifully cut pin-striped suit, cheerful yellow tie and matching yellow handkerchief that coyly peeped from his jacket pocket.

"I offer my deepest apologies for my late arrival," he said, inclining his head in a stately way. He looked slowly around the room. The audience hung on his words as though he were an actor about to deliver a portentous line. "I was unavoidably delayed. Just as I was about to pull into the parking lot, I saw a child fall off his bicycle. I hurried over to make sure he was unharmed." He paused as several people murmured in sympathy. "The poor boy had skinned both knees, so I administered first aid and made sure he reached home."

The chairman smiled. "I'm sure everyone here understands. Fortunately, you're just in time to make your speech."

Dr. Robert Kellman came to the front of the room and spoke without notes. He said that while he was sure his son was a worthy candidate, he was still young and had a young person's unrealistic ideas. He, on the other hand, supported traditional family values. If elected, his actions and ideas would be more in line with community beliefs and sentiments. He would work to put a copy of the Ten Commandments in every school.

JayBee couldn't help rolling her eyes, even as people around her nodded approval. The Ten Commandments! What did they have to do with public school? But she couldn't help noticing that Dr. Robert got a bigger round of applause than Dr. Travis.

When the meeting ended, she made her way to the front of the room. "Hi!" She offered her hand to Travis. "I was in such a hurry to get to school, I'm afraid I didn't thank you properly this morning."

He shook her hand. "Glad I could help out."

He had laugh lines around his dark eyes, as though he might have a sense of humor, so she risked a little joke. "Too bad it didn't happen this evening. Then you could have made a grand entrance because you stopped to help a kitten."

His eyes lit in appreciation and he smiled. "Yes, I'm afraid my dad upstaged me there. What did you think of the speeches otherwise?"

"I think the high school needs some new books and computers a hell of a lot more than it needs the Ten Commandments hanging in the hall."

Georgia glided up and took his arm. "Your speech was absolutely wonderful, Travis. I'm so impressed." She turned her smile on JayBee. "And you must be the new gym teacher I've heard so much about."

JayBee offered her hand. "JayBee Hauser."

Georgia introduced herself in turn. She's got to be his wife, JayBee thought, the way she's hanging on his arm.

"My sister-in-law," Travis added.

"JayBee—what an unusual name," said Georgia. "Is it short for something?"

"Juliet Belinda," JayBee murmured, as though disclosing a shameful secret.

"Oh, yes, I can see why you don't like that—much too feminine for you," said Georgia. "I've seen you zipping around town on your motorcycle. My, you must be a strong woman to handle a big bike like that."

JayBee usually liked being tall and athletic, but tiny, dainty Georgia was making her feel like a gawky giant.

"So nice to have met you, but I'm afraid we must be going," Georgia trilled and began to move toward the door.

Travis lingered for a moment. "I'll try to catch up with you another time," he told JayBee. "I've got some questions about that new club."

Conscious of a feeling of disappointment, she asked, "You disapprove?"

"Not at all! We'll talk later."

"Travis, please!"

"Coming."

JayBee was still looking after him when Denise MacReedy, the home economics teacher, and Charlotte Scott, the history teacher, came up behind her. "Those two were certainly looking cozy," Charlotte commented.

"She's his sister-in-law," said JayBee.

Denise sniffed. "And his ex-fiancée. She jilted him in favor of his older brother."

"That's terrible." JayBee felt a rush of sympathy. Something similar had happened to her once. Her older sister was extremely beautiful. "How could she do that?"

"Which brother would you want? The small-town vet, or the pediatric surgeon?" Denise asked.

JayBee didn't understand the question. "It would depend on their personalities."

"I could put up with a lot of personality flaws if I had Peter's salary to live on," Denise said, with a knowing look.

Charlotte shrugged. "Money isn't everything."

"No, but I'd love to quit this job and be a pampered housewife. Like Dr. Robert's wife." Denise nodded her head toward Dr. Robert Kellman, who was across the room with Alicia clinging to his elbow.

"She's Dr. Travis' mother?" JayBee asked. She could hardly believe it. Alicia could have passed for a woman of forty...at least in dim light.

"Stepmother," Charlotte corrected. With unusual vehemence for the soft-voiced history teacher, she added, "And if there's one person I can't stand, it's Alicia. I had to drop out of the Garden Club the year she was president."

Denise looked amused. "Yep. When she says, 'Jump!' everyone else says, 'How high?'"

"She's beautiful, for a woman that age. She must be in her forties, right?" JayBee asked.

"She's forty-four," Denise answered.

"All the men like her," Charlotte said. "They don't realize that 'helpless little me' thing she does is all an act."

Denise nodded, watching Alicia thoughtfully. Charlotte glared at Alicia with narrowed eyes.

* * * * *

"I hate the way everyone knows everyone else's business in this little town," Georgia said. "Let's go someplace private."

Travis took that to mean she didn't want Peter to know she'd spent time with him. He got into his truck and followed her Volvo down Tecumseh Street and into the park.

Clouds covered the moon. The night's only illumination was a single flickering streetlamp at the park entrance. He could barely see Georgia on the stone path, flitting ahead of him like an insubstantial phantom. Her loose white blouse fluttered in the breeze as she hurried down the wooden steps toward the river. He followed more slowly, wondering why she had chosen this particular spot. Was it mere thoughtlessness, or was she giving another twist to the lance in his heart?

She was sitting on the bench where they had sat together so many times. Not wanting to sit there now, he put his foot up on the bench and leaned on his knee.

Georgia tilted her head back, revealing her long white neck as she looked up at him. "I've always loved the sound of the falls."

"Do you ever come here with Pete?"

"No. I think of it as our special place." She gazed into his eyes.

The most mundane things they had done together seemed to sparkle in his memory. They had sat here often, listening to the river, his arm around her shoulders. He could recall the many evenings when they would linger here, talking, while he could hardly wait to take her back to her apartment and make love to her. Her response to him hadn't been faked. It couldn't have been, not unless she was a world-class actress.

"Travis," she said softly, "thank you for agreeing to meet with me. I know this isn't your problem. You have no reason to get involved…but if you could help me, I'd be so grateful." Her eyes welled with tears.

"You're my sister-in-law." He tried to look away from her. "Family. I'll help if I can."

"You've always been such a good person…I should never have listened to Alicia."

"What does she have to do with anything?"

She sighed. "I listened to something she told me about you. I believed her...and it made me think I'd prefer to marry your brother. I knew he'd always wanted me, so I went after him, but it was all a big mistake."

"What did she tell you?" Travis demanded.

"That you'd gotten a woman pregnant and deserted her. I should have known you would never do something like that."

Travis' hands clenched into fists. "No, I wouldn't. If something like that had happened, I'd have supported the child. Why did you believe her?"

"I don't know." Georgia spoke wearily. "I thought, why would she lie?"

Travis left the bench and went over to the iron railing, looking down at the river. All this time, he had blamed Georgia. He still blamed her, but now he knew what had been behind her decision. Over and over, his stepmother had interfered with his life. Never for his benefit, but always to further her own agenda. His hands tightened on the rail as he imagined confronting her, yelling out his pain and anger.

Georgia joined him, putting her hand on his arm. He shook it off. "Damn it, Georgie, why didn't you talk to me? You know how my stepmother feels about me!"

"I didn't realize she disliked you enough to break up our engagement. I didn't know her very well back then. Why does she feel like that?"

"I've never really understood it, except maybe, in her eyes, I was unnecessary." He shrugged. "She always liked Pete—he was a handsome, polite little boy, so much like his father—and of course she loves her own daughter. But why would she need me around? She was always foisting me off on my grandfather. I was...extraneous."

"Please don't look so angry, Travis. You're scaring me."

"I'm not mad at you," he said, although he knew that was a lie. He tried to calm down. "I'm glad you told me."

"Promise me you won't make a scene with Alicia. It's all water under the bridge now."

Travis looked her straight in the eye. "You expect me to go on as though nothing's happened? That woman has been a curse on my life since the moment Dad brought her in the house."

"But now there's something else going on. Something deep. And lately, I've begun to suspect that Alicia might be at the bottom of it. So you mustn't confront her now. Not if you're going to help me."

"Good Lord, what's going on?"

"You have to promise you won't tell anyone. Do you promise?"

She was looking at him anxiously. He hesitated, wondering what he was getting into. "All right. I promise."

Georgia took a deep breath. "I'm being blackmailed."

Chapter Three

"I can't reach Maman." Katie fidgeted impatiently in the doorway. "I've been trying to call her for two hours."

Travis yawned and sat up in bed. "I'm sure there's a reasonable explanation. She probably just forgot about it. Now go back home and let me sleep."

"No," Katie insisted. "It was the last thing Maman said to me after the school board meeting. 'Don't forget we're going shopping tomorrow morning.' I'm worried about her."

Travis waved a dismissive hand at his half sister. "All right, I'm up. Now get out of here so I can get dressed." He didn't try to hide his irritation. He had been up most of the night, thinking about everything Georgia had told him. Today was Friday, his day off and Katie had to appear at nine-thirty and wake him. "Put on some coffee!" he called after her.

"No time for that! Hurry up!"

Queenie was stretched out over approximately three-quarters of the bed. It had not been Travis' idea to have her sleep there. He had made her a soft bed out of blankets in the kitchen. She had curled up there willingly enough the first night, but later, just as he was falling asleep, he heard her whining at his bedroom door. "Okay, just this once," he'd said and let her in the room. She had immediately jumped up on the bed.

"Don't get too comfortable there," he'd told her. "I don't always sleep alone."

She'd closed her eyes with a funny little grunt of content that made him smile.

Now, stretching and yawning, he got up and threw on the clothes he'd worn yesterday, figuring Katie would have a fit if he stopped to shower.

"Why didn't you run over there yourself if you're so worried?" he asked as they headed out to the truck. Queenie followed them, tail wagging hopefully.

Katie gave him an exasperated look and made room for Queenie on the seat. "Because if something's wrong, I don't want to be by myself."

"Next time call the police," he grumbled as he pulled out onto the road.

"Travis, don't be so mean."

He gave her a quick glance and saw there were tears in her eyes. "Sorry," he muttered. "I just think you're overreacting. I'm sure Alicia's fine."

"I keep thinking…when I was in art school, one of the students didn't show up for a few days. And when some friends of mine went to his place to check on him, they found him dead. And his dog had eaten part of him."

"Monique wouldn't eat Alicia. That overfed poodle won't touch anything tough and stringy, you know that."

"Travis, that's my mother you're talking about."

"All right, I'm sorry. Just calm down."

In a few minutes they pulled up to the handsome oyster-white ranch with its beautifully manicured lawn. "Look," said Travis. "Her car's in the drive. She was probably out doing an errand this morning."

"I'm afraid something's wrong," Katie said, her voice so low he could hardly hear her.

"Sit tight. I'll check."

Travis went to the front door and rang the bell, then listened carefully. He couldn't hear anyone moving inside. He pounded on the front door with his fist, but there was still no answer.

He peered into the garage before he walked back to the truck.

"Dad's car is gone," he told Katie. "Maybe they went somewhere together."

"Then why didn't she call me?"

Travis had no answer for that. "I'll check inside—if you have keys."

Silently she dug her key ring out of her purse and indicated the house key.

Pretty sad, he thought, that he didn't have keys to his own father's house. It was just another one of those little humiliations that Alicia liked to inflict on him.

He unlocked the front door and paused on the threshold, calling his stepmother's name. Queenie pressed against his leg and he stroked her head for a moment, waiting. Nothing answered except silence.

Queenie walked cautiously around the living room, sniffing at the furniture. Alicia had redecorated again, Travis noticed. The room was furnished in her beloved English Country. All the French Provincial furniture had been replaced with upholstered chintz. A hunting horn and a framed fox's brush hung over the fireplace. A large stuffed squirrel under a glass bell drew his eye. Travis frowned at it, wondering why Alicia thought it was attractive to have a dead animal in the living room.

He walked to the hall that led to the bedrooms and called for Alicia once again. Queenie paused by the hall closet, sniffing at the bottom of the door. Snapping his fingers for her to come, Travis repressed a shudder. He was intimately familiar with the interior of that closet—the "punishment closet".

At the other end of the house, he heard a door open, then a scream from his sister. Travis ran through the dining room and thrust the swinging kitchen door open with his shoulder.

The odor assaulted him. It was an odor he was familiar with from dissection rooms…blood and fecal matter.

His stepmother lay sprawled on the kitchen floor, face down, arms outstretched, some type of blood-soaked material bunched up underneath her. A rattan kitchen chair was overturned by her left leg.

"Maman!" Katie stood at the open back door. "Oh my God, Travis!"

Travis felt an almost irresistible desire to run from the room. He was quite sure Alicia was dead, but he forced himself to step forward and touch the back of her leg. Her flesh was cold and rigid.

"She's dead."

In the corner by the stove, Alicia's miniature apricot poodle lay curled in her basket-bed, whining.

The color drained from Katie's face. She cried out, then stumbled across the doorsill and fell to her knees outside, retching.

He glanced at the wall phone. *Crime scene! Get out!* He backed away from the kitchen. Queenie, sitting patiently outside the kitchen door, whined when she saw him and jumped up. Travis hurried through the house and around to the back door. Katie was standing upright, holding her stomach with both hands, her face tear-stained and distraught.

He put his arms around her and she sobbed against his chest. He let her cry for a few minutes.

"Come on, let's sit in the truck."

She nodded, choking on her tears. Climbing back into the truck, she put her head down to her knees while Travis patted her shoulder awkwardly.

He felt his pockets for his phone. Damn! Back home on the dresser. "Got your cell phone?"

Mechanically, she took it out of her purse, but kept it in her hand. "Wait! Are you calling the cops?"

He nodded. She gripped his arm, her eyes searching his. "Travis! Did you have anything to do with this?"

A chill went through him. If the person who loved him most in the world could think that, he was in for a bad time.

"What the hell are you talking about?"

She looked down. "I know how it is with you and Maman."

He took a deep breath. "Why would I hurt your mother?"

"I'm just trying to think about it the way the cops will think. They always look to the family first. I was home by myself last night and you were too. So neither of us has an alibi."

"Katie—"

She was talking quickly now. "But if we say we were together—then who could contradict us? Then we'd both have an alibi."

Travis stared at her. "Why do we need one? Aren't you getting way ahead of yourself?"

"I don't want either of us to go to jail!"

"Some outsider did this. I'm sure the cops will realize it once they investigate."

"But what if they think it had to be a family member? The back door was unlocked! So it wasn't a break-in!"

"It wasn't locked?"

"No! I just turned the knob and it opened!"

Travis tried to picture what could have happened. Alicia would have driven home after the school board meeting. She had been by herself. Perhaps his father had lingered at the meeting for awhile, talking to people. It had been dark by the time the meeting let out and maybe Alicia had forgotten to leave any outside lights on. So instead of putting the car away, she had left it in the driveway, closer to the back door. Someone could have been waiting in the shrubbery, someone who followed behind her and entered the kitchen before she could get the door locked.

But then, when his father came home, he would have discovered the body.

Katie raised a suddenly stricken face to his. "Where's Dad?"

Travis turned out his hands helplessly.

She hid her face against his shoulder and whispered, "I can't take it if they're both dead! Maybe he's in another room—"

"No! His car is gone, remember?"

"Oh, that's right." Her relief lasted only a moment. "But Travis—what if someone came in and killed both of them and took Dad's car? Maybe we should go in the front again. Did you look in the bedrooms?"

"Neither of us is going in there." Gently he took the cell phone out of her hand.

* * * * *

Crime in the village of Priam was usually mundane in nature. The small police force spent most of its time writing parking tickets on the village square and maintaining a speed trap just outside of town. Sometimes the college students "up on the hill" caused trouble, but the campus maintained its own police department. Shoplifting, petty vandalism and an occasional domestic violence incident were the main components in the "Village Police Blotter" that was printed every week in the *Priam Village Chronicle.* The last murder had occurred in 1967, when a man shot his uncle after a drunken argument.

So it was no surprise to Travis when both village police cruisers pulled up, sirens wailing and lights flashing. The police department motto, "We Want to Help!" was painted in black on their sleek gray sides. "'We Want to Help Ourselves to Your Money!' is more like it," one bitter motorist had written in to the paper after being caught in the local speed trap. To which the police chief had replied, "I'll give warnings instead of tickets when the speed limit becomes a *suggestion* rather than the *law*."

That was Austin MacReedy as Travis had always known him, he'd thought when reading the exchange. MacReedy had been two years ahead of Travis in the Priam schools. The son of a bankrupt farmer, Austin had gone into the army at the age of eighteen. No one in Priam had expected to see him again.

But after several years in the army, he had entered the police academy, then quickly risen to become deputy chief in tiny Homerville, on the Ohio River. When Priam's old Chief Goger retired, MacReedy had applied for the job and been hired. Now people proudly pointed to him as an example of local boy makes good.

Travis had hated his guts for years.

As he explained what had happened under MacReedy's intense gaze, he felt himself at a disadvantage. That was the trouble with staying in the same small town all your life. When you met other adults, you couldn't help remembering the stupid stuff from childhood, the bullying and teasing. Sure, you could pretend it was all forgotten—hell, MacReedy's wife even brought her pet chinchillas to him—but it was still always there, just under the surface.

"Tell me again what rooms you were in, Trav," MacReedy said, nodding his head to his subordinate, Officer Luray, who was taking notes.

Travis hated being called "Trav," but it seemed too petty to say anything during this crisis. "Living room, dining room, kitchen."

"You didn't go into any of the bedrooms?"

"Nope."

Queenie sniffed at Officer Ming's polished black shoes. The officer bent slightly to pat her head, then desisted as she caught a glare from her chief.

"Did your sister go in with you?"

"She came into the kitchen from the side door—just a few steps. I walked through the front rooms by myself." Travis added scrupulously, "I should say—the dog was with me."

MacReedy straightened and gave Travis an incredulous look. "Trav, I can't believe what I'm hearing. You brought a dog into a crime scene?"

"How the hell did I know it was a crime scene?" Travis snapped his fingers and Queenie came and sat down by his leg. "Anyway, she didn't go into the kitchen."

MacReedy ran a hand through his crisp red hair. "Did you touch anything inside?" Then he seemed to think better of the question. "I guess it doesn't matter. Your prints would be all over the place anyway."

Travis shrugged. "Maybe not. How long do fingerprints last? This is the first time I've been over here in two—no, three years."

MacReedy's scrutiny intensified. "That's right. You never did get along with your stepmother, did you?"

Travis tried to keep his tone casual. "We argued a lot when I was a teenager. Relations have been cordial the last few years." That sounded too artificial, too rehearsed. "She just came over for dinner with my dad."

Katie had remained in the truck during this conversation, crying into Travis' handkerchief. Now the door opened and she stepped out. She looked ravaged, her eyes red and swollen, her hair awry. Her lips were trembling as she came toward her brother. "Do we have to stay outside here?" she asked, her voice barely more than a whisper. She tripped and stumbled forward. Travis turned to help, but MacReedy was quicker, catching and holding her for a moment as she steadied herself. She leaned close in to the chief, clutching his sleeve. "I just can't believe this is happening!"

"Officer Ming, take Katie into the living room and get her statement," MacReedy said.

The chief directed Officer Luray to tape off the perimeter of the house. "I called the County Bureau of Criminal Forensics already," he told Travis. "They're sending some people out. Coroner'll be coming too and we'll get everything rolling." He cracked his knuckles together, sounding as though he were looking forward to the job ahead—the examination of the body, the inspection of the house for evidence. No doubt a murder like this presented a challenge to him, a break from the boring routine of most days, a chance to get his face on the news. Travis couldn't really blame him, but it didn't make him like the chief one iota more.

MacReedy looked over at the house next door and Travis followed his glance. Mrs. Stansky was outside on her patio, fussing with a potted plant. Alicia had disliked her neighbor, claiming that Mrs. Stansky watched everything that went on at the Kellman house. Travis was sure she would be on the phone soon, informing the old-biddy network that something was going on next door.

Travis wondered if she had seen or heard anything last night. Perhaps she would be able to tell them if Robert Kellman had come home and what time.

MacReedy seemed to follow his line of thought. "We'll be talking to all the neighbors, of course. Unless we get a confession right up front."

Travis said, "I'm no medical examiner, but my guess is that my stepmother died last night sometime. Whoever did it could be five states away by now."

MacReedy gave him a sharp look. "Sure, unless it's a family member. And it usually is."

"No way!" Travis snapped. "Not in this case."

"We'll see." The chief turned to the other man who had come with him, Jerry Davidson, a plainclothes detective. "Jerry, go inside and take Dr. Kellman's statement."

Travis opened the truck, let Queenie jump up on the front seat and cranked the windows down a few inches. The dog lay down with a sigh. Luckily it was a cool, sunless day, so he figured she would be all right for awhile.

Travis didn't know Jerry Davidson, although he looked slightly familiar. Maybe he had seen him at the grocery store or the gas station. Travis followed the big detective into the house, glancing at Katie as they walked through the living room. She looked miserable, hunched at one end of the couch, holding her arms around herself.

"This looks like a good place to sit," said Davidson, glancing into Robert Kellman's study. He took the rolling office chair behind the desk and gestured at Travis to take the other chair across from the desk. Travis sat, feeling uncomfortably like a teenager about to be lectured by his father. That was something that had happened frequently in this room.

Davidson took a detailed statement from him, then asked him to account for his whereabouts of the night before.

"After I left the board meeting, I went to the park. I was there for about an hour, then I went home."

"What were you doing in the park?"

Travis hesitated. "Talking to a friend."

"And who was that?"

"I'd rather not say."

"That's not an acceptable answer, Dr. Kellman."

"It's all I'm going to say right now," Travis answered firmly. Not that he and Georgia had done anything wrong, but if she wanted to keep the meeting a secret from Peter, he wasn't going to blab it to the police.

He thought about MacReedy's comment, "Unless it's a family member."

That was the other explanation for why the door was unlocked. Of course Alicia would have admitted someone she knew—one of her stepsons, her daughter, her nephew—or her daughter-in-law.

It's ruining my life, Georgia had told him in the park. *I think blackmailers are as bad as murderers! I wish I knew who's doing this. If only I knew for sure—that person would be very sorry for screwing around with me.*

It was hard to imagine Georgia, with her dainty gestures, her pretty face, her elegant jewelry, violently killing her own mother-in-law.

An unwelcome remembrance came to mind. Georgia and her parents had moved to Priam from Pittsburgh. Talking about it once, she had said, "Daddy always wanted to move to a more rural area. He loves the outdoors. Do you know, I've been going hunting with him since I was twelve?"

"It's hard to imagine you hunting."

"You should come with us sometime. I'm quite the pioneer girl, in my leather jacket and boots. You should see me field-dress a buck."

Travis had no strong moral objection to hunting and he was well aware that the deer population needed to be thinned occasionally. Still, nothing short of starvation could have induced him to shoot a deer himself.

Would a person who could field-dress a buck have much trouble killing one small woman?

It was a sickening thought. He refused even to consider it further. Georgia would not do such a thing. Killing a deer just wasn't comparable to killing another human being.

And yet…he couldn't deny Georgia had a temper. He remembered the screaming fight over the engagement ring…or rather, her screaming, since he had managed not to raise his voice. He had learned how to keep his temper in a hard school.

He had hoped Georgia would enjoy having a family heirloom. It was his real mother's engagement ring, a beautiful gold ring with a square diamond flanked by emeralds. "I can't believe you're giving me something used!" Georgia had exclaimed, her voice rising in the way that he knew signaled trouble. "Oh, Travis, how could you? I thought you loved me!"

And that hadn't even been their worst fight. When they began planning the wedding, her temper seemed to grow more erratic by the week. At the time, he had put it down to bridal nerves.

Would she be capable of killing someone who might be blackmailing her?

He still couldn't believe it.

Davidson shut his notebook. "Okay, Dr. Kellman. I'm going to leave you alone for a few minutes here while I check something with the chief. Don't leave the room and don't touch anything."

Travis nodded curtly. As the detective exited the room, Travis took Katie's small cell phone out of his breast pocket, debating whether to call Georgia. He wanted very much to hear her reaction to the news. But would it be better to talk to her in person? If he questioned her, he knew her well enough to determine if she were telling the truth.

MacReedy appeared in the doorway. "What the hell are you doing?"

"What does it look like I'm doing?"

"Trav, I don't think you understand how serious this situation is. I don't want you spreading the word around to the relatives—got that? I will personally inform your stepmother's relatives about her death."

Travis could understand that. It was the same thing he'd been thinking about Georgia. Of course MacReedy would want to tell the family, while watching their reactions. "All right, I won't call anyone."

"Give me the phone."

Travis put the phone back in his pocket. "I said I won't call anyone."

MacReedy answered him with a hard stare. "You'd better watch yourself," he said, low-voiced. "You'd better keep your nose clean, or I'll arrest you so fast your head will spin."

"You don't have grounds to arrest me."

"Are you sure about that? It's never a good idea to be the one to find the body, Trav."

In point of fact, it was Katie who had discovered the body. But Travis didn't remind MacReedy of that. The two men glared at each other for a long moment. Then the chief said, "The coroner has a question for you. Come on into the kitchen."

The Tecumseh county coroner was a big man with jowls and a pendulous stomach. He was kneeling by the body when Travis walked into the kitchen. Rising with an effort, he looked up and raised his eyebrows.

"This is the murdered woman's stepson," MacReedy said.

I have a name, you bastard, Travis thought, extending his hand to Thomson. "Dr. Travis Kellman."

"Dr. Mel Thomson," said the big man, shaking Travis' hand. "And this is my assistant, Dr. Velma Wylie," he added, indicating a stern-looking black woman holding a tape recorder.

"Doctor," Velma acknowledged, offering her hand to Travis. She was much more attractive when she smiled.

Well, now we've got all the titles straight, Travis thought irreverently as he shook her hand. What did you say to the coroner who had come to examine your murdered relative? Surely "Nice to meet you," was inappropriate, as was, "Thanks for coming by."

"I wanted to make sure you didn't move the body," said Thomson.

"No. I only touched her leg," Travis answered, trying not to think about the feel of that cold, rigid flesh. Somehow dealing with a human body was so much more troubling than handling a dead animal.

The chief said, "Trav, seeing as how you're a medical professional yourself, do you want to watch the preliminary examination?" There was a hint of a challenge in his voice, as though he were expecting Travis to refuse and then would immediately think less of him.

I don't have to play his macho bullshit game, Travis thought. He really had no desire to watch while Thomson worked on the body of his stepmother.

On the other hand, he did want to know whatever the examination would tell them.

MacReedy was watching him with an ironical look in his narrow green eyes. Travis was suddenly sure the chief was remembering a certain day in the woods…

Travis followed his brother, determined to keep up with the older boys. Jake Duggan was there, Keith Camson and Austin MacReedy. They planned to wade in the creek, down by the Millers' farm where the water was the deepest, but that was forgotten when they found the kitten in the trap.

It must have been there for quite some time, because it was unbelievably thin, its fur disheveled and matted as though it had rolled around frantically in its struggle to escape.

At first they thought it was dead, but as they approached, its head moved slightly and it looked at them. Travis was chilled by the glazed despair in its yellow eyes as it watched them come closer.

"Wow, I wonder how long it's been there," Keith said.

"Let's take it to Doc Henderson," Travis said, dropping to his knees. His grandfather had taught him how to open a trap.

"It'll never make it," Austin said. "I'm going to put it out of its misery." Before anyone could argue, he picked up a big stone and smashed its head. Travis, the closest to it, was spattered with its blood.

It was a horrible moment, but there was worse to follow. It was just too much for him to see the gray and red mass that had been the kitten's head. Turning, he spewed out his guts on the ground.

Only his brother helped him, giving him a used tissue to wipe the blood off his arms. The others began to tease him.

"Aw, did it bother you to see the poor widdle kitty?"

"Are you going to cry about it?"

"Shut up, you guys!" said Peter. "He's only eight years old."

Austin grabbed him by the arm and brought his face close. "Meow! Meow!"

Wrenching his arm free, Travis ran away, hearing the mocking laughter of the others as he made his way back home…

Now, looking up, Travis met the chief's gaze squarely. "I'll stay for awhile."

Two men from the County Bureau of Criminal Forensics arrived shortly afterward and began photographing the scene and taking fingerprints. Meanwhile, at MacReedy's order, Officer Ming walked a still shaking Katie through the house, so that Katie could tell them if anything had been disturbed.

Travis sat in a corner of the kitchen, thinking about how quickly a life could be extinguished. He heard Officer Ming say, "What about this room?" and the murmur of Katie's quavery voice as she answered. Poor Katie, this was going to be a tough time for his sensitive half sister. Travis could still remember the trauma of his own mother dying. He wondered how Peter would feel about it. No doubt Peter would be much more upset than he was, since Peter and Alicia had gotten along quite well.

Things would be different without Alicia, that was certain. She had been such an overwhelming force in all of their lives. It was as if some great personage had died, a queen or an empress. A commanding presence. The person who had always been in control, the person who had always won.

Except not this time.

There was a part of him that was feeling an ugly sense of triumph. It was a part he didn't much like, but couldn't deny was there. Whatever Alicia thought she had on him, whatever secret she thought she could threaten him with, must have died with her. She had given him her ultimatum and he had made his speech anyway. Then she had gone home and someone had murdered her. She couldn't have had time to put her threat into action.

He wondered again what the secret had been. Well, he would probably never know now.

Katie came into the room. Her face was so pale that the faint freckles across her cheeks were more prominent than usual. Quickly, Travis stood and put his arm around her shoulders. "You look like you're going to collapse."

"I'm all right," she murmured.

"How does everything look in the bedrooms?" MacReedy wanted to know.

She spread her arms helplessly. "It's so hard to say. Maman's jewelry is still here. I know the good pieces—her diamond bracelet and her ruby necklace. They're in her jewelry box. And that's in plain sight. Dad's got a hundred dollars in his dresser drawer, right on top."

Officer Ming said, "It certainly doesn't look like a burglary to me."

"There was one strange thing," Katie said. She hesitated, looking from the chief to her brother. "The lower bunk bed in your old room, Travis—it looks like someone slept there."

Travis shrugged. "Maybe Dad and Alicia have been sleeping in separate rooms. You know they weren't getting along at the Reconciliation Dinner."

Katie looked puzzled. "But Maman wouldn't have left the bed like that. You know how she is about unmade beds."

Yes, Travis was well aware of that. He tried to picture a scenario that would explain the bed, but couldn't think of anything. It was impossible to believe that Alicia's murderer would have calmly gone to sleep after committing the deed.

"Show me which bedroom," said one of the men from the Criminal Forensics Bureau. He and Katie walked out together.

Travis turned as he heard a faint whine coming from the dog by the stove. Monique moved as though she were about to stand, then threw up some yellow fluid.

"That's the second time that damn dog's vomited," Thomson said irritably.

Travis bent down to look at the little poodle. "What's the matter, girl, hmm?" he murmured, lifting her up gently and feeling her abdomen. Monique had been known to eat inappropriate things in the past, including a rubber ball and a computer cord.

He saw there was a brown-stained paper plate underneath her. It looked as though something chocolate had been sitting on that plate and she had licked it almost clean.

A paper plate was not something he expected to see in his stepmother's kitchen. Alicia had very firm opinions about what she considered "trashy." Children's drawings on the refrigerator, clothes hanging to dry outside, election posters on the lawn—all of these were indications of people who belonged on Jerry Springer. And paper plates ranked right up there as being totally unacceptable to anyone but trailer trash. Lord knows she had told him that often enough.

The little dog whined and licked his hand. Her stomach didn't seem to be swollen. But if she had been eating chocolate, that was reason enough for her to be sick. Chocolate was toxic for many dogs.

And Alicia knew that. She had listened carefully when Travis told her, at Monique's last appointment, that she was feeding the animal too much and should cut back. "Give her carrots or green beans instead of commercial treats," he had instructed and Alicia nodded seriously. "And mind you, never any chocolate," he'd added, knowing how much Alicia loved it.

"Oh, for goodness sake, Travis, I know that much," she'd answered.

Travis picked up the dog's basket and carried it into a corner of the dining room. Monique curled up again with a sigh. She would probably recover, since she had made it through the night. There wasn't much he could do so many hours later, since the chocolate was already being digested.

He wondered what would become of her now. His father had never liked the little dog who had been solely Alicia's pet. Perhaps Katie would take her.

Travis went back into the kitchen and watched while the photography was completed. Wylie brought in a stretcher. She and Thomson lifted the body up onto it, turning Alicia on her back. The front of Alicia's blouse was covered in blood.

"Stab wound," Thomson said, looking closely at the gaping tear in the front of Alicia's blouse. Travis turned his eyes away.

The body had been lying on bunched-up white material. MacReedy reached down and held it up.

It was a man's shirt.

"Size 16-33," MacReedy observed, looking at the tag.

Travis knew that was his father's size.

He kept his mouth shut, but it was a simple matter for the chief to look in Robert Kellman's closet and find another five shirts of the same brand and size.

Travis followed him into the bedroom. "That shirt doesn't prove a damn thing," he insisted. "It must have been left in the kitchen for some reason and the murderer used it to mop up the blood."

MacReedy's expression was skeptical. "Do you keep shirts in the kitchen?"

That stumped Travis only for a moment. "I've taken off my shirt and run cold water on it when there's a stain."

"Well, it's not enough to make an arrest," the chief conceded.

Travis glanced into his old bedroom. The man from Criminal Forensics turned away from the unmade lower bunk bed, holding up a bag. "Look what I found on the pillow. Hair sample."

"Great!" The chief came into the room to look at it. Frowning, he took the little bag from the other man, holding it up at the level of Travis' head.

The bag held a tightly curled, light-brown hair.

"Just the color of your hair," MacReedy said to Travis, raising his eyebrows.

"My hair isn't curly," Travis retorted, trying to speak calmly. He went back into the living room. His sister looked up anxiously into his face. Apparently she could tell from his expression that something else was wrong. "What is it?" she asked, coming over to him.

"Dad's shirt was underneath Alicia."

Katie gasped, her hand going to her mouth.

"It doesn't mean anything." Travis put a reassuring arm around her shoulders.

"It wasn't Dad!" Katie exclaimed. "It wasn't. Dad loves Maman! He does!"

"Of course he does," Travis said. But he couldn't help thinking of some of the things his stepmother had said at his house that evening. "Men need to keep busy or they just get into mischief." Had his stepmother known something about Robert Kellman that was hidden from the rest of the family? He remembered the argument going on in the dining room while he washed the dishes and the way his father had left without saying goodbye.

"That shirt isn't important," Katie said, going to the chief and looking up at him imploringly.

"It's evidence, Katie," MacReedy said gently. "I'm sorry."

She tossed her head. "They found O.J.'s bloody glove and he was acquitted!"

"But are you saying he was innocent?" The chief's voice was very soft.

Katie looked as though she were at a loss for how to answer that. "That's all irrelevant," Travis said, stepping closer to his sister. "We're talking about Dr. Robert Kellman, not O.J. My father wouldn't take a life. He spent his whole career saving lives!"

"Everyone knows what a good man Robert Kellman is," said MacReedy, which earned him a faint smile from Katie. "But let's look at a hypothetical situation. Suppose he and Mrs. Kellman got into an argument in the kitchen. Say there's a kitchen knife close at hand. In a moment of anger, he snatches up the knife. Maybe he only meant to scare her. They struggle and she winds up getting stabbed. Unpremeditated."

Travis shook his head. "My father knows how to treat a stab wound. He wouldn't have stuffed a shirt under her and left her to bleed to death."

"Well," said MacReedy. "Whatever happened, it would behoove your father to come in and make a statement. If he's innocent, I'm sure he'll have an explanation for where he was last night." He looked intently at Travis. "Are you sure you don't know where he is?"

"I have no idea. I only hope he's still alive."

Katie bit her lip and tucked her hand into Travis' arm. "Come on, Katie," Travis said. "Let's sit down." He didn't want to talk to MacReedy anymore and hear his ugly theories. He was positive that his father wasn't the murderer. No matter what their recent troubles, his father had always treated his wife like a person worthy of great consideration and deference.

Robert Kellman had never used physical force against any of his children, much less his wife. Travis could remember his father saying to him, "Son, only a coward hits a woman." Would a man who believed that be capable of stabbing his wife to death? Travis couldn't credit it.

"I'm so afraid we'll never see Dad again," Katie whispered as they sat down together on the couch. "I think the murderer killed Maman and car-jacked Dad."

"Don't borrow trouble," Travis answered.

"Then where is he?"

Travis said firmly, "He'll turn up." Resting his forehead on his hand, he thought about how a lifetime seemed to have passed in the few hours they had been at the house. He checked his watch. Hell, it wasn't even noon yet.

Dad's alive, he thought. He's got to be alive.

Maybe if he thought it hard enough, it would have to be true.

His stomach growled, reminding him that he hadn't eaten breakfast. It was strange that no matter what kind of trauma of the mind occurred, the body still made its own demands. He found himself regretting he hadn't been firmer with Katie about delaying for coffee.

Officer Ming, sitting across from them, met Travis' eyes in a sympathetic look. "This type of thing is so hard on the family."

"It's awful," Travis replied, with feeling.

Katie made an odd sound—something like a strangled scream. Officer Ming, the chief and Travis whirled around to look at her.

Springing to her feet, Katie pointed at the hall closet.

Slowly, the closet door swung open.

Chapter Four

A small, pajama-clad boy crawled out of the closet on his hands and knees. Blinking at the four petrified adults, he stood up, rubbing his eyes with one hand. "I fell asleep," he said.

Katie was the closest to him. She walked forward like a person in a trance and dropped to her knees in front of the child.

"How did you get here? Who are you?"

The little boy said, "Aunt Gina brought me." His big brown eyes looked scared as he put his thumb in his mouth.

"Don't be frightened." Katie put her arms around him and he let her, although he didn't smile or hug her back. "What's your name?"

"Travis Jeffrey."

A collective gasp went up from everyone in the room.

Travis stood up and took a few steps toward the child. The boy looked at him apprehensively and shrank back, hiding his face in Katie's blouse.

"It's okay." Katie rubbed his back soothingly. "No one's going to hurt you, I promise." She motioned Travis away. "Do you know your last name?"

"Madison."

Travis felt as though his legs would no longer hold him. Sitting again, he took a deep breath.

The chief said sharply, "Travis! Do you know this child?"

Travis couldn't take his eyes off the boy. "I've never seen him before."

"Does the name Madison mean anything to you?"

"I—I dated a Beth Madison—back in vet school."

"What happened to her?" MacReedy demanded.

Travis' heart raced. "She broke up with me—went back to her old boyfriend. She didn't finish school. Dropped out during our third year. I haven't heard from her..."

"Where's Grandma?" asked the boy.

"Grandma?" Katie repeated.

"Grandma said she would make pancakes this morning," the child said. "I'm hungry."

Katie looked from the curly-haired boy to her brother and back again. She spoke aloud what everyone in the room was thinking. "Travis! Could he possibly be your son?"

Travis gripped the arms of his chair, fighting to speak calmly. "I don't see how...I mean...why wouldn't Beth have told me about him?"

If I tell what I know, your whole life will change.

Alicia was dead, but in his mind, Travis saw her triumphant smile.

* * * * *

"There's only one thing faster than the speed of light," Angel liked to say, "and that's the speed of gossip in a small town."

JayBee heard the news at school. The murder was the sole topic of conversation in the teachers' lounge after classes let out. When she came home at four o'clock, she found Angel sitting disconsolate in the kitchen and knew she must have heard about it.

"I thought I was doing well today." Angel looked mournfully down at the table. "I felt so strong after lunch. So I found my sunglasses and my hat and I went to the grocery store all by myself."

"That's wonderful!"

"I was scared when I got there, but I told myself there was nothing to be afraid of, just like Dr. Whirley said. Then I felt well enough to go in. I went up and down the aisles and I was okay. Then when I was in the checkout line, I heard the two women behind me talking about the murder. I couldn't believe it! I was so sure this would be a safe place to live!" She got up from her chair, tore off a piece of paper towel and held it to her eyes. "I started feeling panicky. Everything went dark for a few minutes. My hands were shaking—"

"Were you able to check out?"

Angel shook her head. "I'm so sorry," she whispered.

JayBee put her arm around Angel's shoulders for a moment, laying her cheek against the other woman's. "You tried," she said softly. "That's the important thing."

"All I wanted to do was get home and make sure everything was okay. I kept thinking, I didn't even lock the door yesterday!"

"It's the first murder here since 1967. I don't think the town is unsafe—"

"Oh, it's fine for you, JayBee!" Angel sounded as though she were working herself up into hysterics. JayBee sighed to herself, wondering how to forestall them. Tea? She got up and put the kettle on.

"You're a real tough kind of woman. If someone came at you with a knife, you'd probably kick him in the balls and get away. But I'm not like that. I would freeze, just like—like—"

"I know," JayBee said hastily.

"We should have moved somewhere more isolated. Farther away from town. With an alarm system." Angel sighed, looking down at her hands. "Do you think our family is cursed? Look what happened to our brother."

"Oh, for goodness sake! This murder has nothing to do with our family!" JayBee tried to come up with something to distract her. "Look," she said, getting her knapsack. "I brought you something from school. Someone left it in the teachers' lounge, so I snagged a piece for you."

The cake, wrapped in a sandwich bag, was somewhat the worse for wear. Angel eyed it dubiously as JayBee gave her a fork. "Try it, it's fantastic."

Angel sampled it and her expression brightened. "It's very good," she agreed. "Cocoa in the recipe, I'll bet. Maybe a hint of almond extract, too."

The tea kettle whistled and JayBee went to get it.

"I wish we'd moved away from Ohio," Angel sighed.

"There are murders in every state." JayBee looked around the kitchen. The appliances were old and there were cracks in the ceiling, but she and Angel had done what they could to make the room cheerful, painting the walls yellow, putting up a wallpaper border and hanging new curtains. She felt like she'd already put down roots here. Besides, how many other rental places had a wonderful treehouse?

"Well," said Angel, "maybe it was one of those family things. It's almost always the husband, isn't it?"

"That's hard to believe. I heard her husband speak at the meeting last night. He seemed like such a polite older gentleman."

"Then maybe it was her stepson. The ladies at the store said she didn't get along with her stepson at all."

"Oh, no," JayBee said positively. "No, it couldn't be him."

"Do you know him?" Angel seemed surprised.

"I've met him. He's very nice."

"That's what we thought about Bradley at first."

That irritated JayBee so much that she grabbed the bag of birdseed out of the cupboard, saying, "I'm going to my treehouse."

"Fine. I'd better get back to work, anyway." Angel turned to her laptop computer and opened the software she was using to prepare an index for a college textbook.

In a way, it was a shame that Angel's freelance indexing-editing business, "The Write Angle," had been successful, JayBee thought as she carefully made her way along the tree branch that led to the treehouse window. If her older sister had had to support herself by going to a nine-to-five job outside the house, perhaps her agoraphobia would never have taken such firm hold. As it was, most of Angel's business contacts were through e-mail. She was able to send and receive textbook manuscripts by Federal Express and UPS, choose clothes from online stores and purchase books and CDs from Amazon. If only Priam had had a grocery delivery service, she would never have had to leave the house.

"You'll have to go out sometimes if they give you a foster child," JayBee had told her many times. "A kid won't be willing to stay inside all the time. You'll have to take it to the playground and the movies."

"I'll be able to do it for a child," Angel would always reply. "I'm sure of it." She'd rubbed her stomach gently, just as she used to do when she was pregnant. JayBee wondered if she was even conscious of the gesture. "Oh, JayBee, I wish the wait weren't so long."

"It'll happen. Just be patient."

JayBee pushed through the window and into the treehouse. As always, the cozy little room lifted her spirits. Even the thought of Bradley couldn't spoil the afternoon when she was in here. After what Bradley had done, it was hard for either of them to trust men. Angel's reaction had been to withdraw from the world, stay at home in a comfortable cocoon and not date at all. JayBee wasn't afraid to go outside, go to work, or do the errands, thank goodness. But she often wondered if she'd be able to spot another Bradley. That was the most hurtful thing to remember. She had *liked* him.

She put out the birdseed and stood by the window, watching the squirrel who was balanced on the backyard fence. He sat up, nibbling at something held between his paws.

Too bad she couldn't be a lesbian for real, but she had never had any desire to go to bed with another woman. She liked men…big men…with dark eyes…beards…well, at least that seemed to be the type lately. Bradley was blond, green-eyed and clean-shaven. Somehow her preferences seemed to have changed.

No, she wasn't a lesbian, which meant she had the name without the game. She grinned to herself as she remembered the cashier at the drugstore.

"I was at the board meeting last night," the woman had said in her thick southern Ohio drawl. "Saw you stand up for that club the kids want to have."

"Oh, yes?" JayBee had answered neutrally, bracing herself for some gay-bashing comment. She'd promised herself, when she agreed to be the club's faculty advisor, that she wouldn't go around saying to everyone, "But I'm not a lesbian," as though there were something wrong with being one.

"Yep." The woman had chewed her gum, eyeing JayBee speculatively. "You're a pretty nice-looking gal, lipstick and all."

"Thank you." JayBee wondered where this was going.

"You interested in meeting a great little gal? My sister just broke up with her girlfriend and I know she'd go for you in a big way."

JayBee had managed to excuse herself politely.

Another squirrel approached, loping along the fence toward the squirrel who was eating. The first squirrel made a loud chittering noise. The second one paused, frozen in place. The first one lunged forward and the second squirrel lost his nerve and ran. You've got to be tough to get anywhere in this world, JayBee thought, watching them with a smile.

That would be a good message for her students tomorrow.

She wished Angel could learn it.

* * * * *

Travis went through the drive-through at McDonald's, ordering a Big Mac for himself, a salad for Katie and a plain hamburger for Queenie. Monique was with them too, lying shivering on Katie's lap, but Travis thought he would wait until they got home to feed her. Unpleasant for everyone if she threw up in the truck...

"I don't think I can eat anything," Katie said as they waited for their food.

"I bought you a salad and you're going to eat it."

"Travis!"

He strove for a kindlier tone. "Look, Katie, you haven't had anything to eat today. You're going to have plenty to do the next few days. Promise me you'll eat and keep your strength up. All right?" He remembered how she'd stopped eating after the breakup with Grayson, getting down to a hundred pounds, not nearly enough for her five-foot eight-inch height. Alicia had been beside herself, watching her daughter become more emaciated by the day.

"I'll try," she murmured. The attendant handed Travis a bag of food that turned out to be two Happy Meals. When he finally got the right order, he pulled into a space in the parking lot.

He wondered what they'd give little Travis Jeffrey to eat. What kind of place would he sleep in? Would he be safe from bigger kids? Travis couldn't really imagine what the juvenile detention center looked like—he had never been inside one—but he was sure it would be bleak and cheerless. He'd wanted to bring the boy to his own house, but that was apparently out of the question until the proper bureaucratic hurdles were jumped.

"We don't know who this child is, even if he looks like you," MacReedy had insisted. "I'm going to have to call someone from Family Services."

Katie and Officer Ming had talked to little Travis for a long time, trying to find out as much as they could. He said he was four years old. That worked out right, assuming Beth had gotten pregnant toward the end of their relationship.

The boy had been the mysterious occupant of Travis' old bunk bed last night. "I waked up all by myself," he'd told them. "Then I heard a big noise. So I hid in the closet."

The "big noise" must have been when he pounded on the front door, Travis figured. He wished he'd entered more quietly and found the boy before he concealed himself.

At least it seemed to have been established, after many careful questions from Officer Ming, that the boy was unaware of the terrible events of the night before. Grandma had put him to bed and he'd slept through the night. He seemed to accept, without question, Katie's explanation that, "Grandma had to go away this morning."

Why hadn't Beth ever told him about the boy? She'd broken up with him at the end of their third year of veterinary college, saying she'd decided to return to her hometown boyfriend, Dale Wichowski, the man she'd dated in high school and college. In some ways, Travis hadn't been surprised—she'd talked about Dale more than he was comfortable with. But in other ways, their breakup had been a tremendous blow. Although they hadn't been formally engaged, they'd talked about marriage several times, even discussed sharing a joint veterinary practice.

He tried to understand what had happened. Had she gone back to Dale and then been rejected once he found out she was carrying another man's child?

It was going to be hard to figure out what was going on. Little Travis had told them that his mother was dead. Aunt Gina had been taking care of him, but now she was going to

Indiana with Uncle Ray. He didn't know his address or telephone number. A search through the living room closet had revealed a battered old suitcase filled with clothing, ratty stuffed animals and battered metal cars and trucks. But there was no paperwork, no birth certificate.

The officers had looked through Alicia's purse, the bills she kept on the counter-desk in the kitchen, Robert's desk and every drawer in the house, searching not only for clues to the murder, but anything pertaining to the child. But nothing had turned up.

Maybe the boy wasn't his son at all. Maybe Beth had just liked his name and decided to use it for her child.

He tested that theory in his mind and was surprised at his stab of dismay. Did he want the boy, then? Oh, he knew that if Travis Jeffrey were his son, he'd take responsibility for him. There had never been any question of that. But he was startled to find his heart yearning for the child. The little boy's somber expression was a searing image in his mind.

"They should have let me take him," he said. Katie looked up, startled. "He'd be better off with me than in some detention home. That's a scary place for a little fellow."

"It's only for a night or two. Just until they find a foster parent."

"I wish he hadn't been so afraid of me." He couldn't keep the hurt out of his voice.

"I don't think it was you." Katie put her hand on his forearm for a brief moment. "It's men in general. He was scared of Austin, too."

"The chief's a pretty scary guy. Hell, I'm scared of him myself," Travis answered, going for a lighter tone.

"No, you're not."

His sister knew him pretty well, Travis reflected. No, he wasn't scared of MacReedy, even though the chief wielded a lot of power.

"It's all such a damn mess," he said. "I don't want to speak ill of the dead, but I don't know what Alicia was thinking, playing all these games with me. If she knew I had a child, she should have told me." He thought of what Georgia had said. "I wonder how long she's known about him."

"Not long," Katie said. "Maman wouldn't have been able to keep a secret like that."

"Georgia said Alicia told her I'd gotten a woman pregnant and deserted her. Could she have been talking about Beth?"

Katie shook her head. "I think Maman made that up on her own to get rid of Georgia—she never liked her, you know. Just like she said at Pete's wedding..."

Naturally, that was one family wedding Travis had not attended. "What did she say?"

Katie looked thoughtful. "It was during the dancing. Maman had a little too much champagne. She was watching Georgia dance with Pete and she turned to me and said, 'Well, I certainly outsmarted myself this time. Here I thought I'd saved Travis from that woman's clutches and then she goes and snares Peter.'"

Travis stared at his sister. "So you're saying she broke us up because she didn't like Georgia?"

Katie gave him a "how stupid are you?" look. "Why else?"

Pure malevolence? He didn't say it out loud, just shrugged.

Katie went on, "Maman was awfully upset when you got engaged to Georgia. She used to say to me, 'Travis is just too nice to see what a conniving bitch that girl is. And furthermore, she's unstable.' And honestly, I have to agree. Thank your lucky stars that Pete got stuck with her instead of you. He was telling me a few things that really opened my eyes, the evening we had the reconciliation dinner."

"What are you talking about? Georgia's a very sweet girl. She has a temper, sure, but—"

Katie rolled her eyes. "Travis, believe me—Maman had her number. You should've seen Georgia at the bridal shower I threw for her. She deserved an Oscar for the performance she put on, going on about how she adored every single gift. Then later I heard her talking with her mother, making fun of the presents and our relatives."

"All that means is she knows how to be polite!"

"I can't believe you're defending her after what she did to you. Doesn't it bother you that she dumped you and ran off with our brother?"

"Sure, but I understand it better now. If she thought I'd deserted a pregnant woman—"

"Oh, that's all b.s.," Katie said. "Anyone who knows you wouldn't believe you'd do something like that. Georgia went after Peter for one reason—because he makes four times your income."

"I'm not going to listen to this!" Travis started the truck with a jerk. He drove back to Creekside Farm in silence, not looking at Katie until he heard her sniffling.

"C'mon, let's not fight." He pulled up to the back door of his house. "Want to come in for awhile?"

She shook her head. "I need to be alone."

Travis figured she wanted to call the new boyfriend. "Are you going to take Monique?"

"You keep her for a few days, until she's better."

He'd had a feeling it was going to come to this. Katie put Monique down on the seat.

"Wait a sec." Putting his hand on her shoulder, Travis gave her a kiss on the forehead. "Call me if you need me. Okay?"

"Okay." Tears in her eyes, she climbed down out of the truck.

Travis retrieved Monique's basket from the bed of the truck and carried her into the house, Queenie at his heels. Two cats were watching from the kitchen window as he came in and put the basket by the stove, filled a bowl with water and put it down by the basket. Queenie took a long drink. After a few moments, the poodle joined her, sharing the bowl from the other side. Then Monique whined under her breath, looking anxiously around the kitchen. Travis lifted her into the basket, petting her head until she lay down. Queenie settled herself next to the basket. "Good girl," Travis said, hoping the two of them would keep each other company. Filling a bowl with dog chow, he put it down next to them. Both dogs sniffed it, but apparently it wasn't interesting enough to eat right then.

The two cats watched his every move. Travis opened a can of food and divided it onto two plates. As usual, Puff wolfed his down and then came over to Blackie and tried to eat hers as well. Travis picked him up and placed him outside the back door so Blackie could eat in peace. Snowball ran in from outside and rubbed against his legs a few times until Travis filled the dry-food bowl.

He went into the parlor and sat at his desk. There wasn't much that could be done about the funeral until the body was released—and that would probably take several days, the coroner had told him—but maybe they should go ahead and put the obituary in the paper. Certain people had to be called, too. Alicia's mother lived in a condo in Florida...Travis dreaded giving her the news. Alicia's only sister was dead, but she'd left a son, Alicia's nephew, who lived in town. Not to mention Aunt Prue, their father's sister, who would be mortally offended if someone didn't fill her in on the news before it was revealed to the public.

He wondered if Peter knew yet.

Where was his father? He refused to believe his father had killed Alicia and fled. Could he have been kidnapped by the murderer? That didn't seem like a reasonable scenario.

There had to be an explanation. No doubt his father would return soon and when he did, he would take care of all the funeral arrangements. Possibly with Katie's help.

Just in case he had to be involved, he took a pad of paper out of his desk and jotted down some notes. *Relatives. Funeral arrangements. Obituary. Lawyer.*

He thought of what the social worker had told him, back at his parents' house. "Family Services will file for temporary custody as soon as possible. If you really believe you are the father, you could file as well. You need to find the birth certificate."

"What difference would that make?"

"If the mother named you on the certificate, then Ohio law presumes you are the father. It would make it easier for you to get custody. Otherwise you'll have to wait for DNA tests."

Travis picked up the phone and called his attorney. Ben Misney, a longtime friend, knew his voice right away. "Kellman! I was kind of expecting you to call."

"You were?"

"Yep. They've been running news breaks about the murder since four o'clock on WAKC. Listen, I'm sorry to hear about your stepmother." Misney's tone was cautious, as though he really wasn't sure whether he should be expressing condolences. Misney, of all people, knew how poorly Travis and his stepmother had gotten along.

"Thanks, Misney."

"MacReedy's not giving you any trouble, is he?"

"No. But I'm worried about my dad."

"Got you," Misney said, so quickly that Travis wondered what the newscasters had been saying about Robert Kellman. "Let me know if he needs a criminal defense guy. I know some good people."

"We'll see. Have they said anything on TV about a child?"

"Nope."

Travis breathed a sigh of relief and told him everything he knew about little Travis Jeffrey and all that he could remember about Beth.

"Christ!" said Misney. "What a kick in the balls!"

"Better believe it. Listen, I want to find out as much as I can about Beth. Then I want to know if the boy's my son. If he is, I want to file for custody. Can you help?"

"Sure. I'll do some public record searches tonight. I'll call you as soon as I know anything. Maybe tomorrow."

Travis thanked him.

"Don't let Aussie jerk you around," was the lawyer's parting advice.

Aussie. Travis hadn't heard the chief's childhood nickname in years. He had a feeling MacReedy wouldn't want to hear it either. Maybe it would grate on the chief's ear the way Trav did for him.

Turning the television on, Travis found the local news. They were showing taped segments from earlier in the day, the Kellman house, surrounded by yellow police tape and news trucks…a brief interview with the coroner as he left, saying he couldn't comment until he filed his final report…MacReedy sounding tough and in control as he said, "No, we have no suspects. But we're very interested in talking to Dr. Robert Kellman. Anyone who's seen him should notify us as soon as possible."

Too restless to sit still for long, Travis went upstairs. The house originally had five bedrooms, but two of them had been remodeled into one large master bedroom and bath. He and Georgia had picked out the wallpaper together. She'd wanted a floral but he preferred something plainer, so they compromised on pale blue stripes with a narrow flowered border. That room was finished, as was the guest bedroom, but the other two were in their original state—plain oak flooring, drafty window casings and stained, yellowed ceilings. Well, if he got custody, little Travis could stay in the guest room until he turned one of the other rooms into a boy's bedroom.

He headed up to the attic and found two boxes tucked back under the eaves. Sneezing as the dust flew about, he went through the toys he'd saved. One box held three battered G.I. Joes along with their various uniforms and equipment. The other box contained well-worn stuffed animals and a Super Nintendo game. Four or five generations old by now, in videogame years. Nothing today's kids would be interested in. *Why the hell did I save this stuff, anyway?*

He closed the boxes and shoved them back again, feeling depression sweep through him.

He needed fresher air. Leaving the attic, he went outside to the unremodeled part of the barn. Donning safety goggles and gassing up the chainsaw, he drove down to the creek in his pickup. He'd spent all afternoon last Sunday taking down two dead trees. Now they needed to be cut up for firewood. Last Sunday...he thought longingly of a day before the reconciliation dinner, before Alicia was murdered, before a potentially illegitimate child showed up unexpectedly, before his father disappeared. It seemed like a golden paradise now, with no worries worse than the school board election.

He worked as though an overseer were watching him, whip in hand—worked until his clothes were drenched with sweat and he was shaking with fatigue. He'd driven one big load of split logs to the house and was starting on the second when the police cruiser came slowly down the dirt path.

Travis set his lips, preparing for bad news. Pushing the goggles up on his head, he walked over to meet the chief.

"I heard the chainsaw from the house," MacReedy said.

Travis nodded.

MacReedy ran his hand through his wavy red hair. "I thought I'd come tell you right away, since we're friends."

Even as he braced himself to hear what MacReedy had to say, Travis couldn't help wondering, *he thinks we're friends?*

"What happened?"

"Your father showed up at the house around five o'clock. We took him down to the station and questioned him." The chief sounded regretful as he went on, "I'm sorry, Trav. He's under arrest."

Chapter Five

It was too much for Travis, coming on top of the long, difficult day. "You don't have grounds to arrest my father! What the hell are you trying to do, close this case up fast so you'll look good? Not if I have anything to say about it!"

"Put the chainsaw down, Trav." MacReedy's hand went to the butt of his gun.

Best put the chainsaw down before your "friend" shoots you. Travis set the saw down in the truck's flatbed and tried to gain control over his temper. "You said yourself the shirt wasn't enough to make an arrest! I remember distinctly."

"There's more evidence now."

"What?" Travis snapped. His heart pounded as he waited for MacReedy's reply.

MacReedy sighed. "I don't want to stand out here and talk. Let's sit in the cruiser."

Travis agreed to that but was sorry as soon as he got in the vehicle. They had been on his land, but somehow they were in MacReedy's territory now.

"Where was my father all day?" he asked, trying to keep his voice even.

"Don't know." MacReedy took a package of gum out of his breast pocket and offered Travis a stick, which he accepted.

"What do you mean, you don't know?"

"He won't tell us where he was."

"What did he say?"

MacReedy chewed his gum thoughtfully. "Not much. He made a very short statement. Said he argued with his wife last night and left the house around ten o'clock. Refused to say what he was doing yesterday evening and today, or even if he was with another person. Said he did not murder his wife and can't imagine who did. We gave him his phone call and his attorney advised him not to speak further with us. End of story."

"So you arrested my father because he wouldn't answer your questions?" Travis demanded with growing indignation.

"Of course not. We have additional evidence from the neighbor, Mrs. Stansky." The chief picked up his clipboard, flipped through a few pages and read, "'When asked if she knew what time the victim got home last night, the witness said it was around nine o'clock.'"

"Nine!" Travis exclaimed. "What the hell is she talking about? The school board meeting adjourned at ten to eight."

"'When asked if she was sure of the time, witness said she was watching the clock closely, waiting for *ER* to start. She stated that Robert's car drove up about half an hour after the victim came home. She could hear Robert arguing with the victim because the kitchen windows were open at the Kellman house. The victim was crying.'" MacReedy gave Travis a sardonic look.

"People argue all the time." Travis imagined Mrs. Stansky with her ear to the window, desperately trying to listen in.

MacReedy read on, "'She could not make out any of the conversation.'"

"Then how did she know the person in there arguing was my father?"

"Wait, there's more. 'Witness heard a loud bang and looked outside. She saw Robert leave the house by the back door. He looked very angry. He jumped into his BMW and took off down the street at fifty miles an hour. Witness expressed concern at his rate of travel because there are children living on the street.'"

"Then the murderer must have come over after my father left," Travis insisted. "Didn't Mrs. Stansky hear anything else?"

"No. 'Witness stated that she was in her living room watching ER after that and it was a good episode last night.'" The chief laid the clipboard down. "And there you have it. Independent evidence of an argument. Accused seen fleeing the house. And while Thomson has not yet made his report, he told me informally that your stepmother had probably been dead between ten to fifteen hours when you found her. So time of death fits neatly into the scenario."

Travis took a deep breath, wiping sweat off his forehead. "Hell, this is all circumstantial. My father had no reason to murder his wife."

"Maybe he had a reason you're not aware of, Trav. It might have been anger, or it might have been premeditated. Did your stepmother have any money of her own?"

"I have no idea." Travis was fairly sure she did, but it wasn't up to him to tell MacReedy.

"Well. We'll just have to see who gets the money. Look to the money for a motive—that's what I've learned from being a cop."

"Right. That's a fancy way of saying you think my father did it. Of course she probably left her money to him."

"But did he need it for something just now? That's what the prosecutor will look for. Maybe for a new girlfriend? Or an election campaign?"

"The election isn't that important to him. Don't be ridiculous."

MacReedy gave him an impatient look. "I'm not saying I believe any of that personally. I'm telling you what Jim Percy might use as ammunition when he prosecutes the case." MacReedy took off his sunglasses and polished them. "We're going to move your dad to county lockup tomorrow about ten o'clock. If you want to see him before that, you're welcome to come by."

"Thanks." Travis wondered why the chief was being so helpful.

"If you do come visit, try to talk sense into your dad. Cooperation might do a lot for him. Percy's not a bad sort. If your dad came clean and admitted he acted in the heat of anger, spares everyone a big trial, I'm sure Percy'd give him a good deal. Tell your dad it's not in his best interest to take this high-and-mighty attitude."

Travis' hands, flat on his lap, clenched into fists. "Know something? You've never been my favorite person around here, but I never knew you were lazy. Go ahead, try to railroad my father, I can't stop you—but I'm sure as hell not going to help you do it."

"Now, listen up just one second, Trav—"

"No, you listen to me, Aussie. There better not be any police coercion or manufacturing of evidence or any of the other little tricks you fellows do. You'd best keep everything spic-and-span on this case and play by the rules."

MacReedy froze up. "I've always run a clean station. You won't find anyone around here saying otherwise."

"All right, fine—but this rush to arrest my father makes me wonder."

"Your dad has a shitload of money. I wanted him locked up before he had time to flee the country." MacReedy cracked his knuckles. "Well, it doesn't surprise me that you'd defend your dad. You always thought the world of him, like most other people around here. Just don't be too disillusioned if his adoring public turns on him." Brushing his hand through his curls, he added, "And here's one thing to think about. If we do have the wrong man and the real killer knows we've arrested your dad, maybe he'll get careless. More criminals are caught through their own stupidity than by good detective work."

"I can believe that," Travis said dryly.

"It's no secret. You want a ride up to the house?"

Travis figured that was MacReedy's way of telling him the conversation was over. "No, thanks, I've got my pickup down by the creek."

He was opening the door to his truck when MacReedy pulled up beside him and said through the window, "Get some rest, Trav. You look like hell."

* * * * *

Back at the house, Travis checked on the dogs. Monique seemed fretful, but she hadn't thrown up again. He patted her for a few minutes until she stopped whining. Heading upstairs, he took a long, hot shower. As soon as the water had completely drained from the tub, Blackie jumped in and lay down, willing to put up with some dampness in exchange for the warmth.

He was too restless to go to bed, so he put on clean clothes and went for a walk. He cut through back lots, going toward the village. The full moon gave him plenty of light to see where he was going.

The Scotland Church was one of the oldest structures in the village, built in 1838 by the earliest settlers of Priam. The historical society was always talking about fixing it up but had never raised enough money to do so. The church had sat empty, windows boarded up, for over thirty years.

Behind the church lay a cemetery. Part of it was surrounded by a black wrought iron fence, but part of it was open to the woods. He slipped in noiselessly and walked up and down the rows of tombstones. It seemed unutterably sad to him that so many of the markers had been rendered unreadable by years of weather.

He went to a long, flat monument shaped like a huge shoebox, three feet off the ground and sat down. Too bad he couldn't be buried here someday—it had always been one of his favorite places in Priam—but no new burials had been allowed since 1949.

He wondered where Alicia would be laid to rest. There was a big modern cemetery just off I-675, about twenty minutes from Priam, but it didn't have the charm of these old-fashioned grounds. No doubt his father would decide. Would he be able to attend his wife's funeral? Not unless he was granted bail, but Travis didn't think bail would be permitted in a murder case. Silently he cursed MacReedy for acting so quickly. Couldn't he have spent a few days investigating the case before he arrested Robert Kellman?

Travis still couldn't believe his father would do such a thing. But then, who hated Alicia enough to stick a knife in her chest? Thinking of MacReedy's remark about money, he wondered who wanted her money badly enough.

He needed to talk to Georgia. Before, he wouldn't have accused her or said anything to MacReedy, but everything had changed now that his father had been arrested for the crime. He wouldn't spare Georgia if it meant his father would go to prison or the lethal injection chamber in her place. He felt sure that if he could just talk to her about the murder, look in her eyes, he would know whether she had done it.

* * * * *

JayBee had found the charming old cemetery one day while she was out jogging. Angel used to like making rubbings of old tombstones. JayBee wondered if she'd be able to tempt her outside long enough to come here and see the place.

She especially liked some of the statues, a weeping woman, a cherub with a lyre, an angel of indeterminate sex holding a long sword.

The man was sitting so quietly, like a statue himself, that JayBee didn't realize he was there until she was a mere six feet away. She froze, then sighed in relief as she realized it was Travis Kellman.

"Hi, JayBee." His voice was calm and matter-of-fact. They might have been running into each other at the corner grocery store.

"Hi! I'm surprised to see you here. I thought this place was my private find."

A slight smile crossed his face. "No, I've been coming here since I was a kid. Want to join me?" He patted the stone surface beside him. "It's about the only place to sit around here."

She hitched herself up beside him. "Penny for your thoughts," she said cheerfully, but then could have cursed herself. Naturally he must be preoccupied with the murder.

"Oh...I was just thinking about life and death." He looked around, his gaze seeming to survey the entire cemetery. "Have you ever walked through here during the day? It's interesting to read about why people died. War casualties, childbirth, farm accidents, shark attacks—"

"Shark attacks? In southern Ohio? Must have been a land shark," she said, thinking of the old *Saturday Night Live* routine.

He turned to look at her, startled.

"You know how to avoid the land shark?" she went on. "Just don't answer the door when it says, 'Candygram!'"

He grinned. "A woman with a sense of humor."

The approval she saw in his eyes warmed her, but she felt obligated to speak up for her gender. "All the women I know have a sense of humor. It's just more sophisticated than dirty limericks and fart jokes."

He laughed. "All right, I grant you that. It's just—well, both the women I was engaged to in the past had very little sense of humor."

"Maybe that's why you're not married to either of them."

He seemed taken aback by this view of things. "I never really thought of that before."

Maybe she shouldn't have let on that she knew he wasn't married. Oh well, if he guessed she was interested in him, was that so terrible? Someone had to make the first move.

She was sure he wouldn't turn out to be like Bradley.

In the range of male beauty, he fell somewhere in the "slightly better than average" category. He lacked Bradley's blond, television anchorman good looks. But Travis had something better than a conventionally handsome face. Maybe it was those very kind brown eyes, the way they turned down slightly at the outer corners. Or his impeccably trimmed beard. Or his expression, which seemed to reveal both intelligence and compassion. Really, it wasn't any one feature—something about him as a whole person appealed to her strongly.

He wore jeans and boots, the perfect way for a man to dress, in JayBee's opinion. Suddenly, she thought of Bradley in his expensive Italian loafers, those narrow feet kicking her sister in the stomach. She shivered.

"You're cold," Travis said. "Need a coat?" He took off his hip-length, brown leather jacket and hung it around her shoulders.

"Thanks." She was touched by the gesture. The jacket smelled like him. She inhaled the faint scent of his citrus aftershave.

"Aren't you afraid of running around by yourself at night?" Then he frowned. "Sorry, that sounded kind of threatening. I didn't mean it like that."

"I know." She brushed her hair back, trying to sound casual. "Some of the teachers were talking about you." *Yeah, because I brought you up as a topic.* "You've got a reputation for being a nice guy. Good with animals."

"I'd better be—I'm a veterinarian."

"So I heard. And to answer your question—no, I'm not afraid. I wouldn't live in a place where I didn't feel comfortable walking around by myself."

"We had a murder in town last night." He spoke as though reluctant to mention it.

She nodded. "I know. If anyone attacks me, I'll give them a run for their money. I studied karate for ten years."

"That's an unusual interest." A strange expression had come over his face. Maybe that sounded too unfeminine to him, too tough. Well, it was part of her and she didn't want to conceal that side of herself.

"For a woman, you mean? Maybe. My dad made my sister and me take lessons, starting when we were eight and nine years old. He didn't want us to be helpless." Too bad Angel had quit after a year.

Now he was looking at her as though she puzzled him. "What else do you like to do?"

She wondered if he was asking because he was interested in her, or if he was trying to figure out her true sexual orientation. "Oh, lots of things. Movies, reading, inline skating, working on the house. How about you?"

"All of the above—except inline skating. I'd probably kill myself if I tried that. Do you like music?"

"Sure, especially if I can dance to it."

He smiled. "I like dancing. There's a place out on the highway that has live bands on the weekend. Think you'd like to go with me sometime?"

"Sounds like fun."

He looked deeply into her eyes. Lifting her chin, she gazed back at him. It wasn't enough to be sitting next to him—she wanted him to touch her. She waited, holding her breath, her lips parted.

Leaning forward, he brushed the side of her face with two fingers, the lightest feather touch.

She moved closer, putting her hand on his shoulder. He kissed her, a pleasant, lips-only kiss. Still, something about it made her heart pound. She hated it when guys jammed their tongues down her throat, or pawed at her clothes like a mad dog, or tried to finger private places in the first five minutes. Travis did none of those things. He just kissed her, firmly and confidently, then drew back for a moment, giving her a chance to pull away. Instead, she put her arms around his waist. He kissed her again, a little harder and longer this time.

"What made you do that?" she murmured, her face very close to his.

Still looking intently into her eyes, he said, "I was thinking about that club you're involved with. I needed to know if you're a lesbian. It seemed rude to ask right out."

"And what's your conclusion?"

"You're not." He sounded certain.

She tilted her head, watching his expression. "And if I were? Would that mean we couldn't be friends?"

"We could be friends, sure. But I don't want to think about you the way I'm thinking—if you're not interested."

"I'm interested." This time she kissed him, touching her tongue to his. That seemed to encourage him and he deepened the kiss, pulling her tightly against him. She ached to touch him.

What's the matter with you, girl? she wondered. *It's just because it's been so long,* she answered herself. Still, she couldn't help running her hand through the back part of his hair, where it was longest. He seemed to like that. Leaving her mouth, his warm lips moved down the side of her neck, making her gasp. She slipped her hand up his inner thigh. *Good, I'm not the only one who's turned on.*

He picked up her hand and kissed her fingers.

She heard her own fast breathing in the quiet night, echoed by his. "Wow," she said, finding her voice at last. "Some kiss."

He moved closer, but instead of kissing her again, as she expected, he slowly pushed her hair off her face, tucking it behind her ear. It was such a tender, loverlike gesture that JayBee was startled.

"I was crazy about you the second I saw you looking down out of the tree." The warm note in his voice pleased her. "When can we see each other again? Will you give me your phone number?"

That brought her down to Earth with a bump. "I'm sorry—I promised my sister I wouldn't give it out to anyone. I'll call you, okay?" She stood up to leave, not sure what was going on here. She always liked to be in control of the situation. She wasn't used to feeling overwhelmed like this.

He took his wallet out and handed her a business card. "That's fine—if you really mean it."

"I mean it." She took his jacket off.

He looked disappointed. "Don't you want to borrow it for awhile?"

She grinned. "I'm warm enough from that last kiss." Placing the jacket on his knees, she leaned close to him.

"Then how about one more for the road?" he murmured. He put his hands on her shoulders and kissed her one last time.

"I'd better go," she said finally, surprised by her breathlessness. Instantly he released her.

She hurried off, hoping Angel wouldn't be too upset when she got home. She had stayed out twice as long as she'd intended. Turning once, she saw he was still sitting there looking after her. She waved. Outside the cemetery, she broke into a run.

* * * * *

Back home, Travis got ready for bed, stripping down to his boxer shorts. As he folded the covers back, he imagined JayBee in the bed, her lovely red hair spread out across the pillow.

One of the worst days of his life had taken an unusual upturn…an ending he'd never expected.

He shouldn't be thinking about a woman, with his stepmother murdered, his father in jail and little Travis in a detention center.

But he hadn't gone out to seek her. However attracted he was to her, he wouldn't have spent the evening trying to find her when so many other critical things were going on.

She'd come to him as he sat alone in the cemetery. She'd appeared out of the darkness, unafraid, vibrant with life.

Sometimes things were fated. Sometimes they just…happened.

He lay down, thinking about her warm, soft mouth and the sweet, fresh smell of her hair. God, it had been so long…

A little later, as he was drifting off to sleep, he heard a scratch at the door. Ignoring it, he turned over and pulled the quilt over his head.

Another scratch and a whine.

Finally he went to the door to find both dogs waiting, tails wagging, eyes begging.

"All right, I guess I should have expected this."

Queenie lay down on the bed with an air of great satisfaction. Monique was too small to jump up so he lifted her. She curled up against Queenie's back.

Twenty-eight years old and these were the only females he could find to share his bed.

* * * * *

"Dr. Kellman! Please, just a short statement!"

"Do you believe your father murdered your mother?"

"Do you think there's enough evidence to convict your father?"

Travis paused at the door of his truck. He'd been naïve, he thought, to believe he could come and go as he pleased when news like this hit town. Three vans were present from local television stations, two cars from radio stations, even a reporter from the *Priam Village Chronicle* on her bicycle. "Good Lord!" he said, as numerous microphones were thrust into his face. "What a circus!" He was surprised not to see a news chopper trying to land in his thirty-acre field.

He would have liked to stalk away with a "No comment", but that wouldn't help his father.

Taking a deep breath, he spoke as firmly and convincingly as he knew how. "I'm positive my father is innocent of these charges. He loved my stepmother and had no reason to murder her. The police have been misled by circumstantial evidence. I'm confident that when further investigation is done, the real killer will be found. Now, if you'll excuse me, I'd like to get my truck out of the driveway."

His statement didn't even slow them down.

"What evidence are you talking about?"

"The neighbor says your parents were arguing right before the murder. Do you have a comment about that?"

Travis shook his head and got into the truck. Two of the vans were blocking the drive. Not letting that stop him, he gunned the truck over the grass.

Once on the road, he called Katie. She sounded as though she were just waking up.

"Sorry, I didn't mean to get you out of bed."

Yawning, she said, "That's okay. I took a sleeping pill last night, so I'm still groggy."

"Listen, bad news. Dad's been arrested."

"I know."

Travis wondered who had told her. "I'm going down to the police station to talk to him. Look out if you go outside—

there's a bunch of newspeople outside my back door. Be careful what you say to them."

"I'm not going anywhere today." Katie yawned again. "Tell Daddy I love him."

Travis found more reporters waiting outside the police station. He paused briefly to make the same short statement and went inside.

Twenty years ago, the old police station had been replaced by a new, modern structure. Built a few blocks away from the square, so that it wouldn't conflict with the historic period buildings, the new station was constructed of forbidding gray concrete. Many people considered its erection a rather foolish expense for a village with so little crime. It was rumored that the former police chief had called in many favors to get council's approval. But at least, unlike the old station, the roof didn't leak and there were three separate holding cells instead of one large pen for malefactors.

The inside was depressingly white and gray, like something built in Soviet Russia, circa 1950. Apparently the funds had been expended mostly on the exterior, because all the furniture was of the cheapest possible quality.

Travis went straight up to the desk sergeant. "I'm Dr. Travis Kellman. Chief MacReedy told me I'd be able to visit my father this morning."

The sergeant nodded. "Yes, he left orders. Your brother is already with your father." She told him to walk through the metal detector and gave him directions to the visiting room.

Robert Kellman looked up and managed a faint smile as Travis appeared in the doorway. Robert wore a chartreuse golfing shirt that gave him a youthful air, but his eyes were red-rimmed as though he had been crying. Travis knew his father was a tenderhearted man who cried easily. Sad stories on the news, "Heroes for Today" tales in *Reader's Digest,* a sentimental birthday or Father's Day card from one of his children—all of these could bring on unabashed tears.

"Travis! My son!" His father reached out a hand. Travis took it and his father squeezed his hand. "Thanks for coming."

"Thank God you're alive, Dad! Katie and I were awfully worried, let me tell you."

"I'm sorry about that. How's Katie doing?"

Travis hesitated. "Very upset. She sends her love."

His father sighed. "Take care of her, son."

"I always do." It had been the frequent refrain of his childhood, *Watch out for your little sister, or Go check on Katie, Travis.*

"You're a good brother, Travis. She's going to have a hard time dealing with all this. Help her all you can. You know how hard it is to lose your mother."

"Enough already about Katie!" Peter said. "She'll cope, just like anyone has to when they're grieving. What about you, Dad? Are you going to tell us where you were Thursday night and all day Friday?"

Robert Kellman sat in silence for several long moments. "No."

"Why not?" Peter demanded.

Robert looked from Peter to Travis and back again, his tired eyes suddenly narrowing. "Because it's nobody's business but my own."

"Dad!" Peter's voice rose excitedly. "Dad, you can't take this attitude!"

Robert's face took on a mulish expression that Travis knew well. "Boys, I'm innocent. And under our legal system, a man is innocent until proven guilty. Anyone who knows me should realize I could never commit this type of horrendous crime."

"Apparently MacReedy doesn't know it," Travis said dryly. "Dad, you've got to be careful here. If there's someone who can help, you'd better contact them and get them to testify for you. Surely you weren't out by yourself all those hours, were you?"

"It doesn't matter," Robert said. "I stormed out of the house angry. I admit it. No matter who I was with afterward, that's a fact."

"But that person could testify for you. Tell how you looked when you met up with them. If they could testify that you were calm and pleasant—"

Robert folded his arms adamantly. "I refuse to discuss it."

Travis and Peter looked at each other in consternation. Peter shook his head slightly and then put his hands on the table, palms down. Looking at his knuckles, he said, "You know, Dad, everyone understands overwhelming anger—heat of passion. Everyone has felt that impulse. Anyone who's married knows—you get in an argument with your spouse, you just want to reach over and strangle her. So you're in the kitchen, there's a knife right there—you snatch it up. I understand that, the jury understands it. And it's not even first-degree murder, Dad. You really ought to think about the best path—"

Travis whipped around. "What are you saying, Pete? You think Dad did it?"

Peter's mouth turned down miserably. "What am I supposed to think? Even if he didn't do it, if he goes in there and says to the jury, 'I was with someone right after I left but I'm not going to tell you about it,' then what kind of credibility does he have? No one's going to believe him anyway! So it might be better to make a deal."

"I don't believe this!" Travis exclaimed. "You want him to confess to something he didn't do?"

"I don't know if he did it or not. It's a very flimsy story. I'm just trying to think about what's best for Dad. I don't want to see him go through a long protracted trial and end up on death row."

Nausea rippled through Travis. "Death row! They need an 'aggravating factor' when they ask for the death penalty. I know that much law."

"They've got an aggravating factor. Dad's a surgeon who could have saved Alicia after he stabbed her. His medical knowledge could have saved her and instead he ran out."

"Where the hell are you getting all this?"

Peter looked a little ashamed. "I already ran over to Remus this morning and talked to Jim Percy."

"He was just yanking your chain." Travis became aware of an icy feeling somewhere in the region of his heart. "Dad, don't say another word to the police or to that prosecutor. Don't talk to anyone except your attorney."

His father, who had sat quietly looking down while his sons argued, nodded.

"Dad, you've got to think!" Travis went on. "Was there anyone who was quarreling with Alicia? Somebody, anybody—maybe one of the shopkeepers in town—someone in the garden club? I don't want to believe it's a family member. The murderer must be an outsider."

Robert Kellman turned out his palms helplessly. "I don't know. Everyone loved my beautiful Alicia. She brought a smile to everyone she knew. Why would anyone want to hurt her?"

If Travis had had any doubt that his father was innocent, it was now eradicated. He could tell that in his father's overdramatic imagination, Alicia was rapidly becoming "Saint Alicia", just as Travis' mother had always been spoken of in the sort of glowing terms usually reserved for Mother Teresa. That had sometimes been a sore trial to his second wife. Now she would share the honors.

"All right, then," Travis went on, "just like MacReedy says we've got to look at the money trail. Is there anyone she left money to, aside from you, Dad?"

Robert looked startled. "Of course. I had a tidy little life insurance policy on her, so I told her it was fine to divide her money among you children. I think her nephew gets some, too."

Travis discounted this. He was positive that Alicia wouldn't have left him any money. "What did you two quarrel about last night?"

His father looked off into the distance. "I would rather not discuss that."

Travis drew a deep breath. "Dad, did MacReedy tell you about the child at the house?"

Robert put his hand to his forehead. "He mentioned something about him. Forgive me, son—I really wasn't focusing on that aspect of things. All I can think about is my poor Alicia." He looked up at Travis. "Do you think he's really your son?"

"I don't know. I don't understand what's going on." Travis shook his head helplessly. "He looks like me, I guess."

Officer Ming entered the room. "I have to get the prisoner ready for transport." Her black eyes seemed to dwell on Travis sympathetically. "How's your sister, Dr. Kellman?"

"She's all right," Travis answered, as he and Peter got up to leave. Putting his hand on his father's shoulder, he said, "Dad, I'm going to do whatever I can to get you out of here."

His father laid his hand over Travis' for a moment, then let the officer lead him from the room. Robert Kellman walked slowly, his thin shoulders bowed. Would they handcuff him when they took him to the county jail? A terrible indignity to visit upon an upstanding older citizen like his father…the first of many, perhaps.

As Travis and Peter started back through the station, Denise MacReedy, the chief's wife, came out of the chief's office.

"I can't believe this!" Her short black curls bounced as she shook her head indignantly. "I told Austin he must have the wrong man! Why, your father saved my life when I had cancer two years ago."

Travis murmured, "He's helped a lot of people in this town."

She patted him on the arm, tears in her eyes. "Your father is a wonderful man and don't you ever forget that."

"Thanks." Travis couldn't help feeling pleased that the chief's own wife thought he was wrong for making the arrest.

As he walked down the steps with Peter, he wondered if he should say anything to his brother about the prosecutor. It was hard to break the habit of years, the pattern of Peter as leader and himself as follower. "What made you talk to Percy? Don't you realize he wanted to pump you for information?"

"He's not like that," Peter answered. "He called me because his daughter was my patient last year. It was a courtesy."

"Sounds to me like he wanted to convince you that Dad is guilty. I couldn't believe the way you were talking in there."

Peter stopped and glared at him. "Look, 'innocent until proven guilty' sounds very nice, but most of the time, it's just a fairy tale. An ordinary citizen without a 'Dream Team' doesn't have much chance, once he's been arrested."

"That's a damn cynical view."

"It's a realistic view." Peter looked at his watch. "What are you going to do now?"

"I'm going to my clinic."

"You're going to work? With all this trouble going on in the family?"

Travis shrugged. "I didn't think of canceling everyone until it was too late."

But as he drove over to the clinic, he thought that Pete was right…he should have canceled today's appointments. There was so much on his mind and no time to think.

And yet, there really wasn't anything he could do at this point. The child was in the custody of Family Services. He'd seen his father, but obtained precious little information from him. What else was there to do except go to work?

Travis never knew how he got through that half-day at the clinic. He saw three dogs, five cats, a cockatiel and a ferret. An uncomfortable morning, with so much unspoken between him and his clients. A few people muttered some uncomfortable words of sympathy. No one, not even Thelma the receptionist, dared to ask about his father.

Around one o'clock, Travis let Thelma leave. He straightened the examination room himself and mopped the floor in the waiting room where a scared puppy had urinated. As he was finishing, the door opened to admit the tall, lanky figure of Ben Misney. The lawyer's long face bore a mournful expression, but that didn't alarm Travis. Misney customarily went around looking as though his dog had just died.

"Afternoon, Kellman. I saw your truck out front, so I thought I'd stop by."

"Give me just a second." Travis rolled the mop bucket into the back, dumped out the dirty water and hung up his lab coat. His heart was pounding hard. He knew that Misney wouldn't have stopped by merely to chat.

When he came back into the waiting room, Misney was sitting and reading *Cat Fancy* magazine. Travis knew that Misney was no more interested in felines than he was in learning Sanskrit, it was simply the nervous habit of not being able to sit idle without reading print.

Misney looked up, putting the magazine aside. "I have news about your boy."

Chapter Six

"Tell me over lunch." Travis hadn't eaten all day, except for a quick cup of scalding-hot coffee that morning. "Ming Dynasty? Or Betty's?"

"Grease burgers," Misney decided, so the two men walked over to the square to Betty's Sunny Spot, choosing an oilcloth-covered table in the back. Betty herself waited on them, coming over with glasses of water and her usual cheerful smile. Both men waved away menus and ordered cheeseburgers.

They were silent until Betty was out of earshot. Travis watched the condensation on his glass, tracing a pattern in it with his finger as he waited for Misney to speak.

"I called the social worker this morning," Misney said. "She doesn't want to leave the kid in the detention home, so she's doing an emergency foster placement this weekend. She's already spoken to the foster parent, who's agreed to take the kid today."

"Did she say where the foster parent lives? Are they going to let me visit?"

"I spent a long time talking to the lady—really laid it on good and thick about what an upstanding citizen you are. She explained everything to the foster parent and then got back to me. So here's the bottom line. Everyone knows you're probably the father and that you'll be petitioning for custody. The foster parent will arrange a visit—but she will contact you."

"That's great." Travis wished it could have been a more definite appointment, but this was certainly better than nothing.

"You're really taking this well," Misney observed. "I'd be going nuts if I were you."

"It's sort of a controlled panic." Travis looked up with a wry smile. "And you know I've always wanted kids."

"Kids, right. More fun than a barrel of monkeys. And twice as much trouble."

"Yeah, we got into some real trouble when we were kids." Travis shook his head. "Good thing the adults never knew about most of it."

Misney grinned. "Yeah, I remember."

Misney had been a city child, raised in Philadelphia, but spent a month in Priam every summer visiting his grandparents. Although he was two years younger than Peter's crowd, he'd hung out with them anyway. He went on to Yale Law School, a high-powered litigator's position at a New York City firm and marriage to a socialite. Travis remembered his surprise, leafing through *Vanity Fair* and seeing his friend's familiar, dour face in an article about a swanky Manhattan party. Then it had all fallen apart. Travis never heard the details, but Misney had filed for divorce, left his law firm and moved to Priam. Instead of multimillion dollar lawsuits, he now handled domestic problems, zoning disputes and real estate transactions. "I came back because this was the only place I was ever happy," he had told Travis once.

Misney was facing the door. "Nice rack on her." He lifted his chin for a better view.

Travis turned and saw JayBee seating herself at the lunch counter. His brows drew together. "Watch it—she's a friend of mine."

Misney looked amused. "So what? Am I wrong?" Glancing at himself in the mirror over the counter, he smoothed his black hair back and straightened the collar of his white shirt.

Wanting to get Misney off the subject of JayBee, Travis told him about the school board meeting. It seemed like a century ago.

Betty brought their cheeseburgers. Travis was hungry enough to eat his, but couldn't help noticing there was some scrambled egg stuck to it from someone else's order.

"At least pretend to listen," he said, noticing that Misney's eyes were fixed on JayBee with keen interest.

"See what she's eating?" Misney asked.

Travis took another quick look. The fry cook had just shoved a tall chocolate milkshake and a large order of French fries in JayBee's direction. She was dousing the fries in ketchup.

"Jesus H. Christ, I think I'm in love!" Misney said. "I'm never dating a skinny woman again. I used to take my wife out for a two-hundred dollar dinner and half an hour later she'd be in the bathroom, puking it up. Never again, my friend, never again."

"Too bad you missed the school board meeting." Travis watched the lawyer closely. "That woman's the new faculty advisor for the gay students' collective."

Misney put his fork down with a sharp click. "You're shittin' me!"

"Ask anyone." Travis took another bite of his burger.

"You're telling me she's a dyke?"

Travis felt a prick of conscience. "Did I say that? All I said is she's the faculty advisor."

"What a hell of a thing!" Misney shook his head. "All those looks wasted. Man, I wish I could find myself a girlfriend. Seems like everyone in this town is hooked up already or married. I wish you'd put a good word in for me with your sister. How about it, Kellman?"

"Kind of young for you."

"Well, thanks a whole hell of a lot. Eight years—that's nothing." Misney took a big bite of his burger and washed it down with some water. "Oh, well. She's already got someone, anyhow."

"Thought so. Did you see her with a man?"

"Yeah, they were sitting together at the Paradise, but I couldn't tell who it was. The guy was wearing sunglasses and a cap."

Travis didn't like the sound of that. Who wore sunglasses in a dark bar? Someone who was married and didn't want to be seen with a girlfriend, that was who.

Katie's love life was another good topic to avoid, so Travis changed the subject. "Were you able to find out anything about Beth Madison?"

The lawyer took on a smug expression. "Of course—you're looking at an expert here. I found the death certificate online and sent you all the information by e-mail. Beth was hit by a car last year and died from head trauma."

Travis looked down, thinking about this. He had known since yesterday that Beth was dead, but somehow, hearing the cause of death seemed to make it more real. He couldn't help remembering how he had enjoyed the six months they had spent together.

"I know it's tough to hear about," Misney said sympathetically. "It's always hard when someone dies so young. Anyway, her address was on the death certificate. She was living in Cincinnati. Do you want to take it any further? The next step would be to hire a private eye."

Travis knew that could run into a lot of money. "No, I'll take it from here." Beth's hometown of Galenburg, Ohio, was only an hour away. Assuming no veterinary emergencies came up, he'd drive down there tomorrow and spend the day finding out what he could.

"What about the boy? Were you able to locate a birth certificate?" Travis asked.

Misney shook his head. "Nope. Since you didn't have the birth date or place, I had to make some calls, but no luck. He's not in the Ohio vital records. Your best bet is to look for the sister or Beth's parents and find out where the kid was born."

Travis hoped he'd be able to find Beth's parents. Well, that would be tomorrow's task.

As for today, there was someone he wanted to talk to very much.

* * * * *

JayBee hauled the groceries out of the Toyota Corolla that she and Angel shared, hanging each blue bag over her arms so that she could bring them all in at once. Maneuvering her way through the back door with difficulty, she dumped everything on the kitchen table with a sigh of relief.

"Where have you been all this time?" Angel demanded, hurrying in from the dining room. "You've been gone three hours!"

"I had lunch, then I went to the library and the grocery store."

"The social worker called this morning. She's got an emergency foster placement and I'm getting him! I'm expecting them any minute!"

"Today?"

Angel's eyes glowed with enthusiasm. "Yes, isn't it terrific? I'm so excited!" She hesitated. "There's just one problem. I've got a big deadline Monday. I was going to spend today and all day tomorrow working. I still have two hundred pages to index."

JayBee gave her sister an exasperated look. "Then why did you agree to take the kid this weekend? Couldn't it wait until Monday?"

"No. He's just a little four year old, so Miss Perkins doesn't want to leave him at the juvenile detention center." Angel turned big, pleading eyes on JayBee. "I was thinking, if you'd watch him today and tomorrow, I could keep working."

JayBee sighed as she put away the milk. "Angel, I told you before, I don't want to get involved with this foster child. This is your thing." Angel had gone to licensing classes several years ago, before her agoraphobia overtook her. She'd cared for two foster children when she lived in Dayton, both of whom had been eventually reunited with their mothers.

"I know," Angel said. "I promise I'll arrange things better in the future. It's just for this weekend, okay? I'll give you some money and you can take him to an amusement park or something."

The doorbell rang. Angel rushed off to the living room. JayBee took a quick look around to make sure that everything cold was put away, then followed. She wouldn't have admitted it to Angel, but she was curious to see the child.

The social worker and a young boy stood on the front porch. The boy was solemn-faced, eyes wide and scared. In one hand he clutched a battered red Elmo doll. His other hand gripped the social worker's hand tightly. She was carrying a shabby blue suitcase.

The boy's shirt was small for him, although it was clean. His jeans had tears in the knees.

Angel opened the door with a big smile. "Come in! I'm so glad you're here!"

The child did not look reassured. The social worker tried to let go of his hand so she could shake hands with Angel, but the boy kept hold of her.

Angel dropped to her knees. "Hi, Travis. My name's Angel."

The boy looked down and didn't answer.

Angel's smile faltered, but she kept on. "You're going to live here with me and my sister, isn't that nice?"

The boy drew a little closer to the social worker.

Angel reached her hand forward, then drew it back when the child's eyes widened in fright. Lowering her voice, she said, "We're so happy to have you! We hope you're going to like it here."

JayBee frowned. Angel was coming on strong. She sensed it would be better to remain quiet and let the child get his bearings. Seating herself on the couch, she picked up one of her motorcycle magazines and pretended to be concentrating on it.

"Hi." The child spoke so quietly he could hardly be heard.

"Go ahead into the house," Miss Perkins told him, a slightly severe note coming into her voice. The boy stepped into the house as warily as a wild thing sensing a trap.

Miss Perkins finally managed to get her hand free of the boy's. "Everything he has is in this suitcase," she told Angel.

"What's her name?" the child asked, pointing at JayBee.

She looked up briefly. "I'm JayBee."

For the first time, the boy smiled. "My mommy used to call me by my initials too. 'T.J.'"

"Is that what you want to be called, kid?" JayBee asked.

He nodded. "I saw a motorcycle! Does it live here?"

"Yeah. That's my bike, T.J. You don't want to mess with it. Got that?"

T.J. looked like he was thinking about it, but finally he said, "Okay."

Miss Perkins bent, peering into the boy's face. "I need to talk to your new foster mom about some things. Can you sit quiet and look at one of your books while we talk?"

"I've seen all my books." T.J.'s face took on a stubborn expression.

"I've got some wonderful books you can look at," Angel said with enthusiasm. "Would you like one about dinosaurs?"

"No. I hate dinosaurs!"

"How about this one?" Angel pulled a picture book off the shelf. "It's about some kids at school and all the fun things they do—"

The child shook his head. "Don't want a dumb book about kids at school." His voice sounded as though he were about to cry.

"Want to look at my motorcycle magazine?" JayBee asked.

T.J. thought about that for a few moments, then came over to the couch and climbed up beside her. She laid the magazine in his lap, listening as the social worker talked to her sister. "Now, don't get too attached to him," Miss Perkins murmured. "I took T.J. to the lab this morning for a DNA swab. The father's attorney told me they're going to petition for custody as soon as the test results come in. So don't count on having him more than a few months."

JayBee left the couch, joining her sister and the social worker. "Why doesn't the father have custody now?" she asked.

"It's a strange story," Miss Perkins said. "I was telling your sister on the phone this morning—the mother never told the father she'd had his child. She died a year ago and apparently her sister's been in charge of the boy ever since. It seems the aunt decided to move out of state, so she brought the boy to stay with his grandmother, but—" Leaning closer, she lowered her voice. "That same evening, the grandmother was m-u-r-d-e-r-e-d!" She glanced over at the boy, but he seemed to be absorbed in the magazine.

JayBee gasped. "Are you talking about the Kellman family?"

Miss Perkins nodded. "Yes. And since the father's a professional man, well-known here in town, I'm sure he'll have no trouble getting custody."

JayBee said slowly, just to make certain, "So his father is Travis Kellman? The veterinarian?"

"That's right," Miss Perkins answered. "At least, that's the theory. We'll see if DNA test results prove it."

Miss Perkins gave Angel a list of pediatricians in the area. "We didn't have time to take him to a doctor, but I'd recommend a physical examination as well as some psychological testing. I'm concerned about him being in the house that night."

"Did he see anything?" Angel whispered.

Miss Perkins shook her head. "He was questioned by a police officer at the scene. Fortunately, it seems that he was asleep when it happened. Still, it wouldn't hurt to have a child psychologist talk to him."

Angel nodded seriously. JayBee looked over at the child, who was leafing through the magazine with an intent look on his little face. Now that she'd heard he was most likely Travis' son, she could see a resemblance. What an odd story, though. Travis had mentioned being engaged twice in the past. She knew one of the fiancées had been Georgia—had the other been this boy's mother?

What a lot for Travis to be going through right now. His stepmother murdered and his father arrested for it. People had been talking about it everywhere she had gone that morning. And now this child had turned up.

Part of her wondered whether she was being foolish, getting interested in a man who had so many complications in his life.

* * * * *

Travis spoke softly into the phone. "Georgia? I really need to talk to you."

There was a long pause before she answered. "I'm sorry." Her tone was impersonal. "I really can't take the time to do a survey right now."

He knew Peter must be near. "Could I come see you early tomorrow morning?" Peter usually played golf on fine Sundays.

"Tomorrow morning? I suppose you could call back then. Not before ten, please."

"All right." In the background, as he hung up, he could hear his brother asking, "Who was that?"

Going to his desk, he turned on his laptop and logged on to his e-mail account. As Misney had promised, he'd sent a message containing Beth Madison's online death certificate. She had died at Riverside Hospital in Cincinnati, fourteen months ago.

He wondered where they'd all be if she'd stayed with him. Most likely they'd have picked an early wedding date, once she told him she was pregnant. He'd have encouraged her to stay in veterinary school so they could practice together.

Even if things hadn't worked out between them as a couple, he'd have been there for his son's birth and babyhood. He found it hard to forgive her for concealing that from him.

Deleting numerous spam messages, he saw that he had mail from akkellman@talk.net.

Dear big brother,

I called the police station cuz I wanted to visit dad but they said they moved him to county jail this am. did u know? I called there but no visiting hours til mon 12-4, cd u take me or are u working those hrs? I'm kinda scared to go alone, anyway I'm sure dad wd like to see u too. let me know ok?

Luv, Katie

Travis called up his Monday schedule. Thelma had scheduled forty-five minutes for lunch starting at half past twelve. He sent her a message telling her to call the afternoon appointments and delay each one for an hour. With almost two hours, he and Katie would be able to take a quick run to the Tecumseh County jail and make it back with time to spare.

* * * * *

JayBee couldn't remember when she had been so tired at night. Keeping track of T.J. all afternoon had been an eye-opening experience. She'd taken him to the playground behind Lowden Elementary School, where he'd skinned his knees falling off the jungle gym, gotten into a fistfight with an older kid who made fun of his curly hair and fallen into a big puddle because, "I saw a frog!"

"I only hope you have a child like yourself some day," JayBee's mother had told her one day when she'd been especially naughty. If her mother happened to be looking down from heaven today, JayBee thought, she was sure to be grinning.

"At least he's not a wimp," JayBee told Angel later that evening. "You should've seen him trying to get on a two-wheeled bicycle that was twice his size. I stopped him just in time."

"Can I have a big boy's bike?" T.J. looked up long enough from his macaroni and cheese to ask.

"Someday," Angel told him.

"Everything's always 'someday'," he pouted.

After dinner, Angel went back to her indexing project while JayBee took T.J. upstairs. He didn't want to get a bath and claimed he never went to bed until midnight. "In this house, we go to bed early," JayBee told him in her best "teacher" voice.

"I don't want to get a bath!" His face worked as though he were going to start crying.

Ignoring him, JayBee started the bath water. "Spit-spot into the tub!" If it worked for Mary Poppins, it ought to work for her.

T.J. eyed her resentfully. For several moments, the issue hung in the balance. Finally he began taking his clothes off. JayBee sat on the edge of the tub waiting, biting her tongue to keep from telling him to hurry it up. At least he was doing what she'd told him.

As he stepped gingerly into the bathwater, she gasped. His buttocks were a mass of scars and sores, some of them healed, many of them still fresh and oozing. JayBee's stomach churned. "Did someone give you a spanking, T.J.?"

He nodded. "Uncle Ray gives me a whuppin' with his belt whenever I'm bad."

Trying to repress the quaver in her voice, she asked, "What do you do that's bad?"

That seemed to be a difficult question. "I dunno. Sometimes I make too much noise. Or I give him sass."

JayBee bit her lip until she regained control over her voice. "Could you stay by yourself for just a minute?"

"Okay."

JayBee went to the top of the stairs and called for Angel. There was a note in her voice that brought her sister on the run.

"What's wrong?" Angel demanded as she reached the top of the stairs, breathless.

"I want to show you what Uncle Ray did to that child, but don't make a big thing of it in front of him. Just be sure to take him to the pediatrician on Monday."

Angel nodded, looking puzzled. JayBee beckoned her into the bathroom and told T.J. to stand up.

"Oh, my God!" whispered Angel, staring horrified at the boy's sores. She hid her face against JayBee's shoulder.

"I'm going to put some medicine on your rear end after you finish your bath," JayBee said, speaking in as calm a tone as she could muster. "It'll make you feel better." She still had some of the Bacitracin she'd used the last time she'd fallen off her motorcycle.

"Okay," T.J. said. "Will you read me a story, since I had my bath without making a fuss?"

"Sure."

Angel seemed about ready to cry. JayBee shook her head at her. Gripping her sister's arm, she led her back to the top of the stairs.

"Oh, JayBee, how could anyone treat a child like that?" Angel asked.

"I don't know, but if 'Uncle Ray' ever shows his face around here, there's going to be another murder in town."

* * * * *

On Sunday morning, Travis rose early. It was humid already, unseasonably warm for September. He dressed in sweat shorts and a tank top. Letting the dogs outside, he went to the barn to lift weights.

He loaded a twenty-five and fifty pound weight on each end of the bar and lay back on his bench. For the past few years, he'd been trying to lift two or three times a week. That and the jogging had helped him firm up his midsection and lose a few of the extra pounds that had accumulated once he passed his mid-twenties.

Thinking about Thursday evening in the park, he frowned. Georgia had been so sure he'd be understanding about the reason she was being blackmailed. He wondered how he'd ever given her the impression that he would condone dishonesty, any more than Peter would.

"What else could I do?" she'd asked. "I'd worn the clothes, so I couldn't return them. The store was calling almost every day, demanding a huge payment. Peter had already bitched at me about running up so many bills and anyway, I knew he didn't have much extra himself. So I put my diamond necklace away and then I told everyone the chain broke and I'd lost it. The insurance came through with the money, I paid off the store and everything was fine. It was no big deal, really."

"Insurance fraud is a crime," he'd answered sternly.

"Don't be like that." She stroked his arm. "Don't you see, I had to do it? I was really careful where I wore the necklace after that, but someone must have heard about it and then seen me with the necklace. Because a few months ago, the blackmailer called me."

"Man or woman?" he'd demanded.

"I could never tell." She'd looked puzzled. "But it sounded more like a man."

Travis wondered what kind of blackmailer wanted things instead of money. And such strange things. The first phone call had asked Georgia to mail her sorority bracelet to an out-of-state post office box. She'd done that, hoping the blackmail was over. But six weeks later, another call had demanded a certain tie of her father's. Peter's medical honor society ring had been the third request.

"I'm frightened!" she'd told him. "What if the blackmailer wants to use those things to frame me somehow? Commit a crime and then leave something of mine there?"

"Then you'd have to explain about the blackmail."

"But I have no proof it ever happened!"

He tried to envision a scenario where Alicia was the blackmailer. A lot of the pieces fell into place. She'd tried to blackmail him about the election, after all. If she'd tried to blackmail her stepson, why not her daughter-in-law? He remembered when Katie had told him how upset Alicia had been at Peter's wedding. Maybe she'd been planning to use those stolen items to show Peter that Georgia was a thief.

Perhaps her ultimate aim was to break up the marriage she hadn't been able to prevent.

One thing Robert had drilled into his sons was a strong sense of honesty. Georgia rightfully believed that if Peter found out about the insurance fraud, he'd be horrified.

She didn't mind telling me about it, though, Travis thought.

Did she figure he was still so besotted with her that nothing would change his feelings? Or maybe she just didn't care what he thought of her.

Maybe she'd been desperate for help.

But had she been desperate enough to murder the probable blackmailer?

He'd done two reps of ten and had sat up to take a swig of water when Georgia appeared in the barn doorway. "You and your opera!" she remarked, giving him a bright smile. "I could hear it all the way down the driveway."

He switched off the CD player. "Hi. I wasn't expecting you."

She wore a pretty pink sundress that left quite a lot of breast and thigh exposed. "You called and I came." She walked in, her sandaled feet picking their way carefully across the rough floor. "It's been a terrible couple of days, hasn't it? I don't know how your father could have done this. I'm sure Alicia said something that drove him to it." Sitting beside him, she put her hand on his arm. "How are you feeling, Travis?"

"My father did not kill my stepmother." Travis tried to look into her eyes, but she turned her head and looked down at her knees.

"Pete thinks he did."

"Pete's a fool then."

"Pete is a fool," she agreed softly. "He leaves me alone every single Sunday while he goes to play golf. If I'd married you, would you leave me alone every Sunday?"

"Probably not."

She moved closer to him, caressing his arm. "I know you wouldn't. Every Sunday we'd have stayed home all morning and made love. I remember how good you were in bed."

"Not so good that you didn't dump me for my brother," Travis answered dryly.

She turned tragic eyes on him. "But I told you how that was. I told you how Alicia lied to me." Entwining her arms around his neck, she kissed him.

After the breakup, there'd been so many times he'd wished she would come back to him, so many times he'd imagined this happening. Her mouth was warm and enticing and for just a moment he was tempted. He thought of embracing her, pulling her tightly to him…

She may have murdered Alicia.

It was a thought to chill any amount of ardor. He moved away from her.

"What's wrong? Are you thinking about Peter?" She gave him a sly smile. "Don't you want a chance to pay him back?"

"I didn't call you so we could fool around," he told her. "I want to talk to you about Alicia."

She pouted. "I'll talk if you promise you'll kiss me afterward."

"Look, you chose Pete instead of me. Fine, we both have to live with that. You're my sister-in-law—that's it."

She put her palm on his bare thigh. "But Travis, it doesn't have to be that way." Her voice dropped very low, reminding him of the way she used to talk to him in bed sometimes. "Once a man and a woman have been intimate, there's always a bond. They can always choose to go back." Her hand moved upward. He remembered how it had felt when JayBee touched him, Friday night in the cemetery. He'd wanted to take her then and there, right on top of the tombstone.

Today he didn't have to maintain that iron control. Why was Georgia so sure of him, so ready to kiss rather than talk? Was it because she had something to conceal?

"We're not going back," he said sternly, picking her hand up by the wrist. She winced a little at the strength of his grip and he let go. "Look, we both know you thought Alicia was blackmailing you. Did you kill her?"

"You bastard!" She drew her hand back and slapped him hard enough to make him see stars. He tried to catch her hands but she got up from the bench, walked a few steps away and burst into tears.

Rubbing his cheek, he thought he should have remembered her tendency to turn violent when challenged. He waited until her tears died down, then got up and walked over to face her. "What did you do after we left the park?"

"I went home."

"Can you prove that?"

She shrugged. "Probably not." Her voice was sullen. "I went straight to bed. Pete came in later."

"Where was he that night?"

"Some medical association meeting, I think."

"So you had a reason to kill my stepmother and no alibi. You know what, Georgie? I think you did it. I've thought so all along."

"I didn't kill Alicia! Even if I'd known for sure she was the blackmailer, I wouldn't have killed her!" She bit her lip while Travis tried to evaluate her words and demeanor. Was she upset because she had done it, or because he was falsely accusing her?

Then she startled him by laughing. "I know! I'm innocent and I can prove it! Ask Pete about this if you like. Pete spoke to Alicia about a loan last week. Of course I wouldn't hurt Alicia, just when Pete was going to get money from her." She smiled triumphantly.

"Why does Pete need money?" Travis was skeptical of this whole story. "He's making plenty in his practice, isn't he?"

"I don't know. He hasn't told me why, but I know he needs it badly. It's all he talks about, money, money, money, until I'm ready to scream. He wanted me to ask Daddy, but we borrowed from him last year, so I refused to ask again."

Suddenly it dawned on Travis that here was a motive for the murder. Suppose Alicia, playing her usual games, had promised Pete money and then reneged. Travis knew very well that his older brother's temper could instantly reach flashpoint. Suppose he'd gone over there Thursday night and Alicia said she'd decided against lending him the money he needed. Why, his brother had said the words himself. *So you're in the kitchen, there's a knife right there – you snatch it up.*

Pete was probably expecting money to come to him through the will. Maybe he'd figured if Alicia wouldn't lend it to him, he'd get it after her death.

Nausea rumbled through him. The idea of Pete killing Alicia was as bad as thinking his father had done it.

But right now, it seemed like Pete had a stronger motive.

Georgia said softly, "Last Thursday night, you were so afraid of your own feelings, you wouldn't even sit beside me on the park bench." He looked at her, startled that she knew that. She smiled. "Oh, yes, I can always tell how a man is feeling about me." She put her palms on his chest. "That's why you're puzzling me now, darling. You've changed in just a few days. What is it? You don't really think I killed Alicia, do you?"

"I don't know." All he wanted was to get away from her. "You've given me a lot to think about." He stepped away, sitting down on the weight bench.

Her expression darkened. "Fine, go ahead and act like that, but I'm going to tell you one more thing. I know you and Pete worship that sister of yours, but believe me, little Miss Sunshine isn't as sweet and innocent as she appears. Maybe you should take a look at Katie's motives. She's got a temper, too."

"Katie wouldn't kill her own mother! Don't be ridiculous!"

Georgia tilted her head. "What's the biggest thing in Katie's life? The most important thing to her?"

"Her art." Travis knew that without even thinking about it.

"So if she had money she could stop working at the restaurant. She could spend a year in Paris like she's always wanted. She knows very well she'll inherit money from her mother. Why was she the one to find the body? Because she knew Alicia was dead and didn't want to let her lie there all day." Georgia shook her head. "I'm sure she put on a good act, but really, I'm surprised the police weren't more suspicious."

His hands, slack on his knees, clenched his fists." I'm not going to listen to another minute of this! Katie wouldn't kill someone for money any more than I would. Don't judge everyone by yourself. Katie isn't a hard-hearted bitch like you."

Her eyes widened. Never, in their worst arguments, had he ever used a word like that with her. But this time he was angry enough to mean it.

"You're the one who's judging everyone by yourself. I know you wouldn't kill anyone, Travis. You're so soft-hearted, you can hardly put an animal to sleep. But that doesn't mean Katie's like you. Don't ever forget—she's Alicia's daughter."

With that parting shot, Georgia walked out of the barn. In a few minutes, Travis heard her Volvo start up.

Pushing his damp hair off his forehead, he sighed. A big tabby startled him by jumping down from the loft. Orlando had been the pampered pet of an old woman who had begged Travis to take the cat when she moved into assisted living. She still called every month or two to find out how he was doing.

Travis stroked Orlando's head, trying to calm down as he listened to the big animal purr.

"Katie didn't do it," Travis told the cat.

But he had to wonder about his brother. He thought about how Pete had tried to convince their father to confess. Did Pete really believe their father had committed the crime, or did he see it as a way to get off the hook himself?

Had anyone asked Pete where he was that night?

Chapter Seven

Travis wasn't having much luck in Galenburg, Beth's hometown. He had found her parents' address on an old postcard she'd sent him, but when he located the house, her parents were no longer living there. He'd already suspected that before he drove down, since he hadn't been able to find them in the telephone directory. Still, so many people had unlisted phone numbers nowadays, he thought it was worth the chance.

The young couple who now owned the small colonial had no idea of the Madison family's present location. After a few moments of hesitation, he knocked on the next-door neighbor's front door. From the old woman who answered, he was able to learn that Beth's mother had died three years ago and her father had gone into a nursing home. No, the neighbor didn't know which home.

He remembered the name of the man Beth had left him for—Dale Wichowski, a name that was forever seared into his memory. But there had been no Wichowskis in the phone directory. He had checked not only the local directories, but also the Greater Cincinnati white pages.

Temporarily at a dead end, he decided to eat lunch at the town's only restaurant. If it was anything like Betty's place, a center for local gossip, maybe someone could provide information.

Travis seated himself in a booth not too far from the counter. There were only a few others in the place, two old men arguing at the counter and a young woman reading the Sunday paper. Travis wished he'd thought to bring his own paper along on the trip. He settled for studying the greasespeckled menu instead. What in the world was a "famous dogburger"? Maybe it was better not to know.

A middle-aged woman with a cigarette dangling from her lip came by and gave the red oilcloth in front of Travis a perfunctory wipe. "What'll you have?"

"What's good?"

Apparently it was a question that didn't get asked very often. She pondered her answer for several long moments, rolling the cigarette on her lip. "Egg salad was fresh just the other day," she said at last.

He imagined what Misney would've said to her, something like, "No thanks, I want to survive until tomorrow."

Prudently, he ordered a grilled cheese sandwich and coffee. After she left, he thought about the best way to ask her about Dale Wichowski. Should he offer money? It seemed so crude. But perhaps in a place like this, crude was the way to go. Taking out his wallet, he removed a ten and folded it lengthwise.

Five minutes later she came back with his sandwich. "Have you worked here a long time?" he asked, doing his best to offer a charming smile.

She responded positively, actually taking the cigarette out of her mouth and smiling back. "A good few years."

"I'm in town looking for a friend of mine, Dale Wichowski. He used to live around here."

"Don't know the name."

He moved his hand, drawing her attention to the bill. "Are you sure? It's very important."

She shrugged, which did strange things to her massive, braless breasts. "Hey, you guys!" she shouted, making Travis jump. "Ever heard of a Dale Wichowski?"

The two old-timers at the bar turned and stared at Travis for a long moment. Finally one of them said, "Football team.

Garfield High School. Year we almost won the state championship."

"Does Dale still live here in town?" Travis asked.

"Couldn't say."

That had gone nowhere fast. Travis ate the sandwich and washed it down with coffee that tasted as though it had been sitting on the burner all morning. Handing the check to the waitress with the ten, he left, figuring that five dollars on top of the check was plenty for the non-information. After all, he hadn't learned any more than he'd known already when he came in. He'd heard plenty from Beth about Dale's prowess as the Mustangs' quarterback. It used to irritate him whenever she talked about him, especially in light of how his own father hadn't allowed him to play football.

Back in the truck, he wondered what his next step should be. It would take forever to go door to door, asking folks if they'd ever heard of Dale Wichowski.

Sometimes people kept up with their old teachers or coaches. The high school would have been the next logical place to try…if it had been a weekday.

He drove around the town square. It was a much smaller town than Priam and most of the businesses were closed on Sunday. He remembered one of the Sherlock Holmes stories recommending the "village pub" as a likely source of information, but this town didn't have a bar. Galenburg was probably one of those dry Ohio towns that prohibited liquor sales.

Noticing an attractive Victorian home with a sign out front, he slowed down. He had found the town's public library.

It was a warm day, but the library was cool and inviting. Travis liked the eclectic mixture of old and new—DVDs and books on tape reposed on antique bookshelves and some of the big wooden library tables held computers.

He strolled up and down the shelves in the nonfiction room, glancing at titles. They had a good Civil War collection, he noted, since it was an interest of his. At the shelf labeled "Galenburg Local History" he paused, wondering if anything here would help him. There were only a few books on the shelf—two by Galenburg authors, a street directory, several on southern Ohio history and a collection of Garfield High School yearbooks.

Dale Wichowski had been in Beth's high school class. Travis found the right yearbook and sat down at a table, taking out a notepad.

Beth's class had held fifty-three graduates. He found Beth's picture, feeling a familiar stab of pain as he looked into her wide green eyes. Her curly hair was much longer than he remembered. She smiled at the camera, no foreknowledge in that happy expression, no inkling that in the short span of ten years, she'd be dead. He turned the page quickly.

Dale Wichowski. Looked like a big kid. Blond, big smile full of perfect white teeth. Movie-star handsome.

How the hell was I supposed to compete with him? Travis went through the book page by page, looking for candid photos.

There were several photos of Dale, the star quarterback. "Dale, Tom and Curtis at the pep rally." "Dale and best bud Curtis raise money for the class gift." "Dale and Mike at the Homecoming Float contest."

Travis found Curtis Herman and Mike Jannetty in the full-face photos and jotted their names down. A few pages later, he found a group shot of the football team and wrote more names. Then he got the Galenburg phone directory and looked up those names.

Back in his truck, he took out his cell phone and made calls. At first he had no luck. Mike Jannetty still lived in town, but wasn't home and his wife was decidedly unfriendly and suspicious. No one answered at the Herman household. A few other people he spoke to remembered Dale, but thought he'd moved out of town two or three years ago.

Finally he tried Curtis again and this time, the man answered. For the eighth time, Travis explained why he was trying to reach Dale.

"Dale Wichowski? Sure, we go hunting together every fall. He lives in north Cincinnati now, but he works over at the Ford dealership in Seneca."

"I'm in Galenburg right now. How far away is that?"

"You just take Route 42 West toward Seneca and the dealership's right before you get into the town. Take you about twenty minutes. Hey, say hi for me if you see him, would you?"

"Thanks a lot," Travis said fervently. Maybe the luck was starting to go his way. Would it be too much to ask to find the dealership open and Wichowski at work?

* * * * *

Business was booming at the Shanks Ford dealership and Travis had to park a good distance away from the showroom. Walking down a row of gleaming new Mustangs, he eyed them longingly. Gorgeous…but impractical for a man who lived on a farm.

As he came closer to the showroom, a smiling man came out to greet him. Although eleven years had passed since the high school photographs, Travis had no trouble recognizing Dale Wichowski.

"Hi, I'm Dale! I'll bet you're looking to trade in that old pickup, am I right?" Dale offered his hand.

Travis smiled and shook his hand. "Afraid not. Actually, I came here to talk to you. If you have a few minutes?" Dale nodded, looking curious. "My name's Travis Kellman and—"

Dale's right fist came at him. Travis tried to duck but wasn't fast enough. He rocked back as Dale clipped him on the chin. Shaking his head to clear it, he charged forward as Dale geared up for a second swing. He caught Dale's wrists and held his arms apart as the other man struggled against him. The two were evenly matched in height and weight, but Travis proved the stronger as he slowly forced Dale's fists down.

Guess all that weightlifting finally paid off. Travis experienced a keen sense of triumph.

Dale stopped struggling. "Let me go! I won't try anything else."

"What the hell's wrong with you?" Travis demanded. He dropped Dale's wrists and rubbed his sore chin, still keeping a wary eye on the other man's movements.

"Sorry." Dale hung his head. "Man, I've hated your guts for so many years. I always promised myself I'd give you a good beating if I ever caught up with you."

"I never met you before in my life!"

"Yeah, I know."

"Look, I came to talk about Beth Madison," Travis said. "You willing to answer some questions?"

Dale looked around as though hoping he could escape. A group of people came out of the showroom—a husband and wife and three children, accompanied by a perky saleswoman.

"I don't want to talk out here," Dale said. "C'mon inside."

Travis followed Dale inside to a small cubicle. Travis observed that Dale had won the "Salesman of the Month" award several times. The only picture on the desk showed Dale with Beth. They were on skis, heads together, laughing.

"I'm surprised you sell a lot of cars, if that's how you greet your customers," Travis said.

"I'm not in the habit of beating on my customers. You ruined my whole frigging life, man. Whether you know it or not."

Travis was beginning to get an idea of where this was going. "I could maybe say the same thing about you," he said, his tone ironic. "Beth and I were engaged during our third year in vet school, you know."

"That's a damned lie!" Dale cried. "Bethie was never engaged to you! She never wore your ring!"

"It's true we hadn't made the formal commitment. She made excuses every time we were supposed to pick out a ring."

"That's because she was in love with me."

Travis nodded ruefully, remembering the day Beth had come to see him after being home for the weekend. "It's all over between us," she'd told him, teary-eyed. "I'm going to drop out of school and go back home." He'd been stunned, hardly able to believe what she was telling him. They'd argued about it all night. Finally she'd told him she'd never stopped loving her high-school boyfriend. She was planning to marry Dale.

"I never wanted her to go to vet school in the first place." Dale's face was sullen. "I knew it would cause problems. She had to study so hard all the time, she hardly had a chance to see me. Then she started talking about you all the time. 'Travis helped me study chemistry.' 'Travis and I operated on a dog together.' I got so sick of hearing your name, I wanted to hurl. I used to say to her, 'You sound like you're in love with that asshole.' She would always say, no, she wasn't. Then one day she told me, 'Yes, I am in love with him.'"

"What the hell are you whining about? You won! She went back to you in the end."

"Yeah, sure. She came home and moved in with me and two months later she told me she was pregnant with your kid."

"She specifically said he was mine?" Travis asked.

"Yeah, she was sure. She figured she got knocked up in April and she wasn't sleeping with me until she moved back home in June." Dale sighed. "When she told me, I begged her to get rid of it—even said I'd pay—but she wouldn't hear of it.

Fine, I said, whatever you want. We were still planning to get married, even though all my buddies told me I was a fool."

"But you never married her?"

"No. She changed after she got pregnant. Didn't want to have fun anymore. Wouldn't go to bars. Stopped drinking."

Well, thank God for that! Travis thought.

"She was always making a fuss if I wanted to go out and see my buddies. Always talking about the kid that was coming, blah blah blah, 'til I wanted to scream. We broke up when she was seven months along."

Travis frowned. "So if you two broke up, why didn't she call me and tell me what was going on?"

Dale looked down at the desk, drumming his fingers restlessly. "She was ashamed to go back to you, after she broke up with you over me. Anyway, after the kid was born, we got back together for awhile. We lived together for a year—maybe it was two. But then we started having problems again. Maybe I just wasn't ready to settle down...I don't know. The kid bothered me, too. I wish she hadn't named him after you."

Travis hesitated. He didn't know quite how to ask the next question, something along the line of, "Was Beth a good mother?" And would Dale even be able to judge that? He settled on, "Did Beth have enough money to take care of herself and little Travis?"

Dale shrugged. "Sure, I guess so. Things were okay while we lived together. After we broke up, she moved home for awhile. Then she must have saved up enough to move to Cincinnati."

"Do you know where he was born?"

Dale shrugged. "I think in Kentucky. Bethie stayed with her grandma down there for awhile."

No wonder Misney hadn't been able to find an Ohio birth certificate. "How did Beth's sister wind up with little Travis?"

"Gina was around all the time—she and Beth were pretty tight, especially whenever I was out of the picture. She was Beth's Lamaze coach. So naturally she took T.J. when Beth died." Dale shook his head, looking into the distance. "Man, that was about the worst day of my life—when Gina called me about the accident. I realized what I'd thrown away."

Travis didn't have much sympathy for this. *I wouldn't have wasted my chance, if Beth had chosen me. We could've been happy together. And I wouldn't have missed my boy's birth and babyhood.*

"Gina was doing pretty good with T.J. until she met Ray. That dude is bad news, man. I don't know what makes nice women hook up with losers."

"Yeah, no accounting for it," Travis said dryly.

"Ray bought a used Explorer from me. We had to repo it in six months. He never had a regular job. I think he mostly lived off Gina." Dale looked Travis in the eye for the first time. "Ray didn't like your kid much, from what I could tell. I used to see them in the park together. T.J. was a real spunky kid most of the time—but he sure quieted down whenever Ray was there."

A chill went through Travis that had nothing to do with the air-conditioning vent above his head. "Are you saying Ray was abusive?"

Dale shrugged. "What do you call abusive? He used to holler at the kid a lot. I saw some swats once or twice. Most people know enough not to hurt a kid in public, know what I mean?"

"Yes," said Travis. It was a sickening thought, wondering what might have happened to his son in private. His own childhood came to mind. His stepmother had been quite capable of trotting out her stepsons in their best clothes to pass out canapés and chat politely to her bridge club, so that all the ladies would exclaim over the wonderful sons she had and how well they were being raised. The next day, the slightest infraction might earn Travis an afternoon in the punishment closet.

"Well," Travis said, "thanks for taking the time." He stood up.

Dale rose too, offering his hand. "Hey, man, no offense, okay? Sorry about the punch."

Travis was tempted to refuse the gesture—he still felt the soreness in his chin. But if he ever needed to talk to Dale again, he needed to be on good terms with him. So he shook Dale's hand before he left.

* * * * *

JayBee hummed to herself as she prepared to make sandwiches on Sunday morning. T.J. sat in a kitchen chair, dangling his feet and watching everything with round, wondering eyes.

"Ever go on a picnic before?" she asked.

He shook his head.

She wiped off the dusty picnic basket with a damp paper towel. "Would you like bologna sandwiches, or peanut butter and jelly?"

"Peanut butter and jelly. With the crusts cut off."

"Okay." She took the bread out and began to make the sandwiches.

"Do you think any bears might steal our picnic basket?"

Hearing a note of apprehension in his voice, JayBee answered firmly, "No. There are no bears in the park we're going to."

"Is Angel coming with us?"

"No. She has to stay home and work."

"Goody!"

JayBee looked at him reproachfully. "T.J., you're a very lucky boy to have a nice foster mom like Angel."

He raised his brown eyes to hers. "Why can't you be my foster mom?"

JayBee knew it was irrational, but she couldn't help feeling pleased that at least one male preferred her to her beautiful sister. "Because I already have a job. I go to the high school every day and teach the girls there. You need a foster mom who's home with you during the day." She added a bag of potato chips and some small boxes of juice to the picnic basket. "Well, we're about to get this show on the road. Go say goodbye to Angel. And you know what? I'll bet she'd really like it if you gave her a little kiss on the cheek."

T.J. looked down and shook his head. "I don't want to kiss her."

JayBee sighed to herself. "Well, say goodbye anyway."

T.J. put his head to one side and pursed his lips, as though he were about to refuse.

"Tell you what. Go in there and say, 'See you later, Alligator!'"

T.J. giggled. "Okay!" He ran into the living room. A few minutes later he came back. "You know what? She said, 'In a while, Crocodile!'" He went off in a gale of laughter.

JayBee laughed too, thinking this was the fun part of having a kid around. Even an old chestnut like that seemed funny if you'd never heard it before.

Taking his hand, JayBee started out to the car.

* * * * *

After T.J.'s fifth round driving the kiddie car around the track, he still hadn't tired of it. JayBee handed him another four tickets and he was off to wait in line again.

The little kids' amusement park off I-675 had been one of Angel's better ideas. The only drawback was that all the rides were for children under forty-eight inches in height. Sitting on a green bench watching other people ride was not JayBee's idea of fun.

I'll take him to King's Island someday. That had been one of her favorite places as a child. A day at King's Island had been a treat comparable only to Christmas Day.

Then she remembered that T.J. would be with her and Angel only temporarily.

She wondered if Travis liked amusement parks. She pictured herself sitting in a little cart with him, going on one of those rides where they took you through a dark building and showed you spooky things. She would sit close to him and he would put his arm around her…

Geez, you've only run into the guy a few times and now you're fantasizing being alone in a dark tunnel with him. What's the matter with you, girl?

Of course, sitting and kissing a guy in a cemetery was a little more than "running into" him.

Friday night, she had promised she would call him. It was Sunday now. Would she seem too eager if she called tonight? "Always keep 'em waiting at least a week," Angel used to say in the days when she had fancied herself a femme fatale. JayBee usually preferred the direct route, but noticed that Angel's strategies were often more successful. JayBee had dated Bradley for three months without hearing an "I love you," while Angel had managed to marry him in three weeks.

Not that she wasn't well out of that relationship.

"Men love the hunt. Don't be so darned eager," Angel had told her more than once. Angel would have never let a near stranger sit and kiss her in a deserted cemetery.

Well, then Angel would have missed out on something special. That fifteen minutes in the cemetery…ever since it happened, she hadn't been able to stop reliving it in her mind. Now she wished she had stayed longer, not gone running off like a scared little kid.

"Ms. Hauser!"

She looked up to see Terry, the crimson-haired student who had asked for her help with the Lavender Collective. He had a little blonde girl by the hand. She tugged on his shirt, saying, "Gimmee my tickets!" He gave her the tickets and she scampered off to wait in line with the rest of the children.

"Mind if I sit here?" Terry asked.

JayBee gestured at the empty space to the right. "Feel free. Was that your little sister?"

"Yeah. I got stuck babysitting today."

"Me too."

Terry leaned forward, putting his elbows on his knees. His large hands and feet showed that he hadn't really grown into his height yet. He would be a big man someday. He glanced quickly at JayBee and then looked away.

"I wanted to tell you, I really liked what you said at our first meeting Friday. I thought about it all day. Especially when you said there's a bigger world out there besides high school and we should be ourselves 'cause people in the outside world will be more tolerant than the kids we know here. I just hope it works that way for me."

JayBee felt pleased her words had meant something to Terry. She'd spoken spontaneously, without even thinking about what she was going to say beforehand, but somehow it had struck a chord with this boy. It was one of the rewarding things about being a teacher…most of what you said seemed to go right by the students, but every once in awhile something took hold.

"Thanks. If anything I said was helpful, I'm glad."

"I get discouraged sometimes." Terry leaned back against the bench with a sigh. "My father can't stand me. My stepmom doesn't know what to make of me. Even my little sister criticizes me. On the way over, she said my hair is 'weird'."

"I like your hair."

He brightened. "Thanks. I think it's pretty cool, even if the jocks at school give me a hard time about it." He pulled a strand of hair forward, looked at it, then pushed it back off his forehead. "You know something? I really hate school. It's time to go out there and start living my real life, but school's holding me back."

"You'll like college a lot better. That's how it worked for me, anyway. You're planning to go to college, aren't you?"

"My dad wants me to go into the army." He turned and looked at JayBee, raising his eyebrows. "Is he living in a dream world, or what? Can you imagine me lasting five minutes in the army?"

She smiled. "I think college would be the better choice for you. Try for a large school where there's lots of different types of people."

He nodded, looking down at his hands. JayBee knew he wanted to say something else but wasn't sure where to begin.

"You seem like a really nice person, for a teacher," he announced. "Some of my friends say you push too hard in class, but I don't believe them."

"Some of them need pushing," JayBee said tartly.

He grinned. "I'll bet." The grin faded and soon he was looking down at his hands again.

"Is there something you want to talk to me about?" She kept her voice low and sympathetic.

He nodded, his brows drawing together. Waiting, she prepared to hear something about an unhappy love affair.

"I did something I shouldn't have. I can't stop thinking about it. I was persuaded…" He stopped and swallowed hard, his prominent Adam's apple visibly shifting. "No. I won't blame other people. I shouldn't have done it and that's that."

"Is it something serious?"

Misery drew down the corners of his mouth. "I don't know whether I should say anything."

"Sometimes people feel better if they talk about what's bothering them."

He gazed into her eyes pleadingly. "Teachers are like priests and doctors, right? If I tell you, you can't tell anyone."

She hesitated. "Actually, that's not true. If it's something personal, of course I won't tell. But if it's something illegal—or criminal—I can't help you conceal it."

JayBee saw tears quivering on his lashes. He blinked. "Okay, I get it."

"Is it—something illegal?"

His mouth set in a narrow line. "I'd better keep an eye on my little sister." He got up.

"Terry!"

He paused.

"Terry, please tell someone. Your doctor, or a minister. Maybe even your father—could you talk to him?"

He gave her an incredulous look. "My dad would kill me if he knew about this."

That was pretty stupid of me. I never told my parents anything when I was a teenager. "All right, but tell someone. You can't keep this inside when it bothers you so much."

"I'll think about it." His voice was very soft. "Thanks, Ms. Hauser." He walked up to the exit gate just as his little sister came running out. He took her hand. JayBee could hear him urging his sister to hurry as they left.

* * * * *

Travis sat waiting in a back booth of the Paradise Lounge, drinking a Molson. The Paradise was lively for a Sunday evening, filled with a mixture of college students and townies. The jukebox was playing a country music song filled with wailing harmonicas. Travis figured the selections hadn't been changed in the last ten years. He heard the loud cracks as pool cues hit balls in the back room. The overpowering aroma of

Sid's Spectacular Sausage Sandwiches filled the air, giving the cigarette smoke a run for its money as most annoying odor.

Funny how his tastes had changed. This place had seemed like the epitome of its name when he'd been eighteen years old. Back then, it had been a great treat to borrow his brother's ID, chug a few beers and try to pick up a college girl. Now, he'd much rather be home.

But when he'd called his brother, Peter had suggested they meet on neutral ground.

"What a dump this place is." Peter joined Travis in the booth. "Bring me a shot and a beer," he told Carla as she came by to take his drink order. "Crown Royal and a Heineken."

Travis raised his eyebrows. He'd never known Peter to drink hard liquor before. The two of them had agreed years ago that they never wanted to be like Great-Uncle Bobby, who ruined every family gathering with his alcoholic rants.

"I need a drink," Peter said defensively, frowning at his brother. "Something wrong with that?"

Travis turned one hand out in a "do what you want" gesture. "Just remember, you're the one who lives twenty miles away from here."

"Yeah," Peter muttered. "I wish to God it was two hundred miles. Better yet, two thousand."

Travis nodded. "It's hard to be suddenly notorious."

"We had reporters at the door Saturday morning," Peter said, grimacing. "Can you imagine? Poor Georgia was hysterical. She was afraid to go outside all day."

Travis took another swig of beer while Peter knocked back his shot. Wondering how to lead up to what he wanted to talk about, he finally decided on the direct approach. "Pete, do you need money?"

Peter gave him a narrow-eyed look. "How the hell do you know that?"

"I heard about it."

Peter thought for a moment. "I suppose Alicia told Katie and your little informant turned around and told you."

"Is it true?"

Peter took a deep breath and nodded. "If I don't get some money, I may lose the house. And that means I could lose Georgia."

Startled, Travis said, "She wouldn't leave you just because you lost the house!"

"Oh no? You never really understood her, did you, Travis? I used to laugh inside when I saw you two together. You spent your whole childhood hating Alicia and then you picked out a fiancée who's just like her."

"Georgia is not like Alicia! Don't be ridiculous."

"Of course she is. A little less controlled, maybe. More sensitive. More like Alicia was in her twenties, when she first became our stepmother."

"I think you're way out of line here—"

"You always idealized Georgia," his brother told him coolly. "I know her a little better than you, Travis. I've lived with her for a year now. Believe me, she needs a strong man to keep her in line. God knows I try, but it's hard even for me. You never could have handled her."

Travis was growing increasingly uncomfortable with this conversation. "Shut up about Georgia. How dare you bring her up with me, anyway? You've got a lot to apologize for."

"Not to you, brother."

Travis glared into Peter's eyes. "I've never understood how you could do what you did. If the situation had been reversed, I never would've slept with your fiancée."

"No? Don't be so sure. If a woman you wanted came to you, took her clothes off and said she was dying for you to make love to her, would you be strong enough to throw her out of bed?"

Travis was sure he was no longer in love with Georgia, but even so, hearing this was a stab to the heart. "I don't believe she did that." But even as he spoke, he realized it was probably true.

"I'm not a liar any more than you are," Peter told him. "But believe what you want, it makes no difference to me."

"I don't want to talk about Georgia. Listen, Pete, what's going on that you need money so badly? Is there a problem with your practice?"

Peter looked down at the table for a long moment. Travis waited to be told it was none of his business.

"Gambling," Peter muttered.

"Gambling!"

"Yeah," his brother said, looking up finally. "You know—craps, roulette, twenty-one? You win a little, you lose a little, you lose a little more and then suddenly you look around and you've got markers out for almost eighty thousand dollars."

"Where were you doing all this gambling?"

"Indiana. West Virginia. Windsor. I've gone away a couple times with some other doctors. Most of it was on twenty-one. I really thought I had a system going…" He put his hands flat on the table and shook his head. "It gets ahold of you. You keep thinking the luck's got to turn and you keep playing. I don't know what I'm going to do." Then his expression brightened. "Maybe Alicia left us something in her will. I've got a meeting with her attorney on Monday. I can stave off the creditors awhile if they know I'll have money eventually."

There it was, the money motive. There had to be some subtle way to ask Peter about it. He didn't want to just demand, "Did you kill Alicia?"

"Travis," his brother said, looking him in the eye, "did you kill Alicia?"

"No! Did you?"

"Of course not! Don't turn things around like that. I had no reason to kill her."

"Neither did I!"

Peter gave him a disgusted look. "Don't give me that. I was there, too, the whole time you were growing up. I saw the way she treated you, the things she did to you."

"That's all in the past." Travis waved his hand dismissively. "I don't sit around brooding about it. I've got my own life now, away from her. She was nothing more than a minor irritation the last few years."

"That's one way to look at it." Peter chugged his beer and motioned to Carla, who was waiting on a table across from them. "Bring another round." He leaned forward and spoke quietly. "Here's another way to look at it. All that calm façade of yours, the way you sat back and took Alicia's needling—that was all just an act. You were waiting for your chance to pay her back, once and for all." Peter shook his head. "There was only one place you miscalculated and that was not making it look like a break-in. So now Dad gets arrested for the crime. Or maybe that's what you wanted to happen. After all, Dad earned his share of the blame, too, in your mind. He married her in the first place, right?"

"Are you a surgeon or a novelist?" Travis tried hard to retain his composure. "Let's try an alternate theory. You need money, so you ask her for it. At first she says she'll lend it. Then maybe she changes her mind—you know how she likes to play those little games. There's a murder motive. She refuses you, so you stab her in retaliation."

"You've got your nerve!" Peter stood up fast, jarring the table so that his empty beer bottle fell over. "I should never have made up with you!"

Travis shot to his feet. "Get out of here before I knock your head off!"

"Screw you! You may be taller than me, but I can still take you!"

"Better not try it!"

"Don't worry, I'm out of here!" Peter backed out of the booth, his eyes locked on Travis'.

Breathing hard, Travis watched his brother leave the Paradise. He was trembling with anger and the effort to control it. Ever since the day when he'd stopped by Peter's apartment and caught his brother in bed with Georgia, he'd wanted to fight him. Tonight was the closest he had come to it.

Good thing the argument didn't occur later in the evening, when we had a few more drinks in us.

Travis hesitated, not wanting to head home right away, but not wanting to remain in the booth any longer. Walking up to the bar, he sat next to a blond man and ordered another Molson.

Kevin, the bartender, put his beer down in front of him. The blond man nodded. Travis nodded back, then looked away. He didn't feel like talking to anyone.

"I just got into town yesterday," the blond man said. "You look like a native, though, am I right?"

Travis glanced at him briefly. The other man was wearing pleated pants, a silk shirt and an expensive-looking tie. He had soft, slightly puffy hands and the nails were manicured. "Yeah, I live here." Travis took a long swig of his beer. His sleeves were rolled up. The stranger put his hand lightly on Travis' bare wrist.

"Mind if I ask you something?"

Travis jerked his arm away. "You're in the wrong bar if you're looking to hook up with a guy."

"Whoa, whoa!" The man put one hand up. "You got me figured all wrong. I just want to ask you a question about a woman."

"Shoot." *And then you'd better stop bothering me.*

"Do you know a woman named Angel? Angel Morrow? Long blonde hair, very beautiful?"

Travis shook his head. "Never seen her, as far as I know."

"Are you sure? She's my ex-wife and I'm trying to find her. I'm pretty sure she lives here in town."

"I told you, I don't know her." *Now get the hell away from me, asshole.*

"If you see her, would you call me?" the man persisted, trying to hand Travis his card.

"Look." Travis swung around abruptly. "I am not in the mood for this right now—got it?"

"No problemo," the man answered with an insincere smile. He placed his card carefully on the bar by Travis' elbow and walked away.

The card read, "Bradley Morrow". Travis finished his beer and got up to leave. He didn't take the card.

Chapter Eight

Katie was silent as they drove the ten miles to Remus, which suited Travis fine. He spent the trip thinking about the next round of treatment for the Martins' terrier.

"I can't stand to think of Dad here," Katie whispered to him as they waited for their father to be brought to the visiting room. "He must hate it."

Travis saw the tears welling in his sister's eyes and put his arm around her thin shoulders. "Don't cry. If you cry, you'll make Dad cry."

"I'll try not to." She brushed her hand across her eyes.

Two officers entered the room. The younger one said, "Dr. Kellman, I'm afraid we have to conduct a pat-down search of you and your sister. If you'll stand up and raise your arms?"

Katie gasped, her hand going to her mouth.

"Is this absolutely necessary?" Travis asked.

"Yes, sir, it's necessary if you want to see your father."

"Very well." Travis removed his jacket and put his arms up. The young officer ran quick hands over his body while the older officer watched with a cynical expression. Travis knew he wasn't being accused of anything and the officers weren't really expecting to find contraband. Still, it was extraordinarily humiliating. He was grateful MacReedy had spared him this at the Priam police station.

Katie removed her fringed suede jacket slowly, her eyes downcast.

"Don't you have a matron here for my sister?" Travis asked.

"I'm afraid not, sir," the younger officer apologized. "She doesn't work on Mondays."

Travis remained standing, his eyes silently warning the officer to keep it professional as the man searched his sister.

"They're clean," the young officer told the older man, who grunted.

The two officers left the room and returned in a few minutes with Robert Kellman. Robert was dressed in an orange jumpsuit. Katie gasped. The jail clothes were a shock to Travis as well. Somehow the jumpsuit revealed the seriousness of the situation as nothing else had. He felt a stab of pity as he looked into his father's lined face. Robert seemed to have aged in the brief time he'd been in custody.

"Oh, Daddy!" Katie exclaimed, clinging to her father. "This is so terrible!" She burst into tears.

"Princess," her father murmured, bowing his head. "I wish you hadn't come. This is no place for you."

Travis looked down, clenching his fists. He'd foreseen this would be a difficult visit.

"Daddy, I know you didn't do it," Katie sobbed. "I'm so scared."

Robert rubbed her back soothingly. "Now, listen, Princess. You've got to have faith in our legal system. I'm an innocent man. They won't convict me. That would mean a whole jury would have to decide I'm guilty and that's just not going to happen because I didn't do it. Do you understand?"

She nodded. "Oh, Daddy, I hope you're right."

Travis' eyes met his father's over Katie's head. His father said, "You shouldn't have brought her, son. It's too hard for her."

"She wanted to see you."

Robert held Katie at arm's length. "Listen, Princess. I want you to go find the ladies' restroom. Wash your face and take some deep breaths. I don't want to see any more tears in those pretty eyes. Travis'll take you home in a few minutes, all right?"

She hugged him hard. Both of them were dripping tears. Finally, she whispered, "All right, Daddy." Robert rang the bell for the guard.

As soon as Katie was gone, Robert wiped his eyes and sat down. "They're going to charge me tomorrow. My attorney says the prosecutor will ask the judge to deny bail."

Travis had been afraid of this. "Is there anything you need me to do, Dad?"

Robert shrugged. "There's nothing that can be done. I've got a good attorney. The evidence against me is all circumstantial. Hopefully they won't convict me."

"I hope not either, but innocent people do get convicted, Dad. You read about that all the time."

Robert spread his arms. "Well, if they convict me, it'll all be over."

"What do you mean by that?" Travis demanded.

"Listen, son, I'm too old to become a bitch for some four-hundred pound redneck named Bubba. It's just not going to happen. If I find myself convicted, I will commit suicide."

Travis felt his stomach drop at his father's words. "Come on, you can't mean that. If you're convicted—God forbid—then we appeal."

His father's lips curled slightly upward in a smile that held more sadness than joy. "You know, son, I've had a good life. I had a profession I loved and I was married to two of the best women on Earth. If it's my time to go…then I will go."

Travis set his lips, trying to stay calm. It was awful hearing his father talk this way, but he didn't know what to say to change his mind. "Dad, please! I thought you were a good Methodist. You know suicide is wrong."

His father gave a tiny shake of his head. "I've never really believed that, Travis. There are times when suicide can be absolutely right. Just like the Japanese and their hara-kiri ritual…sometimes suicide is the only honorable course. For instance, if you've done something that causes great shame to your family, then suicide is the right thing to do."

"What are you saying?" Travis wondered if he was listening to an oblique confession. "Did you do something wrong?"

"No, no—it's only an example. The other time when suicide may be right is when a person is caught in a trap. Like a terminal patient in intractable pain. That's the situation I'm facing."

"Millions of people make it through prison. If the worst happens, you've got to be strong."

Robert's hands curled into fists on the table. "Most of them at least have the hope of getting out. If they convict me, it'll be for life, son. For life. I refuse to spend the rest of my days in prison."

"Listen to me." Travis laid his hands over his father's. Travis' were big hands, half again the size of Robert's slender, narrow-fingered hands. "You've got to tell me who you were with that night. You can't let this go on. If there's someone who can testify for you, you've got to speak out."

His father drew his hands away. "I'm not going to say anything. There are ramifications that go beyond this case. I'll tell you one last time—I did not kill your stepmother. And that's all I'm going to say."

* * * * *

Travis sat in the parlor, half-heartedly eating a Big Mac. Puff rolled on his back at Travis' feet, waving his paws. Travis tore off a small piece of burger and gave it to the cat.

The visit to his father had been a harrowing experience for both siblings. Katie, ignoring her father's advice, had cried most of the way home. Travis always hated to see his sister in distress. He had said several heartening things to her, such as, "Dad has a good lawyer," and "I'll bet they won't convict him." Nothing had seemed to help.

Travis wondered if there was any more he could do. The police had settled on his father as the murderer and ceased any kind of investigation. But maybe he could look into things himself. After all, he had managed to track down Dale Wichowski. It hadn't been that difficult. Maybe he could try to figure out what his father had done last Friday or where he had gone that Thursday night.

Should he interfere? He had asked his father if there was anything he could do and his father had refused. Probing further into the matter would involve going through his father's private belongings. The thought of that kind of intrusion was troubling. His father and stepmother had always been very private people. Travis knew that if he asked his father's permission, it would be denied.

The telephone rang and he jumped up to get it.

"Dr. Travis Kellman?"

"Speaking." It sounded like JayBee and yet he wasn't sure…

"This is little Travis' foster mother. The social worker told me you were waiting to hear from me."

Travis hadn't expected to hear from her so soon. Thoughts of his father receded in his concern for the child. "Yes! Thanks for calling. How is Travis?"

The voice seemed to hesitate. "He's doing pretty well. Would you like to see him tonight?"

Travis' heart pounded hard. "Absolutely! Thank you!"

"I'm going to bring him to the playground at Lowden School. Would seven o'clock suit you?"

Travis agreed. She told him she'd wait for him on the bench near the big slide.

Pacing around the room after he got off the phone, Travis thought about how the boy had been frightened of him that first day.

If Gina's boyfriend had been rough with him, no wonder he was afraid of men. Would it do any good to talk to the child about it? Probably not, he was very young.

He would have to earn the child's trust over time.

He changed his shirt and combed his hair. Walking into the kitchen, he planned how he would speak softly to the child, keep sitting to lessen the distance between them, try to seem nonthreatening. Was there anything else that would help quell the boy's fears?

Queenie got up and came to him, whining under her breath.

Some kids were scared of dogs, but lots of kids loved them.

He snapped his fingers and Queenie followed him out the door.

* * * * *

JayBee spotted Travis striding toward the playground, a three-legged dog loping along at his side. He looked terrific in black jeans and a red-and-black plaid shirt. She saw him glance around for the boy, who was at the top of the jungle gym.

"Hi!" JayBee walked up to meet him.

"JayBee!" He smiled, his eyes alight.

"You must be wondering why I'm here. It's a peculiar situation. My sister is the boy's foster mom."

He looked confused. "Was that your sister I spoke to on the phone?"

JayBee nodded. "She was planning to come meet you, but then she decided to send me instead."

"It's great to see you again!" He hesitated. "So you know about little Travis. I just found out about him myself." His dark eyes seemed to beg her to understand.

"The social worker told us all about it. Must have been quite a shock for you."

"Yes." His tone turned serious. "An incredible shock. I'm still finding it hard to accept the way his mother concealed his existence... Well, I don't want to speak ill of the dead. Has Travis been with your sister all weekend?"

"Yes, the social worker brought him over Saturday afternoon. Actually, I've been watching him most of the weekend, since my sister was busy. T.J.'s a really good kid."

"You call him T.J.?" Travis smiled.

"He says that's what his mother used to call him."

They sat on the green park bench near the big slide. "Funny sort of coincidence," JayBee said. "Here we're just getting to know each other and now my sister is the foster parent for your son."

Travis nodded. "Things like that happen in a small town. Anyway, I would have wanted you to know about him right away. I'm going to petition for custody as soon as the DNA test results come in. I feel sure he's my son—but the court will want proof."

JayBee leaned over to pat Queenie, who had seated herself at Travis' knee. "What a lovely dog."

"I hope the boy won't be scared of her."

"Should I call him over?"

She saw that Travis' gaze was following T.J., who was dangling from the top bar of the jungle gym. "Let's wait a few minutes." He looked into her face. "I've been thinking about you all the time, ever since we met up at the cemetery the other night."

"That's another coincidence," she answered. When he raised his brows questioningly, she added, "I've been thinking about you a lot, too."

"I was hoping you'd call."

"Here I am, live and in person. Isn't that better?"

He didn't respond to her flirtatious tone. "There's something important I want to say to you. Maybe this isn't the right time...I don't know."

She waited for him to go on, wondering what could be making him look so serious. Reaching out, he took her hand and held it. She was startled at how intimate the gesture seemed. Feeling the pressure of his big, warm hand was almost like being kissed.

His brows drew together. "Everything's out of kilter in my life right now. My stepmother's been murdered, my father's in jail and now this child...I feel like I hardly dare ask you to get involved in this mess."

JayBee looked into his eyes. He had beautiful eyes for a man, she thought, a rich golden-brown like dark, liquid honey, with a darker brown ring around the edge.

He went on quietly, "I've never met anyone before that I felt so drawn to. The timing is as bad as it can possibly be, but I don't want to let things slide with you."

JayBee looked back at him steadily. "What exactly are you saying?"

He was silent for a long moment. "I guess I'm saying, don't let the situation scare you away. I'd like us to see each other. We could pretend that everything is normal while we're together—even though we know it's not." He sat back against the bench, his expression intent and concerned.

Something in JayBee responded to the honesty of his words. He refused to act as though there were no difficulties, but faced up to them squarely. She tried to match his bluntly direct statement with her own. "I won't pretend I haven't thought about what you're saying. Your stepmother's been murdered, your father's in jail—you've got a lot to think about." She took a deep breath. "But I liked you from the first time we met. So let's go for it."

He smiled and squeezed her hand. "Great! So how about Wednesday night for dinner and dancing? Do you like steak?"

He didn't let any grass grow under his feet, that was for sure. "Sure, steak sounds good."

"Where should I pick you up? What time?"

She hesitated. "Tell you what. I'll come over to your clinic. Six-thirty?"

"Sounds good." He sat up alertly. "Now that we have that settled, why don't you call the little fellow over?"

JayBee asked, "Are you going to tell him you think you're his father?"

He frowned, one hand stroking his beard thoughtfully. "He was afraid of me the first time I saw him. I'm not sure what I should say."

"Are you really certain you're his father?" JayBee asked. "I know the DNA results aren't in yet."

Travis gazed off into the distance, a crease between his brows. "I'm not sure how much the foster care people told you. I dated Travis' mother in vet school. We'd been talking about getting married when we graduated. Then she dropped out of school and went back to her old boyfriend."

JayBee heard the pain in his voice. "That must have been hard for you."

He turned to look into her face. "I hadn't thought about it much in the last couple years. Until this brought it all back." He took a deep breath. "Anyway, I found Beth's boyfriend—the man she left me for. I talked to him yesterday. Beth told him I was her baby's father."

JayBee nodded. "Okay, then I think we should say something, so T.J. can start getting used to the idea. But we won't make a big deal of it, not until the results come in."

"Perhaps that would be best."

JayBee stuck two fingers into her mouth and whistled for T.J. He clambered down the jungle gym and came running, then braked abruptly as he saw that JayBee was not alone.

"T.J., come here and sit beside me." JayBee moved so that there was room between her and Travis. The boy came slowly closer. Queenie stood up, her tail wagging fast.

"What happened to that dog's leg?" the boy asked.

"Queenie here was hit by a car," Travis said. "I took care of her and she got better, but I couldn't save her leg."

T.J. bent over to pet Queenie, keeping the dog between himself and Travis. Queenie wriggled all over with pleasure and made whining noises in her throat. Travis looked at JayBee, raising his eyebrows. "She used to belong to a little boy," he murmured. "Maybe she misses him."

"T.J., I want to talk to you about something," JayBee said. T.J. gave the dog a longing look and sat on the bench beside JayBee, edging as close to her as he could. Travis stood up and walked a few steps away. JayBee felt the boy sigh with relief. Now that a space was vacant, Queenie put her front leg up on the bench and nudged T.J.'s arm to be petted.

"I like this dog," T.J. announced.

"She likes you too," said Travis. T.J. didn't look at him.

"T.J., do you know what a daddy is?" JayBee asked.

He didn't answer this. "A boy in the park had a dog. Uncle Ray said I couldn't have one."

JayBee persisted. "Remember how I read to you about Goldilocks and the three bears last night? There was Baby Bear and Mamma Bear and Papa Bear. It's just like that. Every boy has a mommy and a daddy—"

"I don't. My mommy's dead."

"I know. But this man is probably your daddy. His name is Travis, just like yours."

T.J. continued to pat Queenie's head. JayBee wondered how much he'd understood. He seemed to be an intelligent little boy, but who knew how much a four-year-old child could comprehend?

"Aunt Gina said we were going to find my daddy," T.J. volunteered at last.

JayBee looked up at Travis and raised her eyebrows. He took an eager step closer. "She said that? Then why did she take you to your grandma's house?"

T.J. wouldn't look at him. "I dunno." The boy's face was expressionless, but JayBee thought she detected minute signs of distress. Had his mouth quivered?

She put her arm around his shoulders. "Do you miss Aunt Gina?"

"Uncle Ray said I couldn't go to Indiana with them." He wriggled. "Can I play on the swings now? Will you push me?"

Travis said, "Sure. I'll push you."

"No! I want JayBee!"

"We'll all go over there," JayBee said.

They got down off the bench. T.J. took off running and the dog followed as fast as she could on three legs. JayBee heard Travis sigh.

"He needs time to get used to you," she said.

"I know." He drew a deep breath. "I can wait."

She added quietly, "That Uncle Ray—he abused him. He beat him with a belt."

She saw Travis clench his right fist. "I was afraid of that. How bad is it?"

"He'll have the scars on his butt for a long time. My sister took him to the doctor today. He said T.J. will be fine, but he had to file a child abuse report."

Travis told her what Beth's boyfriend had said about Ray. "I don't know how anyone can hurt a child or an animal," he concluded, his tone bitter. "If I had any idea how to trace that Uncle Ray fellow, I'd make him regret what he did."

JayBee certainly agreed with that.

"Do you think he understood what you told him? About me being his father?"

JayBee shrugged. "I'm not sure. I'll keep working on it."

T.J. played on the swings for twenty minutes, but he wouldn't let Travis push him—only JayBee was allowed that honor. Finally, when it was quarter to eight, JayBee said it was time to go home.

"Bye, Queenie." T.J. bent down and hugged the dog. She licked his face in return.

Travis turned and walked away a few steps, snapping his fingers for Queenie to come to him, while JayBee took T.J. by the hand and began to lead him away. He looked back once, gazing longingly at Queenie.

"Wait!" said Travis. JayBee turned around, surprised.

Travis came over and drew her a few feet apart. "Would you like to take Queenie home with you? Seems like she's found someone she likes better than me."

"We'd love to have her," JayBee said, thinking that maybe Angel would feel safer with a large dog in the house. "If you're sure it's okay."

Travis nodded. Walking up to T.J., he knelt down by the boy, careful not to touch him. "Listen, T.J. Would you like to have Queenie for your very own dog?"

The child stared at Travis without speaking.

"I'll give her to you, but you have to tell me you want her. Do you want her?"

The boy looked down. A long moment passed. Finally, he whispered, "Yes."

Travis snapped his fingers for Queenie. Laying his hand on her head, he spoke softly to her. "Queenie, you're going to be T.J.'s companion now. I want you to take good care of him." The dog looked up at Travis and cocked her head as though trying to understand his words. He set his lips and drew a deep breath. Taking a leather leash out of his jeans pocket, he clipped it on her collar and handed the end to T.J. "Go on, girl! Go with T.J.!" Then he turned on his heel.

The dog whined as Travis walked away without her.

"Come on, Queenie!" T.J. said. "You're my dog now!"

JayBee took the boy's hand and they walked away from the playground. The dog followed them.

* * * * *

The next day at the clinic was grueling, with several emergency calls that had to be squeezed in between regular appointments. The Jacksons' parrot was sick again. The Harpers' new puppy had parvo virus and had to stay at the clinic for treatment. Travis hoped he would be able to save him.

In the middle of the day, when he grabbed ten minutes for a quick lunch of take-out Chinese food, Thelma rushed into his small office with the waiting room television and plugged it in. "Doctor! They're showing your father on TV!"

Sally Rowe, WAKC newscaster, spoke excitedly into the camera. "Robert Kellman was arraigned this morning, charged with the first-degree murder of his wife Alicia. This brutal murder has shocked Tecumseh County. Prosecutor Jim Percy has told WAKC that he hopes to get an early trial date, perhaps as early as next month."

The camera cut to Travis' father being led through a crowd of people in front of the Remus courthouse, his hands cuffed behind his back. Six large cops flanked him, two on each side, one behind and one ahead of him, breasting their way through the crowd.

So they had to show the "perp walk".

The young newscaster went on, "Dr. Kellman's request for bail was denied."

Travis had been afraid of this all along. "Take it away," he told Thelma. He went through the rest of the day numbly, trying not to think about his father.

Late that afternoon, eighty-year-old Sarah Gilly carried in her elderly terrier, who had suddenly lost the use of his legs. Gently, Travis told Sarah it was time to put the dog to sleep. It was a sad ending to a horrible day. The old woman wept as she held the dog. Travis shaved Rascal's leg and gave the injection. They waited together until the dog stopped breathing. Then Travis led Sarah to a chair and took the dog into the back room.

Sarah sat clinging to her purse when Travis returned. "I'm so sorry," he told her, putting his hand on her shoulder. He had known her since his boyhood. He blinked hard, trying to rid his eyes of his unmanly tears.

"I know, Doctor." She peered up at him with cataract-clouded eyes behind her thick glasses and patted his cheek. "You've taken such good care of Rascal these last few months. I know we've done what's best for him." She sighed. "But I'm going to miss him so much. He was the best little dog I've ever had. Do you think I'll ever see him again?"

Travis had no doubts about that. "I'm sure you will."

She smiled wistfully. "That's not what the Church would say."

He looked into her eyes. "As a man of science, let me say this. If any of us have souls, then we all do, humans and animals alike. There isn't that much difference between us."

Sarah was still on his mind when he went home. Blackie and Puff had Fancy cornered under the big sofa, a frequent occurrence. Scolding them, he picked them up and put them outside. He sat down and softly called Fancy's name. Finally she ventured out and jumped into his lap.

"It's a tough life for you here," he observed, scratching her under the chin. She raised her head in enjoyment, her eyes half closing.

A thought occurred to him. Smiling, he went to the telephone.

* * * * *

"It's nice to see you again, Dr. Kellman," Sarah Gilly said, letting him into the living room of her small house. "But I can't imagine what I can help you with." She looked curiously at the cat carrier in his right hand.

"I took in this little cat when the Heymans moved to Europe," he told her. "But the other cats terrorize her. I've been trying to find a better home for her and I thought of you. I know what good care you've always given your animals."

He lifted the small white cat out of the carrier and set her down on the floor.

Sarah pursed her lips. "Well…she is a pretty little thing. But I've never had a cat before, only dogs."

"A cat's even easier to care for," he assured her. "Just feed her and clean out the litter box every few days. I've got one out in my truck that I can give you." Seating himself in a chair, he took a catnip mouse out of his breast pocket and dangled it in front of Fancy. Obligingly, she batted at it, then caught it in her claws and rolled over on her back.

"Oh, isn't she cute!" said Sarah. "Would you like a cookie, Doctor? I just made them yesterday."

"Sure." He wasn't about to turn down homemade cookies. She went into the kitchen and returned with peanut butter cookies on a plate.

Fancy stopped playing with the mouse and went to sit by Sarah's feet, her back straight, her eyes focused on the cookies.

"I'm afraid she's something of a beggar," Travis said.

"Oh, look at that intelligent face!" Sarah exclaimed. Then Travis knew he had found Fancy a new home.

"I'm going to miss your stepmother," Sarah mentioned as they ate. "I used to give her advice when she first married your father. It was hard for her to deal with you two big boys, you know."

Travis had never thought about that aspect of things before. "Really?" It was hard to imagine his stepmother ever having a moment's doubt about how to deal with anything. She'd always seemed to know exactly what she was doing in every situation.

Sarah raised her eyebrows. "She was awfully young when she married your father. Just twenty-one years old."

"I guess so," said Travis. Just a little younger than Katie. He could imagine how badly Katie would cope with two little boys if she were to marry a widower with children.

"She used to come over here, at her wit's end from trying to handle you two." Sarah chuckled. "You and your brother were always roughhousing with each other, always rolling around on the floor, tackling each other. Poor Alicia would get so upset about it. 'Don't worry!' I used to tell her. 'Send them outside to work off that extra energy!' I had three boys of my own, you know. There isn't much about raising boys that I don't know."

"So it was tough for her," Travis murmured. Reluctant as he was to do so, he was feeling some compassion for his stepmother.

"Alicia always took everything hard," Sarah went on. "Why, even last month when we had lunch together after the Garden Club meeting, she was so upset about your father. 'Don't pay him any mind,' I told her. 'More than likely it's just a phase. Don't nag him, just be patient.'"

Travis snapped to attention. "What was she upset about?"

Sarah frowned. She had finished her cookie. Fancy took a long look at her, then jumped up on the couch and curled up beside her.

"I'm letting my tongue run away with me," she said. "Alicia told me in private."

"That doesn't matter now, does it?" Travis asked.

Sarah nodded. "I suppose you're right. She was worried that your father was having an affair."

"That's ridiculous. My father adored her. I'm sure he wouldn't do any such thing." *Good Lord, I sound like Katie.*

Sarah gave him an odd look. He couldn't quite place it, then it occurred to him that her expression was that of an adult wondering whether to fill a child in on some home truths.

"My husband loved me, too, but he confessed to me right before he died that he'd slept with two other women." She adjusted her thick spectacles, looking at him closely. "I didn't say this to Alicia, poor dear. But when a wife has suspicions like that, they're usually correct."

Chapter Nine

Early the next morning, Travis took the key he'd borrowed from his sister and drove over to his father's house. He stopped at the curb to empty the mailbox, overflowing with three days' worth of bills and magazines.

The house seemed unnaturally silent when he entered. He lived alone at his own house and that had never bothered him, although he often thought he'd like to share his home with a woman. But at least his home held the warm, enlivening presence of animals. Sitting down on the couch with the mail, he switched on the television, turning it very low. He felt better having the sound of human voices in the room. Taking his reading glasses out of his jacket, he put them on.

That week's *Time* had arrived, as well as a medical journal for his father and two gardening catalogs for his stepmother. A credit card offer…the electric bill…supermarket flyers.

Maybe this will help, he thought as he found his father's Visa bill. He opened it eagerly, but all the purchases seemed innocuous. Service station, hardware store. No jewelry or furs. Travis' lips quirked up at the corners. That was his father—even if Robert Kellman happened to be seeing a woman on the side, he was smart enough not to buy things for her on his credit card, where his wife might easily see the purchases.

He still didn't know what to think. Alicia's suspicions might not be true.

On the other hand, where had his father been on Thursday night and the following day? If he had spent the night with a girlfriend, perhaps that was why he was reluctant to speak out.

Travis opened his stepmother's Saks bill. She had visited Cincinnati with his father in August and apparently spent over three thousand dollars at that department store. Putting the bill carefully aside, he opened a letter from the Holiday Inn on I-675, just outside of town.

Dear Mrs. Kellman:

I regret to inform you that certain items are missing from Room number 303, rented by you on September 18. I would appreciate it if you would call me immediately and make arrangements to pay for these items, as follows:

1/ 1 clock radio, value $59.99

2/ 1 coffee maker, value $46.99

3/ 2 comforters, value $112.00 x 2 $224.00

4/ 1 lamp, value $185.00

TOTAL $515.98

If this bill is not settled within 14 days, I regret that the hotel will be forced to take legal action under the Fair Debt Collection Practices Act.

Very truly yours,

Jonathan P. Small

Hotel Manager

Travis read through this twice, puzzled. September 18th was last Thursday, the night Alicia had been murdered. How could she have been renting a hotel room?

And who had stolen all those items? He knew his stepmother wouldn't have taken used bedding and cheap electronics.

The school board meeting had ended before eight o'clock, yet Mrs. Stansky's testimony was that Alicia hadn't come home until nine. That would have given Alicia time to go to the hotel, perhaps even see a lover. Travis gripped the arm of the couch, thinking about this. If there were someone in Alicia's life like that, perhaps that person had murdered her.

Then he frowned, wondering how T.J. fit into the picture. At some point, Alicia had taken him from Gina and Ray.

Maybe they were the ones who had stayed at the hotel.

A man who would beat a child was just the type of lowlife who'd steal the comforters off a hotel-room bed, in Travis' opinion. Carefully, he refolded the letter and put it in his breast pocket.

He didn't want to go into the kitchen. He pictured the room as he had last seen it with Alicia's body sprawled across the floor, the coroner bending over her and MacReedy watching over everything with his heavy-lidded cynical eyes. It was hot and airless in the house. He took off his jacket and threw it over a dining room chair, hearing his stepmother's nagging voice in his head, *Travis Jeffrey! Is that the way you're supposed to put away your coat?*

He pushed the kitchen door open. The police tape was still on the floor, outlining where the body had lain. Averting his eyes, he went to the sink and got a glass of water.

Alicia had always kept her bills in the kitchen, on a little low desk that was part of the long kitchen counter. He sat in a chair and went through her bills one by one. He didn't find anything surprising, although he wondered if all women spent so much money on shoes.

A knock on the back door startled him. He went to the door and unlocked it.

Mrs. Stansky stood there with a cherry pie. "Travis, dear. How are you doing? How is Katie?"

"Holding up so far." He really had no desire to talk to this woman whose testimony had helped put his father in jail.

"I made a pie last night. When I saw your truck outside, I thought, this pie will be just the thing for Travis." She put it into his hands. "I know how you men like pie!" She smiled, tilting her head to one side.

"Thanks, that's very kind of you."

"I've been picking up the newspapers every morning, so they don't clutter up the front step." Her expression was anxious. "Do you want them?"

"No, no—thank you. Just throw them out, would you?" He made a mental note to have the subscription halted. "Listen, Mrs. Stansky, I heard about what you told the police. I know my father and stepmother argued sometimes. But my father did not kill my stepmother. I'm sure of it."

She raised her chin. "I never said he did. All I told them was what I heard. They were arguing so loud, I could hear them over at my house. And poor Alicia was crying, too."

"But nothing more than that, right? Nothing like a scream?"

"No. Just arguing and crying. And when I looked out and saw your father leaving, he had the most terrible look on his face. Like something awful had happened."

"I don't remember you saying that in your statement to the police." He hoped she wouldn't repeat that damaging testimony at the trial.

"Maybe we shouldn't talk about it anymore." She drew herself up stiffly. "Good morning, Travis."

He breathed a sigh of relief as she left. Glancing at his watch, he saw he didn't have much time left to look around.

He went into his father's study, sat behind the big walnut desk and opened his father's laptop computer. He waited, impatiently tapping his fingers on the desk as the laptop came to life and the icons appeared against a tropical-scene wallpaper.

His father rarely sent him e-mail, but he seemed to remember that Robert Kellman was an Earthlink subscriber. And there was the square orange icon with the white oval. Travis clicked on it, praying that his father had lazily stored his password.

Yes!—there it was, a row of asterisks in the start screen. Travis smiled and clicked on "Connect".

The toolbar came up, showing that his father had seven new e-mail messages. Most of it spam, no doubt. Travis opened the e-mail facility and clicked "check" and the messages began downloading.

There were two from "akkellman" from early Thursday morning. Messages from Katie. He didn't open those. One from a golf supply place, two from JCPenney, one from Amazon. Cell phone bill. Nothing of real interest.

Checking quickly through the old messages, he saw more messages from Katie, one from Peter, two from Earthlink. Nothing personal, nothing from a girlfriend.

Frowning, he looked back at the new mail and opened the cell phone bill. He glanced at the bottom right of the screen and saw that it was ten after eight. He needed to leave since his first appointment was at eight-thirty.

Hesitating, he was about to click on the exit box when he decided to print the bill instead. It seemed to take forever, but finally the printer began to laboriously spit out the page showing the numbers his father had called. When it finally stopped, he folded the paper and shut down the laptop.

He locked up the house and headed for his truck with the pie when Denise MacReedy waved to him from the sidewalk.

"Hi, how are you?" Travis asked. He never really knew what to call her. He considered her husband his contemporary, but Denise was a few years older than Chief MacReedy and had actually been one of Travis' teachers at Priam High School fourteen years ago. All the boys had been required to take her Home Economics class. Travis had greatly preferred Wood Shop during the second semester.

"Oh, fine. How are you doing?" Her voice and expression were sympathetic.

"I'm all right. Just taking care of the mail."

She nodded with a gentle smile. "Poor Alicia. She'll be greatly missed at our annual flower show. She was really the guiding spirit behind so much of it. I always say she was personally responsible for selling half the tickets."

"True," Travis agreed, remembering how Alicia had usually coerced him into buying twice as many tickets as he needed.

"You'll let me know when the funeral is, won't you?"

"As soon as I know myself." He opened the door of his truck to give her the hint that as far as he was concerned, the conversation was over.

"Because I know my husband will be very interested in attending," she added.

Travis thought about that remark as he started up the Ford. Did MacReedy always attend the funeral when he'd investigated the victim's death? That made sense only if the investigation were still ongoing. But Robert Kellman had been arrested and charged for the murder.

Well, his own investigation was ongoing, even if the chief thought he had caught the murderer. He would keep his eyes open at the funeral, that was certain.

He wondered when the coroner's office would release Alicia's body for burial.

* * * * *

When JayBee arrived at the Kellman Animal Clinic at twenty after six, the parking lot was empty. She rode her motorcycle around to the back where it wouldn't be seen from the street. Dismounting, she took her dress, still in its dry cleaner bag, off the back. Her shoes were in the saddlebag.

She walked around to the front of the clinic just as Travis drove up in his truck. He looked startled to see her in her jeans and leather jacket.

"Is there somewhere inside where I can change?" she asked, holding up her dress.

He got down from the truck and she paused, looking him over. She had thought he might wear a suit, but wasn't surprised to see that his outfit was somewhat more casual. He looked incredibly handsome in gray pants, a pale blue shirt, open at the neck and a black blazer with a black leather collar.

He took her hand. "Where's your car? You didn't walk over, did you?"

"I came on my motorcycle. It's parked around back." She couldn't help herself. Putting her hand on the side of his face, she gave him a kiss. His lips were warm and gentle as he put his arm around her and pressed her close.

He unlocked the clinic's front door. The waiting room was cheerful, the walls an attractive lemon yellow, the furniture two plain vinyl couches. A planter of yellow and white chrysanthemums and a computer sat on the receptionist's desk. One wall held shelves of specialized pet foods, while on another, a bulletin board displayed pictures of adoptable animals, announcements and notes from grateful clients.

Travis led her into the back room and opened the door to his inner office. "Take your time. I'm going to check on my patient."

JayBee looked around curiously as she shucked off her jeans and pulled her dress over her head. Travis' private office was painfully neat, with nothing on the big desk except a computer and an Ohio State University mug filled with pens. Neatly labeled file cabinets reposed behind the desk.

On the wall facing the desk was a framed poster from the Worcester Art Museum showing *The Peaceable Kingdom* by Edward Hicks. In the early American painting, a bull stood next to a lion and little children played on the ground with lambs and exotic cats.

On the side wall, diplomas from Denison University and Ohio State University College of Veterinary Medicine hung beside a framed print of St. Francis of Assisi. The saint stood with birds perched on his hands and mice at his feet. Underneath, the lines read:

Lord, make me an instrument of Thy peace;

Where there is hatred, let me sow love;

Where there is injury, pardon;

Where there is doubt, faith;

Where there is despair, hope;

Where there is darkness, light;

And where there is sadness, joy.

When JayBee came out of the office, Travis was kneeling by a cage at the far end of the room, talking softly to a cocker spaniel puppy and petting its head.

She shut the office door behind her. He turned at the sound and rose to his feet.

"Do you like my dancing dress?" She spun around so he could see how the layered skirt belled out when she moved. "I bought it to wear when I chaperone the homecoming dance." The violet dress had a tight-fitting, low-cut bodice with a built-in bra. Thin straps tied at the back of her neck.

"I don't remember any teachers who looked like you when I went to school," he said, smiling. "Do you really think it's fair to do that to teenage boys?"

She laughed in delight and he came over to her eagerly, taking both her hands. She recognized the hot look of desire in his eyes. That never used to frighten her because she'd always believed she could handle the men she dated—before Bradley. She was suddenly aware they were locked into a solitary place together, a place under his control.

"Let's go, I'm starving!" She tried to sound lively and cheerful, but from the quick glance he gave her, she knew he'd heard something unusual in her voice.

"All right. I'm hungry too." His tone was low and steady. "Give me just a minute." He went back to the cage and knelt down. "Be a good puppy. I'll be back tomorrow morning." His voice held the same note he had just used with her. The puppy lay down with a sigh. Travis checked the cage to make sure it was latched, then went to the sink and washed his hands. All of this had a reassuring effect on JayBee.

He's not like Bradley.

* * * * *

They went to a steakhouse out on I-675, where Travis had reserved a booth. Agreeing on a bottle of Chardonnay and a shrimp cocktail, they faced each other across the table. The waitress lit the flickering oil lamp, which cast uneven shadows over the expanse of white tablecloth between them.

JayBee felt relaxed now, in a comfortably public place.

"Thank you for coming out with me," Travis said. "It's been awhile since I've gone on a date."

"And why is that?" She remembered what some of the teachers had said about him being jilted by his sister-in-law, but she wanted to hear what he would say.

"I was engaged to someone here in town. But she decided she preferred my brother." He sounded as though he didn't want to talk about it.

"Something like that happened to me, too. I was seeing this man...we were getting to a point where we were seriously interested in each other—at least, I thought so—and then he met my sister. One-hundred and eighty degree turn, just like that." She snapped her fingers. "A few weeks later they went to Las Vegas and came back married."

"That must have been tough." His eyes were sympathetic and concerned, looking into hers. "After my brother stole my fiancée, I didn't speak to him for a year. What happened with you and your sister?"

JayBee looked down, tracing her finger along the pattern in the tablecloth, not quite sure how to answer this. "I was horribly angry at first. But I blamed my boyfriend more than my sister. All my life, I've watched men fall for her. She's very beautiful."

"More beautiful than you?" He raised his brows as though he couldn't believe it.

"Thanks—but yes. She's movie-star beautiful. Supermodel beautiful."

"And what does this paragon do for a living?"

"She indexes and edits books at home. She doesn't like leaving the house." JayBee wondered how she could change the subject. That was quite enough about Angel, as far as she was concerned. And Angel would hate it if she knew people were talking about her.

"Agoraphobia?"

JayBee nodded. "She's been seeing a psychologist for it."

"So that's why she didn't come along the other day when I had my visit with T.J. I'd wondered about that."

"She was able to take T.J. to the playground today. I was proud of her for going out. So I think maybe she's improving."

"Does T.J. play with Queenie?"

"They're inseparable. That dog follows T.J. everywhere he goes. T.J. even insists on having Queenie sleep in bed with him."

Travis listened to this with a half-smile on his face. "I miss Queenie, but I'm glad I could give the boy something he likes."

"You couldn't have thought of a better present. Tell me more about Queenie. Did you have her as a puppy?"

"No, I'd only had her about a week. Her owners decided they didn't want a three-legged dog anymore, so they brought her to me to euthanize. But I'd put a lot of time into helping her get better after she got hit by a car. So I wound up taking her home instead of putting her to sleep." He looked up anxiously, as though he thought she might offer some mockery for this soft-heartedness. "That's the hardest part about being a vet—putting healthy animals to sleep just because it's more convenient for their owners."

"Her owners wanted her put to sleep?" JayBee cried. "A great dog like Queenie? Who are they? I want to give them a piece of my mind!"

"I guess I'd better keep that to myself," he answered with a grin. "My brother thought I was a fool for taking her in. He told me if I didn't want to kill things, I should have become a real doctor."

"Since when is a vet not a real doctor? Doesn't he know it's harder to get into veterinary school than medical school?"

He raised his eyebrows. "I don't know if Pete knows that. I know it—but how do you know it?"

"I was doing some reading on the internet. What kind of doctoring does your brother do?"

"Pediatric surgery."

"Well, next time he says anything to you about being a real doctor, just look him right in the eye and say, 'Hey, Pete, I'm a surgeon too. And a diagnostician, an obstetrician and an ophthalmologist. And my patients can't even tell me where it hurts. So there!'"

He took her hand across the table, the look in his eyes warm and appreciative. "Thank you. You're an advocate worth having."

* * * * *

After their steak dinner, they agreed to leave dessert for later and go dancing. Travis drove them to the Holiday Inn a few miles down the road from the restaurant.

"Would you mind waiting in the lobby for a few minutes?" he asked as they walked in. Pulling the letter out of his blazer's inner pocket, he lowered his voice. "The hotel sent my stepmother a letter. I need to speak to someone at the front desk about it."

She gave him a curious look, but said, "Okay."

He went up to the front desk, turning slightly so that he could watch her walk away and seat herself. *Good Lord, what gorgeous legs.*

Travis waited for the teenaged clerk to finish with a woman who was checking in. Several times while in college, he'd brought girlfriends here and rented a room for the night. He hoped they still took the same kind of information at check-in.

When the girl turned to help him, he put a stern frown on his face and slapped the letter down on the counter. "I demand to know the meaning of this!" he boomed, making his voice as deep as possible. "My stepmother sent me to find out why she's being charged for these items. She never stayed here! You people have made a serious error!"

The girl looked scared. "Sir, I'm not sure what to tell you—"

"Pull the record and let me verify her signature!"

Her hands shaking, the girl did as he'd requested. Travis was quite sure she would have refused to pull the record if he'd approached her in a kindly manner, but it didn't make him feel any less guilty. He'd have to do something to make it up to her. Maybe send her an anonymous bouquet of flowers tomorrow.

She showed him the registration record with his stepmother's signature. He scanned it quickly. There it was—license plate AIF 1572. A lead to "Uncle Ray and Aunt Gina."

"All right." He moderated his tone. "Thanks for your trouble." He handed back the registration record, picked up the letter and rejoined JayBee.

"Thanks for waiting." He hesitated for a moment, then went on, "My stepmother charged a room here the night she was murdered. I think perhaps T.J's aunt and her boyfriend stayed here."

"Oh! Of course you want to find T.J's aunt. You must have a lot of questions for her."

He nodded. "Not only that, but she and her boyfriend are likely suspects for the murder. I'm certain my father is innocent, so I've decided to do some investigating on my own."

He was startled at the intent, glowing look she turned on him. "Wow, that's really something. Wouldn't it be great if you managed to track down the real murderer?"

He drew a deep breath, thinking how good it would be to see his father released from jail, his name cleared. "I'm going to do my best," he said quietly. "Come on, let's find the ballroom."

Dancing with JayBee was pure pleasure. She was light on her feet and followed his lead with ease. He especially enjoyed the slow dances when he could hold her in his arms. Taking a deep breath, he inhaled the vanilla scent of her hair.

She looked up at him, eyes shining. "You're such a good dancer!"

"I guess all those years of dancing school have paid off." He smiled. "Lord, Pete and I hated those lessons. We thought our stepmother dreamed them up purely to torture us. But I guess they've come in useful, after all."

"I learned ballroom dancing in college. One of my boyfriends was into it. We used to go every weekend, during my sophomore year."

He frowned, not wanting to hear about her past boyfriends. She gave him a questioning look. Pulling her closer, he gave her a quick kiss on her soft red lips, enjoying the way they yielded under his.

As the song drew to an end, the band leader announced they were taking a break. "Want to stay here, or go somewhere else?" Travis asked.

"You promised to buy me dessert somewhere. All that dancing made me hungry again."

"What would you say to a hot fudge sundae?"

"I'd say, lead me to it!" she said.

"I've got all the ingredients at my house, if you'll come over."

"Oh…I don't know if I should."

There it was again, that odd caution he had noticed earlier. He couldn't understand why she would be willing to go jogging at night by herself and yet be afraid to come over to his house. "Look, honey," he said gently, "if you don't want to come over, that's fine. We can go to a restaurant. But don't be afraid of me. I promise I won't do anything that scares you, ever. All right?"

Sighing, she took his hand. "I'm not scared of you, not when I really think about it. I was in a bad situation once with a man… I can't talk about it. But it makes me—careful—about where I go."

He clenched his right hand at the thought that someone had hurt her in the past. "I'd like you to see my place. I've put a lot of work into it."

"Okay. I can't stay very long though. I promised my sister I'd be home by midnight." At his surprised look, she added, "I think it's another aspect of her agoraphobia. She gets scared when she's alone in the house."

"She's not alone. T.J.'s there. Not to mention Queenie."

"T.J. doesn't count, he's too little. She needs an adult who could run for help or call 9-1-1 if someone tried to break in."

Travis didn't want to argue with her. "Come over for an hour, then. I'll give you the grand tour and make you a hot fudge sundae."

As they drove to his house, Travis wondered what she would think of his home. What if she preferred something more modern? Slick, matching suites of furniture, fancy electronic equipment, a shiny, restaurant-style kitchen? The house was important to him and he wanted her to like it.

"The kitchen's kind of old-fashioned," he said as he unlocked the back door. "In fact, the whole place is old-fashioned. I didn't want a bunch of modern stuff that wouldn't suit the house, so I bought most of the furniture at estate sales and auctions."

She stepped in and looked around. "It's very homey. And so neat!"

"Yes, I like to keep things straightened up. Katie—my sister—accuses me of being compulsively neat, but I'm really not. Well, maybe in contrast to her. She never picks anything up. Drove me crazy when she lived here for awhile." *You're babbling, Kellman. Shut up.*

"Oh, look at the gorgeous cat!" Puff jumped down from the table and wound back and forth around JayBee's ankles. She knelt down on the floor and made clucking sounds. Travis was glad to see she knew proper cat protocol—she didn't immediately grab the cat or try to pull him into her lap, just let him sniff her hand. When he rubbed against it, she petted him carefully, watching to see whether he liked it.

In a few minutes, Blackie came slinking in from the dining room, wanting to get in on the action. Soon JayBee was petting a cat with each hand.

"How many cats do you have?" she asked as Big Bob came peeping around the corner.

"Six right now. Some of them live in the barn." He shrugged at her surprised look. "I hate putting healthy cats to sleep. I figure if they can get along with each other, they can live here." He offered his hand to help her up off the floor. "Come see the rest of the house."

"What a lovely room!" she commented as they went into the dining room.

"Thanks." He waved his hand toward the table. "That's one of the things I bought at an estate sale. It's really amazing—a set like that would cost a couple thousand new, but I bought the whole thing—buffet, china cupboard and all—for just eight hundred dollars." She might as well know his situation right away. "I inherited some money from my real mother and that's what I used to buy this farm. I make a decent living as a vet, but not the kind of money a medical doctor makes."

She nodded. "It's like being a teacher. You have to do it for the love of it, not to make a lot of money."

"Exactly," he said, pleased. "Listen, I promised you some dessert. Take a walk through the downstairs and if you want to see the upstairs, just go on up. I'm going to start the hot fudge."

He went into the kitchen and poured bottled sauce into a pan. While that was heating, he scooped vanilla ice cream into bowls and opened a can of peanuts.

JayBee returned shortly, her cheeks pink from the exertion of running up and down the stairs. "Everything's so nice here. I have to admit I'm relieved. I know I shouldn't be like this, but if I see a guy's place and it's a real pigsty, I feel kind of weird about him."

He pulled out a kitchen chair for her. "Have a seat." He set her sundae in front of her.

"Wow, this looks great!" She dug in immediately. "Mmmm—divine!"

"Glad you like it." He sat across from her. "This is one of the four things I know how to make."

She smiled, her dimples peeping out. "What are the other three?"

"Grilled cheese, hamburgers and scrambled eggs."

Her smile widened. "Then you've got all the meals covered. Breakfast, lunch, dinner and dessert!"

He laughed. "I guess so. I never thought of it that way before."

After they ate, they went into the parlor. She sat in the big armchair and leaned back. "This is so comfortable. I could fall asleep here, no problem."

He sat on the couch, wishing she'd chosen to sit next to him. "I've done that at times. I usually wake up with a cat or two in my lap."

"Does the fireplace work?"

"Sure. I often build a fire when it's cold out. Although they say you lose more heat through the chimney than you gain by the fire. It doesn't really matter, I guess, since it costs a fortune to heat this place anyway. I'm thinking of getting new windows installed…" *You're babbling again, Kellman. Shut up and let her get a word in edgewise.*

"Is that your mother?" she asked, getting up and moving to the small oil painting that hung over the brick fireplace.

"Yes—my real mother. Katie painted that from a photograph."

"She's very good."

"Yes, I think she has real talent."

This time she sat next to him on the couch. "Do you do any farming here?"

"No. I bought the place because I'd always liked it. It was going cheap because the house was in poor condition. I rent the big field to my next-door neighbor. He grows corn every year."

She was close enough that he could smell her floral-scented cologne. "I'm glad we went out," she said, her voice soft. "I've really enjoyed this evening."

"I have too." He took her hand, lifting it to his lips and kissing her fingers. Then he turned it and kissed the palm.

He had to be especially careful, he told himself, because they were in his house. He didn't want to make her feel trapped or uncomfortable. *Take it easy.*

She moved a little closer to him and they looked into each other's eyes. He touched the side of her face gently. "I think…I'm falling for you in a big way."

"Good." She put her hands on his shoulders and they kissed. He kept it light, letting her push things forward. So she was the one who deepened the kiss, who ran her hand into his hair, who unbuttoned his shirt and caressed his bare chest.

It almost killed him to do it, but he pulled away from her. "It's almost midnight."

She gave him a startled look. "In a hurry to get away from me?"

"As far as I'm concerned, you can stay as long as you want." He put his arms around her waist. "I wish you'd stay all night."

Was he imagining things or did she actually look tempted? "No, I really can't do that." He pulled her close and kissed her again, more aggressively this time. When she didn't move away, he left her mouth and kissed his way down her neck. She seemed to like it, letting her head fall back and relaxing under the caress. "Oh…oh, Travis, that's good," she murmured. He loved hearing her say his name…

"Oh, my goodness," she gasped sometime later. "We'd better stop." He moved back from her reluctantly, hating to stop but determined to show he would listen to what she wanted. She sighed.

"Sure you want to stop?" he murmured. But he didn't touch her while awaiting her reply.

"I didn't say I wanted to stop. I said we should stop." A little bit of mischief seemed to dance in her eyes.

"Why don't you call your sister and say you're going to be late? Then…come upstairs with me."

She straightened, putting up her arms to retie the straps of her dress. "No. Not a good idea."

"I think it's an excellent idea."

"Guys always do." She smiled ruefully. "But I never go to bed on the first date. No matter how much I want to. It's one of my rules."

"Good rule—but this is our second date." When she looked at him, surprised, he added, "I consider that our first date took place in the cemetery."

She laughed at that. "Yeah, right. Come on, you'd better take me back to the clinic."

* * * * *

When they reached the clinic, he said, "I've got planks in the truck. We could roll the bike up into the flatbed and I'll drive you home. Then you won't have to change."

"Oh, no! That won't do at all." She sighed. "Remember how I was telling you I had that bad experience with a man? My sister had a problem, too. With the same man, actually. So she and I made a pact that we wouldn't go out with anyone for a year."

"So did you break your promise to go out with me?"

"No—it's been fifteen months. But I didn't tell her I was going on a date. She's been after me to renew our pact for another year." She saw he was waiting expectantly. "But I won't," she added.

He smiled. "Good."

He let them into the clinic and she changed quickly into her jeans and jacket. When they left again, he walked her to her motorcycle.

"Call me tomorrow?" he asked.

She nodded, wishing suddenly that she'd gone upstairs with him. Right at this minute they could have been in bed together. Stop it! she told herself sternly. Well, one more kiss wouldn't hurt. Putting her arms around his neck, she kissed him, then whispered, "I'm falling for you, too."

He looked surprised but happy as she mounted the bike and fired it up.

Watching him from her rearview mirror as she exited the lot, she noticed he didn't get into his truck until she was out on the street.

She headed toward the center of town and buzzed around the square twice out of sheer exhilaration. She couldn't remember feeling this happy in a long time. Since before Bradley had come into her life.

As she traveled down Tecumseh Street, she noticed that a sleek dark car was following close behind. Sighing impatiently, she increased her speed, wondering why people always drove annoyingly close behind motorcycles.

It wasn't until she took the turn for her own street that she realized the car had turned too. Maybe just a coincidence, but it was one she didn't like. She passed her house without pausing and made a left at the end of the street.

She turned onto Prophet Road, exceeding the speed limit by ten miles an hour and made another left at the end of that street. She slowed the bike and put on her right turn signal as though she were going to turn into a driveway. Taking a good look at the car, she saw the Nissan behind her slow to a crawl.

Speeding up again, she headed back to Tecumseh Street. When the Nissan kept right behind her, she was sure she was being followed.

Fortunately, she knew where that concrete monstrosity of a police station was located. She rode around the square again and took the turn-off that led to Troy Road. She drove straight into the well-lit parking lot with a sigh of relief. The Nissan didn't follow her into the lot, but came to a stop out on the street.

"Juliet!" a male voice spoke low.

Only one person had ever called her that. JayBee was shaking, but she jumped off her bike and ran for the police station. Watching from the door, she saw the car speed up and take off.

Chapter Ten

JayBee sighed with relief, lifting off her helmet. She considered calling Travis. She was sure he'd be willing to come back and follow her home if he knew she was in trouble.

Pressing her forehead against the cool glass of the station door, she decided against that. Why drag him into this? She'd deal with her own problems. Briefly, she considered waiting a little while and then heading home without making a fuss.

The thought that Bradley might still be driving around outside forced her to proceed into the station. A motorcycle was just too vulnerable when it went up against a car.

She heard her booted footsteps echoing in the silent hall as she walked forward, looking for signs of life. Finally she spotted the dispatcher, a heavy, middle-aged man with a balding head and prominent eyebrows. He hunched over a desk that contained a half-filled pizza box and a bottle of Pepto-Bismol.

He didn't look up until she tapped on the glass window surrounding his office. "What's the trouble, lady?"

She explained how a car had followed her. He seemed unimpressed. "You can hang around here for awhile, make sure he's gone."

"I've really got to get home!" She decided to come clean and tell him the whole story. "I think the person was someone I know."

He looked skeptical. "Is that so? Did you recognize the car in the dark?"

JayBee didn't like his tone. "As a matter of fact, I saw the car clearly. It was one of those Nissan 350Zs. But that's not how I knew him. Most people use my nickname—but he called me by my real name."

The dispatcher's expression didn't change. "Look, lady, want to fill out a report? I'll give you the form."

"Yes, I want to fill out a report. And then I'd like you to call whatever squad car is out there and have them escort me home."

He frowned. "Lady, this is a police station, not a bodyguard service."

"Oh, right. I guess they're too busy giving out speeding tickets." After only three months in Priam, JayBee had been caught twice in the local speed trap.

The dispatcher didn't reply to this, just opened the desk drawer.

You catch more flies with honey than with vinegar, Angel always said. She put on a pleading expression. "Please, you don't realize how serious this is. I'm sure it was Bradley Morrow out there following me. He's supposed to be in prison for domestic violence against my sister—not to mention assault and battery against me."

He still didn't look very concerned. Was domestic violence such a frequent occurrence in this town that it didn't elicit any type of reaction? "He must be breaking some type of law," she insisted. "My sister had a protection order."

"All that's over once the perp goes to prison," the dispatcher told her. "You and your sister had best see a lawyer if you want another order." He fumbled through the desk, finally coming up with a form and a chewed pen. "Here you go."

JayBee filled out the report, wishing she'd been able to get the license number. Still, how many Nissan 350Zs could there be in town? Damn it, Bradley had been given a three-year prison sentence for what he'd done. How had he gotten released in less than two years?

Oh, she knew exactly how. There were two Bradleys, the charming, public Bradley who had fooled both herself and her sister and the calculating sociopath who was dangerous and violent when he drank. In prison, he must have been on his best behavior, hoping for early release.

She thought of an evening when Bradley had come to pick her up for a party at the stock brokerage where he worked. She had been wearing the sexiest dress she'd ever had, a clinging green layered chiffon with sequined spaghetti straps. Angel had helped her fix her flyaway red hair into a braided knot at the back of her head.

She'd been in the bathroom, making up her eyes, when Bradley arrived. Angel, working on the couch with her laptop, wearing cutoff shorts and an old frayed t-shirt, had jumped up and let him in.

Yeah, when I came out of the bathroom, he could hardly drag his eyes away from Angel long enough to greet me. JayBee still remembered the hurt of that moment. All the way to the party, Bradley hadn't even bothered to conceal his interest, asking questions about Angel until she finally lost her temper.

"Why didn't you tell me to stay home and ask Angel to the party?" she'd demanded. The fight began from that remark. She'd never even made it to the party, but wound up stalking off and taking a cab home.

She'd never worn that dress again, either.

Bradley had called Angel later that same week. "I won't go out with him if it bothers you," Angel had said, but JayBee could tell Angel was intrigued by him.

"Bradley means nothing to me," she'd answered proudly. "Do what you want."

Their quickie marriage in Las Vegas several weeks later had been a shock, but JayBee had weathered it by telling herself, "At least I didn't have to smile my way through a big church wedding." JayBee's relationship with her sister had been strained for awhile, but they made up when Angel became pregnant. "You're the very first person I've called," Angel had told her, sounding happier than JayBee had ever heard her. "Oh, I hope Bradley's as thrilled as I am!"

But he didn't seem to be, at least that was JayBee's impression when the school year ended and she went to visit the newlywed couple for a few days. Bradley was short and sharp with Angel, giving orders like a drill sergeant.

JayBee was startled at the change in her sister as well. Instead of the happy bride or glowing mother-to-be JayBee had expected, she found a drawn woman with apprehensive eyes. When the two sisters went out to lunch, Angel talked feverishly, hardly allowing JayBee to get a word in edgewise.

Finally, as they shared a slice of cheesecake for dessert, JayBee asked, "Angel, what's wrong?"

"Nothing's wrong," Angel told her, opening her blue eyes wide. "What makes you think anything's wrong?"

That evening, Angel began preparing a gourmet dinner two hours before Bradley was supposed to come home. She made an elaborate salad, a potato and cheese casserole and put T-bone steaks in a bowl of marinade. JayBee could tell how disappointed she was when Bradley called just fifteen minutes before he was expected to say that he had to take a client out to dinner.

"Oh, well," Angel said, obviously trying for a cheerful tone. "More for the two of us."

As they sat down to eat, JayBee asked, "Does that happen often?"

"Too often for my liking," Angel admitted. "You wouldn't believe how much food I throw out. I can't eat my dinner and Bradley's and he won't eat leftovers."

JayBee was shocked. In the house where they'd grown up, wasting food was a crime as serious as stealing from the church collection plate.

They stayed up for awhile talking, but the heavy meal had made JayBee sleepy. "It's okay if you want to go to bed," Angel told her, yawning.

"What about you? You look like you could use some rest."

Angel looked frightened. "Oh, no, Bradley would be really upset if I went to bed before he came home."

With difficulty, JayBee refrained from calling her sister's husband a selfish pig and went to bed. Hours later, she awoke from a deep sleep due to a banging noise. As she sat up in bed, she could hear Bradley shouting.

Throwing on a robe, she peeked into the living room.

"I should have called 9-1-1 immediately. That was my big mistake," she told herself often in the months ahead, as she went over and over what had happened. But at the time, she didn't stop to think.

A lamp lay shattered on the floor. Bradley was in his shirtsleeves, his tie askew, his face red with fury. Angel crouched on the floor, her arms vainly trying to protect her stomach.

"You stupid bitch!" Bradley shouted and kicked Angel in the ribs. He drew back his foot to kick her again when JayBee ran at him and kicked him in the back of the thigh. In his drunken state, he didn't seem to feel the pain. With a roar, he whirled around and punched JayBee in the gut. She rolled with it and caught his leg on her way to the floor, bringing him down with her. He clutched at the coffee table with his right arm. As hard as she could, JayBee karate-chopped his forearm. Bradley screamed in pain and threw himself on top of her, pinning her down with his heavy weight and punching her in the face with his left fist.

Someone banged on the door of the apartment. Angel, holding her ribs, crawled to the door and managed to stand long enough to open it.

Henry and Kyle, who lived across the hall, appeared in the doorway. "Thank goodness!" Angel sobbed, sinking to the floor again. Henry ran in and pulled Bradley away from JayBee. Kyle caught Bradley's arms, restraining him until he stopped struggling, then helped JayBee to her feet.

"I think my sister needs to go to the hospital," JayBee gasped, holding her hand to her bleeding nose. She made her way over to Angel and crouched down beside her.

"She broke my arm!" Bradley pointed at JayBee.

"Shut the hell up!" Henry barked, while Kyle grabbed the phone and called 9-1-1.

What an ugly mess, JayBee thought now, remembering the sad aftermath. Her sister had miscarried two days later, whether from the stress or from Bradley's physical violence, they weren't sure. Bradley had made threats against both of them, but it hadn't stopped them from testifying against him in court.

Angel had moved back in with JayBee and started indexing for a living, while JayBee worked another school year. But somehow, Bradley had ruined Dayton for both of them. "Let's move somewhere new, somewhere we've never been," Angel had pleaded. So JayBee had started applying to some other school systems and finally found the position in Priam.

And I like it here. I'm not going to let that bastard scare me off. But what am I going to tell Angel? This is going to be terrible for her.

With a sigh, she handed the report to the dispatcher. He scanned it quickly, then looked up. "The squad car's coming by. They'll follow you home and then they'll take a look around town for that Nissan."

"Thank you!" JayBee told him. She hoped Angel wouldn't be waiting up for her. It would give her a nasty shock to see her sister being escorted home by police.

* * * * *

When Travis arrived home, he was surprised to find Katie sitting in his kitchen. She looked him over, raising her eyebrows. "Where've you been?"

"Dinner with a friend." He removed his blazer and hung it over the back of a chair. Maybe it was the light in the kitchen, but Travis thought his little sister looked peaked. Her face was pale and her cheekbones stood out starkly.

"Georgia?"

He gave her a disgusted look. "No, I was not out with Pete's wife." Sitting down across from her, he asked, "So what's up?"

She pulled a folded paper out of her pocket. "Pete stopped by today and gave me a copy of Maman's will. I thought you'd like to see it."

Travis skimmed through the beginning legalese quickly. Alicia had appointed her husband as executor, with Peter to act if her husband was unavailable.

Half of her estate was left to her "beloved daughter, Alicia Kathleen Kellman", with no restrictions on the inheritance. No surprise there.

Twenty percent of her estate was left to Peter Robert Kellman, her stepson, with the following restriction, "Any personal use which benefits Peter's wife, Georgia Kellman, is prohibited. The inheritance must be used solely for the improvement of the medical practice of Peter Robert Kellman." Travis thought he could almost hear his stepmother saying the words. He knew that Peter was not going to be pleased with this restriction. "The improvement of the medical practice" probably didn't include paying off gambling debts.

Travis' eyes widened in surprise as he read that twenty percent of the estate was left to him for the following purposes, "First, Travis is to pay off any remainder of the money his father lent him to buy his veterinary practice. Second, the inheritance may be used to purchase or benefit any animal or animals, as Travis sees fit. The inheritance may not be used to improve the house at Creekside Farm, since he bought it against my express advice."

The final ten percent was left to Alicia's nephew Terry Gordon, for college tuition and expenses.

Travis put the will down and looked at his sister. "I can't believe Alicia left me money."

"She could hardly leave Pete money and none to you," Katie answered.

He shrugged. "It was her money. She could do whatever she wanted with it. I never expected this."

"It's a lot of money, too," his sister said. "Pete says Maman's estate is worth close to a million dollars."

Travis whistled. "That much?"

Katie nodded. "Most of it was her inheritance from Grandpa. Maman told me once he'd made some excellent investments."

"I guess so!" He wondered what he could do with that much money. Maybe add on a room at the Clinic for unwanted animals until they could be adopted.

He was confused, happy and sad, all at the same time. He could put that money to some good uses...yet he had never wanted to take anything from Alicia. How typical of her to put the restriction in about Creekside Farm. And yet, how kind of her to leave him money to help animals.

Katie got up and opened his refrigerator. "My goodness, Travis, don't you have anything to eat around here?"

"I'll make you something. Grilled cheese?"

She sighed. "No, I can't eat cheese this late."

"I've got hot fudge I could warm up. How about a sundae?" Reaching over to the stove, he removed the lid from the fudge pan and waved the pan enticingly under her nose.

"Well...maybe just a little one."

Katie was wearing sandals, a pair of Sixties-style low-rise jeans with embroidered flowers and a muslin shirt. Her elbows and collar bones stood out sharply. She and JayBee were about the same height, but JayBee had to have twenty pounds on his sister. Not that JayBee was fat, but she was nicely padded in all the right places. Stirring the fudge as it heated, he found himself having a pleasant daydream about JayBee's lovely breasts.

She had said, "I'm falling for you too."

"You look like you're in la-la land," Katie's voice brought him back to Earth.

"Just thinking about this evening."

Katie looked at him reproachfully. "I don't see how you can be going out on dates when we're having all this trouble in the family."

Travis had questioned that himself, but it didn't stop him from feeling annoyed that Katie was saying it. "Everything good doesn't have to stop just because of our troubles. You've got a boyfriend, haven't you?"

"No, I broke up with him."

"Sorry to hear it." He scooped some ice cream into a dish, poured the hot fudge over it and handed it to Katie. There really wasn't anything else he could say without being rude, but he knew he was lying. Actually, he wasn't at all sorry to hear that Katie had broken it off. The last thing she needed was another married boyfriend.

"I feel like I'm all alone in the world," Katie went on. "No boyfriend…Maman's gone…Dad's in jail…"

"So what am I, chopped liver?"

Her dark eyes peered up at him sadly. "Don't forget, you're a daddy now. You're going to be busy with little Travis, once you get custody."

"Sure, but I was hoping you'd give me a hand with him. He's your nephew, you know."

"I don't know much about kids."

"Neither do I. We'll learn together, all right?"

She nodded. Slowly, she ate some of the ice cream, taking tiny little spoonfuls. It was quite a contrast to the way JayBee had attacked her helping. He smiled to himself, remembering how much she'd enjoyed the dessert.

Katie's next remark took him by surprise. "Travis, do you think whoever killed Maman will go to hell?"

He sat down again, stroking his beard thoughtfully. "I'm not sure I believe in hell."

She looked up from her sundae, startled. "Don't you think bad people should be punished? People like Saddam Hussein and Osama bin Laden?"

"I don't know. I'm hoping God manages better than that. What would be the point of endlessly torturing souls?"

"Deterrence?"

He gave her a half-smile. "Sure, you can see how well that works."

"Well, I think evil should be punished. I don't see how it can work any other way."

"I guess we won't know until we die."

Katie nodded, taking one last scrape of the bowl with her spoon. Carrying the bowl and the pan to the sink, she washed them. "You really need to get a dishwasher."

"I hope you'll be able to sleep after eating this late."

"Sleep?" she repeated, as though he'd said something outrageous, like suggesting she join the Hare Krishnas. "I've hardly been able to sleep since...since what happened to Maman." Still with her back to him, she said, low-voiced, "Have you ever done something...something that you can't stop thinking about? Something awful?"

"Well, sure," Travis said. "Everyone has."

She whirled around, looking at him intently. "Really, Travis? I can't remember you ever doing anything wrong. I mean, really, really wrong."

"I have a bad conscience about certain things."

"What?" Katie demanded.

"I shoplifted a cassette back in junior high school."

She gave him a scornful look. "That's your worst thing?"

It seemed to be important to Katie that he answer honestly. "I guess most of the things that keep me awake at night are things I didn't do. Things I participated in that I knew were wrong but I didn't try to stop. Pete and his buddies used to tease Andy Tantello. I don't think I actually ever did anything to the poor kid myself, but I was there when they used to say things that made him cry, or took his cap or his books and ran off. And sometimes things went on in vet school that I should have spoken out about." There was one other thing, but he certainly wasn't going to talk to his sister about the woman in Cincinnati. "So, what is it you're feeling bad about?" he asked.

She opened her mouth as though she were going to speak, then sighed. "I know you hate hearing about my love life. I'll just keep it to myself."

"Sure you don't want to talk about it?" he asked, trying to hide his relief.

"No. I'd better get going." She went to the door. "Thanks for the sundae."

Yawning, Travis picked up his jacket and headed upstairs. Monique left her basket and followed at his heels, whining until he lifted her up onto the bed.

As he undressed, he thought uneasily about the things Katie had said.

"Maybe you should take a look at Katie's motives. She's got a temper, too," Georgia had said. He still couldn't believe that his little sister would have murdered her own mother. But he wondered if she had really been talking about her love life just now.

It was a strange time for her to break up with her boyfriend, right now when she needed support and comfort.

Of course, grief could put extra stress on a relationship that almost certainly already had complications...

An ugly thought occurred to him. What if it were Katie's mysterious boyfriend who had murdered Alicia? If Katie were shielding him for some reason, it would explain why she was feeling so guilty.

No, that didn't make sense. What kind of motive could Katie's boyfriend have? And surely Katie wouldn't shield an ex-boyfriend at the expense of her father.

Unless she were implicated some way in the murder.

* * * * *

Midday, JayBee sat at her desk in her tiny office in the back of the girls' locker room, noting down comments about that morning's gym classes. As she worked, she kept her ears open, listening to what was going on in the dressing area. She didn't check to make sure the girls showered, figuring that was their own business, but she was always alert to the possibility of fights or gang-up teasing. If she heard anything like that, she would walk through and make sure it stopped. No *Carrie*-type incidents in her locker room, thank you.

The door opened and Charlotte Scott came in, holding a long white box. "I was in the office when this came for you," she said, smiling. "Aren't you lucky! It's got to be long-stemmed roses."

JayBee smiled back. She wasn't surprised that Travis would send flowers after their date. She ripped the white paper off the box and opened it. Charlotte leaned forward.

The two women gasped in bewilderment.

Had the florist made some terrible mistake? But no, this had been done purposely. Brown and wilted daisies and roses filled the box. Mixed among them were prickly thistles. In addition, the whole thing smelled as though it had been sprayed by a skunk.

An envelope lay on top of the arrangement. JayBee picked it up and took out the card.

Just a little token to show you how much I appreciated eighteen months in prison.

Tell Angel I think about her every single day. You'll be seeing me soon.

It was unsigned, but JayBee had no doubt who had sent it. Carefully, she put the card into her purse.

"It's just a joke," she told Charlotte, who didn't look convinced. No wonder—JayBee could hear the shakiness in her own voice. "Keep an eye on the girls for a few minutes, would you, please?"

Charlotte nodded and JayBee closed the box and took it outside to the dumpster at the back door of the school.

JayBee stopped by the office after lunch to get her mail. On the counter, there sat a small white china vase filled with purple violets, lilies of the valley and baby's breath. A violet bow tied around the neck of the vase completed the lovely arrangement.

The secretary looked up. "Oh, JayBee! Those are for you. My, two flower deliveries in one day! What it is to be young and pretty!"

"Thanks, Mrs. Carson," JayBee said, taking the vase. She waited until she got back to her office before she opened the envelope.

Dear J.B.

Thanks for a terrific evening.

Travis

It was so nice of Travis to send flowers. And purple violets, too, one of her favorite types. She was so glad he hadn't sent common roses. Had he chosen purple flowers because she had worn purple on their date?

She smiled, feeling like this second delivery had somehow blunted the ugliness of the first set of flowers. Blushing a little at her own sentimentality, she kissed the card before putting it away in her desk.

* * * * *

Travis glanced up at the big station clock, fidgeting impatiently as he waited for MacReedy to finish with his subordinate. Damn it, he had called ahead before coming over to the station—he'd hoped MacReedy would do him the courtesy of seeing him right away. His next appointment was at half past one and it was already ten after one.

Finally, MacReedy's door opened and Officer Ming came out, her cheeks flushed, her eyes downcast. She gave Travis a quick look and whispered, "Watch out. He's in a foul mood today."

Great, just what I need.

MacReedy looked ostentatiously at his watch as Travis walked into his office. "Okay, Trav, what is it?" he asked brusquely. "And make it snappy—I've only got a few minutes."

Travis decided he could act just as rudely in return. Uninvited, he pulled a chair up, took the hotel letter out of his breast pocket and slapped it down on MacReedy's desk. "I found this letter in my stepmother's mail. It turns out she rented a room for my son's aunt and her boyfriend, Gina and Ray. I followed up with the hotel and they gave me the license plate of their car. That's it, written on the bottom."

"You followed up with the hotel?" MacReedy sounded offended. "You should have brought me this letter immediately."

Travis shrugged. "I thought I'd see if anything would come of it before I brought it in. And I didn't know if you'd follow up the lead unless I pushed."

"From now on, I'd advise you to leave the investigation to us."

Travis fixed him with a cold stare. "Why? I'm not exactly impressed with the thoroughness of the investigation so far. You arrested my father after one day."

MacReedy put his head down, rubbing his forehead with both hands. "Yeah, yeah, you don't have to tell me—I know your whole family is pissed off with how fast your father was arrested. Well, let me tell you something, Trav. If your wife gets murdered, your shirt is under the body and you won't tell the police where you've been, it looks bad. Very bad. And if you have a lot of money and you're a flight risk, then the safest thing all around is to put you in jail. Ninety-nine out of a hundred cops would have done the same thing I did."

"Fine. You've done your job. But you can't blame me if I think your whole case is full of crap."

"Jim Percy doesn't think so. He says he's sure he can get a conviction."

"I don't believe that."

"No?" MacReedy looked at him thoughtfully. "Did you know your father had a huge life insurance policy on your stepmother?"

"Everyone has life insurance on their spouse," Travis snapped.

"For years, the policy was for two hundred thousand dollars," MacReedy told him. "Then just six months ago, your father increased it to a million."

"Coincidence." But Travis felt a chill go through him.

"Right," MacReedy drawled, picking up the hotel letter.

"With that license number, you can track the owner of the car, maybe even locate this Ray and Gina in Indiana," said

Travis. "For all you know, one of them is the person who murdered my stepmother. I'd advise you to start looking."

MacReedy threw him a disgusted glance. "I hardly think one of them could be the murderer. What would have been the point? Drop the kid off and then murder the person they left him with?"

"Maybe they didn't know how wealthy my stepmother was until they saw the house. Maybe it was Gina's idea to leave the boy and then Ray went back to try to take some money off her. My stepmother was one tough lady. Suppose Ray went over to rob her and she refused to give him anything. So then he got mad and killed her. The point is, you don't know unless you spend some time looking into it."

MacReedy put his hands out. "Okay, okay. No one's saying we won't try. But you have to realize it's a long shot. Indiana's a big state. It's going to be difficult to track them unless they get picked up for some type of crime."

"Give it your best shot," Travis told him, leveling a serious gaze into the chief's eyes. "Or I'm going to start talking to the papers about what a piss-poor investigation this has been."

MacReedy returned stare for stare. "You do that and you'll just alert Ray and Gina to the fact that we're looking for them."

Travis nodded curtly. "And I'd like to be told when you locate them. Even if they're cleared in the murder investigation, I want to talk to them about the child."

"We'll cross that bridge when we come to it."

Travis got up to leave. Just as he reached the door, the chief asked, "How's your sister holding up?"

"She's very upset."

"Not surprising." The chief shook his head, his expression sad. "It's a tough situation. Well, all right, Trav. I'll let you know if we make any progress."

* * * * *

Heather Ridgely was a petite brunette with stern manner. She bred Dalmatians and would have been a profitable client for Travis, if he hadn't alienated her in his first few months of practice. Ever since the day when they had disagreed about a treatment for one of her chief studs, she'd been taking her dogs to a vet in Remus. The fact that he'd been right hadn't brought her back. The incident had taught him a valuable lesson about dealing with clients. A veterinarian had to be tactful, especially with clients who thought they knew more than the trained professional.

"Thanks for letting me come by," he said, following her out to the kennels behind her house.

She gave him a sympathetic look. "I can't imagine how it must have been, finding poor Alicia's body. I can't bear to think about it."

He knew Heather had been one of his stepmother's closest friends. "It was awful," he murmured.

They had arrived at the fenced part of her large backyard. As she opened the gate, four large Dalmatians bounded up to greet her. Travis followed her in, holding out his closed hands and letting the dogs sniff him. One of them jumped up, paws to his chest, while another took his wrist playfully in her mouth.

"My dogs always did like you," Heather observed as he distributed pats and fondled ears.

"Most dogs do." He felt in his pockets but had only one dog treat on him, so he left it where it was.

"Do you have any theories about who murdered my stepmother?" he asked as they went into the barn that had been remodeled for dog kennels.

She looked surprised. "There's a lot of evidence against your father. I know that must be hard for you to face—"

"Circumstantial evidence only," he insisted. "The police rushed to make an arrest. So I've decided to do a little investigating myself."

"What can you do that the police didn't do?" Her tone was skeptical.

"I don't know, but I'm going to try."

"Alicia always said you were terribly stubborn." She motioned him to join her at one of the large crates. "As long as you're here, maybe you could take a look at Daisy's eye. I'm afraid she has an infection."

Well, he didn't mind giving her a free veterinary visit, if it would encourage her to help him in return. She found a flashlight and he got down in the straw to examine Daisy, a pregnant bitch who looked as though she would be whelping any day now. He spent a few minutes talking to Daisy while Heather worked, filling food and water bowls. Then he examined Daisy's eyes and wrote a prescription, which Heather stuck in her jeans pocket. "Thanks, Doctor."

Travis helped her fill a big metal bucket at the pump. "I hoped you'd tell me whether Alicia was quarreling with anyone. Whether she had any enemies."

"All strong women have enemies," she said. He took the bucket and filled the large watering trough in the yard while she spread fresh straw in one of the crates.

"I can only think of one person," she told him when he returned for more water. "Charlotte Scott."

"Charlotte Scott!" he repeated. She was one of his clients—and one that he liked very much.

"I'm afraid so. She and Alicia never got along, from the moment Charlotte moved here."

"Any particular reason why?"

Heather sighed. "It all started at one of our garden shows. Alicia and Charlotte had each entered arrangements in the 'all natural' category. Charlotte won first prize and Alicia filed a complaint with the prize committee, claiming that some of Charlotte's flowers had been dyed."

"And were they?" Travis asked, raising his eyebrows.

"It was a difficult decision. The committee found for Charlotte—by one vote only. But Charlotte never forgave Alicia for bringing the complaint."

"Interesting," said Travis, thinking it all sounded like a tempest in a teapot, "but hardly enough to be a motive for murder."

Heather hesitated. "There's more. But I don't know the whole story. So perhaps you'd better talk to Charlotte herself."

"I'll do that."

She walked him to the gate. "You know, Travis, in cases like this, it's almost always the spouse."

"Not this time," he answered firmly.

* * * * *

Travis put a TV dinner in the oven. It had been a long day, from his early-morning visit to the village florist, to the midday talk with MacReedy, to the interview with Heather Ridgley. Not to mention a full day of patient appointments.

He hoped the pimply-faced, vacant-eyed clerk at the florist shop had gotten the flowers right. Perhaps it hadn't been a good idea to order the two things at the same time, the little white vase for the hotel clerk and the twelve red roses for JayBee. Too bad he didn't know her address, but he had done the best he could, sending her the flowers at school.

Going to his desk, he took out the list of numbers on his father's cell phone bill and began to call them.

In twenty minutes, he had identified the numbers as his father's tailor, a bakery in Remus, his father's sister Prue and a men's store at a mall in Dayton. Aunt Prue kept him on the phone the longest by asking a thousand questions about Alicia's funeral that had not yet been decided.

Finally, the very last number on the list yielded different results.

"Miss Fairfield's office. This is her secretary speaking. May I help you?"

Travis hesitated for just a moment, then said, "I'd like to speak to Miss Fairfield, please."

"She's with one of the girls right now. Is it important?"

"Yes—very important."

"Very well. Who may I say is calling?"

"Dr. Kellman."

Travis waited, enjoying the "on hold" music—Satie's *Les Trois Gymnopedie*, a piece he'd always liked.

The music clicked off abruptly and a warm, contralto voice spoke excitedly. "Robert, darling! I'm so glad to hear from you! Did they let you out of jail?"

Chapter Eleven

"I'm sorry," Travis answered gently. "This is Dr. Travis Kellman."

A long silence ensued. Finally, she said, "Robert's son. How did you get this number?" Her voice was distinctly chilly now. "Did your father ask you to call me?"

"No, he knows nothing about this." Travis was afraid she was going to hang up, so he said quickly, "It's vitally important that I talk to you. Would you be willing to meet with me? If you'll just name a time and place—"

He heard her sigh. "It's very difficult."

"Please! You know my father's in jail. I'm trying very hard to help him—"

"All right," she interrupted. "I'll get in touch with you soon. Do not call this number again." And she hung up.

* * * * *

Travis stood looking into the mirror, remembering how his stepmother had commented on the length of his hair at the reconciliation dinner. Should he have his hair cut for the funeral?

Cutting hair at a death was a ritual in some religions. It would be a way to honor Alicia. If he wanted to honor her.

He thought about the last time he'd seen JayBee, their kisses on the couch, how good it had felt when she'd put her hands into his hair. She seemed to be a woman who liked a man with longish hair.

He brushed his hair, deciding to leave it just the way it was.

The coroner had released the body to the funeral home on Thursday, although his report had not yet been issued. Katie was in charge of the funeral arrangements for her mother. She'd asked Travis to help. They'd spent Friday picking out a coffin, choosing flowers and ordering food for the post-funeral lunch.

Katie had been pale and silent throughout the day, coming to life only once, when talking to the minister about the service. "I want to say a few words about my mother before we go to the cemetery," she'd said, a spot of color coming into her cheeks.

"Are you sure you're up for that?" Travis had his doubts.

"I want to," she'd repeated. The minister had nodded gravely, so Travis said no more.

Putting the brush down, he got his jacket out. It was time to go to the Dayton airport to pick up Alicia's mother.

He wondered how much he should tell Alicia's mother. T.J. was no blood relation to her. Should he mention that she now had an illegitimate step-great-grandson? If he did tell her, would she want to meet him?

He parked the truck and waited in the baggage area for her. He felt a stab of pity as she hobbled down from the transport cart and come toward him. She was an elegant older woman of seventy with silvery blue hair and a carefully made-up face.

No one, no matter what age, should have to lose a child. And this woman had lost two, Alicia's sister Laura, who had died eight years ago from breast cancer and now Alicia as well.

"Travis!" She stood on tiptoe to kiss his cheek. "Thank you for coming to get me, dear."

He put his arm around her shoulders briefly. "I'm so sorry about what's happened, Grandma."

She sighed, clinging to him for a moment. "Let's not talk about it. Do you know which carousel we need?"

Travis had already found out it was carousel four. She pointed out her two large old-fashioned suitcases, a matching makeup case and a hatbox. As he staggered out to the truck under the load, he wondered uneasily how long she was going to stay.

She looked unfavorably at his truck. "My goodness, Travis, you should have borrowed one of your parents' cars to come get me."

"Sorry, didn't think of it." He helped her into the front seat. "Are you planning to stay at Alicia's house? I borrowed a key for you."

She gave him a look as though he'd suggested she take up residence in a brothel. "Travis, can you really be thinking I would stay at a house where a murder took place?"

"Should I take you out to Pete's house?"

"Certainly not! You know I don't care for his wife."

Travis suppressed a sigh. Since Katie's barn apartment had no guest room, that left only one place for Alicia's mother.

"I'll be staying at your house, dear." She nodded decisively.

When JayBee had called him Thursday evening to thank him for the flowers, they'd talked about going out Saturday night. He'd hoped she would be willing to come back to his house again after their date. Well, this unexpected guest had put an end to that plan.

* * * * *

Travis was disappointed when JayBee called early Saturday morning and cancelled their tentative date. T.J. wasn't feeling well and she didn't want to leave him.

"Is there anything I can do?" Travis asked.

"No, I don't think so. He's got a slight fever and a stomachache, but I called the pediatrician and he told me what to do."

"Children's Tylenol, plenty of fluids and rest," Travis guessed.

"Exactly right!" JayBee sounded surprised.

"It's not rocket science. Medicine is medicine."

"I think you're going to be a great dad." Her voice was warm with approval.

That made him feel good for awhile, but when evening came, depression settled over him like fog creeping into a valley. Alicia's mother had gone to bed at eight and after that, no television or music was permitted in the house. "I'm sorry to be so sensitive," she'd told him with a deprecating smile. "But I can hear it from my room and then I can't sleep." Travis was too restless to read but not in the mood to go for a walk or work out. So when Misney called, Travis agreed to go drinking with him.

"Aussie told me the next time I get picked up for DUI, he won't let me off the hook. So maybe you won't mind being the designated driver?"

"Sure, I guess I can stick to one beer," said Travis.

"Wish I had your discipline."

"Well, I don't want to be hung over at Alicia's visitation tomorrow. Bad enough without that."

Travis picked his friend up and they went to the Paradise. It was still early enough to get a booth near the front. Misney liked to keep an eye on who was coming in. "Maybe if the right person comes along, you won't have to give me a ride home," he said.

"Keep dreaming," Travis answered. When the waiter came over, Travis ordered a Molson. Misney requested a strawberry daiquiri.

"I love those, too!" exclaimed their handsome young waiter, giving Misney a radiant smile.

Travis was hard put to keep from laughing. "Yeah, you can probably go home with him."

"I can't help it if I like sweet drinks."

"Let's hope he puts a cute little umbrella in it."

"Shut up. Hey, did you see those two brunettes over there? They were definitely checking us out."

"Don't get me involved in that tonight."

"You know what, Kellman?" Misney asked. "You've got to get past this thing with Georgia."

"Georgia!" Travis repeated. "That's all over. My brother's welcome to her."

Misney looked closely at his expression. "Are you seeing someone new?"

Travis changed the subject. "I think the college students must have found another hangout. I don't see anyone here except locals tonight."

Misney glanced around the bar and agreed. "Same old dull crowd. I wonder how many of the women in here have turned me down? I see at least ten without even turning my head. Janet Malcolm—now there's a bitch. Kelly Carow, Marie Dowlich—why isn't she home with her kids? And there's Lisa Angstrom. She actually went out with me three times before she blew me off. Denise MacReedy—too high-strung for me."

"You went out with Aussie's wife?"

"Years ago, before she married Aussie."

"Isn't she older than you?"

Misney shrugged. "She likes 'em younger. She's six years older than Aussie, you know. Maybe that's why she always dresses so young. My granny had a saying about that—" Misney looked down, frowning, at the tabletop. "I got it. 'Mutton dressed as lamb.'"

Travis chuckled and took a surreptitious glance at Denise. She was wearing a bright-red blouse and a skirt that revealed too much of her plump, middle-aged legs. Did the chief have any idea his wife was at the Paradise? She was leaning across the table, deep in conversation with a blond man. Travis couldn't tell who he was since the man's back was to him.

Well, he shouldn't criticize her, even inwardly. The chief had an important job and left Denise alone much of the time. Perhaps she was lonely. Since they had no children, there was no one to keep her at home. Just like anyone else, she needed to unwind on the weekends.

Misney was watching Denise too. "That's why I divorced my wife. Everything else I could put up with, but when I found out she was screwing another man, I divorced her ass."

"Just because she's out drinking doesn't mean she's having an affair," Travis said. "Anyway, I give her credit for being able to live with a prick like Aussie."

"The chief's not so bad." Then Misney looked chagrined. "Oh, sorry. I kind of forgot about your dad there, for a minute."

"It's not just that," Travis said. "Hell, the stuff with my dad I can almost understand, looking at it from the chief's point of view. I've got other reasons for hating his guts."

Travis thought of an autumn when he'd been eleven years old…

He was excited to be going on his first deer-hunting trip with his father, Pete, Austin MacReedy and Carl, Austin's father. His grandfather had taught him how to handle the big twelve-gauge shotgun and he'd gotten pretty good at shooting tin cans that summer.

It was a chill fall twilight and he was sitting in the deer-hunting station with his father and Austin. Where was Pete? Maybe back at the cabin, reading. Pete had gotten his buck the year before and no longer had to prove himself. Carl was at the cabin, too. Austin's father had spent most of that trip drinking. So it was just the three of them, sitting there sharing a pair of binoculars, waiting to spot a deer.

Austin had seen it first. With excited gestures, he'd handed the binoculars to Travis.

Seeing a deer on television or in the distance in a park was not the same thing as observing it closely through binoculars. His father always had fine equipment. He could make out the buck's soft eyes and quivering nostrils. He saw it raise its head and look around alertly, then go back to drinking at the river.

His father grinned broadly and passed him the shotgun, giving him a thumbs up signal. Travis took the shotgun and found the buck in the sights. He knew exactly how to do it—get the right spot in the cross-hairs, then gently squeeze the trigger.

The buck could be his. He had the shot. In just a few minutes, the animal would be dead. He pictured it in his mind, the dead buck strung up across the roof of their Chevy Blazer.

All that vibrant life would be ended, just so he could say he'd shot his buck.

He had a moment of absolute clarity. He'd been looking forward to this trip for months, he had practiced shooting all summer…but now he knew he wasn't going to shoot the buck. Somehow he felt if he squeezed off that shot, he would lose something, something vitally important.

So he lowered the shotgun, shaking his head and handed it back to his dad.

His father gave him a questioning look. "Are you sure, son?" he asked in the faintest whisper.

He nodded. His father would have probably let it go, but then Austin had to butt in, trying to impose his thirteen-year-old will on Travis.

"Take the shot, you little wimp!"

Travis whispered back, "No. You shoot it if you want."

"You baby! You chicken!"

"Shut up!"

Their voices, getting louder, were heard by the animal. Robert Kellman, watching it through the binoculars, said, "Darn it—you scared him off."

"Asshole!" MacReedy said.

"Shut up, dickhead!" Travis answered.

"Now, boys, none of that. Let's head back to the cabin."

"Dad?" Travis asked his father later that evening, when they were roasting potatoes in the fireplace. "You're not mad because I didn't shoot the buck, are you?"

His father looked at him seriously. "Would you have done it if we'd been starving and needed the meat?"

"Well, sure. I had the shot."

"Then all I can say is that it was your choice. I wish you had done it once, just for the experience. But I'm not mad." And his father patted him on the shoulder.

There were times when Travis didn't feel close to his father, times that he resented him for leaving the rearing of his boys to their stepmother. Robert Kellman worked long hours. Travis was often in bed and asleep before his father came home.

But at that moment, he knew how much he loved his dad.

Travis thought that would be the end of it, but Austin wouldn't let it drop. The next morning, he kept bringing it up and that got Peter started too. The two of them mocked him until Travis attacked his brother. They got into a vicious rough-and-tumble that resulted in a black eye for Peter, a sprained wrist for Travis and a broken tooth for Austin. All three boys were in trouble with their fathers and the older boys blamed Travis.

When the school year started again, Austin made a point of telling everyone that Travis had been too much of a wimp to shoot a deer…

Now, as he finished his beer, he thought, *I'm still glad I didn't kill that buck.*

His cell phone rang, startling him. He took it out of his shirt pocket.

* * * * *

JayBee came down the stairs and announced, "T.J.'s finally asleep. Poor kid, he kept complaining he was hot. I sponged him down with rubbing alcohol and that seemed to help."

"Thanks for taking care of him while I'm working."

"That's okay." JayBee retrieved her jacket from the back of a dining room chair. "I'm going out on my bike. I may be gone several hours, so don't worry."

Angel's eyes flickered over her. "Where are you going?"

"Just riding around."

"Oh, really? You're not heading out for a fling with the new boyfriend?"

JayBee stopped and stared at her sister. "How did you know about my new boyfriend?" She thought she had been really careful about not saying anything.

Angel smiled smugly. "You just told me."

"Don't be so sharp, you'll cut yourself," JayBee muttered.

"So who is he?"

JayBee hesitated, but she couldn't think of a good reason for not revealing the information. "T.J.'s father."

"T.J.'s father! I'm surprised you would get mixed up with that guy." Angel looked at her reproachfully. "Anyway, I thought we weren't going to date for awhile."

JayBee zipped her leather jacket. "Look, maybe it's time to stop beating ourselves up over Bradley. Okay, he fooled both of us. That doesn't mean we have to live like nuns for the rest of our lives."

"I knew I shouldn't have sent you on that visit with T.J." Angel frowned into the fireplace, shaking her head.

"I met Travis before we got T.J."

"Well, all I can say is, I'd be careful if I were you. I've always thought this whole thing with T.J. is a very suspicious story."

"I don't know what you're talking about." JayBee glared at her sister.

"Why did T.J.'s mother never tell him he had a child? Why didn't she sue for support? For some reason, she didn't want him to have a relationship with his son."

"You don't know him." JayBee drew on her driving gloves with a sharp snap. "He's a really nice guy. I don't know the whole story, but I'm sure Travis would have done the right thing, if he'd been told about the boy."

Angel looked skeptical. "Maybe T.J.'s mother knew something about him that you don't. People thought John Wayne Gacy was a cute clown—until they found all those bodies under his house."

"Shut up!" JayBee slammed the door on her way out.

She took off down the street on the motorcycle, thinking of all the things she should have said to Angel. This wasn't a big city where you met people by chance and had no way of knowing their real backgrounds or relations. Travis had lived in Priam most of his life. He was a settled professional man with a well-known family.

Yeah and a stepmother who was just murdered.

But that isn't Travis' fault. It isn't fair to hold that against him.

And it wasn't like she hadn't checked him out. She had talked to several of her fellow teachers about him. Cheryl Kaufman and Bob Souter had said what a nice man he was. Her friend Charlotte Scott had almost sounded like she had a crush on him. "He's always been so good to my son. He's really great with kids." She'd smiled mischievously. "Too bad

I never date men younger than myself." Even Gary Bright, who seemed to dislike everyone and everything, had said, "Kellman the vet? Yeah, I wouldn't take my dog anywhere else."

She thought of Travis' very kind eyes and felt reassured.

"I won't do anything that scares you, ever," he had told her.

He's just what you need. Someone who's gentle and kind. She thought of all the nice things he had done…bought her dinner, took her dancing. Made her a sundae, sent flowers.

Maybe he was too nice.

She had to admit that he wasn't the type of man she'd been attracted to for most of her life. Somehow she'd always been drawn to bad boys, guys in black leather, guys with tattoos.

Right, she told herself, haven't you outgrown that type? She thought of some of her college boyfriends. Slade…good-looking, but a lazy idiot who couldn't even keep a job at the local food mart. Mac had a cool motorcycle and he'd been fun in bed, but he took money out of her purse and sold weed for a living. She hadn't let herself fall in love with Miller, knowing he wouldn't be a good long-term boyfriend. But goodness, he'd looked sexy in his black leather pants.

She couldn't imagine Travis in black leather pants.

She'd been trying to get away from attractive but irresponsible males. Bradley had seemed like a perfect choice…handsome, yet a hard-working man, holding down that good stockbroker's job. Fancy car and beautiful, tailored clothes…

Yet now that she thought about it, everything she'd known about him had been outward details. She hadn't known if he'd ever done one altruistic deed in his life. She had no idea if he was generous to his mother, gentle with old people, or kind to children.

At least she knew that Travis was good to animals.

Thinking about that session on his couch the other night, she wondered what he would be like in bed. He had been a little more passive than she really liked. She hoped he wasn't one of those guys who lay back and expected the woman to do everything.

On the other hand, she wouldn't have liked it if he hadn't stopped when she asked.

What was wrong with her? She didn't know what the hell she wanted.

She had reached her destination. She had made a list and called the hotels and motels within a twenty-mile radius of Priam. On the fourth call, she had found that Bradley was staying in the Embassy Suites in Remus.

At the front desk, she asked the clerk, "Could you dial Bradley Morrow's room and tell him he has a visitor?"

The clerk did as she asked, but then reported, "I'm afraid there's no answer."

JayBee thanked her and went to a chair in the lobby where she could see the front door. Pulling out a paperback novel, she waited.

* * * * *

"Hello?" Travis said. Only a few people had his cell phone number—his father, sister and JayBee.

"Dr. Kellman? This is your son's foster mother. I hope this isn't too late to call?"

"No, it's okay." He put his hand over his other ear, trying to shut out the noisy bar. "Is T.J. all right?"

"He's fine—I just checked on him. I'm calling because I'd like to talk to you. Can you possibly drop by?"

Travis agreed and she gave him the address.

"I hope you don't mind if I leave for awhile," he told Misney. "I'll come back later and see if you need a ride home."

"Sounds good. I'm going to go talk to those gals in that booth over there." Misney smirked. "If I'm not here when you get back, you'll know I got lucky."

Travis drove up to the gray, asbestos-shingled house on Forest Avenue. The house that JayBee and her sister shared had a sagging front porch and its trim needed painting, Travis could tell that much even in the dark. But there were cheerful ferns hanging in pots from the porch roof and two white wicker chairs, which gave it a homey, comfortable look. JayBee's sister was waiting for him in one of the chairs.

She stood as he got out of the truck, watching him as he made his way up the driveway. She seemed to be as tall as JayBee but much thinner. Her long blonde hair was tied back severely.

Holding out her hand as he came up the steps, she said, "Hello, Dr. Kellman." As he had noticed the first time she called him, her voice sounded very much like JayBee's.

"Hi. Call me Travis." He shook her ice-cold hand. This close, he could see that JayBee had been correct—her sister was beautiful. Her face was a flawless oval with full lips, a pretty nose and large, sad eyes. And yet, there was something about JayBee's less perfect face that this woman's face lacked. Something lovable, that certain something that had made him long to kiss JayBee the very first time he saw her.

"Is JayBee here?" he asked.

"No, she's out. Won't you have a seat?"

They sat in the wicker chairs. Having heard from JayBee about her sister's agoraphobia and reluctance to meet men, Travis wondered what was up.

"I wanted to meet you because I know JayBee's been seeing you."

"Right," Travis said cautiously. "We went out to dinner."

"I wanted to see what you were like." Her tone was very formal. "I wondered what kind of man could have such turmoil going on in his life and still take time to be going out on dates."

Travis frowned at this. He had already heard this from his own sister—he'd be damned if he was going to take it from JayBee's sister. "I've already discussed that with JayBee. It's her business…and mine." He left the words "not yours" unspoken.

"JayBee doesn't always know what's best for her. She's still very young and impulsive. Aside from that, she isn't over her last love affair, which ended very badly." She took a deep breath. "She doesn't need more trouble in life. You should leave her alone."

Travis waited a few moments to answer this. He was angry, but he didn't want to answer sharply and further alienate this woman who was JayBee's sister and his son's foster mother.

It was so quiet on the street, he could hear crickets chirping. The murmur of a television show drifted over from the house next door. Up and down the street, windows glowed with light.

"I'm not sure you have the right idea about me," Travis said. "I'm a veterinarian…I have a good reputation here in town. I'm not seeing JayBee because I want a one-night stand. I care about her—"

She interrupted him. "If you truly cared about her, you'd give her more time to recover."

"If she asks me to, I will."

"I'll tell you straight out, Dr. Kellman." She leaned forward, her blue eyes boring into his. "I have a lot of questions about the type of man you are. Why did T.J.'s mother never tell you about his birth? Why did she feel she had to keep his existence a secret?"

Travis was shaken, but tried not to show it. "I'm not sure. As far as I can tell, she was trying to make a life with her high-school boyfriend and leave me out of the picture."

"I think she knew something about you—something no one else knows."

"That's not true!"

"It's a lot more likely than the reason you just gave me."

"I don't know what I can say to disprove it," Travis said impatiently. "T.J.'s mother is dead, so it's not like we can question her. I wish to God I could! I'd like to get some answers myself."

"So you refuse to leave my sister alone?"

"I won't stop seeing her on your say-so."

* * * * *

JayBee looked up as the doors opened. Her eyes narrowed. Bradley had entered the hotel.

Prison hadn't changed him outwardly. Stylishly dressed in a tailored silk jacket and neatly pressed trousers, he strode in confidently, looking straight ahead.

She called out, "Brad!" He whirled around. She stood and beckoned to him.

Advancing with a big grin, he said, "Juliet!"

She took a step back. "My name is JayBee."

He tilted his head to one side, still smiling. "Now, look, sweetie, you know what I always thought of that silly, seventh-grade nickname. You'll always be 'Juliet' to me."

"Don't look happy to see me. This is not a friendly visit."

"What else am I supposed to think, when you visit me late at night in my hotel?" Reaching out, he took her hand. "We don't want to discuss our business out here in the lobby, do we? Come up to my room."

JayBee snatched her hand away, considering it a victory that she didn't slap his face. "Right here is just fine." She sat in her chair, waving her hand at the chair next to hers. "I filed a police report after you followed me the other night. And I saved the card from the dead flowers. There are anti-stalking laws in this state, you know."

He sat too, lounging back comfortably in his chair. "Anti-stalking laws! Such harsh words, Juliet. It's not stalking if I'm concerned about my ex-wife and her sister."

JayBee leaned forward, staring into his eyes as menacingly as she knew how. "Listen to me, Bradley Morrow. Angel and I are doing just fine without you. Neither of us wants to see you again. That's what I came to tell you. Stay away from us. I'm warning you."

He smirked. "Oh, Juliet. You always like to pretend you're so tough."

He was maintaining a mask of good humor, but she had the feeling that something inside him wasn't laughing. Something was there, scrutinizing her, peering at her cautiously like a weasel venturing out of its sordid den. She tried to speak to that Bradley.

"I'm going to tell Angel you're back and then we're going to get a protection order. If you violate that, you'll go back to prison. Do you understand? I'm sure you're out on parole. If I tell your parole officer you're stalking us, you'll go back inside."

He sat back, looking smug. "That might work if I were the old Bradley you knew before. But don't think you can control me that way. I can disappear, just like that." He waved his hand. "I have no intention of reporting to a parole officer like a good little boy. I'll disappear and then I'll come back when you least expect me."

"I'll be waiting for you with a gun. And don't think I'll hesitate to kill you, if you come near me or Angel."

He laughed with what sounded like honest delight. "Then you'll be the one going to prison. I'd almost let you try it, just so I can see you behind bars."

"I wouldn't go to prison if I were defending my home."

"That's what you think. I've left a letter with my attorney, stating that you're insanely jealous because I married your sister instead of you. If anything ever happens to me, no matter how far away I am from you, you'll be investigated. If a car hits me in Timbuktu, the police are going to show up at your door. So you'd better hesitate before you do me any harm."

JayBee took a deep breath. "You have no idea how much I hate you."

"Juliet—Juliet. So unforgiving!" He stood up. She didn't want to sit while he loomed above her, so she stood as well. He wasn't as tall as Travis, so their heads were on the same level. She stared into his reptilian-green eyes.

"You weren't always so cold with me," he said softly. "I remember how much you enjoyed it when I made love to you."

For the first time, she lied. "I faked it. Every single time."

"I don't believe that." He put his hands on her shoulders.

"Don't touch me!"

His smile broadened and he tightened his grip. She brought her knee up fast and hard, connecting with his testicles. He doubled over, his breath coming out in a high, keening gasp, like an animal caught in a trap.

"That was for Angel." She turned and left the hotel.

* * * * *

"I'd like to see T.J. before I go," Travis said.

For a moment JayBee's sister looked as though she were going to refuse. "All right." Her tone was begrudging. "If you promise not to wake him."

She led the way up the staircase and into the first room on the right. T.J. sprawled across a single bed with Queenie curled up at the foot of it. The dog sprang up alertly as Travis paused in the doorway, then wagged her tail and jumped off the bed. Travis fondled her ears, his eyes fixed on T.J. The boy looked very young, asleep with his thumb in his mouth. As Travis watched, he moved a little and Queenie turned and licked his arm.

My son, Travis thought, *my own flesh and blood.* If only he could have the boy at his own house. He'd give him a goodnight kiss and teach him to say his prayers, just like his own father had done.

But he'd promised not to wake him. He contented himself with whispering, "Good night, son."

Queenie wagged her tail again, hearing his voice and jumped back up on the bed, lying down with the little grunt that always made Travis smile.

"Thanks for letting me see him," Travis said as he followed JayBee's sister back down into the living room. "I'd better get going," he added, thinking of Misney at the Paradise.

She nodded, walking him to the front door.

"By the way, I don't know your name."

"I'm Angel Morrow."

"Angel Morrow! That's interesting—I met your ex-husband just last week. He was looking for you—"

The color drained out of her face. Travis was just in time to catch her as she fainted.

Chapter Twelve

Travis carried Angel to the couch and laid her down gently. Kneeling, he took her pulse, which was racing. Just as he was about to call 9-1-1, she opened her eyes.

"Are you all right?" he demanded. "Good Lord, you scared the hell out of me!"

"I'm fine," she answered, but her voice was languid. "It was…just…the shock."

He was still holding her wrist. Yanking her hand away, she struggled to sit up.

"Do you want some water? Should I call someone?"

"It was just the shock," she repeated. "Where did you see my ex-husband?"

"He was at the Paradise, asking about you." When she looked at him blankly, he added, "It's a bar. One block off the square, in the shopping center."

"Of course," she murmured. "Where else would Bradley be found?" She looked up into his face. "You'd better go now."

"Don't you want me to stay until JayBee gets back?"

"Absolutely not." Her eyes narrowed. "I'd like you to go…right now, please." She stood up, staggering slightly and opened the door. Travis hoped she wouldn't faint again as soon as he left, but there was nothing he could do if she wouldn't accept his help.

"Goodbye, Dr. Kellman." He heard her throw the deadbolt as he went down the steps.

* * * * *

The visitation was to have a closed casket, but the family arrived early to see Alicia in her coffin.

Travis was sure the embalmer had done as well as he could, but this cold woman did not really resemble the stepmother he remembered. Alicia's makeup had always been subtle. The garishly noticeable blush and bright red lips made her look like some other woman, not like Alicia Kellman at all.

Alicia's mother and Katie clung together, holding hands. Peter and Georgia took a long look and then Georgia walked away and sat, sniffing into a handkerchief. Peter remained by the coffin for several minutes, his expression unreadable.

There were plenty of times I didn't like you very much, Travis thought, looking down at the body. *Still, you didn't deserve to die like that.*

Travis hadn't realized what an ordeal the visitation would be for the family. He'd gone to several of these "showings," as the older relatives called them, in his life. But his mother and grandparents had died when he was too young to participate in the "meet-and-greet" part of the business. He wondered why protocol required such an effort of the family. Perhaps the idea was to take their minds off their grief.

Almost two hours passed before all the visitors had passed through the receiving line. Robert Kellman's absence was felt by all but mentioned by none.

So many people had sent flowers that the coffin was surrounded with them and more arrangements were to be found on every surface. Katie's allergies were acting up. She had to keep drying her tearing eyes and sneezing into a tissue.

"We should have said 'no flowers' in the paper," Travis murmured to his sister.

Katie shook her head. "They're so beautiful. Maman would have loved them."

When they were finally able to leave the receiving line, Travis led Katie to a couch and found her a box of tissues. As he bent over her, she whispered, "Can you believe what Georgia's wearing?"

He hadn't noticed what his sister-in-law had on, except that it was black and a dress.

"That neckline!" Katie went on. "What does she think this is, a country club party?"

Travis sat in a chair near Katie, stretching his long legs out. It felt good to sit after two hours of standing.

He found his thoughts drifting to JayBee. Sometimes he liked to remember her as he had first seen her, those big brown eyes looking down at him through the leaves. Just thinking about her was like finding an oasis in the desert.

Georgia came up behind him and touched him on the shoulder. "Mr. Carney wants to see you."

He followed her out to the hall and into the funeral director's office. Mr. Carney was nowhere to be seen.

"He'll be back." Georgia handed him a cup of coffee. "Here, I made this for you. Just the way you like it, with sugar."

"Thanks." He sat down in one of the chairs facing the desk. Georgia perched up on the desk and crossed her legs. Her skirt was hiked up and he could see quite a bit of her creamy thighs. He looked away uncomfortably.

"How are you doing?" Georgia asked softly.

He shrugged. "Fine."

A long silence fell. Finally, she asked, "Don't you care how I'm doing?"

He felt irritated, wondering what she was getting at. "How are you?"

She threw her hair back. "It's nice to know you care. Here I told you my very deepest secret—about being blackmailed—and you don't even ask me about it."

Letting his annoyance creep into his voice, he said, "I've been busy, you know. My whole life's a mess."

"Not too busy to go out dancing, apparently."

It was simply amazing, how gossip got around in a small town. He raised his eyebrows. "I gave the death of our relationship a full year of mourning. That's enough."

"I'm surprised at you, Travis. Why would you take a woman out when she's known to be a lesbian?"

"She's not a lesbian."

"That's not what I heard."

"Then you heard wrong."

She wrung her hands. "You're just doing this to get back at me, aren't you?"

More annoyed than ever, he snapped, "Everything isn't always about you."

She stood up, so he stood as well. "Do you still think I killed Alicia?" She came close to him, laying her palms on the front of his jacket, looking up at him pleadingly.

"I don't know who killed her." *And I haven't ruled you out yet.*

"I didn't! I didn't do it!"

He looked down into her face, seeing her eyes brimming with tears. But he tried not to let that sway him. He knew what a good actress she was. "I'd better go check on Katie."

"How can you be so cold?" she whispered, catching his sleeve as he turned to go.

"You put me through hell for a long time. You'll have to excuse me if I choose not to go back there."

She stared at him, her mouth twisting. Then she fled the office.

With a sigh, Travis sat and picked up his coffee again. Would he ever be able to be around Georgia and treat her like just another person? The memory of being in love with her lingered, no matter how he tried to repress it.

He wondered if Mr. Carney had really wanted to see him, or if that had been Georgia's way of getting him to herself. He found out when the funeral director came into the office. "Dr. Kellman! I've been looking all over for you. There's a woman downstairs who says she wants to talk to you."

"A woman? Do you know who she is?"

"No, I don't believe I know her."

Immediately he thought of JayBee. He followed Mr. Carney down the stairs to the large basement of the funeral home, where there were meeting rooms and a banquet hall.

Mr. Carney opened the door of one of the meeting rooms. A lovely, slender woman was seated at one of the tables. She looked up gravely. She was perhaps ten or fifteen years older than himself, Travis judged.

Her dark hair was tucked into a bun at the back of her head. She wore a gray tailored suit. A blue scarf around the neck was the only hint of color about her. As soon as Mr. Carney shut the door behind Travis, she rose.

"Hello, Dr. Kellman. I'm Louisa Fairfield." She offered him her hand, which he shook.

Travis was surprised to see her, as he'd only half-believed that she would ever contact him. "Call me Travis. Thanks for coming."

Music drifted in from an intercom, a gooey, overblown arrangement of a song he didn't recognize. Travis wished he knew a way to turn it off.

Her eyes scrutinized his face. "You have such a look of Robert about you," she said softly. "Especially your eyes and mouth."

Travis was pleased. People often said that about Peter, but not often about him, probably because he and his father were built so differently. "Thanks. I can't think of anyone I'd rather look like."

"It's nice to hear someone say something good about Robert. Such terrible things have been happening and the media seem to have him tried and convicted already." She sighed. "When you told me on the phone you were trying to help him, I knew I had to see you—no matter what the cost to myself."

They sat down across from each other. "Yes," Travis said eagerly. "I want to help my dad. That's why I wanted to see you. I've been trying to investigate on my own."

"How did you find out about me? I talked to Robert on Monday and he swore he hadn't told anyone."

Travis told her how he'd found the phone number, adding apologetically, "Ordinarily I wouldn't snoop through my father's things, but in this case, it seemed like the ends justify the means. Listen, Ms. Fairfield—"

"You may call me Louisa."

"All right—Louisa—I don't know how you fit into the picture, but my dad loved my stepmother. Even though they've had some problems lately, I can't believe he would have murdered her."

"Of course he didn't! Robert is the kindest, gentlest man I know."

He was supposed to be questioning her harshly, but his first reaction was that he liked her. This was not the way to conduct an interrogation.

Good Lord, Kellman, you'd make a lousy cop.

He leaned forward across the table. "My father won't tell anyone where he was the night my stepmother was murdered. We know he left the house around ten o'clock and didn't return until five the next day. Was he with you?"

"Yes."

Travis tried to quell his rising enthusiasm. Finally, finally, he knew where his father had been that night. "What was he like when you saw him? Did he seem like—well, like his normal self?"

"He'd had a long drive to join me at the hotel. I had a conference in Akron the next afternoon and he drove up to spend the night with me. He got there about two in the morning. He was perfectly normal and cheerful…he brought sandwiches and coffee with him. We sat up and talked for awhile, then we went to bed." She looked straight into Travis' eyes. "Robert is a sensitive, caring man. He would have to be some kind of crazy psychopath to kill your stepmother and then be so calm and happy with me a few hours later. You know your father better than that."

"Why haven't you come forward?" Travis demanded. "Don't you think your testimony would help him?"

She smiled slightly, shaking her head at him. "You're not thinking it through," she said, sounding like a teacher with a slow pupil. "Robert and I discussed it. We thought it would be better not to mention me at all. Without me in the picture, he had no motive to murder your stepmother. But with me, it sounds like some kind of nasty, vulgar love triangle."

"Or maybe everyone will think you committed the murder and my father's covering for you."

"Let me set your mind at ease." She reached into her purse and drew out a credit card receipt. Travis looked at it carefully. It was from the Marriott in Akron, for the night of September 18.

He handed it back to her. "Conceivably, you could have murdered my stepmother and then left for Akron. Or you could have signed for that earlier and then driven back down here to murder her."

"I left my school at eight o'clock that night, which people there can verify. I signed into the hotel around midnight. The police can check the time on credit receipts, you know. Robert will tell you that we spent the rest of that night together, if you ask him."

"Unless he's covering for you."

"I don't think he'd do that at the expense of going to prison himself, do you?"

Travis thought about it. He could imagine his father being in love with this woman, but not so much that he would let her get away with murdering his wife.

He spoke slowly. "I still think it would have been best to tell the police the whole story. Part of the reason they arrested my father was that he wasn't forthcoming about where he'd been that night—"

"You don't understand!" she cried, her expression suddenly distressed. She took a tissue out of her purse and held it to her eyes. "Robert and I have been so careful the last few years…not only because he didn't want to hurt Alicia, but because of my situation."

Travis opened his hand toward her, inviting her to keep talking, but not making her any promises.

"I'm the principal of a girls' private high school in Dayton. I have a lot of difficulties with my board—the board of trustees. Several of them would like to push me out of my position—we've butted heads many times—but I have a contract. That contract could be broken if I were to be involved in this kind of scandal." She lowered her head, looking down at her hands. "That's mostly why Robert has kept silent."

That sounded like his father. Travis frowned, stroking his beard thoughtfully. He would have to talk to his father and make sure his story and hers coincided.

"Very well," he said at last. "I won't say anything…for now."

"Thank you." She stood up to leave. "If you need to call me again, I'd prefer you use my cell." She handed him a small sheet of paper with a number written on it. Folding it, he put it carefully away in his wallet.

* * * * *

Travis hurried upstairs, wondering what Katie would say if he told her, "I just met Dad's girlfriend." Well, no reason to upset her, even if he hadn't told Louisa he would keep quiet about her existence.

Glancing around, he saw that Katie was still on the couch where he'd left her, talking to Austin MacReedy. The chief rose as Travis walked up and shook his hand.

"Hi, Trav. Sorry about your loss."

"Thanks, Austin." Travis looked for Denise, but didn't see her. "Did your wife come with you?"

"She's in the bathroom, repairing her mascara. This whole thing has her damned upset."

Travis nodded. Many of Alicia's fellow garden-club members had teared up as they passed the coffin.

"Oh, look, Travis!" Katie said, sitting up. "Terry finally got here. I was beginning to think he wasn't coming."

Travis looked over and saw their cousin Terry Gordon, the son of Alicia's deceased sister. He was standing in front of the coffin, talking to his grandmother. His bright crimson hair seemed incongruous with his dark navy suit.

Travis had always liked Terry, who'd lived through a similar situation to his own, losing his mother at a young age and having her replaced by a stepmother whom he didn't care for. Alicia had seemed to have a fondness for her nephew, occasionally including him in family get-togethers. Like Katie, Terry was artistic. Alicia had two of his paintings hanging in her house.

Travis watched as Terry turned away from his grandmother and knelt on the padded rail in front of the coffin. His hands went to the side of the coffin and he leaned his forehead on them.

The crowd had thinned out now and the room was quiet as people talked to each other in low tones. When Terry sobbed, everyone heard.

Travis watched for a moment, seeing the boy's shoulders shaking. He felt uncomfortable, witnessing Terry's grief. And yet, he couldn't help thinking how odd it was that unrestrained grief at a funeral home seemed inappropriate.

He'd better do something. Walking up to the coffin, he put his hand on Terry's shoulder. "Calm down, Terry. I know you're going to miss your aunt—"

Terry stood up, his face twisting with anger in spite of the tears that rolled down his cheeks. "Miss her! No way, man! She made me do it—and now it can never be right again!" He broke down, sobbing, hiding his face in the crook of his elbow.

"What are you talking about, son?" MacReedy asked, coming up on Terry's other side.

Travis looked at the chief across Terry's shoulders. MacReedy's tone had been low and sympathetic, but his eyes were hard and gleaming.

Travis put his arm around Terry's shoulders. "Come on, Terry. Let's go find somewhere to talk." He glared at the chief. "Just the two of us."

MacReedy opened his mouth to speak.

Travis said quickly, "Terry's my cousin. Let me handle this, Austin."

"Not if it's a police matter."

"Who says it is?" Travis' heart was pounding hard.

"We'll see, won't we?" MacReedy walked out into the hall, beckoning Travis and Terry to follow him. The three men went into Mr. Carney's office. MacReedy closed the door.

"If you've got something to confess, you'd better get it off your chest, son," MacReedy said, holding Terry in a serious gaze.

"Now, wait just a minute!" Travis interrupted, before Terry could speak. "If you're going to question him, don't you have to read him his rights?"

"I don't have to do a damned thing," MacReedy drawled. "We're all just talking, right?"

"Listen to me, Terry." Travis looked intently into Terry's sad eyes. "If you've done something wrong—something that's a crime—you'd better watch what you say. Better yet, don't say anything. I'll call my friend Ben Misney. He's a lawyer." It almost killed him to say that. Was he preventing Alicia's murderer from speaking out? But there was no way he was going to stand aside and let MacReedy railroad the boy.

"Look, Trav," MacReedy said, frowning. "I could run your young relative in just on the strength of what I heard him say with my own ears. Now shut the hell up and let him talk."

"You shut the hell up, Austin! I don't know what you're doing here today."

"I came here to show respect to your family." MacReedy stood up. "But right now you're interfering with police business. I could arrest you for that."

"Go right ahead!" Travis was suddenly furious. He shot to his feet, matching MacReedy's glare. "That'll look good in the papers—'Priam police chief arrests man at his stepmother's funeral.' Don't think Misney won't be able to get some publicity out of that."

"You really want to sit in jail until Monday's arraignments, Trav? Believe me, it won't be fun."

"Guys, please! I'd rather tell about it," Terry whispered.

The two antagonists looked at him as though they'd forgotten he was there.

"Please," Terry went on. "I can't stop thinking about it. Even if it's a crime, I want to speak up."

"Well, Terry, if that's your choice, I can't stop you." Still holding MacReedy's gaze, Travis sat down. After a long moment, MacReedy sat as well.

The chief's voice was reasonable and persuasive. "What did you do, son? Tell us all about it."

"Aunt Alicia—she was blackmailing someone. I helped her make the calls." Terry buried his face in his hands and began to sob.

Travis sighed, feeling like a deflating balloon. "That's it?"

Terry looked at him as though he were crazy. "Yes! Isn't it bad enough? Don't you see? Whoever she was blackmailing—maybe that person killed her!"

"Do you know who you were calling?" MacReedy asked.

"No, Aunt Alicia always dialed the number. She had everything written out like a script. I never even heard the person's voice."

"How much money was involved?" Travis kept his tone casual. He didn't want to let on to Austin that he knew anything about this.

"It wasn't money. She wanted things," the boy explained. "A bracelet. And a tie."

MacReedy's puzzled eyes met Travis'.

"Did she make the calls from home?" the chief asked.

Terry shook his head. "No. Pay phones."

"And you had no idea who you were calling?" MacReedy asked again.

"No, sir. But I think it was a woman. One time I asked who it was and Aunt Alicia said, 'Someone who's going to be sorry she ever crossed me.'" Terry looked at MacReedy uncertainly. "Are you going to arrest me?"

The chief frowned, seeming to think it over. "I could arrest you, you do understand that? You've been an accessory to blackmail."

Terry nodded, his expression miserable.

MacReedy tilted his head and pursed his lips. "Tell you what, son. I want you to come in tomorrow and make a statement as to what you've told me. Will you do that?"

"Yes, sir!"

"Then I'll think it over. If you keep your nose clean and stay out of trouble—well, then, maybe I'll let you off. It all depends on you, son."

"I won't get into any more trouble. I promise!"

MacReedy got up and opened the door. "Run along now."

Terry left the office with a visible sigh of relief.

"Well? What do you make of that?" the chief asked as soon as the door had closed behind Terry.

Travis hesitated, wondering whether he should tell MacReedy what he knew. He couldn't help feeling uneasy that he was concealing evidence. On the other hand, he was fairly certain now that Georgia was not the murderer, even though Alicia had been blackmailing her.

He thought of MacReedy's rush to arrest his father. Would Georgia undergo the same treatment? He was no longer in love with her—of course not—but even so, the thought of her in jail was horrible.

And most of all, he had promised Georgia not to tell anyone. He took that promise seriously.

"Strange story."

MacReedy was watching him closely. "You sure you don't know anything about this?"

"I wasn't close to my stepmother and I haven't seen Terry in months."

"All right, Trav. If anything occurs to you, be sure to let me know." MacReedy stretched, cracking his knuckles. "I'd better go collect my wife. She's probably looking for me."

When Travis emerged from the office, the visitation was winding down. Only a few people were left. He found his sister and grandmother. "Come on, you two. I'll take you out to dinner."

He wondered whether he should tell Georgia what he'd learned.

* * * * *

What a way to start the week, JayBee thought as she sat in church at the funeral of Alicia Kellman. She hadn't been to church in months, not since the last time she'd visited her father and attended Sunday service with him to please him. He would have liked this church, though. Her father hated ornate, statue-filled churches, greatly preferring a plain, New England-style. This sanctuary was large and airy, with nothing over the altar except an unadorned wooden cross.

The half-day substitute teacher had been a little late, which meant that JayBee hadn't made it to Alicia Kellman's service as early as she'd wanted. The church was packed and she'd had to find a seat off to one side, passing by several glaring older women. Well, too bad—she certainly wasn't going to stand for the entire service after having been on her feet all morning at school.

She spotted Travis in the front row. His face was somber, almost stern, very different from his usual good-humored expression. He was sitting next to a dark-haired young woman. There was something similar about their faces. JayBee assumed she was his sister.

JayBee's thoughts drifted as prayers were recited and hymns were sung. She mulled over the argument she'd had with Angel on Saturday night. Her sister had been furious when JayBee got home. "You knew Bradley was in town and you didn't tell me! And then you leave me alone for hours!"

"I was trying to take care of the problem," JayBee had explained, telling Angel how she'd confronted Bradley at his hotel. "Hopefully I gave him something to think about."

"Yes, more reasons to hurt us," Angel had answered bitterly. "And let me tell you, I wasn't very impressed with your new boyfriend. He asked to see his son and then he just stood there. He didn't even give the boy a kiss. I think he's going to be one of those emotionally distant fathers."

That had made JayBee angry in turn. "I don't agree with that at all! He probably didn't want to frighten him. He knows T.J. is scared of men."

JayBee sighed and tried to pay attention as the minister spoke about the deceased for a few minutes, saying she had been a loving mother and a pillar of the community, a woman who would be sorely missed by the village of Priam. Travis' expression never changed throughout, although his sister was crying into a handkerchief. JayBee wondered what Travis was feeling. This service was bringing the death of her own mother to mind. Those three months of her mother's final illness had been the worst thing that ever happened to her, even worse than losing her brother.

"And now," the minister announced, "the deceased's daughter, Alicia Kathleen Kellman, would like to read a poem she wrote about her mother."

Wow, JayBee thought, looking at Travis' sister with respect as she came up to face the congregation, *I could never have done that when my mom died.*

Travis' sister lifted her chin and surveyed the congregation. She was a tall, thin figure, clad in funereal black and yet somehow her full skirt and turtleneck had an artsy-funky look. Maybe it was the fringe on the skirt or the beaded vest she wore over the turtleneck. She started strongly:

Where are you now, O my mother?
Are you with the moon and the stars?
Dwelling in Nirvana?
Living in one of the mansions of which Jesus spoke?
Reincarnated as a beautiful animal?

Your life cut short,
Betrayed,
The Guilty One, accursed and afraid,

The wrath of God shall find you –

Suddenly she sobbed and covered her face with her hand. The congregation sat quietly, but JayBee could feel the tension as they wondered whether she would be able to continue.

As the moments dragged on, Travis rose and went to his sister's side. Putting his arm around her waist, he said something to her quietly. She handed him the paper. Taking a pair of glasses out of his jacket, he put them on, cleared his throat and read in a dry, emotionless voice:

Vengeance is mine, saith the Lord,
And I will repay.

O my mother,
Dwell on the Other Side,
With Buddha,
And Mohammed,
And Krishna,
While we live on without you,
Missing your frail grace,
And your beautiful face.

He nodded to the congregation and then led his sister back to her seat.

Well, JayBee thought, she's a better artist than a poet. And yet, something about the scene had brought tears to her eyes.

When they went to the grave at the new cemetery outside of town, it was drizzling. JayBee wasn't surprised. Every funeral she had ever attended had been in terrible weather. She remembered standing by her mother's grave in February. Shivering, she recalled the bitter cold of that day and the slushy, snowy ground.

The service at the grave was short. The minister said a prayer, everyone threw carnations at the coffin and it was over.

"The family would like to invite everyone to a lunch at Creekside Farm," the minister announced. "That's near the intersection of Crocker and Pine, folks."

JayBee, lingering at the edge of the crowd, didn't think Travis knew she was there until she found him at her elbow.

"JayBee, honey, thanks for coming." He looked handsome and distinguished in his gray overcoat. "I didn't think you'd be able to get away from work."

"They let me have a substitute for half the day."

"How's T.J.?"

"He's fine today. Fever's all gone."

"That's good. You're coming to the lunch, aren't you?" As she hesitated, he added, "Please come. I want to see you."

She couldn't resist the longing in his eyes. "Okay, for a little while."

* * * * *

Back at the house, Travis took off his jacket, rolled up his sleeves and played host for a time. Katie and his grandmother helped him put out sandwiches, cold fried chicken, potato and macaroni salad and soft drinks.

"We should have planned a restaurant meal," Travis told his sister, patting the sweat off his forehead with a handkerchief.

"No!" Katie said. "This is much nicer. Homier."

Seeing that Great-Uncle Bobby had arrived, Travis locked the china cabinet that held the liquor and pocketed the key. He went looking for his brother and found him in the parlor. The two of them hadn't spoken at the visitation, with the animosity of their meeting at the Paradise still lingering.

"Hey, Travis," Peter greeted him warily.

"Hi, Pete. Uncle Bobby's here. Keep an eye on him, okay?"

"Yeah, I'll take him outside if he makes a scene."

Nodding his thanks, Travis turned to see Ralph Peterson carrying a large carton. He hastened to take it from the older man. "You know you shouldn't be carrying this," Travis scolded, knowing Ralph had arthritis. "Why didn't you tell me to come get it?"

"Got room for it on your desk?" Ralph took out a penknife and opened the box.

"I'm very pleased with the way they came out." Unfolding one of the election brochures, Ralph smiled proudly. Travis studied it with mixed emotions. Ralph had taken the photograph on the front, which showed Travis in his lab coat, looking down and petting Ralph's gray tabby.

Well, it's a good picture of the cat.

The inside detailed Travis' platform and listed his credentials.

"When you go door-to-door, hand them out," said Ralph. "Even if people say they're voting for your father. You never know, they might change their minds when they read your brochure."

Right, if they read it before it goes in the trash. Somehow, the election had lost its zest for Travis. Running against a man who was in jail charged with murder was like being in an auto race against a bicyclist.

The next twenty minutes were spent greeting guests as they filed in. Finally, when most of the guests were seated, balancing paper plates full of food on their laps, Travis grabbed a chicken leg for himself and went to find JayBee.

He found her sitting by herself, halfway up the staircase, a heaping plate beside her. "This is a great lunch," she told him enthusiastically, moving over to make room for him on the stair.

It felt so natural to be with her. The day had been one long ordeal, but her presence had changed everything, made everything brighter.

"So," said JayBee, "you finally met my sister."

"Is she all right?" Travis asked. "She fainted while I was there."

"Yes, she told me. She's upset about her ex-husband coming to town."

He nodded. "I don't think your sister cared for me too much. We didn't hit it off."

"So she didn't try to flirt with you?"

"Flirt? I should say not. She told me to stay away from you."

JayBee smiled. "But here we are together."

He smiled back. "Just the way I like it. I wish you'd stick around for awhile after the guests leave."

"Help you clean up, you mean?"

He laughed. "No. You can sit in a chair and look pretty while I clean up. How about it?"

"I wish I could, but I promised T.J. I'd take him to the park this afternoon."

He sat silent, disappointed.

She said tentatively, "I wish I hadn't promised…"

"That's all right. I'm glad you're taking such good care of him."

"I should have thought maybe you'd need cheering up. I know you must feel bad about your stepmother."

Not wanting to shock her, he said only, "I feel bad about the way she died."

JayBee took his hand with a sigh. "It's so hard when people pass away. My mother died four years ago, but I still think about her every single day."

"I still think about my real mother, too. She died when I was five."

JayBee squeezed his hand. He felt very close to her.

"Hey, Travis?" Katie called from the dining room. "Is there any more ice?"

Apparently it was time to be the host again. "I'll be back in a few minutes."

"Okay," JayBee said. "I'm going to run up to the bathroom."

Travis went into the kitchen and opened the second bag of ice just as Misney came in. The lawyer folded his arms and looked at him sardonically. "So she's a dyke, huh? A dyke who sits and holds your hand?"

"She's trying to make me feel better. Because of my loss."

Misney snorted. "Yeah, I can see how broken up you are because Alicia's dead. So how long have you known that woman?"

"Not very long." Travis started filling the ice bucket. "I told you before, she's a friend of mine."

"A friend, huh? Are you getting any?"

Travis stopped what he was doing and looked up. "Is that any of your business?"

"Yeah, because I figure it this way. If you're actually doing her, I'll back off. But if you're just friends, maybe I'll ask her out."

"You go near her and I will personally knock your head off."

"Are you shittin' me?" The lawyer sounded incredulous.

Travis walked up to him and stood toe-to-toe. Misney was several inches taller. Travis raised his chin and looked his friend in the eye. "I'm dead serious. And you know I can take you."

"I'm not so sure about that," Misney muttered. "Besides, I'm an attorney and I'll sue your ass."

Travis grinned. Misney raised his hands, palms out. "All right, don't worry. I won't poach on your territory."

"Good!" Travis walked into the dining room with the ice bucket.

* * * * *

JayBee peeked in the open bathroom door and saw that Georgia was standing at the mirror, holding a wet washcloth to her face.

"Excuse me," JayBee said. "I'll use the other bathroom."

"No, that's all right. I'm finished." Georgia put the cloth down on the sink. Spots of high color flamed in her cheeks and her eyes were red and swollen.

"Are you okay?"

"Funerals affect me very badly. Here you go, it's all yours." Georgia walked past her into the hall.

JayBee closed the door. When she came out again, she found Georgia waiting for her. JayBee looked at her inquiringly as Georgia's eyes raked her up and down.

"Are you sleeping with him?" Georgia demanded.

"Who?" JayBee asked, although she had a pretty good idea who Georgia meant.

"Travis, of course!"

"How is that your concern?"

Georgia looked closely at JayBee's expression. "That means you aren't. Well, I'd be careful if I were you. He has some rather—peculiar—tastes in bed."

"Good! I like a lover with imagination."

"I'm just trying to warn you for your own good. You're a woman—I'm a woman. I want to save you from what I went through." She turned and went down the stairs.

JayBee stood there for a long moment, looking uncertainly after the woman's back.

Travis glanced up with a smile as JayBee made her way down the stairs and sat down next to him. Only five minutes apart and he'd already missed her company.

She answered his smile with a frown. "Excuse me for saying so, but your sister-in-law is very odd."

Startled, he asked, "Did she say something to you?"

"She asked me if I was sleeping with you—not that it's any of her business. She warned me that you have peculiar tastes in bed."

"What?"

"You heard me." She looked at him speculatively.

Damn Georgia anyway. He tucked JayBee's hand into his. "Don't let her spoil things between us before we even get anywhere with this relationship."

She was still giving him a penetrating look. "I'll say this right up front. I'm not interested in anything sexual involving animals, pain, or more than two people."

"I'll leave the sheep at home then." He gave her hand a squeeze.

"I'm serious."

He looked at her earnestly. "Look, honey, Georgia was just trying to yank your chain. I'm a pretty ordinary guy. And I won't push you to do anything you're not comfortable with."

"I'm going to ask you a question. I want you to answer right away, because if you hesitate, I'll know you're not telling the truth. Okay?"

"Shoot."

"What's the most unusual thing you've ever done, sexually?"

"Made love with Beth on the roof of my apartment at OSU. During the daytime." After a moment, he added, "As a matter of fact, I'll bet that's when Beth got pregnant. We didn't use a condom that day. She claimed it was a safe time for her, but I guess she was wrong."

Somehow the sense of harmony between them was gone. She stood up. "I'd better get going. It's after three."

"All right. I'll walk you out."

They went outside. Morrie, the police dispatcher, was leaving as well. Travis paused to shake hands with him and thank him for coming.

"Have any more trouble with that Nissan?" Morrie asked JayBee.

"No, everything's been fine, thanks."

"What was that all about?" Travis asked as they walked over to the motorcycle.

She seemed reluctant to talk about it. "Nothing."

"It must have been something if Morrie knows about it."

"If I say it was nothing, it was nothing!"

"I'm only asking because I'm concerned."

"If you must know, I was followed home after our date last week. I know who it was and I handled the problem. Okay?"

He frowned. "No, it's not okay. What are you doing out on the bike if you're having a problem like that? Look, how about if I follow you in my truck? I want to make sure you get home safely."

"Don't treat me like a six year old," she said irritably. "I can take care of myself."

"I know. I'm just concerned. I care about you—"

"Well, maybe you shouldn't." She looked down. "I don't have good luck with men. I never have. Maybe I ought to listen to my sister and your sister-in-law. I don't really know anything about you—"

"But you'll never get to know me if we don't keep seeing each other!"

"I don't know. I used to think I could trust my instincts, but then I found out that wasn't true."

As they looked into each other's eyes, her expression was doubtful. He felt frantic inside, panicky at the thought that he could lose her. *Do something!*

Roughly, he pulled her close and kissed her. Throwing her arms around his neck, she kissed him back just as hard.

Perhaps it was the high emotions of the day, the near-fight they had just had, but something flared between them, something that was almost out of control. He imagined slinging her over his shoulder, striding into the barn, throwing her down on the hay and pounding into her for hours. Shocked at himself, he loosened his grip.

She stared at him. "Wow! You never kissed me like that before."

Fighting for calm, he put his hands on her shoulders. "Listen, JayBee. There's something between us—it could be the most important thing to ever happen to us. Give us a chance, that's all I'm asking."

"I'd better go."

He couldn't read her expression. "Call me."

She put on her helmet and started the bike. "I need…time to think."

He stood there a long time, watching as she disappeared down the road.

Chapter Thirteen

Travis came back into the house wanting to shake Georgia until her teeth rattled. Perhaps Angel had tried to infect JayBee with doubts, but Georgia's cruel remark had changed the atmosphere. He went over the conversation in his mind, thinking he should have taken everything more seriously from the beginning, not made the stupid joke about the sheep. But the whole thing had seemed to come out of left field. It had been so unexpected that he hadn't known how to handle it.

I could tell her how hard Georgia's been working to get back into my bed.

But then he rejected that thought. Somehow he knew that JayBee would not be impressed with a man who boasted about his conquests.

The house was still full of guests. He wanted desperately to be by himself, even for just a few minutes. Taking the stairs two at a time, he went up to his bedroom.

Maybe he would feel better if he changed into casual clothes. He got a pair of jeans out of the dresser and hung up his suit pants. Putting his dress shirt into a bag for the dry cleaner, he looked for a clean, comfortable shirt.

The door opened and Georgia stepped into the room.

"Didn't you ever hear of knocking?" he demanded. "And haven't you caused enough trouble today?"

She rolled her eyes. "Well, let's not pretend I've never seen you in your underwear before." Nonchalantly, she strolled farther into the room.

"Right, back in the old days when I was being so 'peculiar' in bed." With a glare in her direction, he grabbed his jeans and tugged them on.

She tittered. "Oh, I'm sure your little girlfriend knew I was teasing."

If he said anything more, he would have to admit that JayBee had taken the remark seriously. So he changed the subject. "I found out something about your blackmailer."

Georgia dropped her casual pose. "Oh, Travis, really? I've been so worried about it!"

He thought of using his knowledge as a bargaining chip, demanding that she contact JayBee and tell her she hadn't meant that comment. But maybe that was making more of it than was warranted. JayBee had to show some measure of trust in him, make up her own mind, not let one ill-natured remark ruin their budding relationship.

"I shouldn't even tell you, after you tried to mess me up with JayBee."

"I didn't mean anything." She sat down on the bed and looked at him pleadingly. "I'm just…jealous. I admit it. It's hard for me to see you with another woman."

Perhaps it was time to have this out with her, once and for all. He sat down beside her, turning so he could look into her eyes. "But you chose Pete instead of me. Right? I don't know what's wrong between the two of you, but you should concentrate on making things work with my brother. Pete's a good guy—"

"I don't know. I'm scared of him. He can be so harsh sometimes—not like you, Travis. And I keep thinking, what if he killed Alicia?"

Travis was startled. "Do you think he did?"

"I don't know. Ever since we talked in the barn that day and I realized Pete would inherit some of Alicia's money, I've wondered about it. I know he needs money. Plus, he's been acting so strange lately. I don't know what to think."

"I don't believe Pete would commit murder. I still think it was an outsider, not a family member."

"I don't know...I just don't know," she said in a half-whisper. "That day he came home from the medical meeting—the night Alicia was murdered—there was blood on his shirt."

Travis frowned. "That doesn't necessarily mean much. Pete works in a hospital, after all."

"But he never came home with blood on his shirt before."

"Did you ask him about it?"

"He told me he was making morning rounds when one of his diabetic patients pricked her finger to check her blood sugar. The blood spurted all over." Her brow creased as she seemed to think about the conversation. "Is that even possible, Travis?"

He nodded. "It can happen. She may have nicked a blood vessel." Assuming Pete had told the truth... "Is that shirt still around?"

"No, he took it to the dry cleaners the next day. So I guess that could never prove anything."

Travis wasn't sure—he knew that blood residue could linger for a long time. Still, he could just imagine what a good defense lawyer would say about evidence like that. "Ladies and gentlemen of the jury, my client is a medical doctor—a surgeon. He's around blood all day. Naturally, some of his clothing may have blood residue."

"Tell me what you found out about the blackmail. Please tell me." As Travis sat silent, frowning, she added, "You promised you would try to help me, Travis."

So he had. "It was Alicia. For sure."

"How did you find out?"

He hesitated, not wanting to betray Terry.

"Tell me—or I won't know whether to believe you."

"I'm not a liar, Georgia. I know for sure it was Alicia. But I can't tell you how I know. You're going to have to take my word for it." His voice was firm. She looked uncertainly at him, then seemed to accept that was all he was going to tell her.

"All right. Thank you."

"I'd better get back to my guests." As he left the room, he wondered whether he should have kept his big mouth shut.

* * * * *

Alicia's mother was adamant that she wanted to visit Robert Kellman in jail. Travis, thinking of all the steps into the place, didn't think it was a good idea. But Helene insisted she had to do it. "And don't give me any more arguments," she told him sharply. "I want to talk to your father face to face. If you won't take me, I'll find some way to get there myself!"

So Tuesday afternoon found them at the visiting area, waiting for Robert to be brought in. Helene was dressed as though she were going to a fancy tea party, elegant violet suit with a silver pin, lace blouse and teetery high heels. She looked precisely like an older version of her daughter. Travis wondered if his father thought so too, because a look of pain crossed his face as he took in his female visitor.

"Helene!" Robert said, putting his hand to his forehead. "What a shock to see you here! I never would have imagined this."

She stood, looking into his eyes. "None of your playacting, Robert, if you please! I want you to tell me—with no prevarication—did you murder my daughter?"

Travis was taken aback at the question, but his father showed no emotion, sinking heavily into a chair. "Helene, Helene, what a thing to say! How could you even think that?"

Helene sat as well. "Robert, let us have plain words. No one knew as much about Alicia as I did. I spent hours on the phone with her over the last few months, listening to her troubles. We both know that things weren't going well between you. Now I ask you again, did you kill her?"

Robert sighed. "I adored Alicia. She meant everything to me."

Helene rolled her eyes. "Oh, please, Robert. I'm well aware you have a woman on the side."

Both the Kellman men stared at her. She said impatiently, "I didn't raise any stupid children. Alicia knew all about this Louisa Fairlawn—"

"Fairfield," Robert corrected, his tone subdued.

"So naturally she told me about her. Alicia was very unhappy about the whole thing."

Robert sat staring down at the table. "Sometimes I thought she suspected," he mumbled at last. "But she never confronted me."

"I advised her not to," Helene said. "I thought you were having a midlife crisis—a *late* midlife crisis—and it would all blow over." She gave him a piercing look. "Perhaps I made the worst mistake of my life."

Robert shook his head vehemently, then turned toward Travis, his expression miserable. "Son, I'm so sorry. This must be a shock for you—"

"Actually, Dad, I found out about Louisa on my own." Thinking it was high time he took part in the conversation, Travis turned to face his grandmother. "I talked to Louisa myself, Grandma. Dad was with her the night Alicia was murdered. Louisa told me he seemed perfectly normal and calm, not at all like someone who had just murdered his wife—"

Helene snorted. "My goodness, Travis, you can certainly be naïve for a grown man. Don't you know, after all these years, what a good actor your father is? To my mind, he's perfectly capable of killing my poor darling and then going to his mistress without a care in the world."

"That's damned unfair!" Robert exclaimed. "You're talking about me like I'm some sort of monster!"

"You were a surgeon, Robert." Helene's eyes were steely. "Blood and knives aren't that upsetting to you, are they? Oh, I'm not saying you planned it all in advance. I'm sure it was a spur-of-the-moment thing." She leaned forward, her voice dropping to a near-whisper. "But now that I've spoken with you and looked into your eyes, I'm sure you did it."

"No!" Travis exclaimed, as his father said, "I didn't! I didn't do it!"

She sat back, folding her arms over her big purse. "Deny it all you like, Robert. I know what I know."

Travis frowned. Maybe he was naïve, as his grandmother said, or perhaps just plain stupid would be a better description. He'd never dreamed that Helene's purpose in coming here had been to accuse his father.

"Grandma, really—the evidence against Dad is all circumstantial. The neighbor said she heard them arguing—so what? Didn't you ever argue with Grandpa?"

"Not so loudly that the neighbors could hear it," she answered triumphantly.

"All married people fight sometimes," Robert said. He cocked his head, looking at his mother-in-law. "You never liked me, did you?" he asked, his tone sad. "You tried to talk Alicia out of marrying me in the first place, all those years ago..."

"Of course I did! I knew what a burden it would be to my poor Alicia, to take on your two rambunctious boys! What a thing to ask of a beautiful young girl!"

"How dare you! Alicia had a good life with me—clothes, trips, a new car every three years, a luxurious home!"

"And look what it all came to. Being murdered in her own kitchen." The old woman's face crumpled. She drew a tissue out of her purse and began to sob into it.

"You'd better go," Robert murmured, ringing the bell to call the guard. "Damn it, Travis, you shouldn't have brought her."

Travis hurried to his grandmother and put his arm around her shoulders. "Come on, Grandma."

As the guards arrived to take Robert back to his cell, Helene gave him a poisonous look. "You'll be sorry, Robert. Mark my words!"

* * * * *

Early Wednesday was Travis' standard time to perform operations. This week he had two dogs to neuter and a cat to spay before his morning appointments began. He didn't particularly mind doing the operations—after four years of veterinary college and three years of practice, he had done hundreds of them—but he much preferred working with conscious patients. Even if he had gone to medical school as his father had wanted, he would never have gone into a surgical specialty.

He had finished the first dog and was just about to prep the second when Thelma's voice came over the intercom. "Doctor, your sister-in-law is calling. She says it's urgent."

"Did you tell her I'm operating?" he asked, not even trying to hide his irritation.

"Yes, of course, but she was so insistent…I thought I'd better see if you had a moment to talk to her."

"All right. Put her through." Line two lit up on the phone. He punched it and put her on the speaker.

"Travis?" Georgia sounded excited.

"What is it? You're on the speakerphone," he warned, hoping that Thelma wasn't listening in.

"I'm at your parents' house. I borrowed Pete's key."

"What the hell are you doing over there?"

"Don't be mad. I came over to look for those…things…your stepmother borrowed from me." She spoke cautiously, but Travis caught on to what she meant. She had to be looking for the items Alicia had asked for when blackmailing her. "And I found something! Something that may clear your father!"

"What?" he demanded.

"I was looking through the bedroom—ohhhh!" Georgia cried out and then Travis heard a thud.

"Georgie? Are you okay? Georgie!"

A few seconds passed. Then a click sounded as someone on the other end hung up the phone at the Kellman house.

Swearing, Travis frantically dialed 9-1-1 and reported what had happened. Then he stripped off his gloves and surgical greens.

"Got to go—it's an emergency!" he told Thelma, patting his breast pocket to make sure he had his cell phone. "Cancel my first four appointments. I'll call you in an hour and let you know what's going on."

Travis arrived at his parents' house just as a police cruiser drove up. Officer Ming and plainclothes detective Jerry Davidson jumped out of the cruiser.

Georgia's Volvo and Katie's Civic were in the driveway.

The scene was like a nightmarish reenactment of two weeks before. Katie knelt outside the back door, retching into her mother's prize rose bushes. Through the open back door, Travis could see Georgia lying face down in the kitchen. Ming and Davidson pushed past him into the house.

"What's going on?" Travis demanded, grabbing his sister by the arm. She straightened, deathly pale. "What are you doing here?"

"I came over to bring in the mail," she whispered, hiding her face against Travis' chest.

"Sit down!" he ordered her roughly, snagging one of the patio chairs and propelling her toward it. Then he strode into the kitchen and bent over Georgia.

There was blood on the floor, flowing sluggishly from a wound on the back of Georgia's head. A large piece of firewood lay beside her.

Officer Ming, taking Georgia's pulse, looked up. "She's still alive!"

Travis grabbed a wad of paper towels and pressed it hard to the back of Georgia's head as Officer Ming called for an ambulance. Taking deep breaths, Travis tried to think through what this all meant.

Jerry Davidson came back into the kitchen and knelt beside him. "I've been through the rest of the house," he said. "No sign of an intruder. I'm going to talk to your sister and find out what she saw."

Travis just nodded, intent on his task, worried about the amount of blood Georgia had lost already.

Austin MacReedy arrived a few minutes later, cutting through the backyards from his house, which was on the other side of the block. "I heard the call come in," he explained briefly. "Is Mrs. Kellman alive?"

"Yes, thank God," Travis answered.

Katie stepped into the kitchen doorway, hanging on to the doorjamb with both hands.

"What happened?" MacReedy asked, addressing Katie.

"I just told Officer Davidson…I came over to get the mail. I opened the back door and I saw her lying there…" Katie bit her lip. "Oh, God, I thought she was dead. Just like Maman. What's wrong with our family? I can't believe this!" She buried her face in her arms.

The chief went over and patted her on the back. "Steady, Katie. Take deep breaths."

She grabbed his hand. "Oh, Austin, why do these things keep happening?"

He detached himself from her. "Calm down, Katie," he said, a warning note in his voice.

Katie burst into tears and fled the kitchen, going into the dining room. MacReedy nodded to Officer Ming. "Go keep an eye on her. Make sure she's all right."

Davidson looked in the back door. "Chief, I'm going to take a look around the neighborhood."

The chief nodded, making a "go ahead" gesture.

Travis tried to keep a tight rein on his emotions. No matter how hard he had tried to purge Georgia from his heart, there was still some lingering feeling for her. He hated seeing her like this, so still and pale. Looking up briefly, he said, "I was on the phone with Georgia when it happened. She said she found something that might clear my father."

The chief came closer. "Did she say what it was?"

Travis shook his head. "She was about to, then I heard her gasp. Whoever did this must have come in behind her."

"Jesus!" The chief sounded disgusted. "Do you see anything out of place in here?"

Travis looked around quickly, not leaving Georgia's side. He shrugged. "It's hard to tell. Everything looks the same as it did last week."

He heard sirens outside and sighed with relief. The towels he was using to close the wound were drenched in blood. Georgia desperately needed better medical attention than he could provide.

MacReedy walked out of the room and returned a few moments later with a brown leather Coach purse. Methodically, he began going through it, taking out Georgia's wallet, brush, makeup bag and sunglasses, laying them one by one on the kitchen table.

A gold charm bracelet and a man's ring were held together by a tie with a knot in it. MacReedy held up the conglomeration, looking accusingly at Travis. "Now we know who was being blackmailed."

Four paramedics rushed in, quickly taking over from Travis. Going to the sink, he began to wash up. His hands and forearms were covered in blood.

Katie came back into the room, holding a damp washcloth to her face. Officer Ming trailed behind her.

"Katie, call your brother Pete and tell him what's going on," MacReedy ordered. As she started over to the kitchen phone, he snapped, "Not that phone! Do you have your cell on you?"

She took it out of her pocket and held it up.

"You may have to have him paged," Travis added. "He's probably in surgery."

Katie went outside to make the call on her cell phone while the paramedics loaded Georgia on a stretcher and took her out. Travis debated whether he should follow the ambulance to the hospital. Checking his watch, he decided reluctantly to go back to his clinic, at least for a few hours. There was nothing he could do at the hospital except wait. He didn't want to cancel a whole day's worth of clients.

Perhaps Katie would be willing to go to the hospital and wait for Pete.

Damn it, why hadn't he anticipated that Georgia would go running over to the house to look for the items Alicia had taken? He had told her the blackmailer was Alicia to set her mind at ease, but he should have kept quiet.

"All right, you'd better tell me what's going on here," MacReedy said. "Let me see if I have this right. Mrs. Kellman—your sister-in-law—didn't know who was blackmailing her, because Terry was making the calls. But after we talked to Terry, you shot off your big mouth to Mrs. Kellman and told her the blackmailer was your stepmother. So then Mrs. Kellman came over here and got knocked in the head by…someone." MacReedy leveled his finger at Travis' chest. "I thought you knew more about this blackmail than you were letting on."

"All right," Travis said. "Georgia told me she was being blackmailed. I couldn't tell you about it. I'd given her my word."

"Given your word!" MacReedy repeated, jabbing Travis with his finger. Officer Ming, watching with frightened eyes, took a step back from her chief. "What the hell do you think this is? Let me set you straight, Trav—this is a goddamned murder investigation! What were you thinking, withholding that kind of information?"

Travis knocked the chief's hand away. "Why the hell should I tell you? So you could rush to arrest Georgia as fast as you did my dad? Anyway, what happened just now should prove her innocence!"

"It doesn't prove a damned thing! This could be a completely unrelated mugging!"

"That's ridiculous! It's clear to me the murderer is still around. That person must have seen Georgia come in here, hit her on the head and took whatever evidence she'd found."

"So you think the murderer is watching the house?" MacReedy asked, his tone dripping with sarcasm.

Put like that, it didn't seem very likely. But Travis didn't back down. "Why not? Maybe it's a neighbor!"

MacReedy waved his hand, as though dismissing that as nonsense.

Travis went on, "To my mind, this proves that Georgia's innocent—and my dad as well. Why the hell don't you do something, instead of standing here arguing with me?"

MacReedy's eyes narrowed. "Don't tell me how to do my job. For all I know, you're the one who hit her on the head."

Travis opened his mouth, outraged, but Officer Ming spoke before he could say anything. "Oh, no! Dr. Kellman drove up at the same time we did!"

MacReedy whirled on her, his face furious. "That doesn't mean a damned thing! He could have attacked Mrs. Kellman, left, driven around the block in his truck and then come back to make it look good!"

"Oh, for God's sake, you know me better than that!" Travis exclaimed. "Anyway, my receptionist can vouch for me. I told you, I was at my clinic when Georgia called me. I called 9-1-1 from there before I drove over."

Katie, coming back in, was just in time to hear the last exchange. "How dare you?" she demanded, striding up to MacReedy and getting right in his face. "My brother would never hurt a woman!"

MacReedy took a deep breath. "All right, folks, let's calm down." He gave Travis a sharp-eyed look. "Aw, hell, I guess I really don't suspect you. I remember you were too much of a wimp to shoot a deer." He pointed at Officer Ming. "Call his receptionist and check out his story, though."

Travis was so infuriated with MacReedy for bringing up ancient history that he wanted to jump the chief and slug him, the way they used to go at each other when they were boys. "I've got to get back to my clinic," he said, desperately trying to calm down and keep his temper. "Katie, I wish you'd go to the hospital and wait for Pete. Take Georgia's purse with you in case they want her medical card. And call me if—if anything happens."

"Anything like what?" Katie asked, gazing at him wide-eyed. "She'll be all right, won't she?"

"Hard to say." The words "traumatic brain injury" kept running through his head. "She has a concussion, at least."

MacReedy turned to Katie. "You got here before your brother. You sure you didn't see anyone leaving the house?"

"No, I didn't see anyone."

It crossed Travis' mind that MacReedy was being singularly unsuspicious about Katie's presence at the scene. She could have hit Georgia on the head with the wood as easily as he could have. But of course he didn't say anything, not wanting to arouse any more suspicions in MacReedy's mind than the chief already held.

"Can I have a drink of water?" Katie asked in a whispery voice.

Travis, seeing how white her face was, pulled out a kitchen chair. "Sit and put your head down," he told her, than turned toward the sink. But MacReedy was already getting a glass from the cupboard.

* * * * *

It was a long, horrible day for Travis. He had Thelma cancel as many appointments as she could, but there were still a lot of patients to see. Instead of eating lunch, he spent that hour doing the two operations he had missed that morning. It was hard to concentrate because he kept wondering what was going on with Georgia. He was annoyed that no one called him to fill him in on what was happening.

He drove straight to Tecumseh County General Hospital when the day was over and found out that Georgia was in the Intensive Care wing. Taking the elevator upstairs, he discovered his brother outside Georgia's room, reading her chart.

Peter turned as Travis came down the hall.

"Pete, I'm so sorry about Georgia. How's she doing?"

Peter gave him a slight smile. "Twenty-five stitches, but I'm hoping she'll be all right."

"Conscious?"

Peter's smile broadened. "She finally woke up about an hour ago. She's very confused, but she knew me, thank God."

"That's great," Travis said sincerely. He had feared that, like so many head-injury patients, she would awaken with impaired memory. "Did she say who attacked her?"

"No, she doesn't remember anything about that."

Travis was surprised to see tears in his brother's eyes. "I'll tell you, this has made me see things in a whole new light," Peter said. "Do you know how easily that could have killed her? I could have lost my wife! For good!" He swiped at his eyes with his sleeve. "Jesus, I'm as big a crybaby as Dad."

"You've got a right to be upset."

"I'll tell you," Peter went on, "I haven't been that great a husband. I'm going to try to do better from now on."

Travis clapped him on the back. "That's good to hear."

"Now that I almost lost her, I can understand how you must have felt when I stole her away from you. I want you to know…I'm sorry."

Travis raised his brows in surprise. Peter's emotions were certainly running high to let him make an admission like that. "Well," he answered, "maybe it all worked out for the best, after all. Is it okay if I go in and see her?"

"Sure, just don't stay too long. She needs to rest."

Travis went into Georgia's room and sat down in the visitor's chair. She opened her eyes and smiled at him.

"Travis," she whispered. "Oh, thank goodness you're here at last!"

"Were you waiting for me?" he asked, startled.

"Of course!"

Did that mean she wanted to tell him what she had found at the house, the thing that would clear his father? "I'm glad you're awake. How are you feeling?"

"Woozy. My head aches."

"That's no surprise. Do you know what happened to you?"

"Peter told me someone hit me on the head. That's funny, isn't it? Why would someone want to hit me on the head?" she wondered dreamily. "I thought everyone liked me. Well, except for Alicia. She doesn't like me."

"You don't know who hit you?"

"No. I don't want to think about it, anyway." She smiled weakly at him. "Poor Travis. I'll bet you've been worried sick about me. You know what? I've been lying here thinking about that family ring you wanted to give me."

"What?" It took him a moment to follow what she was talking about and then he remembered how she'd been angry when he'd tried to give her his mother's ring to mark their engagement.

"Daddy told me I was being a selfish brat for giving you grief about it."

"Georgie, please…don't worry about that now."

"No, Daddy was right," she said, her voice getting firmer. "So I've decided it will be fine. If it's what you want, darling, I'll wear it for my engagement ring."

Chapter Fourteen

Travis pressed his hand to his mouth, leaning over Georgia. It took him a moment until he felt like he could talk without his voice shaking. "Georgia, what year is it?"

His heart sank at her answer. She thought it was a year ago, when they'd been engaged. She yawned. "I'm sorry, but I have to go to sleep. Will you give me a kiss goodnight?"

Bending, he lightly kissed her forehead. She closed her eyes and fell asleep immediately. Travis sat and watched her for awhile, thinking. If he was engaged in a competition with his older brother, Georgia had just handed him four aces.

In one quick flash, he saw it all. If her memory loss was permanent, he could have her back. Marry her, without Alicia's interference this time around. She'd come live with him at Creekside Farm and share his bed in the room they'd decorated together.

He was damned sick of celibacy, of living alone. And hadn't she shown over the last few weeks that she'd regretted marrying his brother?

Of course, it would be a terrible blow for Peter. But so what? It would be no worse than what Peter had done to him.

Then he thought of T.J. If the boy was his son, anything he did would have to take him into account. Would Georgia want a child who was not her own? Or would he be perpetuating another generation of cruelty to a stepson?

And anyway, where did all of this leave JayBee?

The mere thought of her made him realize how impossible it would be to settle down with Georgia. Everything had changed, his life had moved on. His tastes had altered in this last year. Or maybe, now that he knew that someone like JayBee existed, he wasn't willing to settle for anyone else.

Even though their last meeting had ended badly, he believed they'd be together again. At least he wanted to believe it. The thought of that last kiss encouraged him. He couldn't have been the only one who'd been altered by what surged between them.

Leaving the room, he waited while Peter finished his conversation with another doctor.

"Georgia's asleep," he told his brother. "Listen, Pete—she's very confused. She thinks it's last year."

Peter nodded. "That can happen after head trauma. Hopefully, she'll start getting her memory back as the wound heals."

"Pete, she thinks she's still engaged to me."

Peter's face changed and he looked at Travis with suspicious eyes. "Didn't you set her straight?"

"I didn't want to upset her."

"Are you sure you didn't have another reason?" Peter stared into Travis' eyes, frowning.

I could have had her in the barn that day if I'd wanted. Lucky for you I held back. "I thought I'd leave it up to you, since you're her husband." Travis put his hand on his brother's shoulder. "Just…be gentle with her, okay?"

Peter turned away. "I think I know how to deal with my own wife."

As Travis left, he wondered if he had done the right thing. He hoped his brother would be kind to her.

* * * * *

When Travis got back home, Helene was annoyed no one had told her what was going on until she called Katie at home.

"I would have liked to send poor Georgia a small bouquet of flowers. And a card as well."

"Send the things tomorrow, Grandma. She'll be in the hospital for a day or two."

"I'll order something tonight." The old woman clucked disapprovingly as she ran the feather duster over the mantel. "Perhaps this will teach Georgia to always lock a door behind herself. I never leave the door unlocked at my condo. One never knows what kind of hooligan could enter."

"This wasn't a mugging," Travis said. "I think whoever killed Alicia saw Georgia over there and went after her as well."

Helene eyed him thoughtfully. "So you still hold to your theory that your father is innocent? Well, poor Alicia always said you were the most stubborn person she knew."

"Dad is innocent and to my mind, this proves it."

"Nothing is proved. Georgia's a lovely woman. Probably, if we knew the truth, Katie's arrival prevented a rape from occurring. My goodness, Alicia's house is only a mile from the college. I'm sure there are hundreds of lusty young men there who are quite capable of hitting a woman on the head and having their will of her."

"Then maybe it was one of them who murdered Alicia." Travis wondered if Austin, in his rush to arrest Robert Kellman, had done any investigating up at the college.

Helene shook her head. "I called the coroner to inquire. Dr. Thomson was most helpful. Poor Alicia was not—interfered with—in that way. We have that much, at least, to be thankful for."

"Thank God," Travis said. It would have been horrible to think that Alicia's killer had raped her as well.

Although he couldn't help thinking that such a scenario might have proved his father's innocence.

Helene clicked her tongue as she dusted the lamp. "Don't you ever dust this room?" she scolded.

"Dust?" Travis asked vaguely. "I have a maid service that comes in once a month." Sitting down at his desk, he began to go through the day's mail.

"Once a month isn't nearly enough, not with all these animals in the house."

Travis paused as he encountered a long envelope from the DNA laboratory. Weighing it in his hand, he wondered what it might contain. If T.J. was his son, then he would be responsible for him for years to come…school, college…guiding him through boyhood and adolescence. There would be hard work ahead to win the child's trust and affection.

Or, if he were a stranger's child, no relation, he would either remain in foster care or return to Beth's sister. His mind flinched at the thought of that. No matter what, he would do whatever he could to keep the boy away from "Uncle Ray".

Ripping open the envelope, he scanned the letter quickly.

"The DNA test results are here," he announced, surprised that his voice sounded shaky. "T.J. is my son." He felt as though a huge weight of uncertainty had been lifted from his shoulders. Drawing a deep breath, he realized there was one person he ached to share the news with…JayBee.

Helene sniffed. "Well, you needn't sound so happy about it."

"Were you expecting me to hang my head in shame?"

"There's never been a bastard in our family before."

Travis gave his grandmother an exasperated look. If he'd been properly married to Beth, the first grandchild in the family would have been cause for rejoicing. There would have been baby showers, birth announcements and a christening party.

"I'm not ashamed of him." Travis folded the letter carefully back into its envelope and put it in his desk drawer. "I've always wanted a kid and now I have one. And I don't want him to feel bad—ever—about existing."

"Well, I suppose I had better meet him before I return to Miami Beach. Can you arrange it?"

Travis was surprised. Although he had told her about T.J. the first day of the visit, Helene had never before expressed a desire to see the child.

"I wasn't going to waste my time with the boy, unless he turned out to be your son," she explained. "But now I believe it is my duty to become acquainted with him."

Travis smiled. "Are you up for a picnic, Grandma?"

When Helene agreed, Travis wrote a short note to Angel, inviting the household to a picnic at Tecumseh Park on Saturday.

* * * * *

T.J. kept begging to see the treehouse. "All right," JayBee agreed at last. "But you can only come here when I'm with you. Do you promise?"

The little boy nodded seriously.

JayBee made him wait under the tree while she went along the branch and through the window. She opened the big trap door and let down the rope ladder. This way into the treehouse would be easier for him.

She climbed down the ladder quickly, showing him how to hang on to each rung, then stood back and let him climb it. She thought he might be frightened, but he was like a little monkey, scrambling up even faster than she could and popping through into the treehouse with a triumphant shout.

She followed him up and then dragged the ladder in and shut the trap door. "There, now no one can come up here unless they come along the tree branch."

"I like this," he said, plopping down into one of the beanbag chairs with a grin. "I wish Queenie could come here."

"It's not for dogs. Only for people." She looked around with satisfaction. Really, it was such a cozy little place, carefully designed and built. She didn't know how or why and she had never asked anyone in the neighborhood if they knew. Without that knowledge it seemed more like hers to enjoy.

There was a big braided rag rug on the floor, two beanbag chairs and a small rattan chest. JayBee had brought the chest in herself, which hadn't been easy. She opened the lid. She kept a variety of items in there, a few paperback novels, candles and matches and snacks. Fishing out a small bag of potato chips, she threw it in T.J.'s direction. He ripped it open gleefully. "Don't tell Angel," JayBee said, sitting in the other beanbag chair. "So what did you do all day?"

"I played in the sandbox with Nicole." Frowning, he added, "Tommy came over, but I don't like Tommy."

"Why not?"

T.J. looked stubborn and tried to change the subject. "Can we go to the playground later?"

"After dinner. Why don't you like Tommy?"

Looking down, the little boy murmured, "He said I don't have a daddy."

"What did you say about that?" JayBee asked. Angel had received the DNA results from the social worker. JayBee had spoken to T.J. about his father several times. She wondered if her words had meant anything to the child.

"I said I had a daddy."

"That's right," JayBee said encouragingly.

"He gave me Queenie," T.J. went on. "You know what? I'll bet if we put a big basket on the ground, Queenie would get in it and then we could pull her up into the treehouse!"

"That's a smart idea. But if she got scared and jumped out of the basket, she'd get hurt."

T.J. nodded. "Yeah, I guess so."

"Did Tommy say anything else?"

"He asked me why my daddy doesn't live with me. Why doesn't he?"

"He has his own house. And pretty soon you'll go to live with him there. Remember I told you about his farm? He has some cats and a dog and a big house with lots of land around it. And Queenie can come live with you there."

"Will you and Angel be there?"

"No, we have our own house here. But you can come over here and see us." After all, JayBee reflected, Travis worked all day. He would need someone to watch his son. Perhaps he and Angel could come to an agreement for day care. Angel could certainly use the extra income.

Hastily, JayBee began to talk about how much fun T.J. would have, living with his father. She knew that Travis' attorney would most likely press for an early court date. JayBee wanted the boy to be prepared for the move.

As she told T.J. again what a nice man his father was, how much he would enjoy living on the farm and all the things he and his father would do together, it occurred to her that if she really believed everything she was saying, she ought to listen to herself. She knew she wouldn't have spoken to the child like this if she hadn't known the father personally. Some deep part of her meant those words. She truly believed Travis was a good, decent person.

He could be a good father and still have "peculiar" sexual tastes, she reminded herself. But maybe she had been wrong to pay attention to what Georgia had said. She didn't really know anything about the woman or what had broken up the engagement. And after all, some women made a lifestyle out of being bitchy to other women.

That last kiss had been incredible. She needed to make up her own mind about him, not let herself be influenced by other people.

Thinking of the look on his face when she'd said, "I need time to think," she knew she had hurt him.

With a sigh, she said to T.J., "I'm making dinner tonight. Let's go back in the house."

"What's for dinner?"

"'Snips and snails and puppy dog tails,'" she quoted.

"JayBee!"

She laughed. "It's a joke. What do you say to hotdogs? And maybe some macaroni and cheese?"

"Yummy!"

* * * * *

Charlotte Scott had been a client of Travis' for the last three years, ever since she'd moved to Priam with her young son David. A tall, generously proportioned woman with a glorious mane of naturally blond hair, she taught history at Priam High School.

"Thanks for letting me drop by." Travis seated himself on a high stool at the counter.

"How about a piece of chocolate cake?" When he hesitated, she urged, "It's homemade. You're not going to turn that down, are you?"

"Thanks, very kind of you."

"I'm always happy to have company in the kitchen." She gave him a sweet smile as she cut a good-sized piece and handed it to him on a plate. "I hear we have something in common," she said, taking a package of chicken out of the refrigerator.

He looked at her questioningly.

"We're both single parents."

Travis nodded. "So you heard about T.J."

She threw an amused glance over her shoulder as she washed the chicken. "You know what gossip's like in this town."

"You bet I do. My son's in foster care, but now that I have the DNA test results, I'm hoping I'll get custody soon."

Charlotte looked concerned. "That will be a big change for you."

"Yeah—I guess I'll be cutting down on the wild parties and impromptu trips to Europe."

"I didn't mean anything like that. It's just—you can't imagine how much having a child changes your life. Not until you have one and you see what it's really like."

Travis put his elbows on the counter and leaned forward. "All right, I don't mean to be sarcastic. But it's not like I'm living some out-of-control bachelor life right now. If I'd had my way, I'd have married T.J.'s mother and settled down five years ago."

Charlotte dipped the chicken in flour then moved it to a pan. "Is it true your son was in the house when your stepmother was murdered?"

Travis tried to examine her expression, but he could see only a bit of her profile. He reminded himself that just because he'd always liked Charlotte, that was no reason to let his guard down. "He was there, but fortunately he was sound asleep."

Charlotte shook her head. "What a terrible thing. I always felt safe in my house until that awful murder. The day after the news broke, I put chains on all my outside doors."

"Very wise," Travis commented. "The police arrested my father, but I still think it was some outside person who committed the murder. As a matter of fact, that's why I'm here today. I've decided to look into things myself, see if I can turn up anything the police investigation missed. So I've been talking to some of Alicia's friends."

Charlotte turned away from the pan and gave him a speculative look. "I hardly consider myself in that category. Are you talking to me as her friend or as a possible suspect?"

"I'd heard you didn't get along with her." When Charlotte's brows drew together, Travis added quickly, "Not that I blame you for that. Believe me, I know just how difficult Alicia could be."

"Difficult!" She snorted. "I couldn't stand to be in the same room with her." Her green eyes glittered unpleasantly.

"I heard about the flower show incident."

Charlotte tossed her head. "That isn't the half of it. Just a month after that happened, someone reported me to Family Services."

Travis' brows drew together. "For what?"

"This person claimed she saw me hitting David in public. It was utter nonsense—I've never hit David, I don't believe in physical punishment—but you wouldn't believe the trouble it made for me. I had social workers making home visits for the next two months."

"And you thought it was Alicia who called Family Services?"

She shrugged. "I don't know anyone else who dislikes me enough to make a false report."

The door burst open and David himself came running into the kitchen. "Did you call me, Mom?" he asked, then came to a halt as he spotted Travis. "Hi, Dr. Kellman!"

He was a tall, wiry twelve year old, but he didn't resemble Charlotte in the slightest. His father had been from Yemen. David had his father's olive skin and black hair. Travis wondered if that ever bothered Charlotte. He'd always liked the fact that T.J. resembled him, even though there was nothing special about light-brown hair and brown eyes.

"Hi, David. How's Bingo?"

"I'm taking him for a walk right now."

"Go ahead," Charlotte told him, "just be back by six." Before he could leave, she grabbed him and kissed the back of his head, which made him protest, "Mom! Stop it!"

She grinned as she came back to the counter. "They hate showing physical affection after the age of nine or ten. Keep it in mind." She tilted her head. "What am I saying? I'm sure you remember what that was like."

"It was never a problem with my stepmother," Travis said dryly.

Charlotte put the chicken in the oven and came over to stand in front of him. Travis remembered that he'd heard Alicia refer to her as a "peasant milkmaid", but he'd always liked her looks. Even her extra pounds were arranged pleasantly on her voluptuous figure.

"She always struck me as being very non-maternal," Charlotte said, "although to hear her talk, she was the world's greatest stepmother. Do you remember when you asked me out two years ago?"

"Sure," he said, wondering uneasily why she was bringing that up now.

"I didn't tell you the whole truth about why I didn't accept."

"I thought the age difference bothered you." Charlotte was six years older than he was. Travis hadn't seen that as a problem, but she had.

"It did, somewhat, but mostly I couldn't stand the thought of dating Alicia's stepson. I figured if things turned serious between us, I'd have to be around her all the time, or else cause a rift between you and your family. So I thought it was better not to get involved."

As Travis drove home, he mulled over what Charlotte had told him. She had always struck him as a straightforward, honest person and their conversation hadn't changed his opinion. If she had murdered Alicia, surely she wouldn't have been so forthcoming about the Family Services incident.

It was a motive, but perhaps not a strong one. The damage was done. Alicia had made the false report—if she had really been the culprit—social workers had investigated and then it was over. Was there really any point to killing Alicia for it, other than revenge?

He remembered being somewhat hurt when Charlotte hadn't wanted to go out with him, but he'd accepted the reason she'd given at the time, that she didn't date younger men. And to think it was really because of his stepmother! Just another way she'd managed to affect his life, this time without even trying.

* * * * *

On Friday, his day off from the clinic, Travis went to see Georgia during afternoon visiting hours. When he entered her room, he was relieved to find her sitting up in bed wearing a pink bed jacket. Her hair was combed, her makeup was perfect and only the large bandage wrapped around her head showed why she was in the hospital.

"Feeling better?" He pulled a chair up to her bed.

"The headache's almost gone," she said with a bright smile. Her hands smoothed the white sheet covering her legs. "Heavens, wasn't that a close call? I was a big silly to go over to that house by myself."

"I wish you'd waited for me," he agreed. "I'd have gone with you. Do you remember why you were there?"

"I think so. I was looking for something in your parents' bedroom." Her brows drew together. "I remember I found Pete's tie." She bit her lip, looking confused. "I don't know why I was looking for Pete's tie. But he's my husband, I know that now. He showed me our wedding album."

"Do you remember being married to him?"

"Sometimes. Some of it comes back to me, here and there." She reached out and picked up his ringless left hand. "But you're not married. Are you?"

"No. But I'm seeing someone that—that I'm very interested in."

"I remember her. Isn't that funny? She's a tall redhead with a black leather jacket."

"That's JayBee." Travis couldn't help smiling.

She dropped his hand and restlessly began to smooth the sheet again. "It doesn't seem quite real to me that I married Pete instead of you." She looked up, her eyes pleading with him. "I wonder what would happen if I left Pete."

"Why would you do that?" Travis asked.

She murmured, "To come back to you."

Travis drew a deep breath. "That would be a mistake. You and Pete love each other." He hoped those words were true. "And anyway, would you want to be a stepmother?"

She sighed. "Perhaps you're right. I forgot about the little boy. Have I ever seen him?"

"No, not yet."

"I didn't think so..." Her voice trailed off.

"Do you remember what else happened at the house?" Travis asked, his voice very quiet. "Besides finding Pete's tie?"

"I found something else. I know it was important. I remember I called you. But I can't remember what I said." Her voice rose in frustration.

Travis put his hand over hers, holding it still. "I don't mean to upset you, Georgie. But if you remember why you called me, will you let me know right away?"

"Was it important?"

"Possibly."

A nurse came in with a basin of water, giving Travis a look that told him he was in her way. Hastily, he moved the chair, but bumped the back of it into the basin. Some of the water sloshed onto the nurse's shoes.

"Oh! I'm so sorry!" Travis said, springing to his feet.

"Don't worry about it," the nurse said. She put the basin down on Georgia's tray table. "I'll be back in a minute."

Georgia gasped, pointing at the nurse's shoes as she exited the room. "Travis! I remember!"

"What?" he demanded.

"At Alicia's house! I was looking through things in her bedroom. She had all her shoes stored in their original boxes, stacked in the closet. So I started looking through them and that's where I found Pete's ring. I kept looking and I found someone else's shoes!"

"How did you know they weren't Alicia's?"

"They were the wrong size, silly! Alicia wore a size five. These shoes were size seven." Georgia frowned with the effort of recalling that day. "They were beige—all streaked with something dark. That's what reminded me—when I saw the streaks of water on the nurse's shoes."

"Streaked with something dark," Travis repeated thoughtfully. "Blood?"

Georgia shuddered. "That's what I thought. I could just picture it—the woman stabbing poor Alicia and the blood spurting over her shoes."

"They were women's shoes?"

"Yes! That's why I thought they would clear your dad. I picked them up, holding them with a tissue and I went into the kitchen to call you. I think I was holding them when—when I was hit."

"But there weren't any shoes found with you," Travis said.

"Because whoever hit me must have taken them," Georgia said, her tone bitter.

* * * * *

Austin MacReedy came down to the hospital to take Georgia's statement.

She told him everything she could remember and described the shoes as tan flats with one-inch heels, very plain.

"But you still can't remember who hit you?" the chief asked.

Georgia shook her head. "I was standing by the kitchen sink, looking out the window when it happened. I remember thinking that Alicia's roses needed pruning."

"Thank you, Mrs. Kellman," MacReedy said, shutting his notebook.

"That's it?" Travis asked impatiently. "Don't you see, this proves my dad wasn't the killer! Why else would someone have taken the shoes and hit Georgia over the head? Because the killer was afraid the shoes would identify her!"

MacReedy frowned and held up one hand for silence. "Mrs. Kellman, excuse me—I'm going to have to get back to the station. Trav, come out into the hall with me."

Travis looked at Georgia, concerned. She lay back against the pillows. "Go ahead, Travis," she murmured. "I'm going to take a nap until Peter comes."

"All right. See you later." Feeling MacReedy's ironic gaze on him, Travis bent and kissed Georgia on the cheek before following the chief into the hall.

They walked down to a small waiting area at the end of the hall and sat in two plastic chairs.

"Look, Trav," said the chief. "I doubt that the prosecutor will pay any attention to this information. I'm just telling you for your own good."

"Why do you say that?"

"Have you ever heard of false memory?" the chief asked.

Travis paused, taken aback. "Yes. But I don't think it applies here."

"Sure it could. What were you talking about with her before she remembered?"

"She knew she'd found something at the house, but she couldn't remember what. And then the nurse came in and what happened with the water jogged her memory."

"Or else she knew you wanted to hear what she'd found, so her subconscious made something up to please you." MacReedy shook his head. "If the shoes had been found, then we'd be getting somewhere. But without the actual evidence…"

"Sure, it would be a lot of work to open the case again," Travis said, his right hand clenching into a fist on the arm of the chair. "You and Jim Percy think you've got a tidy little case against my dad and you don't want to look at any other evidence. I still think my son's aunt and her boyfriend need to be investigated, particularly now that Georgia found a woman's shoes—"

"Oh, I've been meaning to tell you," MacReedy said, flipping through some pages in his notebook. "We've done some work on that aspect of the case. They've been cleared of suspicion."

"What? When did that happen?"

MacReedy gave him an exasperated glance. "Weren't you the one pushing for us to look into their activities that evening? We identified the boyfriend, Ray Patterson, through the license number you brought me. The hotel supplied the credit card number he was using that evening in the bar. He was charging drinks in the bar from approximately nine-thirty that evening until almost two-thirty the next morning, when the hotel bar closed." MacReedy flipped through a few more pages. "Now the coroner estimated the time of death for your stepmother between nine o'clock and midnight."

"What if Gina was using the credit card while Ray went out and murdered my stepmother?"

"That theory doesn't hold water," MacReedy said. "Detective Davidson talked to the hotel bartender. He said they were there all evening."

MacReedy pointed to Davidson's notes and read, "The bartender stated, 'I kept my eye on them most of the time. The guy, he was one tough-looking dude. Him and his girlfriend, they were putting away so much beer, I was kind of thinking I might need to call Security. I was expecting they might get rowdy, you know? But they left when I told 'em to, right around two-thirty when we close up. The girlfriend had to help the guy to the elevators. He was having some trouble walking, you know? They must have went up to their room. I didn't see them anymore after they left the bar.'"

"Maybe the coroner's time of death is wrong," Travis argued. "Maybe they left the hotel and went over to my stepmother's house at that point."

MacReedy shook his head. "I don't think so. Davidson talked to Delbert Nolan at the hotel, too—he's the head of Security there. Security was called to their room twice—at three a.m. and at three-thirty—due to complaints from guests on the same floor. Apparently Gina and Ray were arguing loudly and Security had to warn them to quiet down." He looked at Travis earnestly. "From the neighbor's statement, we know your stepmother was still alive between nine and ten. We have the approximate time of death from the coroner. Even if he's off by an hour or two, Alicia couldn't have died later than two a.m. So it just doesn't seem like Ray or Gina could have done it, not when people at the hotel saw them until three-thirty in the morning."

Disappointment held Travis silent. He realized how much he had been counting on Ray and Gina being involved in the murder. It had seemed like the perfect scenario to him, Ray, seeing the luxurious home Alicia lived in, deciding to get some money from her. Alicia refusing and Ray, angry, killing her in retaliation.

After all, a man who would beat a tiny child was capable of anything.

"The pediatrician who saw my son filed a child abuse report," Travis said.

"Yep. That came over my desk," the chief replied.

"So what will be done about that?"

"Nothing, unless Ray Patterson comes back to Ohio. We don't try to extradite for that type of minor crime."

Travis had expected as much, but he couldn't help saying bitterly, "Right, beating up a child isn't an important crime."

The chief tilted his head. "We have to be realistic here. However, I do have one piece of information you might want." He flipped through the papers and handed Travis one with nothing except a typed address:

4104 Anderson Road

Indianapolis

"Gina Madison's new address," he told Travis, who folded it and put it away carefully in his breast pocket. "And mind you—you didn't get that from me."

Chapter Fifteen

T.J. was turning cartwheels in the front yard when Travis drove up to the house on Forest Avenue. Queenie pranced around the boy, tail wagging fast. Monique, balanced on Helene's lap with her nose stuck out the window, saw Queenie and barked shrilly.

"I'm glad we have such beautiful weather for the picnic," Helene said. "I've always adored Indian summer in Ohio."

Travis nodded. Although it was October now and the leaves were changing color, it was as warm as a summer day. He pulled his father's BMW smoothly into the driveway just as JayBee stepped out of the house, a pair of inline skates slung over her shoulder. She was wearing tight cutoff denim shorts that revealed her long, shapely legs. Standing on the porch for a moment, she flipped her red hair behind her shoulders.

"Who's that girl?" Helene asked. "She's not the boy's foster mother, is she?"

"No, that's Angel's sister. Her name's JayBee."

Helene sniffed. "What was their mother thinking, giving them names like that? Put your eyes back in your head, Travis, it's rude to stare."

JayBee called T.J. to her. He hurried up the steps and took her hand. Watching with envy, Travis wondered if he would ever have that type of easy, trustful relationship with the boy.

Angel came out the front door, carrying a beverage jug and locked up the house.

Still holding T.J. by the hand, JayBee approached the car and Travis made introductions. The little boy glanced quickly at his great-grandmother, then lowered his eyes shyly.

"What do you say?" JayBee prompted him.

"Hello, Great-Grandma," he said, his voice little more than a whisper.

Helene smiled. "Good afternoon, T.J." To JayBee she added, "I see you've taught him some manners, at least."

"He's a good kid," JayBee answered, ruffling his hair as he climbed into the back seat.

Travis walked around to the other side of the car to open the back door for Angel. Inwardly dismayed by the cool, brief smile JayBee gave him, he kept his thoughts to himself.

"How's everyone been this week?" he asked as they started on their journey. *And why didn't you call me?* he silently questioned JayBee. Adjusting the rearview mirror so he could see her, their eyes met for a quick moment, then she looked away.

Angel answered him, chatting about inconsequential matters. Travis listened with only half his attention, wondering if he'd be able to get JayBee alone. He needed to have things settled, one way or the other.

* * * * *

JayBee jumped out of the car the minute Travis pulled into the parking lot. She eyed Travis covertly, watching as he walked around and helped his grandmother to her feet, then opened the back door for Angel, offering his hand as she got out of the car. Angel took it with a glowing smile.

He looked damned good today, JayBee thought, in his tan Dockers and brown-plaid cotton shirt. The neck of the shirt was open and she could see the faint, curling hairs on his chest.

T.J. clung close to her. He'd hardly said a word since Travis arrived at the house.

Travis bent down to speak to his son. "Since we're the two men here, why don't you help me get the picnic things out of the trunk?"

Looking pleased at the idea, T.J. tugged on JayBee's hand. "You come too."

Angel said to Helene, "Let's go find a picnic table."

"Get one with a grill," Travis told them. Turning back to T.J., he said, "Come see what I've got in the trunk."

The boy came closer, his eyes wide with curiosity. Travis opened the trunk to reveal a boy's blue bicycle with training wheels.

"This is for you, T.J." Travis lifted it out and set it down carefully.

T.J. gasped in delight. "For me?" The new bicycle sparkled in the midday sunlight.

"That's right. You can learn to ride it with the training wheels, then when you get a little bigger, I'll take the training wheels off and teach you to ride it without them."

"Wow! Great bike!" JayBee said. "Look, T.J., it's got a horn. See if it works."

T.J. squeezed the bulb, sounding the horn. A startled Queenie barked at it and T.J. grinned. "Look, Queenie! It's my very own bike! Just like Tommy's, only brand-new!"

Queenie wagged her tail, responding to the excitement in the boy's voice. Travis held the bike steady while T.J. climbed on. "Don't go too fast just at first," he cautioned his son. He already sounded like a father, JayBee thought, watching them with a smile.

T.J. started out tentatively. The bike rocked a little from side to side as he got used to balancing. Queenie tried to follow him, but Travis grabbed her collar, holding her back. T.J. rode fifteen feet away from them, then turned the handlebars and started back. He waved at JayBee. "Look! I'm riding my bike!"

"You did great!" Travis said. "You know what? I'll bet Angel and Grandma would like to see your bike." He lifted a big cooler out of the trunk.

"I can take something." Spotting a bag of charcoal, JayBee hoisted it out of the trunk.

"I'll come back for that," Travis protested.

"That's okay. I got it." She lifted it up on her shoulder and started off toward the picnic table. T.J. hurried after her, walking the bike.

"Look! Look what Daddy gave me!" he told Angel with a big grin as they reached the picnic area.

There were twenty tables scattered over a quarter-mile area, about half of them with in-ground grills. An open-wall shelter was nearby. JayBee wondered why anyone would want to be under a roof on such a lovely day, but there were several groups of people in there.

Helene and Angel examined the bike, making admiring comments. Travis went to the grill.

"It was so sweet of you to get him a bike," Angel said, walking over to Travis as he slit open the bag of charcoal with a penknife.

"Something JayBee said gave me the idea."

Angel smiled at him, tossing her blonde hair behind her neck with a casual gesture. "He's been talking about a bike since the day he came to us."

He poured charcoal into the grill and took a can of lighter fluid out of the cooler. "I really appreciate everything you've done for him. I know it's been a lot of work, taking care of him all day."

"Yes—but he's worth it." She put her hand on Travis' arm. "He's such a smart little boy. But that's to be expected. You have to be really intelligent to be a vet, don't you?"

JayBee listened to this with growing indignation, wondering just what Angel was up to. She watched Travis' face, wondering how he would react to Angel's overt flattery.

Travis sprinkled the charcoal with lighter fluid. The pungent odor filled the air. "To be a vet? You have to like animals. And not be bothered by vomit and feces."

Angel, looking startled, made a face.

T.J. tugged at JayBee's sleeve. "I want to ride my bike some more."

She took him back to the parking lot and watched while he mounted the bike by himself and started pedaling. Opening the back door of the car, she took out her inline skates, kneepads and helmet.

After donning her equipment, she began performing slow circles in the empty part of the parking lot. It was too bad Tecumseh County didn't have a real skating park, like there had been in Dayton.

Sometimes it was easier to think when she was moving around, doing something athletic. Okay, suppose she told Travis that she didn't want to get involved right now. Of course, she knew she didn't like seeing him with Angel. There had always been a competitive spirit between them, not to mention Angel's theft of Bradley. But suppose Travis was with some other woman…would that bother her?

She tried to imagine him with Charlotte Scott, someone she liked, a nice woman who could use a good man in her life. Travis would be a fine stepfather for Charlotte's young son and little T.J. certainly needed a mother. She pictured them all on a picnic together, just like today. Travis would prepare the grill while the two boys played ball together. Charlotte, coming up behind him, would put her arm around his waist. He would turn and give her one of those sweet, exciting kisses…

JayBee's stomach lurched unpleasantly.

Well, that was clear enough.

She might be scared to get involved with a man again, but nothing would be worse than seeing him with another woman.

She skated to the far edge of the lot, picking up speed and then jumped over a concrete parking-space divider. When she turned back, she found Travis leaning against the BMW watching her, his arms folded across his chest.

She came toward him fast. He straightened, putting his hands out to catch her, but she stopped a foot away.

"Don't worry, I know what I'm doing," she said, laughing and lifted off her helmet.

"I can see that. You're really good! I couldn't believe it when I saw that jump." He smiled into her eyes. "I thought about you a lot this week." His voice was low. "Seems like no matter what else I'm doing, I'm thinking about you."

She came closer to him as he reached up and gently pushed a stray lock of hair away from her face. Something might have come of that, except that T.J. rode his bicycle up at that moment.

"I'd better get back to the grill," Travis said. JayBee stayed behind for awhile, watching T.J. When he got tired of riding the bicycle, they rejoined the picnic group.

JayBee went over and sat by Angel, who was hugging her arms around herself, looking down.

"Depressed because he wouldn't flirt with you?" JayBee asked.

"I wasn't flirting."

"Give me a break."

Angel flipped her hair back. "Okay, maybe I was, but not because I'm interested in him. I was testing him. You don't want another boyfriend who would dump you just because I smiled at him, right?"

"Don't do me any favors."

Angel shivered and wrapped her arms around herself more tightly.

"Are you cold?" JayBee asked, trying not to sound overly sympathetic.

"Just feeling a little anxious," Angel answered with a wan smile.

JayBee tried to hide her disappointment. Angel had been outside with T.J. several times in the last week and JayBee had had high hopes that her sister was getting over the agoraphobia. "You don't want to leave before we eat, do you?" she asked anxiously.

"No, I think I'll be all right," Angel said, taking a deep breath.

* * * * *

Travis grilled hotdogs and steak shish kabob, his attention partially on his task and partially on his son, who was playing ball with JayBee and the two dogs.

The sun was shining, making the grill cook's job a hot one. He rolled up his shirtsleeves and opened his shirt one button lower.

The bicycle had been a success. He knew you couldn't buy a child's affection. Still, children remembered who had given them things. He recalled the circumstances of every bicycle he had ever received, the Christmas he had gotten an electric train set and his tenth birthday catcher's mitt.

If only the child would talk to him. It hurt every time T.J. looked at him with those scared eyes, as though he were some kind of tyrant concealing a whip. Animals usually trusted him after a short while, even sick, frightened ones. Why couldn't he make any headway with his own son?

He watched T.J. running through the grass, those busy little legs pumping hard. The child spun around laughing as JayBee threw the ball to him.

Even though he'd met his son only two weeks ago, he loved him already. It was a tremendously powerful feeling and not what he'd expected. He'd always known he would have children someday. He'd thought love would grow slowly, increasing as the children grew older. But this wasn't like that—it was more like being hit with a bolt of lightning, a jolt that had knocked him out of his old life and into a new state of mind. Everything now would have to be looked at in terms of the boy.

He thought of places he'd liked to go as a boy. Niagara Falls, the beach, amusement parks. All that could be enjoyed again, this time sharing it with his son.

His eyes lingered on JayBee. He and his son needed her. He'd never known a woman like her before. But now that he knew she existed, he'd never be happy without her.

As for T.J., now that he had seen the boy interacting with both Angel and JayBee, he could see which one was the boy's real foster mother.

JayBee came over to the grill, looking eagerly at the food. "Wow, look at those shish kabobs! Did you make 'em?"

"If I say yes, will you be impressed?"

Her eyes laughed at him. "They're from Pooley's, aren't they?"

"That's right," he admitted. "I got the potato salad there too. And the pasta salad. Remember, I told you right up front that I don't cook."

"Then how are you going to feed T.J. when you get him?" JayBee asked.

Travis had been turning the shish kabob, but now he stopped dead, looking at her. "Good Lord, I never thought of that."

She snickered at the expression on his face. "Don't worry, I'm sure you'll be able to learn some easy recipes."

"I hope so. I was always good at chemistry. Cooking's pretty similar, right?"

Her lips twitched. "Keep the emergency numbers handy."

"Maybe my sister Katie will help. She's a great cook."

"Is she all right?" JayBee asked. "I heard she was in the hospital."

"No, it's my sister-in-law who was hurt, not Katie. She was released last night."

"What happened?"

Travis told her about the attack on Georgia. JayBee frowned, thinking it through. "But if a woman's bloody shoes were found in the house and the shoes didn't belong to your stepmother, they must have belonged to the murderer!"

Travis nodded. "That's my theory." He spread his hands helplessly. "But without the shoes, there's no evidence. Georgia made a police report. I talked to the prosecutor myself. But everyone acts as though the shoes are irrelevant." He told JayBee about his unsatisfactory meeting with Jim Percy, the prosecutor. "He said right to my face that he won't take Georgia's word about what happened."

"I can't believe that! To me, this means your father couldn't have done the murder."

"I agree. But the prosecutor has a good case against my dad. He's not willing to let it go because of some 'possibly nonexistent shoes'." His brows drew together. "Even if the shoes had been found, it's not so easy to match them to a person. Georgia said they were common tan flats. Size seven."

JayBee looked down at her own feet. "Rules me out. I wear a ten."

"I did a little research on the internet. Size eight is the most common size for women. So seven must be fairly common too."

JayBee nodded. "I think so. Angel wears a seven."

"So does my sister. Anyway, the shoes don't prove the murderer had to be a woman. It could have been a woman helping a man." He thought of Gina and Ray. No matter what

MacReedy said, he still wondered if one of them had killed Alicia.

"I'm glad your sister-in-law recovered. My goodness, she might have been killed too!"

"She hasn't totally recovered. It's going to take some time."

JayBee looked concerned. "Will she be all right, do you think?"

"I'm not sure." He looked at JayBee cautiously. "It was pretty upsetting there for awhile. She had a memory gap when she first woke up. Thought it was last year. If I were a certain type of man—well, let's just say I could have gotten back at my brother for stealing my fiancée."

JayBee got it at once. "You mean she thought she was still engaged to you?"

"Something like that," he admitted.

JayBee's voice was deceptively calm as she said, "That must have been tempting. You were terribly in love with her at one time, weren't you?"

He met her eyes squarely. "It was briefly tempting, yes. But then I thought about you. And I thought about T.J.'s welfare, too."

JayBee's eyes narrowed. "That was the major consideration? Which of us would be the better mother for T.J.?"

"I didn't say that."

"It sounds to me like you were thinking it."

"I think you misunderstood—"

JayBee's breath came fast and short. "When I'm with a man, I expect to be loved for myself!" she told him. "Not because I can cook—or because I make a good salary—and certainly not because he needs someone to care for his kids!" She put her hands on her hips. "Is that why you kissed me in the cemetery?"

"No!"

"Wasn't it the same day you found your son?"

"The kiss had nothing to do with that!"

She looked at him for a long moment, her lips set in a thin, straight line. "I have three words for you."

He stared at her, expecting she would tell him to go to hell.

"Hire a nanny!" She strode away to the picnic table.

* * * * *

"Were you fighting?" Angel purred as JayBee sat down next to her.

"No," JayBee lied, but it was never easy for her to hide her feelings. She sat silent as Angel helped Travis unpack the lunch. Travis was quiet, too, as they ate. Angel and Helene had found they shared a love for musical theater and talked about it extensively during the meal.

As soon as he'd eaten a hot dog, washed down with orange pop, T.J. went back to playing with the dogs. JayBee watched him chasing Monique and then being chased by her in turn. The little poodle looked like she was having a wonderful time with the boy.

T.J. fell, catching himself with his hands, then let out a loud wail. JayBee jumped up and ran to him.

Travis, who'd been throwing away the lunch paper plates, hurried to the boy as he kept on crying.

"T.J.! What's wrong? What is it?" JayBee demanded, thoughts of broken bones filling her mind. The child clung to her, choking and sobbing so hard that he couldn't catch his breath. She put her arms around him, but he only cried harder. "T.J.!" she exclaimed, feeling helpless and panicky.

Travis knelt down and put his hand on his son's shoulder. He spoke in a deep, quiet voice. "T.J., you're scaring Queenie. You don't want to scare her, do you?"

T.J. made a visible effort to get control over himself. He reached out and petted the dog, who was nudging him with her nose. "It's okay, Queenie," he said, choking back his sobs. He held out his hand toward JayBee. "Look!"

Travis took his hand by the wrist, holding it up. JayBee saw a large, reddish welt on the boy's palm.

"Looks like you got stung by a bee," Travis said. He picked his son up and carried him over to the picnic table, asking, "Anyone have tweezers?"

JayBee, following along feeling useless, didn't even have her purse with her, but Angel was carrying a purse that contained a makeup bag, including tweezers.

"Wait," said Helene, retrieving a small silver flask from her purse. "Better sterilize them with this."

Travis raised his eyebrows at his grandmother's contribution, but took the flask without comment, pouring some of the alcohol over the tweezers. Seating himself at the table in front of T.J., he took the boy's hand and looked seriously at him. "Now, T.J., this may hurt a little bit, but I have to pull the stinger out. Do you understand?"

T.J., his face frightened, jerked his hand away. He looked desperately at JayBee for help.

She came over and sat down beside him on the tabletop. "Let your daddy take the stinger out, T.J. Then you'll feel better."

"Do I have to?"

"Yes, you have to. Give your daddy your hand and I'll tell you a story. Which one would you like?"

All the adults held their breath while T.J. pondered what JayBee had said. Finally, he held the stung hand out to Travis. "Tell me about the elves making shoes."

JayBee took his other hand and began to tell the story in as bright and lively a manner as she could muster.

"Ow!" the boy exclaimed.

"Sorry!" Travis said. "Look, T.J., I pulled the stinger out. It's all over."

T.J. sobbed a few times, his mouth trembling, while Travis took a clean handkerchief out of his pocket, wet it with the alcohol and cleaned around the welt.

"You were a brave boy." JayBee gave him a hug.

T.J. managed a faint smile. "I'm going to play with the dogs now."

Travis, a rueful expression on his face, watched as the boy slid down from the table. "My first long visit with my son and he has to get hurt."

"If it doesn't need stitches, it's not that serious," Angel told him. "It seems like we were at the emergency room every other week when we were kids. JayBee was always banging herself up."

T.J. and the dogs played for awhile without incident. Gradually, they moved farther and farther away from the picnic area as T.J. threw the ball and they raced after it. Then JayBee saw Queenie lie down and roll on the ground, her three legs waving in the air.

"Uh oh," Travis said. "Looks like Queenie found a mud puddle." Jumping up, he called to her. She sprang to her feet and stood listening. He called again and this time she galloped toward him, T.J. and Monique following.

Queenie's glossy coat was caked with wet gray mud. Shaking his head, Travis scooped up Monique and handed her to his grandmother. "I'm going to take Queenie down to the creek. Keep an eye on Monique and don't let her follow us. She's too little to play in the creek. I don't want her to get hurt."

"Can I come too?" T.J. begged. "I want to see the creek!"

Travis looked surprised, then smiled. "Sure, you come too."

The two of them walked off together, Queenie loping along at T.J.'s side. JayBee began to wrap up the leftover food. Tearing a half-eaten hot dog into smaller bites, she put it on a plate for Monique. The little poodle jumped down from Helene's lap and wolfed the pieces.

"There's that nosy man again," Helene said, sounding annoyed.

"What man?" JayBee asked.

"In the shelter. He has binoculars—he was watching us as we ate lunch."

Angel stood up, shading her eyes with her hand and squinting. "Oh my God, I think it's Bradley!" she whispered.

JayBee gritted her teeth. "Damn it, I told him to let us alone!" She laid down the dish she was wrapping. Angel caught her arm.

"No, JayBee—just ignore him! Let's pretend we never saw him!"

He walked out of the shelter, sauntering slowly toward them. JayBee shook off her sister's hand. "The hell with that. I'm going to give him a piece of my mind!"

She strode out to meet him, thinking, *damn it, I'm not going to let him scare Angel.* Monique followed along at her heels.

"What are you doing here?" she demanded as soon as she was within speaking distance.

He stopped and folded his arms, giving her a sly smirk. "Just keeping an eye on you and my lovely wife."

"I told you to stay away from us!"

"It's a public park, Juliet. So, which of you is dating that man who had lunch with you?"

"He's the father of our foster child. And you'd better leave before he gets back!"

"I'm not scared of him, or of you either, Juliet." He looked down at Monique, who stared back at him and barked shrilly.

He aimed a kick at her. Jumping away, she barked again. Bradley laughed. "Did you bring the baby poodle along to intimidate me? I'll let you in on a little secret—it's not working."

"Brad, I don't understand what you want. You need to get on with your life and let us get on with ours."

"I don't have a life anymore. They take away your stockbroker's license once you commit a felony, did you know that? I've got only one thing to think about now—revenge."

Monique had kept up a steady barking while he spoke. Suddenly, Bradley bent and snatched the little dog off the ground, holding her by the throat and letting her legs dangle. She squealed and moved her head, trying to bite, but he twisted her collar, restraining her head.

"Let go of her!" JayBee cried, darting forward.

"No, no, no!" he warned her, thrusting the dog out at arm's length. "You come another step forward, Juliet dear and I'll break her neck!"

"You wouldn't!"

"I'd like to do it, just to see your face!" He tilted his head, laughing at her. Squeezing the dog's neck, he listened as she squealed again. JayBee measured the distance between them, wondering if she could kick him in the balls before he could kill Monique. She had no doubt he would do it.

"Brad—please! Don't hurt the dog. Put her down!"

His smile was sickening to see. "Remember how you broke my arm, Juliet? I'd like to break yours, just to show you how it feels. But you're a lot stronger than this little bitch. So maybe I'll just break her leg, instead."

"No!"

He held Monique's right front paw in his hand and jerked it up suddenly. But he had loosened his grip on her neck. Moving her head like a snake striking, Monique bit his hand. With a roar, Bradley dropped her to the ground.

JayBee leaped forward but he was faster. Cradling his bleeding, bitten hand, he took off running. She pounded after him, but stopped when she heard a high, keening wail from Monique. She couldn't just leave Monique back there, injured. Reluctantly, she returned to the little dog.

Monique sat on the ground, frantically licking her dangling right paw. Tears ran down her cheeks as she picked the dog up, cuddling her in her arms.

"Give her to me," said Helene, walking forward. There were tears in her eyes, too. "Run down to the creek and find my grandson. He'll know what to do."

Chapter Sixteen

JayBee ran toward the creek at full speed, heedless of stones and tree branches, stumbling as she almost tripped on some slick mud. She caught her balance and kept going, her mind centered on one thought, find Travis.

Travis and his son were standing side by side, watching Queenie swim toward a large stick. The dog got it in her mouth and moved toward the bank, her head lifted triumphantly.

"Travis!"

He seemed to know immediately that something was wrong. Perhaps her voice had given her away. Turning, he came toward her quickly. "What's the matter, honey?" He touched the tear tracks on her cheeks.

Hearing the concern in his voice made her feel slightly better. "Monique's hurt! I think her leg's broken."

"What happened?"

T.J. ran up, his brown eyes wide and anxious. JayBee realized she couldn't tell Travis the real story, not in front of the boy. "She—uh—she jumped down off the table and slipped."

Travis' brows drew together. Before he could say anything, JayBee added, "Come on, she needs help!"

Quickly, they made their way back to the picnic area, where a white-faced Angel was loading the last few dishes back into the cooler. Helene held Monique, trying to keep her calm by petting her.

Travis took the dog carefully from his grandmother and examined her leg. "Broken," he told everyone. "I'll take her to the clinic." He looked at the three women. "Do the rest of you want to stay here or should I take you home?"

"I want to go to the clinic with you," JayBee said. "I can help, if you need someone to hold her." She looked anxiously at her sister. "Do you want to be taken home first, Angel?"

"No," said Angel, her voice firm. "We'll all go to the clinic. If that's all right with you, Helene?"

Helene nodded.

JayBee whispered, "I'm proud of you," as she got into the car beside her sister.

Angel murmured, "I'd think I'd be more afraid at home alone."

* * * * *

At the clinic, Helene and Angel stayed in the waiting room with Queenie while JayBee went into the examining room to help Travis if she could. She tried to get T.J. to stay with Angel but he said he wanted to help Monique too. "That's all right, let him come in," said Travis.

As he worked on the little dog, he explained everything to his son. "I'm going to give Monique a shot. It will relax her and take away her pain."

"I hate shots," T.J. said.

"No one likes them, but sometimes they're necessary," Travis said, giving Monique the injection between her shoulders. She whimpered a little, but held still for it.

"Tell her she's a good dog," Travis suggested.

T.J. reached up and patted Monique's head, saying, "Good dog! Good dog, Monique!" She licked the boy's hand.

After a few minutes, the little poodle closed her eyes and fell asleep. Travis carried her to another room to x-ray her leg.

"Angel took me to the doctor," T.J. mentioned to JayBee as they waited for Travis to come back. "He gave me a lollipop."

"That's right," JayBee said.

"Is Daddy a doctor for dogs?"

"Yes and for other kinds of animals. He takes care of cats and birds, too."

"What about gerbils?"

"Probably."

"What about cows?"

"I don't know. You'll have to ask him."

"Did he ever give a shot to a lion or a tiger?" T.J. asked, his eyes growing wide at the thought.

JayBee was spared from having to answer when Travis came back into the room. "It's a simple fracture," he told them, sounding relieved. While the poodle slept on, he set her leg in a spoon cast and put a shield around her neck. The poor dog looks like she's wearing a lampshade, JayBee thought.

"What's that?" T.J. asked.

"That will keep her from chewing on the cast," Travis said. "We're all done here, T.J. Go tell Grandma and Angel we're going to leave in a few minutes."

As soon as the boy left the room, Travis turned to JayBee, his expression stern. "Now tell me what really happened."

"What do you mean?"

"You wouldn't have been that upset just because the dog fell off the table."

"Okay," JayBee admitted. "It was Bradley."

"What?"

"Bradley Morrow, Angel's ex-husband. He was watching us from the shelter. I went over to confront him and Monique followed me. He picked her up—he was threatening to break her neck. But instead he broke her leg…"

She trailed off as she observed Travis' reaction to her story. His usual expression of tolerant good-humor had left his face. His eyes flashed and he was white around the mouth with anger. "Are you telling me he hurt my dog purposely?" he demanded. "You're certain it wasn't some kind of accident?"

"It was revenge for when I broke his arm," JayBee explained.

"Broke his arm! When did that happen?"

JayBee let out a strained sigh. It wasn't a story she liked to tell, particularly since she hadn't won the fight. And anyway, it made her sound a little too tough and unfeminine, not the impression she wanted to give this man. "It happened back when he was married to Angel. He was hurting her, so I tried to stop him. We got into a fight and I karate-chopped his arm and broke it." She looked at him apprehensively.

"Good for you!" JayBee heard nothing but admiration in his voice. "Too bad it wasn't his neck. Do you know where he's staying?"

"Why?"

"Because he's going to answer to me for what he did."

"He was staying at Embassy Suites last week. But I'll bet he'll check out. What he did—isn't it a crime? Cruelty to animals?"

"Purposely injuring a companion animal is a first-degree misdemeanor."

"I'll fill out a police report tomorrow," she told him.

He drove them home as T.J. questioned him excitedly about what kinds of animals he'd worked on. "No, I've never treated a lion or a tiger," he told his son, who looked disappointed. "But I helped clean an elephant's teeth, when I was in vet school."

"Did it try to bite you?" T.J. asked.

"No, she was a very friendly elephant." He added reflectively, "I was bitten by a snake once."

JayBee asked, "A poisonous snake?"

"Actually, yes." He shook his head. "I was careless that day. Luckily we had anti-venom handy."

When they got to the house on Forest Avenue, Travis unloaded the bicycle for his son. JayBee prompted T.J., "Say thank you to your daddy for the nice day."

Travis raised his eyebrows, giving her an ironic look. But T.J. seemed to have forgotten the bee sting as he said, "Thank you, Daddy. When can I ride my bike without the training wheels?"

Travis put his hands on the boy's shoulders. "I'll come over and take them off this week, if Angel says it's all right. How would that be?"

"Okay."

Travis bent and kissed the boy's forehead. "Good night, son." Turning quickly, he started back to his truck.

T.J. took JayBee's hand. "Can I have my bike in my bedroom?"

"No. I'll put it in the garage." When he looked unhappy with that, she added, "Your bike can keep my motorcycle company."

"Okay," he said, cheering up again.

"Go inside and see what Angel's doing."

"I don't want to."

"Go inside now," JayBee said, using her stern teacher's voice. T.J. pouted, but went inside.

JayBee walked over to Travis' truck. She watched him belt up, knowing him well enough now to read the sadness in his face.

"I had a good time—at least up until the end," she said.

"I shouldn't have left you alone."

"None of us knew that Bradley would show up. It wasn't your fault." He had his elbow leaning on the windowsill. She put her hand on his arm. "I think you're really good with T.J."

"I don't know…I feel like I didn't make any headway."

"Sure you did. He just needs time. Come over tomorrow and see him, if you like. I'll make it okay with Angel."

He looked interested at that, but then his face fell. "I'm sorry, but I can't. I have other plans."

She wondered what could be more important than spending time with his son. Feeling that she had reached out to him and been rejected, she said coldly, "Okay. See you later."

"Wait!" he said as she turned to leave. "I wouldn't want you to think… Sunday's the only day I can do this, because it's going to take some time. I have an address for the boy's aunt, Gina Madison. I'm going to go see her tomorrow."

"Oh! How did you find her?"

"Don't ask. She's in Indianapolis, so I'm going to leave early in the morning, probably around seven o'clock." He frowned. "Let's see—if I leave at seven…" His voice dropped off as he added up the time. "Maybe I could come over around four o'clock tomorrow. But don't tell T.J. I wouldn't want to disappoint him if I don't make it back that early."

"Okay. See you tomorrow, then." She watched him drive away, wishing they hadn't fought at the picnic. She'd have liked a goodbye kiss.

Wheeling the new bike into the garage, she locked the door.

* * * * *

On Sunday morning, Travis was coming out of the barn when his sister hailed him from her doorway. "You're up early," he commented.

"I was painting. The light's so good this morning. What were you doing?"

"Working out." He wiped his forehead with his handkerchief.

She stood back from the doorway, motioning him in. "Come have some coffee. I just made it. Oh and I borrowed your Sunday paper. You probably want it back…"

"Yes, I certainly do," he said, coming into her kitchen. It was a worse mess than he'd ever seen it. Several weeks' worth of dirty dishes littered every surface. The trash was overflowing and there were three other filled bags that she had not yet taken out. He frowned to see his newspaper scattered all over the table in pieces.

"Sorry, I need to straighten up today." She poured him a cup of coffee. "Let's go into my studio." She looked through several pieces of the paper until she located a particular section. "Read this," she told him, handing him the paper as they went into the studio. She cleared a chair by moving the paint tubes and rags that were on it to another chair.

Travis sat and opened the paper. Katie pointed to a full-page feature article about Alicia's murder.

"Great," muttered Travis. "Just what we need, more publicity."

"Wait until you read the quote from Grandma."

Travis skimmed the article, which retold all the facts about the murder and the evidence against Robert Kellman. There were comments from some of Alicia's friends and neighbors, most of them critical of Robert, although Denise MacReedy was quoted as saying, "I can't believe it was Dr. Robert Kellman. He saved my life when I had cancer."

But the most damaging quote was from Helene. "Of course Robert must have done it. And I know why. He has a mistress. I'm not going to name names, but she's the principal of a private girl's school in Dayton. My poor daughter Alicia was just in the way."

"Can you believe that?" Katie demanded, reading the article over Travis' shoulder. "Where did she get all that? It can't be true!"

Travis refolded the paper. "It is true," he said quietly. "It doesn't mean Dad is a murderer, but it looks bad. It gives him a motive for murdering Alicia."

"Dad has a mistress?" Katie asked in a near-whisper. "Are you sure, Travis?"

"I'm afraid so."

Katie looked horrified. "But this is terrible! Up until now, there wasn't any reason for Dad to do it. But now they'll say he wanted to get Maman out of the way because of this other woman!"

Travis nodded. He had been hoping the information would never come out. Damn Helene anyway.

"Travis, if Dad didn't murder Maman, who did?" Katie asked, looking at him intently.

"Hell, Katie, if I knew, would I sit here and let Dad stand trial?"

"I don't know," she murmured. "You didn't like Maman."

"I didn't dislike her enough to kill her!" he retorted.

"Even though she was blackmailing you?"

Travis stared at his sister. "How do you know that?"

Katie gazed down at her feet. "I overheard her talking to you. The day of the reconciliation dinner. When she took you into the parlor, I opened the kitchen door so I could hear."

He gripped her arm. "Katie, I swear to you, I didn't kill her. Even though she tried to blackmail me." He looked directly into her eyes. "All right, you asked me a hard question. I'm going to throw one right back at you. This mysterious boyfriend you were seeing—did he have anything to do with the murder?"

She let out a short bark of laugher. "No! He'd be the last person to do something like that."

"Who is he?"

She licked her lips, then shook her head. "I don't want to tell you."

"Why not?"

"Just let it go, okay? It's my business."

Travis frowned, wondering if it would do any good to press her about it. But it really was her business, so he decided not to badger her.

Possibly to distract him, she said, "Come look at my new painting." She had a large canvas by the window, covered with a sheet. "I think it's going pretty well. Actually, it's almost done."

He walked over and stood in front of the canvas. She whisked away the sheet.

Travis found himself staring into the eyes of his stepmother. It was a life-size head and upper torso view, with an abstract background of swirling, pulsing reds and purples. Alicia's eyes looked challengingly from the canvas. Her lips were crimson, the way they had been at the showing. A matching crimson rose, pinned to her bosom, brought to mind the stab wound that had killed her. Her blonde hair fluttered as though a strong breeze blew through the background. He gazed at the portrait in horrified fascination. There was something both compelling and repelling about it.

"What do you think?"

"It may be the best thing you've ever done," he said slowly. And yet—he couldn't put his finger on why—it was somehow deeply disturbing.

Katie carefully covered it again. "I hope Dad gets a chance to see it someday. I was really painting it for him." Her mouth trembled. "But maybe I'll keep it, now that I know he has a mistress."

Travis said gently, "It doesn't mean he didn't love your mother."

"Maybe." She tossed her head. "Anyway, I still believe he's innocent. Don't you?"

"Absolutely."

"And he's innocent until proven guilty. Isn't that right? So they can't convict him."

Travis hesitated. "I don't know, Katie. Innocent people do get convicted." He sighed. "Dad just doesn't deserve to have his life cut short over something like this."

Katie's eyes opened wide. "They wouldn't give him the death penalty, would they?"

Travis said hastily, "No, probably not."

"Then why did you say that? What exactly did you mean?" Her dark eyes bored into his.

"Well…life in prison is a scary prospect. I'm not sure Dad can face it."

"He said something, didn't he?" she demanded.

Travis wished he'd never gotten into this conversation. He didn't really want to tell Katie what their father had said, but he'd backed himself into a corner. "He said he'll kill himself if he's convicted."

Her eyes filled with tears. Half-whispering, she asked, "Do you think he meant it?"

Travis said, "No, probably not." But he could tell from Katie's expression that she knew he was lying.

* * * * *

Back in his house, Travis showered and dressed. It was already seven o'clock, so he decided he would grab a bite to eat on the road rather than take the time to eat at home. He had just finished replenishing the animals' food bowls when he heard the roar of a motorcycle coming up the gravel drive.

Travis stood watching as JayBee dismounted from her motorcycle, thinking what a welcome sight she was in the early morning. She lifted her helmet off, shaking her head and her glorious red hair spilled out around her shoulders. Her outfit was western-oriented today—faded jeans with studs down the sides, brown leather boots with steel toes and a dark-green, long-sleeved shirt with snap fastenings.

He came out on the back step. "Going to the rodeo?"

She grinned, her dimples peeping out. "I'm so glad I caught you before you left. I wanted to tell you, Angel and T.J. are going to Dayton to see my father and they're staying overnight. So you won't be able to visit today. I'm sorry."

"Why didn't you call me?"

"I didn't want to wake up your grandmother." Reaching into the saddlebag of her motorcycle, she pulled out her purse. "Besides, I thought maybe I'd come with you today."

She wants to come with me. His first reaction was a glowing happiness that she had sought him out to spend time with him. But then caution set in. "I don't know if I ought to let you."

"Why not?"

"This Ray Patterson, Gina's boyfriend—he sounds like he could be trouble. And I've got a bone to pick with him."

"Exactly. So it's good for you to have backup."

"Back-up! The last thing I want is for you to get hurt."

"Okay, forget I said that. I'm just coming to meet T.J.'s aunt." She looked at him carefully, apparently able to tell from his body language that he was about to refuse to let her accompany him. "Besides, if I don't ride in the truck, I'll just follow you on my motorcycle."

"Then I guess all I can say is, get in the truck."

* * * * *

As they drove along the highway, JayBee asked, "How's Monique doing?"

"So far, so good. My grandmother's flying home today and she's going to take Monique with her in a carrier." Travis smiled. "I thought it was kind of nice, to have Alicia's dog go to Alicia's mother."

"That is nice," said JayBee. "I could tell she was fond of Monique."

"I went looking for Bradley last night, after I dropped everyone off," Travis went on. "He'd checked out of Embassy Suites. He wasn't at the Holiday Inn or Day's Inn, either, at least not under that name." JayBee nodded as though she weren't surprised. "Kevin, the bartender at the Paradise Inn, knows who he is," Travis continued. "I gave him a twenty. If Bradley shows his face in there again, Kevin will call me and get another twenty for his trouble."

"Good," she said, giving him a smile. "I went to the police station last night and filled out a report. So I guess we've got all the bases covered."

After two hours in the truck together, Travis decided that JayBee was a great traveling companion. She wasn't a chatterbox, like Alicia and Georgia and even Katie at times. During part of the journey they talked, but when he turned on the radio, she listened to NPR with him and made several intelligent comments. Their political views were similar. Believing strongly in women's rights, she spoke movingly about her concern for women in third-world countries.

Moving on to lighter topics, they discussed sports and found they were both football fans. It didn't surprise him to learn she was a woman who liked sports. "I like baseball, too. And pro wrestling," she said.

"Pro wrestling isn't a sport."

Her dimples were peeping out again. "Whatever it is, I like it."

"What do you like about it?"

Her grin broadened. "Where else can I see great-looking hunks wearing tight outfits?"

Travis found that so annoying that he turned on the radio again.

As they traveled on, he found his mind drifting away from the program. JayBee had tucked her chin down and closed her eyes. So far, they'd managed to avoid any discussion of their personal lives. He wasn't sure how he felt about that. Remembering how they'd clashed the day before, he decided it might be for the best. He would need all his energy to deal with Gina and Ray.

* * * * *

JayBee looked dubiously up at the apartment building. Each front window had an outside balcony, but the wrought iron railings were rusted. The windows on the top floor were boarded up. The grass around the apartment hadn't been mown in weeks. A sign in front of the building had once proclaimed its name to be "Crestview Arms", but green and purple graffiti now defaced it.

She opened her door and jumped out, not waiting for Travis to come around to her side of the truck. There were empty beer bottles on the tree lawn and she barely avoided stepping on one.

"Apparently they're not doing very well," Travis said, looking around with a frown of distaste. "Dale told me that Ray mostly lived off Gina."

"What kind of job does Gina have?"

"I don't know. She was still in high school when I knew her sister." He offered JayBee his arm as they walked toward the building. She took it, happy to have the comfort of physical contact when they were approaching a strange place.

JayBee reeled back as they walked into the vestibule. The odor of vomit was overpowering.

"The aftermath of Saturday night," Travis murmured. He punched the doorbell for apartment 210, which had the label "Patterson-Madison".

As the buzzer sounded, JayBee grabbed the door handle and they headed up the stairs. A blonde woman appeared in the doorway of 210, barefoot and wearing a bathrobe. "Did you buzz me?"

Travis stopped. "Hi. Are you Gina Madison?"

Eyes wide, she nodded. "Who are you?"

"I'm Travis Kellman, your nephew's father. Mind if we come in?"

"I just got up. Can you go out back and wait? There's a picnic table out there."

"All right," Travis agreed.

He and JayBee walked out and around to the back of the building. If possible, it was even more cheerless than the front. A row of garages held various rusty beaters. The picnic table, chained to a tree, was missing one of its slats on top. JayBee sat down, stretching out her long legs. "Think she'll really come down?" she asked.

Travis sighed. "I hope so."

"Well, if she doesn't, we've just wasted several hours."

He smiled and took her hand. "Time spent with you is never wasted."

"I was just thinking, what if she doesn't want to talk to us? Maybe I should go out front and make sure she doesn't take off."

He tightened his hold on her hand. "No way. We'll stick together in this neighborhood."

In a few minutes, Gina came walking down the back fire-escape stairway. She was a short woman with large breasts and thick legs. Her cutoff denim shorts didn't meet her skimpy black t-shirt, revealing several inches of overweight flesh.

"Thanks for coming down to talk to us," Travis said.

"Yeah, well, sorry I couldn't invite you in. Ray's super hung-over today. He'd be mad as hell if we woke him up." She sat down facing them.

Travis gave an understanding nod. "This is my friend, JayBee Hauser. JayBee and her sister are taking care of little T.J. right now."

Gina looked puzzled. "The cops told us about T.J.'s granny getting herself murdered. But why isn't the kid with you?"

"There was nothing to prove he was my son, until DNA test results came in," Travis explained. "So he had to go into the foster care system."

Gina put her hand to her forehead. "Well, shit! I don't get it. Your name's on the birth certificate."

"Did you leave the certificate with Alicia?" Travis asked. "We didn't find any paperwork in the house."

"It's in the kid's suitcase. There's a slit in the lining of the bottom and I put all the papers in there—his birth certificate, medical records and some pictures. His granny knew..."

Travis and JayBee looked at each other. She could tell exactly what he was thinking. If only they'd known about those papers, T.J. would never have had to go into foster care.

"She was murdered before she could tell anyone. Well, perhaps it's all for the best," Travis said. "T.J. and JayBee here have bonded. She's been a great foster mom."

Gina gave JayBee a longing look. "That's good to hear. I miss the kid, but him and Ray just didn't get along. So I thought it would be good to take him to his granny." She looked at Travis. "It was tough, 'cause I really love him. I promised Bethie I'd look after him. But then I thought, well, maybe his daddy would like to have him. I tried to call you all afternoon one day, but I kept getting your answering machine. Then I saw another Kellman's name listed right before yours, so I called that number and got your mom. When I said who I was, she told me to bring T.J. to her."

Travis was nodding along with this. "So that's why Alicia had him."

"Yeah. Then when she told us to meet her at the hotel, I was surprised. She didn't seem to want us at her house. I thought, that's cool, maybe her house was kind of run-down and she didn't want me and Ray to see it. Then when she met us at the hotel, I figured she'd bring you along with her, but she didn't."

"She didn't tell me about T.J." Gina looked surprised and Travis added, "I'm sure she was planning to, but she was murdered that evening."

"I know!" Gina said. "That cop who talked to us—he thought we had something to do with it. Can you believe that? Good thing we stayed in the bar all night. Why the hell would we leave T.J. with his granny and then kill her? We'd be assholes to do that."

"The theory was that maybe you left him with his grandmother and then Ray went back to try to rob her and wound up killing her." He looked down at Gina's feet, clad in scuffed clogs. "What size shoe do you wear?"

She stared at him, seeming to be taken aback by the question. "Size nine. Why?"

"Shoes were found at the house—they could have belonged to the murderer. But they're size sevens."

"Ray wears a thirteen. He's a big man." She hesitated. "He's done some bad things in his life—but he wouldn't murder anyone."

"Yeah, but he'd hurt a little boy," Travis said caustically.

Gina looked embarrassed. "I told him he was being too tough on the kid, but he wouldn't listen."

JayBee had listened intently to Gina's conversation and scrutinized her body language. She was convinced that Gina was telling the truth, as far as she knew it. But sometimes women were blind about what their boyfriends were really like.

"Are you sure Ray was with you that entire evening?" she asked. "He didn't slip out for a little while?"

"Are you kidding? After a few hours, he was so shit-faced he couldn't hardly walk. I had a god-awful time getting him up to our room." She shook her head, seeming to remember that night with unhappiness. "I got wasted too and then when we went up, we got into a fight. Man, that was awful. I wanted to sleep so bad, but he was screaming at me about moving to Indianapolis. He wasn't cool about it, but I had a job offer here."

"Why didn't Beth ever tell Travis he had a son?" It was the question JayBee had most wanted to ask. She hoped Gina knew the answer. She waited, drawing a deep breath. Her future with Travis might depend on what Gina said.

"Oh, she wanted to marry her dopey high-school boyfriend," Gina said scornfully. She looked at Travis. "I used to tell her it wasn't fair, 'cause you had a right to know about the kid. But she would say, 'I want me and Dale and T.J. to be a family. I'm not getting into that whole visitation thing. I know Travis—he'd want to be a big part of the boy's life and Dale would be jealous. So it's better just to leave Travis out of it.'"

Travis gave JayBee one of his raised-eyebrow looks. She interpreted that to mean, "See? Isn't that what I told you?"

A barrel-chested man appeared on the second-floor staircase landing. He had a scraggly beard and large, tattooed forearms. He was clad only in a pair of dirty jeans held up by a thick leather belt. Its shiny silver buckle sported a skull. "Gina!" he roared. "Who the fuck are you talking to down there?"

Gina rolled her eyes. "Oh, Christ, he's awake," she murmured. "Hold on." Going to the stairs, she called up, "It's T.J.'s father! He came all the way from Ohio to talk to me!"

"Well, get rid of him! I'm starving!"

"The coffee's all made, sweetheart!"

"Fuck the coffee! Get your ass up here and fry some eggs!"

Travis joined Gina by the stairway. "Ray, my name's Travis Kellman. I'd like you to come down here. I have something to discuss with you."

Ray gave him a long, baleful stare. "What the hell do you want? I don't know you."

"We need to talk," Travis said. "Now are you going to come down, or am I coming up?"

"All right, hold on." Ray disappeared. When he came back to the stairway, he had added a t-shirt and motorcycle boots to his outfit. Coming down the stairs, he demanded, "Okay, here I am. What the hell's so fucking important?"

Travis' arms were loose at his sides, his hands clenched into fists. JayBee left the picnic table and came up behind him.

"I wanted to see what kind of man beats a little child." Travis stared into Ray's eyes. Ray was taller than he was and probably thirty pounds heavier, JayBee thought. Travis took a step closer. "Didn't think you'd ever have to answer to anyone about that, did you?"

The big man tried to bluster his way out of it. "What the hell are you getting in my face for? You weren't around when the kid was acting up! You shoulda heard the mouth on that young 'un, before I took him in hand!"

Gina pulled on Travis' sleeve. "Hey, don't make him mad, now."

Travis turned slightly. "Gina, you're the boy's aunt and you're welcome to come see him anytime." Turning back to face Ray, he went on, "As for you, don't show your face in Ohio again! You hear me? Not only will I see you arrested, I will personally kick your ass."

"You threatening me?" Ray demanded, grabbing Travis by the collar.

"Get your hands off me!" Travis punched him in the mouth.

Ray reeled back, holding his hand to his mouth, eyes wide. Then he charged forward, aiming a blow at Travis' gut. His hangover had to be slowing him down, JayBee thought, watching Travis dodge. Catching Ray by the shoulders, Travis punched him in the face again. Ray bellowed with rage and hit Travis in the ribs, bringing him to his knees. Ray followed him down, pummeling him with both big fists. They rolled on the ground, punching and kicking.

"Stop it!" Gina screeched. "You guys! Stop it!"

JayBee held her breath, unsure who was winning. Ray's mouth was bleeding and Travis had a bloody nose.

Travis seemed to be getting the better of Ray as he got in two more punches to the face. Ray tucked his head down, rolling on to his side and reached down to his boot. JayBee gasped as something glinted in the sun—a six-inch hunting knife.

Her timing had to be perfect. She stepped forward as Ray raised the knife. She took careful aim. Kicked hard.

The knife spun out of Ray's hand. Ray howled, grabbing his right hand with his left and glared around to see what had happened.

JayBee ran after the knife, snatching it off the ground and securing it in her purse.

Travis leaped forward and pinned Ray, punching him a few more times in the face as the other man struggled to throw him off. JayBee was mesmerized by the furious, menacing look on Travis' face. She had never dreamed the gentle veterinarian could look like this wild man, with blood on his face and his hair standing up.

Ray gasped, "Hey, man—I'm sorry, okay? C'mon, let me up! You're killing me, man! I give—I give!"

Travis got off him and stood up, fists still raised, watching him. Ray lay there for a few moments, shaking his head groggily.

"Next time you go after a kid—" Travis panted, "—better find out if there's a father around somewhere."

Ray raised himself on one elbow. "Okay, man, I hear you," he muttered.

"Give me your belt," said Travis.

"What?"

"I said, give me your damn belt!"

Ray, staring at Travis, slowly removed his belt and handed it over. JayBee held her hand to her mouth, wondering what Travis meant to do. Could he possibly be planning to beat Ray with the belt, the way his son had been beaten?

"Look, man, I said I was sorry," Ray said sullenly.

Travis rolled up the belt and jammed it into his front jeans pocket. "Now get the hell out of my sight!"

Ray looked at Gina, who came to him cautiously, putting her hand on his shoulder. He reached up and Gina helped him get to his feet. Holding his face, he said, "I think you broke my fucking jaw."

"Get out of here!" Travis said again, his voice low and menacing. He watched as Ray, with Gina beside him, limped to the fire escape.

Only when Ray was out of sight did Travis slowly pull a bandanna out of his pocket and hold it to his sluggishly bleeding nose.

JayBee looked up into his face. This was a side of him she had never expected. He looked back at her, his expression questioning. "Are you upset about all that?" he asked tentatively.

She touched the side of his cheek. "You were wonderful!"

Chapter Seventeen

They headed back to Ohio, JayBee driving while Travis cleaned his face with tissues and bottled water. After an hour, they stopped for lunch at a Denny's. Travis disappeared into the bathroom while JayBee ordered cheeseburgers for them.

When he came back out and sat down across from her, he looked much more presentable with his hair neatly combed. He had rinsed out his blood-stained shirt and now wore only the black t-shirt he'd had on underneath. JayBee eyed him covertly, surprised to see what a broad, muscular chest he had, now that it wasn't concealed under a button-down shirt.

He took her hand. "You sure you're all right with what happened today?"

"Did you expect me to scream and faint? I'm tougher than that! How does your nose feel?"

"Sore."

She made a sympathetic face. "Maybe you should put some ice on it."

"No, I'll be fine," he said impatiently.

"So, were you planning all along to fight that guy? Because it seemed to me you were provoking him."

Travis grinned sheepishly. "I wanted a piece of him ever since I heard he abused my son." He added, "At least T.J. won't have to worry about him anymore."

"Wow, I didn't know you could fight like that."

"Well, you helped! Thanks for kicking that knife away."

JayBee squeezed his hand, thinking how differently the day might have gone if she hadn't come with him. He could have been wounded, even killed. She shivered, imagining how she would have felt, hearing the news that he was dead.

"My turn in the bathroom," she said, trying to speak cheerfully. She knew he had heard something in her voice, because he gave her a concerned look. Picking up her purse, she left the table.

She took Ray's knife out of her purse and looked at it distastefully, wondering what to do with it. Finally she wrapped it in paper towels and threw it in the waste bin.

Travis could have been killed. And I would be devastated. She stared at her reflection in the bathroom mirror. Her lower lip was trembling. She wanted to go back to the booth, throw her arms around him, kiss him until they were both dizzy. Would he be thrilled or embarrassed by a public display? A tiny grin came to her face as she pictured his reaction.

When, exactly, had he come to mean so much to her? Goodness, she had known him—she counted back—not even three weeks. Somehow he and his son had become as important as her own blood sister and father. Like family.

Brushing her hair, she tried to gain control over her emotions. When she returned to the booth, instead of resuming her seat across from him, she sat beside him, needing the closeness. Looking pleased, he put his arm around her shoulders.

Not that she wanted to be with a man like Slade, who got into a fight every time they went to a bar together. But it was good to know Travis could defend himself if necessary. He had fought a man bigger than himself, a man armed with a knife, because he wanted to teach him a lesson.

She admired courage and she honored him for what he had done.

* * * * *

When they got back to Travis' house, it was five in the afternoon. "Why don't you come in?" he asked. "We could order a pizza or something."

"I have to go home and let Queenie out."

Travis was disappointed. Although neither of them had said anything about the evening, he'd hoped they would spend it together.

JayBee looked at him speculatively. "If you don't mind eating leftovers, I have lasagna at my house."

She could have said "dog food" and he would have agreed to come over. She started up her motorcycle and he followed in his truck, parking on the street when he reached her house. He brought in his shirt, but she took it away from him. "Don't you dare wear that damp shirt. I'll put it in the dryer."

Queenie, left by herself in the house all day, seemed ecstatic to see them. She leaped impartially on both of them, trying to lick their faces. JayBee unlocked the back door. "Can you keep an eye on her while I change? I have to get out of these hot jeans."

"Sure." He took Queenie outside and waited while she relieved herself. She found a ball under a shrub and brought it to him, tail wagging furiously and dropped it at his feet. Throwing it for her, he thought about how much he'd missed her since he'd given her to his son.

JayBee appeared at the back door, utterly enticing in a short denim skirt and a lacy peach top that left an inch of skin bare at her slender waist. "Come on in, I'm microwaving the lasagna."

He went into the dining room and found that she'd put a tablecloth and unlit candles on the table. Two places were set across from each other at the end closest to the kitchen.

She brought out a basket of bread and a bottle of wine, then returned to the kitchen. When she came out again, she was carrying plates with big squares of lasagna.

Handing Travis the bottle of wine and a corkscrew, she dimmed the lights and lit the candles. He thought this was even better than the night they'd gone to the steak restaurant, because now they were alone.

Travis couldn't stop looking at her as they ate. The lasagna was delicious, but he couldn't really give it the attention it deserved. He was too intent on wondering what would happen this evening. Was she trying to make up her mind where to go with the relationship? He had the feeling that tonight might be the make-or-break point. Somehow he had to convince her that they should be together.

He helped her clear the table and load the dishwasher when they finished eating. *See? I'm a modern guy—I help around the house,* he told her silently. She was very quiet as they worked together. Nervous? he wondered.

Finally she asked, "Want to go for a walk?"

Leaving the house was the last thing he wanted. "Let's just sit and talk."

"We can't talk while walking?"

He smiled. "I want to look at you while we talk."

She smiled back, seeming pleased at the implied compliment. "All right. Let's sit in the living room."

A large red couch faced the fireplace in the living room. It would have been the perfect spot for a cozy conversation, if it hadn't been covered with papers and books. Travis looked at it with a frown. JayBee said apologetically, "Angel always spreads out when she works." Shoving papers together, she moved them to the coffee table.

He seated himself at one end of the couch. She sat a few feet away—not really far away, but not close enough that he could put his arm around her. He moved a little closer and took her hand. "Thanks for dinner. Did you make the lasagna yourself?"

"I don't have a cook! It's my mother's recipe."

"It was great." He played with her hand for a moment, admiring her pink nails and the pretty gold rings she wore. "I was thinking about something you said at the picnic. About whether I was looking for a woman just to be a mother to my son."

She didn't answer, just tilted her head expectantly, waiting for him to continue.

"I was also thinking about what a good storyteller you are. I didn't remember that one—*The Elves and the Shoemaker*—until you started telling it. Anyway, I thought I'd tell you a story."

She leaned forward eagerly. He could tell he'd surprised her. "A story? Really?" There was a laugh in her voice.

"Yes. And it starts like all good stories." He looked into her eyes. "'Once upon a time'—there was a man who had almost everything he wanted. A house, a profession he loved, a reliable truck and lots of pets. But he wasn't happy, because there was one important thing he didn't have. Do you know what that was?"

"A Corvette," JayBee guessed, a gleam of mischief in her eyes.

He laughed. "No. He didn't want a Corvette—well, not much, anyway. What he wanted was a girlfriend. In spite of having seven cats, he was lonely. So anyway, one day he was out running, because he always tried to keep in shape. And he came to a big tree.

"He heard a rustling in the tree and he looked up and saw the loveliest face he'd ever seen. Two pretty brown eyes, pink cheeks, long red hair…the man was completely enchanted. He knew he was seeing a wood nymph—a dryad—and she'd put him under her spell."

"What did the dryad do?" JayBee asked as he paused.

"She fell out of the tree, so the man caught her. As soon as he had her in his arms, he knew he was never going to let her go."

"Oh and what did he do then? Did he kiss her?"

"He wanted to, badly, but he was too polite. She made some excuse about having to go to school and ran off. And the man was very upset. He thought she was a high-school student."

JayBee laughed. "Not really! I'm sure she didn't look that young."

"Who's telling this story, you or me? He thought she was a high-school student," Travis said firmly. "When he found out she wasn't, he was happy again. At least, until he thought she might be gay."

"But she wasn't gay, either," JayBee guessed.

"No, she wasn't. She proved that the next time they met, when she sat and kissed him in a cemetery."

"Was she a good kisser?"

"Since she was a dryad, her kisses were magical. The man couldn't think about anything else afterward.

"So things were going along well, until the dryad started having doubts. She'd had a previous love affair with an evil—an evil—"

"Stockbroker," JayBee murmured.

"An evil wizard and things hadn't gone well. So now she was afraid the man would treat her badly. She thought maybe he just wanted her as a mother to his son. What she didn't realize—" Travis took a deep breath "—she didn't realize he'd fallen for her from the moment she tumbled into his arms. Before he even knew he had a son."

"Dryads can be silly sometimes," JayBee said softly.

"Not silly. She just needed to learn to trust him."

"And did she?"

"Of course. And then they were happy together—happy ever after."

He had hoped she would like the story, but he wasn't prepared for her reaction. Moving closer, she threw her arms around his neck and gave him an all-out kiss. He kissed her back intensely, his tongue exploring her mouth, remembering how she'd liked it in the driveway that day. He pulled her onto his lap, one arm around her shoulders, the other caressing her thighs.

"You forgot an important part of the story," she whispered at last.

"What was that?"

"The part where they go to bed together." She pulled away from him and stood up. Reaching out her hand to him, she whispered, "Come upstairs."

* * * * *

JayBee's bedroom expressed a blatantly feminine side of her that Travis hadn't expected. The furniture was white wicker, graceful and elegant against a pale-blue wallpaper of flowers and swooping birds. She closed the door behind him and turned down the white coverlet on the bed. "Do you like my room?" she asked. "I hung the wallpaper myself." She sat on the bed.

"Very nice." He took a quick look around. He had papered two rooms himself at his own house, so he knew how difficult it could be. "Makes me feel like I'm outdoors." He sat beside her, taking her in his arms. She leaned back against the pillows, pulling him down to lie beside her.

Her kisses were incredible. He'd known that already, from the night they'd kissed at his house, but the memory wasn't as good as the real thing. Her mouth was hot and eager under his, infinitely arousing. Their tongues stroked each other and his excitement grew. All he could think about was how much he wanted her naked underneath him. He unbuttoned her blouse and kissed the sweet spot between her breasts.

Suddenly she stiffened and raised her head.

"What's wrong?" he asked.

"I thought I heard a car."

"Oh, hell," he muttered. "Maybe it was next door."

She slid out from his grasp and went to the door that led to the outside porch. Opening it, she looked out. "Angel and T.J. are back. Damn it!" She came back to the bed and sat down.

"I thought you said they were gone for the night."

"Angel must have changed her mind." JayBee sounded as though she were near tears. "Travis, I'm so sorry—but we're going to have to stop. T.J. will come looking for me in a few minutes and the bedroom door doesn't lock." Swiftly, she rebuttoned her blouse.

He sat up with a rueful smile. "Guess it's a good thing we're still dressed." He could hear them now, downstairs. A door banged and Queenie barked.

JayBee's face changed, lighting up with a big smile. "I just thought of something! We can go to the treehouse!"

"What treehouse?"

She grabbed his hand and led him to the porch door. The treehouse was about five feet away from the end of the porch, anchored to a huge branch of the big oak tree in the backyard. "You're not afraid to walk along the branch, are you?" She kicked off her sandals and shoved her feet into a pair of tennis shoes.

"I can do it." He wasn't about to let something like that stop him, not when making love to her was the prize at stake.

"Let's go before anyone comes upstairs." She walked across the porch, went over the rail and stepped carefully onto the tree branch. A few quick steps and she was opening the window to the treehouse and boosting herself over the sill.

Travis followed more slowly, not as sure-footed in his boots as she was in her soft-soled shoes. But he made it. Once he got his shoulders through the window, the rest was easy.

She laughed. "You did it!" Flinging her arms around his neck, she kissed him exuberantly. "This is great! No one will bother us now. Angel's too scared to walk the branch and T.J. knows he isn't allowed." There was a shade above the window, which she pulled down. "Should I light a candle?"

"I can see pretty well," he said. It wasn't dark out yet.

Being in the treehouse seemed to have energized her. "I always wanted to make love out here," she told him, her eyes dancing. "Sit down and get comfortable."

He sat on one of the beanbag chairs and started to unbutton his shirt. Laying a hand over his, she shook her head. "No—not yet."

He leaned back in the chair, waiting. She smiled at him, a sweet, mischievous smile that was so intimate it took his breath away. Leaning over, she shook her hair, then brought her head up sharply. Her red hair was wilder now, spread out around her shoulders.

She stepped out of her shoes and pushed them neatly to the side. Next to go was her blouse. Underneath she was wearing a lacy, peach-colored bra that reined in her large breasts. She looked so pretty standing there in her lingerie. It was nearly impossible to sit still and wait.

She stepped closer to him. Her breathy voice was almost a whisper as she said, "Unzip my skirt."

He reached up and unzipped her denim skirt. She put her thumbs in the waistband and wriggled it off her rounded hips. Her panties were a wispy bit of lace that matched the bra.

His hands went around her, pulling her close, holding her buttocks. His face was at the level of her thighs. He buried his face in them, inhaling her scent, enjoying the feel of her hands in his hair.

Reaching around, she unclasped her bra and discarded it. He looked up, feasting his eyes on the sight of her breasts. They'd been on his mind ever since the evening she had visited his house. He held them gently, rubbing his thumbs over the nipples. Throwing her head back, she closed her eyes and moaned under her breath as he continued to touch her. Eagerly, he stood up.

She pulled away, commanding, "Now you—undress." She stood back and waited.

He removed his shirt while she watched intently. "Oh!" she said, as pleased as a little girl getting a special toy on Christmas Day. "Your chest is gorgeous!" Travis grinned and flexed his arms, proud of his chest and the cut muscles of his shoulders and arms.

She ran her hands over his biceps. "You must work out," she said, sounding surprised. "You look like an athlete."

"The first time you saw me, I was jogging."

"That's right. But somehow I thought you were one of those bookish types." Her touch was exciting as she stroked his chest, her fingers dwelling on his nipples. "Most guys with a chest like yours would be running around in a t-shirt two sizes too small for them."

"Well, that's not me." Bracing himself against the rattan chest, he pulled off his boots, which brought him closer to her height. He dug out his wallet and took out a condom, then stepped out of his jeans.

She raised her eyebrows. "Were you expecting to get lucky tonight?"

"I always carry a couple. Just in case a dryad seduces me."

To his relief, she smiled. He reached for her and she flowed into his arms and kissed him. Then, taking his hand, she led him to the beanbag chairs.

"It's too bad I don't have a bed in here," she said.

"We'll be fine like this," he answered, following her down.

His heart pounded as he sucked each of her nipples in turn, then moved back to enjoy the sight of them, glistening and erect. He was aroused to a painful degree, but he wasn't going to rush this encounter. So he tried to ignore the demanding heat in his groin as he kissed his way down her stomach.

She was delightfully responsive, moaning as he licked her navel, raising her hips to help when he eased her panties down. He kissed her mons. She gave a deep sigh and opened her legs.

He moved farther down and stroked her with his fingers. Her tiny mew of pleasure encouraged him to lower his head and taste her.

"Travis—yes!"

He'd never known a woman like her before. Gusty and outspoken, yet so gentle with his son. He'd known she was special since the day he'd seen her peering down from the tree.

He wanted her badly. But he already knew that one night with her wouldn't be enough. He was determined to be the best lover she'd ever had.

He slipped his palms under her butt to raise her to his mouth. At first she lay quiescent, merely trembling slightly at each stroke of his tongue. After a minute or so, she gasped and raised her hips, increasing the contact with his mouth.

He lifted his head. "Tell me—is there anything you especially like?"

"You were doing it—don't stop!"

He'd figured that would be her answer. Deciding to alter his technique slightly, he moved his hand and teased her clit with his thumb while thrusting into her with his tongue, imitating the rhythm of intercourse. Her low moans told him how much she liked that. Her hips jerked in response to his thrusts. It wasn't long before she cried out, then went limp, her head thrown back.

He put on the condom, thinking he couldn't remember ever being this hard and hot before. Moving forward, he positioned himself between her legs, leaning down to kiss her first. She gazed into his eyes, smiling and returned his kiss.

He knew he'd die if he waited another minute. He slid into her slick channel, feeling her orgasm still pulsating through her body.

"That's it—so good…"

Her words spurred him on. Her hips rose eagerly to meet his thrusts, her hands gripped his shoulders. She'd never been more beautiful to him than now, with her cheeks flushed and her lips slightly parted.

Each thrust was like pushing into hot, molten silk. He increased his speed, addicted to the feel of her surrounding his cock. She wasn't speaking now—instead, she cried out each time he moved.

"I love you," he gasped and kissed her one more time.

She stroked down the length of his body and gripped his butt with both hands. The extra stimulation brought him over the edge. With a groan, he sank into her, pleasure surging through him.

* * * * *

"You were wonderful," JayBee murmured, caressing his beard. She put her head on his chest, snuggling close to him and promptly fell asleep. Smiling, he kissed the side of her face and her ear. She reminded him of a dainty little cat, utterly relaxed and trusting.

He lay still for awhile, watching her sleep. He didn't know if he'd told the story well enough. He'd wanted to express to her the depth of what he felt, the sense of enchantment he'd experienced, seeing her lovely face appear out of the tree. And now, after having made love to her, all his feelings had intensified.

He was so happy he didn't want to waste any of his time in sleep, but eventually he dozed for a short time. When he woke, he stroked her hair, wishing they could stay like this all night. His arms tightened around her. She opened her eyes and smiled, her face very close to his.

"Did you mean what you said? While we were doing it?"

"I don't know—what did I say?" he teased her, but he knew very well what she meant.

"You said you loved me."

"Of course I do." He pressed his lips to her neck and she sighed happily.

"Oh, Travis—I love you too."

Caressing her hair back from her face, he looked deeply into her big brown eyes. "I never made love up in a tree before. But I guess I should have expected that, when I fell for a dryad."

She laughed softly, her hand stroking his chest and stomach. His eyes half-closed as he reveled in her touch.

"I think you would have been more comfortable on my bed," she told him. "But at least it's private out here."

"It's so quiet…I almost feel like we're marooned on a desert island together." Remembering all the trouble in his family, he added with a sigh, "Too bad we're not."

"Silly—you'd get tired of seeing only me, day after day."

"Sure I would, after about a hundred years." He kissed her. "Make that two hundred."

Her arms went around his neck as his lips moved sensually over her shoulders and downward, between her breasts. "A desert island might be more fun than an Ohio winter," she said.

"You bet it would. We'd lie on the beach together, enjoying the warm sand, listening to the ocean." He loved the soft, yielding texture of her skin. "Every day I'd find a different flower for you to wear in your hair."

"What would we eat?"

"We'd dig for clams and catch fish. There'd be coconuts, bananas…" Cupping her breasts in both hands, he tasted each nipple with his tongue. "Look, I just found some grapefruit."

She giggled. "Tell me more."

"We'd shower under a waterfall and go swimming every day. Instead of cats and dogs, we'd have monkeys and parrots for pets." Her face flushed as he moved his hands downward over her hips and stomach, then slowly caressed her inner thighs. He watched, pleased, as her lips parted and her breath came quick and fast. "And every day we'd wake up together and I'd make love to you. And every night we'd lie on the beach together, looking up at the stars and we'd make love again."

"I'm not sure exactly what you mean," she murmured. "How about a hands-on demonstration?"

That sounded like a good idea to him.

"Travis?"

"Hmm?"

Her breath was warm against his ear. "Remember that fruit you mentioned? I think I just found a banana."

* * * * *

Travis returned home in the middle of the night. JayBee had finally given him her phone number and it was tucked securely into his breast pocket.

"Come over and have dinner with me tomorrow," he had urged her.

She'd clung to him, her arms around his neck. "I'll try. But I have to see what kind of mood Angel's in. She's more frightened than ever about being alone, now that we know Bradley's around."

She'd lowered the rope ladder for him so he was able to leave without going back through the house. He'd watched her walk back along the branch and go safely into her bedroom before he went to his truck.

He was yawning as he let himself in the back door of his house. It was going to be hard to work tomorrow, after so little sleep. But it had been worth it.

It was an incredible feeling, being in love again. He had hated leaving her in the middle of the night. Too bad JayBee didn't live alone. Then he shook his head at his thoughts. She was the best thing that had ever happened to his child.

He couldn't wait until tomorrow. All he wanted was to see her again. Hold her again. Make love to her again.

The light on the answering machine was blinking. He debated whether to leave it until tomorrow. After all, he couldn't return any calls at three in the morning.

The cats' dry food bowl was empty. He poured some food in, smiling as Puff glided in from the dining room, closely followed by Blackie.

Getting himself a glass of water, he hit the "play" button on the machine and stood listening to the three calls.

Austin MacReedy had called at five o'clock, seven o'clock and eleven o'clock. By the last call, he sounded almost frantic, so unlike his normal, taciturn self that Travis was startled.

"I don't know where the hell you are, Trav, but this is a friggin' emergency! Jesus, I've been trying to reach you for hours!" A long pause and then he said, "All right, I wanted to explain in person, but I'm going to tell you what's going on. Your sister Katie drove to the county jail in Remus today—where your dad's being held—and confessed to the murder of her mother."

Chapter Eighteen

How quickly things could change. One of the best evenings of Travis' life had suddenly turned into the worst.

He couldn't believe it. He couldn't imagine how it could have happened—his sensitive, artistic little sister, suddenly stabbing her own mother to death.

His stomach churned as he counted up the strikes against her. She had discovered Alicia's body. And Georgia had found blood-stained shoes in her size at the house. Katie had been at the house when Georgia was attacked.

She must have been the one to attack Georgia.

He thought of Katie's moodiness lately, the way she wasn't eating or cleaning her apartment. He had put it down to grief, but maybe that was the wrong word. Maybe it was guilt, not grief, that she was experiencing.

He paced back and forth in the kitchen, trying to think it through.

Remembering her scream when she found her mother's body in the kitchen, he marveled at her capacity for acting. He had certainly believed she had been horrified and grief-stricken.

Still, anyone could scream. And he hadn't been there with her when she found the body, hadn't seen her expression.

He frowned, thinking about how she had thrown up in the rose bushes. That, too, wasn't always involuntary. Most people could induce vomiting with a finger down the throat.

He tried to recall every detail about that day. He had held her in his arms, trying to comfort her. Then they had gone to sit in the truck.

And she had talked about how they might both need an alibi.

At the time, in the midst of things, he hadn't thought much about that. Tragic events affected people differently, brought strange ideas to mind. But if she was the murderer, she had almost given herself away right then and there.

His head throbbing, he went to the liquor cabinet, poured a scotch and drank it. Blindly, he walked through to the parlor.

Pacing to the end of the room, he paused by the mantel, looking at the portrait of his real mother. Katie had painted her with her eyes downcast, a faint smile on her face. Her hair, precisely the light-brown color of his own, fell softly around her face and shoulders.

The portrait had completely replaced his dim, boyhood memories of what his mother looked like. He could remember bits and pieces about her—the way she used to tuck him into bed, the violet scent of her perfume.

Unlike Alicia, she had loved him.

Help me. I can't take this. I really, really can't.

With a deep sigh, he went to his desk and sat down. If only there were someone he could talk to.

A white envelope lay on the desk, his name written on the front. He stared at it for a moment, then ripped it open.

Dear big brother:

By the time u read this, I'll have confessed to killing Maman.

I know it's hard to believe but u know how M could be. I was so mad I couldn't help it! We got into a big argument about the man I was seeing. The knife was sitting on the table and before I even knew what I was doing I stabbed her! I never thought the police would arrest Dad, I can't let him go to prison when I'm the guilty one!

Remember what I said in my poetry, the Guilty One, Accursed and Afraid well you did not know I was talking about myself.

Do NOT visit me in jail, I know how sad u will be and maybe mad too and I can't take it, I know u have always taken care of me but there is nothing u can do about this!

Luv,

Katie

Travis set the letter down and put his hands to his face.

* * * * *

JayBee wished she didn't have to go to work on Monday. It would have been a perfect day to lie in bed and daydream about Travis, but unfortunately, she had to work for a living. If there's another life after this one, I want a gigantic trust fund, she told herself as she showered and dressed. She was yawning and heavy-eyed as she came downstairs and made a cup of instant cocoa and a Poptart.

Angel was already up and working when JayBee entered the living room with her breakfast.

"You certainly made a mess of my papers last night." Angel glared in JayBee's direction.

"Good morning to you, too." JayBee could have given Angel a variety of sharp answers but she was too happy this morning to be sarcastic. "T.J. up yet?"

"He was up at six, wanting to see his bicycle." Angel smiled fondly. "I could barely get him to eat any breakfast."

"And how's Dad?"

"Dad's just fine. He was crazy about T.J.—taught him how to play checkers. He thinks T.J.'s very smart for his age." Angel hesitated. "I told Dad about our problems with Bradley. He thinks we ought to come back home, so we'll be safe."

"I hope you told him that's completely out of the question. I'm not about to drive an hour to school every day. Not to mention we have a lease here."

Angel didn't answer. JayBee asked, "Well, what did you tell him?"

"I said we'd think about it."

"Have you forgotten about T.J.?"

"Of course not. Dad thought it would be fine to have him there for a few weeks, until Travis gets custody." Angel looked at her pleadingly. "It's really not such a bad idea, JayBee. We could sublet this place. And it would throw Bradley off our trail."

"Angel, if you want to move back home at the age of twenty-eight, I can't stop you. But I'm staying right here."

Angel sighed. "I can't very well leave you all by yourself. I was so worried about you yesterday that I didn't feel comfortable about staying at Dad's." She looked into JayBee's face accusingly. "Can you imagine how I felt when I got back and the doors were unlocked and you were nowhere to be found? I thought you'd been kidnapped!"

"I was in my treehouse."

"I figured that out, eventually." Angel jumped up, went to the dining room and returned with Travis' shirt, which JayBee had left in the dryer last night. "And you weren't alone out there, either."

Busted! thought JayBee.

"Did he have to walk that branch to get in there?" Angel asked. When JayBee nodded, Angel said, "Well, he's got guts, I'll say that for him. I wouldn't do that for a million dollars."

"Fortunately for me," JayBee muttered.

"So, how was the dashing doctor?"

A number of descriptions flashed through JayBee's mind—words like "wonderful" and "fantastic". But remembering how Angel had tried to flirt with him at the picnic, she settled for, "Above average". After all, it wasn't a lie—she just hadn't said just how far above average he had been.

* * * * *

It was such a lovely day that some of the teachers decided to take their lunches outside. JayBee sat down next to Charlotte and popped the top of a can of Pepsi, yawning.

"Late night out?" Charlotte asked her with a smile.

"Late night in," said JayBee.

"Sounds like fun."

"It was, but I'm not used to staying up until three in morning, not on a school night."

JayBee moved over on the picnic table seat as Denise MacReedy joined them.

"I swear this incoming class of freshmen is the most obnoxious bunch I've had in fourteen years of teaching." Denise set her tray down with a thump. "I had to send two little smart alecks to the office today and I threatened the whole second period class with a detention if they didn't settle down. Anyone got aspirin?"

Charlotte found some in her purse and shook them into Denise's hand.

"I don't know," Charlotte said, pushing her long blonde hair back behind her shoulders. She was lovely for a middle-aged woman, JayBee thought, almost as beautiful as Angel, except for being about eighty pounds heavier. "I haven't had too much trouble so far. We've got a much nicer group of kids here than when I was teaching in Cincinnati, believe me. What do you think, JayBee?"

"I always start out mean to put a scare in 'em. One of the girls gave me a smart remark the first day of school and I made her do twenty push-ups. After that the rest of them toed the line."

"Yes, you can make them do push-ups or run laps to punish them." Denise sounded envious. "I can't very well do that when I'm teaching Home Ec."

JayBee decided to change the subject. After all, shouldn't they be able to get away from the students during their brief lunch period? "Do you think it's possible to settle down with someone and still be happy years later? Would you ever get married again, Charlotte?"

The blonde woman tilted her head to one side as she thought about it. "Sure, I think so. He'd have to be a very different kind of man from my first husband."

"Marriage!" Denise rolled her eyes. "Isn't it tiresome how we're all raised to want it so badly? We're given bride dolls and pretend bridal gowns as girls—our mothers talk about 'when you get married' as if it's the only possible future. We're so brainwashed."

Charlotte nodded. "It was certainly one of the worst choices I ever made—except that I got David out of it. Having my son made it all worth it."

Denise looked at JayBee. "But do you have that expectation if you're gay? It must give you a whole different mindset."

Charlotte looked amused. "Why ask JayBee? She isn't gay."

Denise's eyes seem to probe JayBee's face and figure. "You're not gay?"

JayBee said, "Nope."

"Then why are you running the gay students' collective?"

"It's for 'queer folk and friends'. They were having trouble getting a faculty sponsor, so I said I'd do it."

"Then you're probably just like all the rest of us. Dying to get that ring on your finger."

"Actually," said JayBee, "marriage has never been that important to me. Two of my friends from college are divorced and they're not even thirty yet. Not to mention my sister. I think it must be awfully hard to make it work. It seems like people just aren't interested in being faithful anymore—especially men."

"Absolutely right," Charlotte sighed. "My husband started fooling around as soon as I got pregnant with David."

"Men are like dogs," said Denise. "When they stray, they have to be taught a lesson. A sharp lesson that they'll remember."

"Easier said than done," murmured Charlotte.

JayBee was hard put to keep a straight face, imagining Denise disciplining her police-chief husband by whacking him with a rolled-up newspaper. "What kind of lesson are you talking about?"

Denise surveyed her thoughtfully. "You have to make them very, very sorry. And that's all I'm going to say."

JayBee frowned, baffled.

Charlotte said, "When I found out about my husband, we fought constantly for the next six months. It really wasn't worth it. I should have just walked out, without all the fighting. Too much stress."

"I completely agree," said Denise. "Fighting doesn't get you anywhere."

JayBee thought it was hard to imagine Travis being unfaithful, so maybe it wouldn't be a problem if their relationship deepened into something more serious. Infidelity involved constant lying and he seemed so very honest.

* * * * *

"But, Doctor!" Thelma protested. "What should I tell them? And you already cancelled Mrs. McCloskey last week."

"Tell them I'm sick." The way Travis felt today, it wasn't entirely a lie. "I've got to get to the county jail before visiting hours are over."

"Did something come up with your father?" Thelma asked, giving him a sympathetic look.

"Uh—yes." So far, Katie's confession had not broken in the news and Travis wanted to keep it that way as long as possible. He hung up his lab coat and shrugged his shoulders into his brown leather jacket. "See you tomorrow, Thelma."

It was already three o'clock by the time Travis made it to the Tecumseh County courthouse and asked to see his sister.

The desk sergeant consulted the computer, then looked up at Travis over thick glasses. "I'm sorry, Dr. Kellman. She refuses to see visitors."

Travis remembered what Katie had written in her note, but he hadn't believed she'd meant it. "Are you absolutely sure? Could you check with her again and tell her that I'm here? Be sure you say her brother Travis. I'd appreciate it."

The desk sergeant tapped his fingers thoughtfully against the side of the desk. "All right. Give me a minute."

Travis paced back and forth, hands in his pockets, as he waited. This facility was much older than the modern police station in Priam. A strong smell of disinfectant pervaded the room and the green-and-gray linoleum was scuffed and worn. Even the American flag hanging from the wall seemed faded, the white stripes yellow with age.

The desk sergeant was shaking his head as he returned to his post. "She said she doesn't want to talk to anyone."

Travis felt as though he'd been sucker-punched in the gut. He managed to say, "Thanks," before he turned away. He went back to the lobby of the courthouse, away from the lockup area and sat down. Hitting his fist against his thigh, he tried to plan his next move.

At last he went up to the fourth floor, to the county prosecutor's office and asked to see Jim Percy. He had to wait for almost an hour, but was finally admitted into Percy's inner office.

Percy was a tall, lean man, prematurely balding, with a sharply intelligent expression. Travis had met him the week before, after Georgia's memory had returned regarding the shoes. Percy had not taken much interest in the idea of Alicia's murderer being the person who attacked Georgia.

"Dr. Kellman," Percy said, shaking his hand. "Have you been visiting your sister?"

"I tried, but she refused to see me." Travis took a chair across from Percy's big oak desk.

"Interesting," said Percy, sitting down and steepling his fingers together.

"What do you mean?"

"It could mean she's afraid to face you, with this crime on her conscience. Or it could mean she doesn't want you to talk her out of what she's trying to do."

"Which is what?" Travis demanded.

"Come now, Dr. Kellman, you're an educated man. You're surely aware that every time there's a notorious murder, crazy people confess to it."

"And you think my sister's crazy?"

"No, but I don't find her story credible, either. She may be a mixed-up young lady who's trying to get her father out of jail."

Travis drew a quick breath as he remembered how Katie had questioned him about their father the day before. It certainly made more sense to think of her sacrificing herself for her father's sake, rather than being her mother's murderer.

"Here's the transcript of what Miss Kellman told the police yesterday," Percy said, handing over a folder of papers. Travis skimmed them and learned that Katie had told the police the same story she had told him in her note. She had driven to Alicia's home late that night, around half past ten. They had started arguing. She had snatched up a kitchen knife and stabbed her mother. Her father's shirt had been hanging over a chair. Snatching it up, she had tried to stanch the bleeding, but the wound was too deep and she couldn't get the bleeding to stop. Terrified, she had washed her hands and left the house.

Detective Brown. What did you do with the murder weapon?

Kellman. I hid it in my shirt and took it with me. Then I drove out to the park. I was crying and shaking, trying not to throw up. I pulled off the road and buried the knife.

Detective Brown. Could you find that area again?

Kellman. No, I have no idea where it was. I was driving around at random.

Detective Brown. What about the attack on Mrs. Peter Kellman? Were you also responsible for that?

Kellman. Yes. I went over to get the mail and I saw Georgia in the kitchen. So I picked up a piece of wood and hit her over the head with it.

Detective Brown. Why would you do that?

Kellman. I didn't like her snooping around over there.

Detective Brown. Mrs. Kellman claims that she found something at the house. Did you take anything away from her?

Kellman. No.

Travis looked up. "You know Georgia called me from the house that day."

"Yes, yes," the prosecutor said. "We discussed that last week." He took the folder back from Travis.

"Whether you believe it was shoes or not, Georgia found something. Otherwise she wouldn't have called me."

"I believe she called you. The police substantiated that with your receptionist," Percy conceded.

"So Katie must be lying about the attack on Georgia. And if she's lying about that, her whole story may be false." Travis frowned, working it through to the obvious conclusion. "So, really, there's no hard evidence against Katie."

"Only her confession."

"Katie was always our father's pet," Travis said. "It's been very distressing for her to see him in jail. When the news came out about Dad's girlfriend yesterday, it was a shock to her. She realized right away that it made your case against him stronger."

The prosecutor was nodding along. "Yes. As I said at the beginning, this may certainly be a false confession made in the hopes of freeing her father."

"Then are you going to release her?" Travis demanded.

The prosecutor sighed. "Dr. Kellman, your sister confessed to a murder. I can't do anything hastily."

"Why not?" Travis glared at the other man. "You certainly charged my father with no delay."

"If you want to help your sister, I suggest you get her an attorney. Now, if you'll excuse me, I have a very full schedule today."

* * * * *

Travis sat in the kitchen, phone in hand, waiting for Misney to pick up. He should have known all along that Katie wouldn't raise a knife in violence. Even as a young child, if another child punched her, she was much more likely to come home in tears than to fight back. He should have remembered that.

With a sharp click, the "on-hold" music stopped and Misney came on the line.

Travis explained what was going on. "So what do make of that? I don't understand why Percy doesn't release her, if he really believes she didn't do it."

"Jesus, your sister has some guts," Misney said, his voice filled with awe. "Can you believe she was willing to do the time just to get your father out of jail? What a woman!"

"To save our father's life," Travis corrected him. "We're afraid he may kill himself if he's convicted."

"Even so. Man, I wish someone loved me like that. Incredible."

"So do you know someone who can take her case? Or could you do it yourself? They've either got to charge her or release her, right?"

"That's right." Misney paused. Travis could hear him tapping the keys on his computer. "I'm looking at my schedule…I've got to be in court tomorrow at eleven, but I can go out there earlier and talk to Katie. Hmm…I'll bet Percy will try to get her to recant. Otherwise, this has muddied the waters."

"How do you mean?"

"He's got to be worried the defense will use it against him. Well, I'll see what I can do tomorrow."

When Travis hung up, he felt that he had done everything he could for his little sister. He wondered if she had a cellmate and if so, whether the woman would be nice to her. It's just county jail, not a women's correctional institution, he tried to tell himself, but he couldn't help feeling uneasy. He wished he could have seen her today, found out how she was really doing.

* * * * *

JayBee was annoyed as she headed over to Creekside Farm on her motorcycle. She had stayed late at school, coaching the women's field hockey team. When she'd finally arrived home after five, she had asked Angel, "Did anyone call me?"

"No," Angel had answered. "Were you expecting someone?" Her expression was ironic.

"Not really." *He's probably still at the clinic.* She made a meatloaf and put it in the oven, then sat down with T.J. and read him a story. All that time, the phone stubbornly stayed silent.

By the time six-thirty came around, she was getting angry. So he thought he could sleep with her and then just blow her off? After everything they'd said to each other?

"I'm going out for awhile," she told Angel.

"Will you be back before dark?"

"I don't know."

Angel looked at her pleadingly. "You won't stay out all night? Promise?"

"I promise."

When JayBee got to the farmhouse, she found Travis' truck in the driveway and the back door unlocked. There was no doorbell, so she knocked.

There was no answer, no footsteps. She entered the kitchen. Travis' leather jacket was hanging over a chair.

"Travis?" she called.

Still no answer. She pushed through the kitchen door and walked through the dining room and into the parlor.

He was lying on his back on the couch, with Blackie on his lap and Puff curled on his chest. Her anger melted away as she looked at him. He was boyishly handsome as he slept, his mouth faintly smiling. Bending down, she kissed him.

He jerked and woke up, struggling up to one elbow. Blackie gave JayBee the evil eye and slid off, sneaking behind the couch.

"JayBee!" Blinking, he pushed his hair off his forehead. "What a great surprise."

"Don't you remember you asked me over for dinner?"

He looked confused as he sat up. "Good Lord, I forgot all about it. I'm sorry."

She turned away, biting her lip. "You forgot? Well, I don't want to intrude. I'll go."

He caught her hand. "Wait! Let me explain. Please—sit down."

She gave him a look to tell him he'd better have a damned good explanation, but sat on the couch. Sighing with relief, he said, "Let me get you something to drink. Glass of wine? Beer?"

"Wine, please," she decided.

Travis left the room. After a moment, JayBee heard the water running in the kitchen. When he came back, JayBee saw he'd combed his hair. Handing her a glass of white wine, he held up his own glass. "Here's to you and me." He tapped the glasses together.

"To you, me and T.J.," she answered.

He smiled, looking pleased with her amendment.

"Let me tell you what happened when I came home last night." Seating himself beside her, he told her about the message on his answering machine and why he hadn't slept at all the night before.

His voice sounded troubled. "I want to do something to help my sister. I've always been able to step in before. But she wouldn't even see me."

JayBee pictured it all as though it were happening in her own family. Her father, innocent but accused, facing the rest of his life in prison…Angel sacrificing herself for him…she herself, convinced they were both innocent, but powerless to help.

She put her arms around him. "Travis, I don't know how you can stand it."

He hugged her back for a long moment, then gently disengaged himself. "Listen, honey, I know you must be hungry. Should we order pizza or go out for something?"

She looked into his face, realizing that he didn't want to seem weak in front of her by appearing to need comfort.

"Let's go to the Paradise." She tried for a cheerful tone. "I've been in town for months and I've never had one of their sausage sandwiches."

He grinned. "You sure you're up for that? I hope you've got a strong digestion."

"You bet. And you know what I'm going to have with it? A mug of the darkest beer they've got."

*****

As soon as they got to the Paradise, JayBee used a trip to the ladies' room as an excuse to walk through the entire bar, looking for Bradley. She remembered what Angel had told her—Travis had been in the Paradise when Bradley had been asking about Angel. And knowing Bradley's love for alcohol, it seemed a likely place to find him.

Bradley wasn't in the bar, but she saw several other people she knew. Linda Morgan was there with her husband, sitting in the back. JayBee gave her a smile and a wave. She also saw the drugstore clerk who had tried to fix her up with her sister. And Denise MacReedy was sitting by herself in a booth in the front of the bar, reading, with a glass of wine on the table.

Travis was watching her keenly as she returned, with an expression in his eyes that didn't seem to be his usual admiration when he looked at her.

"So is he here?"

"Who?" she asked, bluffing it out.

"I'm a little slow on the uptake today from lack of sleep, but I eventually figured it out. You thought Bradley might be here, right?"

"It did cross my mind," she admitted.

He raised his eyebrows. "And just what do you think you're going to do if he shows up?"

JayBee's plan had involved karate-chopping Bradley's other arm, but she said prudently, "I've got my cell phone on me. I thought I'd call the police. I filed a police report—don't you think they'll come arrest him?"

Travis grimaced. "Doubtful. Our illustrious police chief isn't exactly known as an animal lover. Here's what I think we should do. I'm not sure I remember what Bradley looks like—so you point him out to me and I'll confront him."

JayBee thought about it. "What does 'confront him' mean, precisely?"

"I'll give him a chance to explain what he did to my dog. And if I don't like what I hear, then I'll invite him outside to 'discuss' it some more."

"Don't you believe what I told you?"

Leaning across the table, he took her hand. "Of course I do. But I can't just go over and start beating on him. He needs to know why, at least."

"I'll confront him and you can be my backup."

Travis gave her an exasperated look. "What kind of man would I be to sit back and watch while my girl confronts a dangerous snake? Don't be ridiculous."

"It's not ridiculous. His quarrel is with Angel and me—Monique just happened to get in his path. In a way, it doesn't involve you at all."

"Honey—" He squeezed her hand. "If it involves you, it involves me. Okay?"

She couldn't believe it—she liked to think of herself as a tough person—but his words and tone brought quick tears to her eyes. Squeezing his hand in return, she said, "Okay."

Carla, the well-endowed waitress, finally sauntered over to take their order. She had a big smile for Travis. "Hi! I haven't seen you for a whole week. How are you, doll?" JayBee didn't miss the way she put her hand on Travis' shoulder. She always hated it when a waitress touched the man she was with.

They ordered Beck's beer, a sausage sandwich for JayBee and two slices of pepperoni pizza for Travis.

"Don't you want onions on that?" Carla asked. "You always order onions!"

"Not tonight, thanks."

JayBee gave her a dirty look as she disappeared into the kitchen. "She'd better keep her hands to herself or I'll kick her ass, too."

Travis, his eyes alight, picked up her hand and kissed it. "You are a constant delight to me, do you know that?"

She smiled back at him, glad she could take his mind off his troubles for awhile. To lighten the mood, she spoke of T.J., telling Travis about the friends T.J. had made in the neighborhood, his desire for his own sandbox and his continuing fascination with JayBee's motorcycle. The subject seemed to be of endless interest to Travis. Every time JayBee ran out of things to say, he asked a question to elicit more stories.

"I can't wait until I get custody," he said, a world of longing in his voice.

"That's fine for you, but I'm going to miss him terribly."

Travis looked intently at her, about to say something.

"Oh my God," JayBee said, lowering her voice. "I think I see him."

Travis turned to look.

"Don't let him see you!" JayBee warned him.

She watched as Bradley came into the bar, took a quick look around and then slid into the booth with Denise MacReedy.

Chapter Nineteen

"Maybe I should distract him, while you come up on the other side," JayBee said, springing to her feet.

"He doesn't know who I am."

"Yes, he does! He was watching us through binoculars while we were picnicking. He asked me who you were."

"He's going to learn all about who I am." Travis strode up the aisle toward the other booth. Bradley lifted his head and their eyes met across the room. With a quick word to Denise, he was out of the booth and pushing his way through the crowd, heading for the door.

"See, I told you!" JayBee exclaimed. Travis quickened his stride as Bradley reached the door. Just as Bradley fled outside, a group of college students came in, blocking the exit. "Excuse me—excuse me!" Travis said, trying to make his way through without actually shoving anyone.

"Hey, asshole, what's your problem?" said one of them, putting himself in Travis' way.

JayBee darted around them and got through the doorway. "Bradley!" she shouted.

"Sorry!" Travis told the student, pushing past him, frantic to catch up with JayBee.

With a screech, Bradley's car pulled away from the curb. JayBee ran toward it. Travis burst through the door. He rushed after her and grabbed her arm. "What the hell are you doing?"

She struggled to free herself from his grasp. "Let me go! He's getting away!"

"Too late now."

She gave him an exasperated look. "I was going to get in front of his car! Why did you stop me?"

He pulled her close, glad that he had reached her before she put her plan into action. "I was afraid of that! Are you crazy?"

Tilting her head to one side, she considered this. "I don't think he would have dared to actually hit me with his car."

"Look what he did to Monique! He could've run you over!" Still holding her tightly, he closed his eyes for a moment, thankful she hadn't been hurt. His heart pounded as he imagined what could have happened.

She sighed. "I wish we'd been able to get hold of him. Let's go back in. I want to talk to Denise."

"Oh, do you know her?" Travis asked.

"Of course. I know all the teachers at Priam High."

Back inside, Denise was sitting by herself, sipping her wine.

"Hi, Denise. Mind if we join you?" JayBee asked.

Denise's expression was not particularly friendly as she looked up and nodded.

Travis wondered if she had come to the bar expecting to meet Bradley. He had never seen the chief's usually conservative wife dressed in a low-cut pink t-shirt before. He was quite sure she wasn't wearing a bra. And in spite of the bar's smoky atmosphere and the aroma of onions and sausages, he could clearly smell Denise's musky perfume.

JayBee sat and folded her hands on the table, looking at her fellow teacher with a slight frown. "Denise, I don't know how well you know Bradley Morrow, but I wanted to warn you about him. He's a convicted felon and a truly bad person."

JayBee was nothing if not direct, Travis thought as he slid into the booth beside her, across from Denise.

Denise looked unconcerned. "I know he's been in prison. He's been very open with me about his problems."

"He was convicted for assaulting my sister and me." JayBee's knuckles were white as she clenched her hands. "And now he's in town because he's angry with us and wants revenge."

"Really, JayBee!" Denise took a sip of her wine. "I think you're exaggerating. When we first met, right here at the Paradise, Bradley told me he had some problems due to alcohol in the past. I was impressed with the way he was so honest with me. He's trying hard now, sticking to soft drinks, making changes in his life. He needs supportive friends, not evil gossip about the past."

"Gossip!" JayBee's brows snapped together.

Travis said, "The other day, he broke a dog's leg, just to scare JayBee and her sister." Denise had pets of her own. Perhaps this would open her eyes to the truth.

"Did you see it happen?" Denise demanded.

"Well…no," Travis admitted.

"Bradley told me all about it. The dog was snapping at his ankles, so he tried to pick it up. It bit him so he dropped it."

"That's a bold-faced lie!" JayBee exclaimed. "That's not what happened!"

"There are two sides to every story." Denise sniffed. "I believe I've heard enough." She exited the booth and left the bar, her walk slightly unsteady in her pink spike heels.

JayBee and Travis gazed at each other in consternation.

A giggle sounded over their heads. "I've been looking all over for you guys!" Carla had arrived with their food.

Later, as they drove back to Travis' house, JayBee asked, "Travis? You believe me, don't you? About Bradley?"

He gave her a quick smile. "Honey, the one time you lied to me, about Monique falling off the table, I knew right away you were fibbing. So you'd better stick to the truth because you're not a good liar." He took her hand. "I believe everything you've told me about Bradley. And don't worry, we'll catch up with him one of these days."

She sighed. "I wish Denise believed me."

"Maybe you can talk to her at school. Explain more about what went on with you and your sister."

"Maybe." JayBee sounded doubtful. "Do you think she's in love with him?"

"I've never seen her so dolled up before," Travis admitted. "If she is, her husband has only himself to blame. He's a workaholic and he neglects her." As he pulled into the driveway, he asked, "Do you want to come in for awhile?"

"I'd better go home. It's getting dark out and I promised Angel I wouldn't be gone too long."

He put the truck into park, not turning it off. She moved closer and they put their arms around each other. Stroking her hair, he looked into her eyes. "You're not even gone yet and I'm already missing you."

"Why don't you come for dinner tomorrow? We eat at six."

He agreed to that and they kissed goodnight.

"Aren't you going in?" she asked as she opened her door to leave the truck.

"I'm going to follow you home."

"You don't need to do that. I'm sure I'll be fine."

"I'm sure, too, because I'll be right behind you."

To his relief, she didn't argue. Perhaps she was more worried about Bradley than she would admit.

He followed her to the house on Forest Avenue without incident, watching from the street as she put the motorcycle in the garage, walked around to the front and entered the house safely.

* * * * *

On Tuesday, Travis was washing his hands after his last appointment and trying to decide what he should take to JayBee's house when Thelma's voice came over the intercom. "Doctor, your sister's here."

"My sister! Let her in!"

"She says, can you come out here and pay the cab?"

"I'll be right there!"

Travis rushed out to the waiting room. Katie was standing by the front desk, an anxious-looking cab driver hovering behind her.

Travis had seldom seen such a welcome sight in his life. Pulling his sister into his arms, he gave her a hug. "Thank God they let you out!"

She smiled, hugging him back. "Hi, Travis. I hate to ask, but can you pay the cab driver? I'm a little short at the moment."

He paid the driver, then told Thelma she was free to leave. "I'm impressed," he said, sitting on one of the waiting room couches. "I know Misney is a good lawyer, but this is really fast."

"It wasn't Ben. I refused to see him."

"Katie—"

"I know you were trying to help when you sent him. But I didn't need a lawyer for what I was trying to do."

"You should have known that Dad wouldn't want to be free at your expense," Travis told her. "That wouldn't make things any better."

She tossed her long hair behind her shoulders. "I thought it would be better than having him kill himself. Well, it's all come to nothing, thanks to my ex-boyfriend."

"What does he have to do with it?"

"He went to Jim Percy and gave a statement saying he was with me the night Maman was murdered."

Travis frowned. "That's all it took? Why did Percy believe him?"

Katie sighed. "It's what they call a 'statement against interest'. My boyfriend is a married man. If it came out that he was having an affair with me, his wife would be furious."

Travis shook his head, still not sure she was telling him the whole story. Katie and her married men! Well, it seemed to have worked to her benefit this time. At least the man had been decent enough to make the statement and get her released.

"That was kind of him, then," Travis said. "Especially since you broke up with him awhile ago."

Katie blushed, looking down at her hands. "He didn't want to see me go to prison. I guess he still cares about me. I just hope no one tells his wife. Jim Percy swore he wouldn't, but you know how gossip can get out."

"So is that why you thought you needed an alibi, the night of the murder?"

"Yes. I was with my boyfriend that night, but I knew I couldn't say that in my statement. But it sounded so lame to say I was alone that night and it wasn't true anyway. I was afraid that big detective, Jerry Davidson, would be suspicious and start prying into things." She opened her eyes wide, looking at her brother. "My boyfriend's wife is so clingy and possessive. One other time—two years ago, before he knew me—my boyfriend had an affair. She found out and she made his life hell for months and months!"

"Most women would," Travis said dryly.

"Would most women kill their pet chinchilla and put it in their husband's shoe? I don't think so!"

Pet chinchilla! Travis stared at his sister, then slammed his hand down on the couch. "Katie, were you sleeping with Austin MacReedy?"

"Oh!" she said, her hand going to her mouth. "You know Denise keeps chinchillas?"

"Of course I know! I'm their vet!" Travis shot to his feet, incredulous. His thoughts whirled frantically as he paced the room, trying to recall any link between his sister and the chief. The only thing that leaped out at him was when Georgia had been hurt. MacReedy had seemed to be curiously unsuspicious about Katie's presence at the scene.

Of course…because he knew already that she wasn't Alicia's murderer, so she had no reason to go after Georgia and take the shoes.

"I know you don't like Austin…" Katie said in a small voice.

"I've hated his guts since we were boys," Travis told her. "Good Lord, Katie, how could you? He's older than I am—he's married—and he's tough as nails!"

"He is not 'tough as nails'! He's a good man."

"Then why did you break up with him?" Travis demanded.

"Because he arrested Dad."

"I rest my case."

Travis took his sister home, filled with conflicting emotions. He was immeasurably relieved that she was no longer in jail, but found it hard to accept that she had been having an affair with MacReedy. Next time he saw the chief, he would have a few choice words to say to him.

"What are you going to do now?" he asked Katie as he stopped the truck by her door.

"I'm going to take a long, hot bath," she said. "There were roaches at that jail—it was really disgusting."

Before she got out of the truck, he kissed her on the forehead. "Try to stay out of trouble."

She gave him an "okay" sign and headed into her apartment.

* * * * *

JayBee checked her watch, wishing Travis would get here. She was tired of sitting on the floor by the closet.

She heard quick steps on the stairs. It sounded like Travis was taking them two at a time, which meant Angel must have told him they were having trouble with T.J.

Queenie, lying beside her, stood up and went to Travis as he came in. JayBee jumped up as well. "Thank goodness you're here!" she whispered. "T.J.'s hiding in the closet and he won't come out."

"Why?"

"He saw a man in the supermarket—he was a big guy, looked sort of like Ray—but it wasn't Ray. I told him that, but I don't think he believes me."

Travis nodded and went over to the closet. "T.J.," he said, in his deep, quiet voice, "I'm here now. You don't have to be scared. Come on out of there."

JayBee sat down on the bed, holding her breath, wondering whether T.J. would obey him.

"I want to stay in here," the boy answered.

"Then I'll have to take Queenie home with me." Travis' tone was stern. "Because Queenie doesn't want to live in the closet with you."

"No!" The boy's white face appeared in the closet doorway. "Queenie's mine! You gave her to me!"

"You can keep her—if you come out of there."

Slowly, the boy edged his way out of the closet. Travis bent and reached out to him, probably intending to give him a hug, but the boy slid by and ran to JayBee, throwing himself onto the bed. She glanced away from Travis' disappointed face. Putting her arms around T.J., she kissed him. "Oh, T.J.," she murmured, brushing the dust bunnies out of his hair. "Don't ever hide from me again."

Travis sat on the edge of the bed. "T.J., I'm glad you came out, because I have something to give you." He pulled Ray's belt out of his jeans pocket and laid it on the bed. "Do you know what this is?"

T.J. looked up from the shelter of JayBee's arms, staring at the belt like a bird mesmerized by a deadly snake. "Belt," he said finally, his voice barely a whisper. "Are you going to whup me?"

"Of course not!" Travis said, his voice loud in the quiet room. "Listen, T.J. This is Uncle Ray's belt. I told Uncle Ray he was never allowed to hit you any more. And I took his belt away so he couldn't hit you with it, ever again. Do you understand me, T.J.?"

JayBee could feel the boy trembling. "What if I'm naughty?"

"If you're naughty, I'll think of another way to punish you, but I'll never hit you." He picked the belt up and offered it to the boy. "This belt is yours now, T.J."

T.J. reached out cautiously and touched the belt with one finger. "It's mine?" he asked, as though he hardly dared to believe it.

"It's all yours. What would you like to do with it?"

T.J. bounced free from JayBee's arms. "Can we cut it up into a million zillion pieces?"

Travis smiled. "If that's what you want to do."

JayBee smiled, too. "I'll get the hedge clippers."

They headed downstairs, where the delicious aroma of frying pork filled the rooms. Travis sniffed appreciatively. "What's for dinner?"

"Angel's making pork chops."

"Oh, boy!" said T.J., running ahead of them into the kitchen. "I love pork chops!"

He certainly seemed like a different boy from the cowering child who had hid in the closet for the last two hours, JayBee thought.

They followed T.J. into the kitchen, where Angel was standing by the stove, turning the pork chops with tongs. "Look, Angel!" T.J. said. "It's Uncle Ray's belt! Daddy says I can have it!"

Angel looked puzzled.

"We're going to cut it up, so Uncle Ray can never hit any boys with it again," JayBee explained to her sister.

"Oh!" The expression Angel turned on Travis seemed to hold a look of respect. "That's a good idea."

JayBee brought the hedge clippers in from the garage. Carefully, Travis cut the belt into small pieces while T.J. watched.

"Now, what should we do with the pieces?" Travis asked.

"Flush them down the toilet!" T.J. said gleefully.

"No, that would back up the toilet," Travis told him. "Let's think of something else."

"Throw them into the ocean and let a whale eat them!" said T.J.

JayBee grinned. "We're kind of far away from an ocean. How about if we put the pieces in a shoebox and bury it?"

"Goody!" T.J. grinned back at her.

Travis gave her a raised-eyebrow look. Obviously, he knew who was going to be digging the hole. "After dinner," he amended.

They ate in the dining room, enjoying pork chops, mashed potatoes and peas and carrots. T.J. was talkative, telling them all about his day and how he had played house with the little girl down the street. Travis listened with a half-smile, his eyes never leaving his son's face.

Angel gave JayBee a surprised look. JayBee knew exactly what her sister was trying to tell her. *He's never this talkative.*

JayBee answered with a smile and a shrug. Whatever Travis thought he was accomplishing by cutting up Ray's belt, it seemed to have worked.

After dinner, JayBee found a shoebox. Travis dug a hole in the back west corner of the yard, where the ground was soft and they buried the belt in the shoebox.

T.J. tugged on his father's sleeve. "Daddy, will you take the training wheels off my bike now?"

Travis went to his truck and returned with a toolbox. He removed the training wheels while T.J. observed, fascinated. Then JayBee and Angel sat on the front porch and watched as Travis ran up and down the street, holding the bike while his son pedaled.

"He's good with the boy, I'll say that for him," Angel said grudgingly.

After twenty minutes, Travis and T.J. joined them on the porch. Travis apologized for not bringing anything with him to dinner. He said he had been planning to go to the bakery in Remus after work, but his sister had been released from jail unexpectedly.

"Oh, I'm so glad she's out," JayBee told him.

He nodded and JayBee realized he didn't want to pursue the topic further.

"I made a chocolate cake today," Angel said, "so it's fine that you didn't bring any baked goods."

"And you mustn't give any to Queenie," JayBee told T.J. "I saw you give her your peas at dinner. But she can't have cake. Chocolate can be poisonous for dogs."

"I won't give her my cake. Can I have a really big piece?" T.J. asked as Angel brought it outside.

"You can have a piece today and a piece tomorrow," Angel answered.

"Great cake," said Travis, as he took a second bite.

"It's 'mmm-mmm good!'" T.J. quoted the soup commercial. He looked pleased when all the adults laughed.

"I like cake," T.J. continued. "JayBee likes cake—Daddy likes cake—even Grandma likes cake!"

"Don't talk with your mouth full," Angel admonished him.

Travis raised his head sharply. "When did you see your grandma eat cake?"

"When I stayed at her house. She had some cake. But I didn't get any," said T.J., continuing to eat with enjoyment.

JayBee saw Travis take a deep breath. "Do you mean when you stayed with Grandma Kellman?"

T.J. looked confused.

"The house where Monique used to live," Travis added.

T.J. nodded his head. "Monique was there. Grandma put me to bed, but I couldn't sleep."

"So did you get up out of bed?"

T.J. looked scared, as though he thought he might be getting himself in trouble.

"It's okay," Travis said soothingly. "Did you want something from Grandma? Maybe some water?"

"She told me not to get out of bed. But I was thirsty."

"Did you see her in the kitchen?" Travis asked.

Again, T.J. nodded. "I opened the door a little bit. I saw Grandma eat some chocolate cake."

"I wonder where she got that cake from," Travis said in a conversational tone.

"A lady brought it for Grandma."

"How do you know that?"

T.J. gave Travis an exasperated look. "I saw her give it to Grandma. At the kitchen door."

"Did Grandma say thank you for the cake?"

"She said, 'thank you, please come in'."

"What color hair did the lady have? Brown, yellow, red?"

T.J. shrugged. "I dunno."

"Did the lady do anything else?" Travis asked.

JayBee looked from Travis to his son, suddenly afraid of what she was going to hear. Was it possible that T.J. had seen the murder?

"She went over to pet Monique. I didn't want her to see me. I thought they'd be mad 'cause I got out of bed."

"So what did you do then?"

"I went back to my room." T.J. looked thoughtful. "My room had bunk beds. Can I have bunk beds when I come live with you?"

"I suppose so. Did you ever see that lady again?" Travis asked.

T.J. shook his head. He had finished his cake. "Can I look at your motorcycle magazines?" he asked JayBee.

She glanced at Travis, wondering if he had any more questions. When he didn't say anything else, she told T.J., "Okay. Wash your hands first."

T.J. ran into the kitchen to wash his hands, while Travis sat back in his chair, putting his hand to his forehead. "Do you realize what T.J. just said?"

JayBee said cautiously, "Someone came over your parents' house that night—a woman—and brought a cake."

"The murderer," Travis said. "It all fits together. Monique had been eating something chocolate that made her sick. Maybe she finished the cake after Alicia was killed. And it fits in with Georgia's story, too." He took a deep breath. "It must have been someone Alicia knew. A friend or a neighbor."

Or possibly Georgia, JayBee thought. Could Georgia have hit herself on the head to divert suspicion? It would take a brave woman to strike herself with a piece of wood hard enough to cause memory damage. Knowing that Travis had been in love with her, JayBee didn't speculate out loud.

"I wonder if T.J. would recognize the woman, if he saw her again," Travis mused.

"I don't want that boy involved in anything dangerous!" Angel said.

Travis frowned at her. "Of course I wouldn't involve my son in anything dangerous."

"Maybe you could take him to a school board meeting," JayBee said. "Almost everyone in town turns up at those."

"But what reason would he have for being there?" asked Angel. "That might alert the murderer that the child was looking for her."

"Well, I'm glad you made cake, anyway," Travis said. "Otherwise we wouldn't have known that T.J. saw the murderer."

Angel sighed. "It was good, but not quite as good as the cake JayBee brought home from school that one day. I was trying for something like that, but I didn't quite get it."

"That cake from school…" JayBee said slowly. "That was the day after the murder. Wasn't it? Remember, we talked about the murder when I came home? You'd heard about it at the grocery store."

"That's right!" Angel said. "Could it have possibly been the same cake?"

"Long shot," Travis commented. "Plenty of people make chocolate cake." But he looked thoughtful. "I had some awfully good cake at Charlotte Scott's house."

"It couldn't be Charlotte. She's a friend of mine," JayBee said.

"What were you doing at her house?" Angel asked Travis. JayBee glared at her sister, knowing she was trying to cause trouble.

"I went to talk to her about Alicia. Someone told me they didn't like each other."

"I can't believe Charlotte would kill anyone," JayBee insisted. "She's just not that kind of person."

"I agree," Travis said. "I don't know her as well as you do, but she's been a client of mine for years. She doesn't strike me as the murderous type, even though she didn't like my stepmother."

"Easy enough to settle it," Angel said. "Introduce T.J. to her and then ask him if she was the woman he saw at his grandmother's house."

"T.J. is the key," Travis agreed. "We've got to think of some way for him to meet some of the women in town. Of course, even if he can point someone out, proving it will be another matter. I wouldn't want T.J. to have to testify in court."

"I don't want him doing anything dangerous," Angel said again.

"Whatever you feel for the boy, it doesn't hold a candle to what I feel." Travis thumped his chest with his fist. "I'm his blood relative—his father."

"Fine," Angel said, "but what a man thinks is dangerous might be a lot different from what a woman thinks."

"Let's not argue," JayBee said. "It's time for T.J. to go to bed, anyway." She opened the screen door, looking over to where he was sitting quietly in the living room. "T.J.! Bedtime!"

He put the magazine down and came over to the porch. "Do I have to go to bed while Daddy's here?"

"I'm leaving in a minute," Travis said, getting up.

"Come on, let's get you ready for bed," JayBee told him.

The boy looked from JayBee to his father. "I want Daddy to read me a story."

Travis looked touched to be called upon.

"Okay," JayBee said, "but only if you get into your pajamas very quickly. It's already half an hour past your bedtime."

"Goody!" said T.J., making a run for the stairs. Queenie raced him to the top. Travis and JayBee followed at a more leisurely pace.

* * * * *

JayBee shut the door softly. "There, that's done." She sighed with relief. "He was pretty good tonight. Sometimes it takes him a long time to settle down. That Gina and Ray, they didn't have a regular bedtime for him. I think he was allowed to stay up as long as he wanted."

Travis caught her hand, stopping her before she started down the stairs. "I want a goodnight kiss, too."

Turning, she put her arms around his neck. He pulled her tightly against him, then bent to her lips. As he kissed her, his hands went to her backside. She moaned as she felt him caressing her, pressing her against his pelvis.

"We'd better stop," she murmured. She kept her arms around his neck, but turned her face away so he'd have to stop kissing her. It didn't help, his lips moved to her neck and then nibbled her earlobe. She didn't want to be so aroused when she knew nothing could come of it this evening. It was too public in this house, with Angel downstairs and the child next door to her bedroom.

"When are we going to see each other again?" he asked.

"See each other, or sleep together?"

"Both, I hope." He raised his head, stopping what he was doing long enough to look into her eyes. "I was thinking...I'd like to have T.J. come for an overnight visit this weekend. He needs to start getting used to being at my house. You should come too, so he has a familiar person there. He can have the guest room and you can spend the night with me."

That was a very tempting thought, spending the night in Travis' bed. She wanted to make love again…lie in bed talking to him…fall asleep with him holding her. "What about Angel? She won't want to stay here alone."

"Doesn't she have a friend she can stay with?"

"Maybe. Or she could go stay with Dad—"

From downstairs, Angel called up excitedly, "Hey, Travis! Your father's on television!"

They hurried down the stairs. Channel 8 news was recapping the story of the murder, with shots from the aftermath of Robert Kellman's arraignment. They showed the past footage of Robert Kellman being taken away after pleading not guilty.

They switched to a live report, prosecutor Jim Percy on the steps of the Tecumseh County courthouse.

As cameras jostled for position and microphones were thrust in his face, Jim Percy announced, "Today, Robert Kellman changed his plea to guilty in the voluntary manslaughter of his wife."

Chapter Twenty

"I still believe my dad is innocent."

No matter how many times he said it, it didn't change the fact that Robert Kellman had decided to plead guilty to the crime.

Travis let himself in the back door of his house. His stomach was churning. He'd felt sick ever since seeing Jim Percy's smug face on television.

Thank goodness JayBee had been standing next to him when he heard the news at her house. Her calmness had helped steady him. "Travis, I don't understand," she'd said, putting her hand lightly on his arm. "Why is your father doing this?"

The concern in her face had made him feel slightly better. "I don't know," he'd answered, "but you better believe I'm going to find out."

As he came into the kitchen, the phone was ringing. Snatching it up, he was startled to hear the frantic voice of Louisa Fairfield. "Travis! Did you see the prosecutor on television?"

"Yes, I saw him."

"Why is Robert pleading guilty? I talked to him last week and he was planning to stand trial. He kept saying since he was innocent, he was sure he would be acquitted!" To Travis' discomfort, he heard Louisa start to cry.

"I'm not sure what's going on. This was a complete shock to me, too."

"He couldn't have done it! Robert would never have murdered his wife!"

"I still believe my dad is innocent," Travis said, in the most reassuring tone he could muster. "And furthermore, I think I have a good lead to the real murderer."

Louisa sniffed back her tears. "Really? What?"

Travis hesitated. He considered her a long shot to be the murderer...but still, there was a slight chance. Thinking about her story and the time frame she had outlined, he wondered if she could have gone to Alicia's house, killed her, then taken a flight to Akron in time to meet Robert at the hotel.

But would Alicia have let her in?

Perhaps...if Louisa had said something about being Robert Kellman's mistress. Maybe Alicia's curiosity would have outweighed her caution.

But he couldn't quite imagine Louisa showing up with cake.

"I don't want to discuss it on the phone," Travis said. "Do you think you could come over tomorrow evening?" Somehow he had to arrange it so that T.J. could get a good look at her.

"Tomorrow? I have a meeting in the evening, so it would have to be later. How about nine o'clock?"

Damn. He knew Angel and JayBee never let the boy stay up that late. But he couldn't very well uninvite Louisa now.

Maybe he could take her picture. He'd make some excuse, perhaps tell her he wanted his father to have it, then he'd have a photograph he could show to his son.

"That's fine." Travis gave her the address. "Come to the back door."

After he got off the phone, he put out food and water for the cats and walked restlessly through the house. He hoped that Louisa wasn't the murderer.

But she had a better motive than anyone else.

Perhaps Louisa had hoped that with Alicia out of the way, she could become Robert's third wife. She hadn't sounded entirely happy when she talked about her position as head of the girls' school. Maybe being the pampered wife of a wealthy, retired surgeon sounded a lot better to her.

He should have done more to check her story.

Louisa claimed she had driven to Akron, but suppose she had killed Alicia around ten o'clock. Would she have had time to get to the airport, take the flight, then reach the hotel by midnight? It seemed like it might be possible.

He should have told Austin about her and had him check the flights to Akron. Travis frowned, knowing that he hadn't wanted to suspect Louisa because he liked her.

He still needed to check out other possibilities. If the murderer wasn't Louisa, perhaps it was someone whose motive he didn't know. Someone who had a grudge against Alicia for some reason. He had to think of some way for his son to meet some of the people in town. JayBee's idea of taking him to a school board meeting…now, that had been on the right track. It had to be something like that, where T.J. could see a lot of people, but it also had to be something that wouldn't make the murderer suspicious.

He sat at his desk and took a pad of paper out of the drawer. The box of election flyers that Ralph Peterson had brought over were still sitting on top of the desk. That gave him an idea…

The back door banged. "Travis?" It was Peter's voice.

"In the parlor," he called, turning his chair.

"Jesus, it's dark out and that back door's standing wide open!" Peter came through the dining room into the parlor. "Don't you lock your doors?"

"I lock up when I go to bed," Travis told him impatiently. "Did you come about Dad?"

"That's right. I've been trying to reach you all evening. Where the hell have you been?"

"Visiting my son."

Peter frowned. "Oh, yeah, I forgot about the kid." He sat in the worn velvet chair, pushing his hair back wearily. For the first time, Travis noticed his brother had faint lines on his forehead. Well, Pete was four years older than himself…thirty-two. And these last few weeks had been hard on all of them.

Peter leaned forward intently. "Dad called me about seven tonight. I was able to go down there and talk to him."

"Did he tell you he was going to plead guilty?"

Peter nodded. "He wanted to tell me about it before he talked to Percy again. He said Percy had offered him a deal. Plead to voluntary manslaughter, no possibility of the death penalty."

"I don't understand. What's the deal? What does Dad get out of it?"

Peter sighed. "Percy was going to charge Katie with hindering prosecution. Because of her false confession. That's a felony, Travis."

Travis stroked his beard, thinking about Peter's words. He had been afraid there would be repercussions from Katie's confession…but he hadn't imagined this.

"That bastard Percy…he talked to Dad for a couple hours today. Painted quite a picture of what the Marysville Women's Correctional Facility is like. Talked about some of the things that go on there. Mistreatment by correctional officers, rapes, fights between the prisoners…Dad was in tears when he told me about it. 'I can't let my little Princess go through that,' he kept saying. So finally Percy made it clear that he would drop all the charges against Katie, as long as Dad would plead to voluntary manslaughter."

Travis closed his eyes in pain. How miserably ironic, that Katie's attempted sacrifice, instead of saving her father, had led to worse problems. Standing trial, their father had had a chance of being acquitted. Pleading guilty would condemn him to years in prison…or the suicide he had claimed to be considering.

"Isn't there anything we can do?" Travis asked. "We could send Katie out of the country—she's always wanted to go to Paris. Then Dad could renege. He hasn't changed his plea in court yet, right?"

Peter shook his head. "I tried to bring up something like that, but Dad wouldn't hear of it. 'I gave my word,' he told me."

The two brothers sat silent for a few long moments.

Then Peter said bitterly, "I hate to have our name dragged through the mud like this. At least with Dad going to trial, I could hold up my head and say, 'My father didn't do it! It's all a mistake!' But what am I supposed to say now? Everyone's going to think I'm the son of a murderer!"

"Maybe you'd better worry about what this means to Dad instead of thinking about yourself."

"And maybe you won't be so high-and-mighty when your practice goes downhill," Peter retorted. "Don't you think some of your clients will leave because your father's a murderer?"

"I don't need clients like that. I'm sure some of them will stick by me. And if they don't, I can always go practice elsewhere." But his mind shied away from the thought of leaving Creekside Farm.

"Fine!" Peter said, standing. "Go on living in your dream world! But I'm telling you, this is a fucking tragedy!"

"It's been a tragedy all along," Travis answered, sadness heavy in his voice.

* * * * *

"My sister made this cake last night," JayBee said, cutting it into small pieces and putting the pieces on paper plates at the teachers' lunch table. "It came out pretty well, but not as good as that cake someone brought in a few weeks ago." She waited, hoping someone would volunteer that they had made the cake. "If anyone knows who made that, let me know. Angel wants the recipe."

None of the eight teachers at the table said anything, except Bruce Souter. "Looks good," he said enthusiastically, taking a piece.

Later, Charlotte Scott stopped by JayBee's small office near the girls' gymnasium. "She didn't say anything when you asked about the recipe," Charlotte said, looking puzzled. "But I think I know who made that cake you were talking about."

* * * * *

Travis left work the next day around four o'clock and headed over to Angel's house. To his disappointment, JayBee was still at school. He explained his plan to Angel.

"I don't know," she said doubtfully. "Do you really think T.J. can handle it?"

"I think so," Travis said. "If I explain it the right way."

"Very well. Have him back by six o'clock."

T.J. seemed pleased to go for a ride in Travis' truck. He was even more pleased when Travis parked in front of his parents' house and brought the Radio Flyer red wagon out of the truck's flatbed. "This is for you, T.J.," Travis said.

"Oh, boy, a wagon!"

"I thought I'd take you on a ride around the block."

"Goody!" the boy answered, clambering into the wagon.

"We're going to play a game," Travis told him. "We're going to go from house to house and give everyone a flyer." He lifted the box of election flyers out of the flatbed and put it in the wagon behind the boy. Kneeling down beside the wagon, he looked directly into his son's eyes. "Now, here's the game. We're going to look for the lady you saw at Grandma Kellman's house. Remember, the lady who brought Grandma the cake?"

T.J. nodded, his dark eyes intent on his father's face.

"If you see the lady, don't tell me in front of her. We're going to have a secret code word."

T.J. looked excited. "What's the code word?"

"The code word is 'hungry'. So if you see her, you say something like 'Daddy, I'm hungry'. All right?"

"Okay."

Travis started pulling the wagon to the next house, which was a peach-colored split level. When he'd been a child, an old lady had lived there, but now he had the vague idea that it had been bought by a young couple.

He pulled the wagon up the long driveway, picked up one of the flyers and went to the door. T.J. jumped out of the wagon and followed him.

The woman who answered the door had a baby in her arms and a toddler clutching her pants leg. Travis couldn't help feeling bad about disturbing her during a busy time of day, but he smiled and went into his spiel about running for school board.

She interrupted, asking him, "Is that your little boy?"

"Yes, this is my son, T.J." Travis put his hand on the boy's shoulder.

"So you'll be sending him to the Priam schools?"

"Yes, ma'am. Next year he'll be starting kindergarten."

"All right, I'll take one of your flyers." She opened the screen door a half-inch.

That wasn't too bad. Travis and T.J. went back to the wagon as the woman closed the door.

"T.J., are you hungry?" Travis asked, bending to peer into the boy's face.

T.J. grinned. "No, Daddy, I'm not hungry." As he sat down again in the wagon, he said, "I like this game."

Hope you still like it after another ten houses.

Well, he would have to take it a little at a time. A few houses a day, so that the child wouldn't get bored with it.

An hour later, they had covered only eight more houses, making it halfway around the block to the street behind his parents' house. At two houses, no one had answered, so Travis had merely left flyers. The old woman at the corner house was Mrs. Oliver, who had known him as a boy. She fixed Travis with a gimlet eye and sternly told T.J. to go sit in the wagon.

"Go ahead, T.J.," Travis said. "Are you hungry, son?"

"No, Daddy." T.J. headed back to the wagon.

"Travis, where did this child come from?" Mrs. Oliver demanded. "I know you're not married!"

"T.J. is my son from a prior relationship."

"You ought to be ashamed of yourself! Well, I always told Alicia you would turn out badly! I haven't forgotten how you and your brother put rotten eggs in my mailbox a few years ago!"

"Twenty years ago!" he protested. "I'm very sorry about that." Hell, he'd been sorry twenty years ago, when his father grounded him for two weeks.

She glared at him and slammed the door shut.

Well, that's one vote I won't get. Checking his watch, he went back to the wagon. It was twenty to six, almost time to start heading back. Maybe they could get two or three more houses done.

The next house was a brick ranch belonging to Chief MacReedy and his wife. Travis noted that the bushes and shrubs were cut with military precision.

Travis and T.J. went to the door. Travis let his son ring the doorbell. After a few moments, Denise came to the door.

"Hi, there," Travis said, a little uneasy with her as he remembered their last conversation. "Since I'm running for school board, I'm trying to talk to everyone in the village and pass out my flyers."

Denise bent down, speaking directly to T.J. "And who are you, young man?"

"I'm T.J." Tugging at Travis' sleeve, he said, "Daddy! I'm hungry!"

Travis' head jerked as he turned to look at his son. He was so shocked that he forgot to conceal his surprise. "Are you sure?"

"Uh-huh."

Travis turned back to Denise, thinking that his son had to be mistaken. Or perhaps T.J. had forgotten the terms of the game and he really was hungry. Denise was looking at the boy with narrowed eyes.

"T.J.'s my son," Travis said hastily. "I don't know if Austin mentioned him."

"Yes, I heard all about it. Poor boy, Austin said he was at his grandma's house the night she was murdered."

"Yes, but fortunately he was asleep when it happened."

"That's something to be thankful for, then."

"Absolutely," Travis said. "Well, I'm going to have to get going. It's time for dinner—as you heard, T.J.'s hungry."

"Aren't you going to give me one of your flyers?"

Travis, with an insincere smile, handed her a flyer.

Good Lord, Kellman, you'd better stay off the stage. You're certainly a failure as an actor.

"Aren't we going to any more houses, Daddy?" T.J. asked as they started back around the end of the block, heading toward the truck.

"No. The game's over for today."

It wasn't until they were both belted into their seats in the truck that Travis asked, "Was that the lady who came to Grandma's house?"

"Uh huh."

"T.J., tell me again what she did when she came to Grandma's house."

"I dunno." T.J. seemed to be bored with the whole topic.

Travis frowned, thinking that even if he could get Jim Percy to listen to T.J., the boy would not make a good witness in court. "Did she give Grandma some cake?"

The little boy nodded.

"What kind?"

"Chocolate."

"And then she petted Monique?"

"Yes. Are we going to eat dinner now?"

"Just answer one more question, T.J. Are you absolutely sure it was that lady?"

"I told you."

JayBee was sitting on the front steps with Queenie when Travis drove up to the house. The dog bounded forward, thrilled to be reunited with T.J. JayBee looked up eagerly and ran to meet Travis as he got out of the truck.

"I have such news!" she told him. "I found out who brought the chocolate cake to school!"

He put his hands on her shoulders. "Let me guess. Denise MacReedy?"

JayBee's mouth opened in a little round "o". Her eyes were huge, boring into his. "Yes! How did you know?"

* * * * *

Travis was so intent on thinking about what had been revealed that evening that he didn't even notice Puff winding back and forth between his legs as he walked into the parlor. Sitting at his desk, he opened his laptop and booted it up.

He had stayed at JayBee's for a few hours, eating dinner with the sisters again. They had put T.J. to bed early and then talked about Denise MacReedy.

Angel had argued that until they obtained hard evidence, such as the shoes that Georgia had found, or the murder weapon, T.J.'s testimony would not be enough to convict Denise. "In any case, just because she brought cake over to your stepmother's house doesn't mean she killed her," Angel had pointed out.

"Then why didn't she ever say she was over there that night?" Travis had retorted. "That's evidence and she withheld it! If she came after my father was home, that proves Alicia was still alive when my dad left. But Denise never spoke up."

"I don't know what to think!" JayBee had said. "We don't have a motive for Denise, either. Did she have some reason to dislike Alicia?"

Travis had thrown up his hands. "Not as far as I know."

All of them had agreed that accusing the police chief's wife was a tricky proposition.

Travis began typing a list of everything he knew that pointed to Denise. The shoes Georgia had found. His son's identification. The cake at Alicia's house. Put together, it didn't look like much.

What would be the best way to use this evidence? Convince his father to plead not guilty and then use it as part of his defense? Take it to Jim Percy? He shook his head as he thought about that. Jim Percy and Austin MacReedy seemed to be hand in glove. Would Percy be willing to consider Austin's wife as a suspect?

Maybe it would be better to go to the police in Remus. Could he convince the Remus police chief that Denise had committed the murder? It was hard to imagine that working. The Remus chief frequently worked with MacReedy. Would he be willing to go to a judge and get a search warrant? Would a surprise search of MacReedy's home even yield hard evidence? If Denise really was the murderer, she had had plenty of time to get rid of the shoes and the murder weapon.

Did Austin know? That was the most important question of all. Had he been engaged in a cover-up of his wife's crime all during these events, arresting Robert Kellman in order to set up a smoke screen? Or had he acted in an upright fashion all along, making the arrest because he truly believed Robert was guilty? Travis didn't know how to answer that.

He looked up sharply as he heard the kitchen door bang shut.

* * * * *

JayBee sat down on the couch and switched on the television. Lying back, she put her feet up, thinking about Denise MacReedy. It was hard to believe that someone she worked with every day, ate lunch with, spoke to in the teachers' lounge, was actually a murderer.

And yet, she didn't know Denise very well. She had never become real friends with her, the way she had with Charlotte Scott.

JayBee jumped and Angel sprang to her feet as they heard a loud, metallic crash outside.

"What was that?" JayBee rushed to the window. She couldn't see anything except the quiet street.

"It sounded like it was right in our driveway!" Angel answered.

JayBee went to the back door. "Someone's car hit our Corolla!" she exclaimed, looking out into the driveway. She couldn't see the make of the car, but it seemed to be a small, dark American car, perhaps a Ford Focus. Its bright lights were on.

JayBee threw the deadbolt, opened the door and rushed down the back stairs. Her first thought was that the rowdy college students from next door had gotten drunk and pulled into the wrong driveway.

There was no one in the car that had rear-ended their Corolla. As JayBee peered in the passenger window of the strange car, a rustling came out of the darkness. Then she felt something long and cold against her cheek.

"Hello, Juliet."

* * * * *

"Hello, Travis." Denise MacReedy stood in the archway between the parlor and the dining room. Her pink blouse and gold bracelets contrasted bizarrely with the shotgun she held in her right hand. Her left held something else, something concealed in plastic.

Oh, God! Does she really know how to shoot that thing? Can I rush her? Travis took a few steps forward. Denise moved back, laid the plastic bundle on the dining room table and raised the shotgun.

"Don't come one step closer!" she warned him. "Austin taught me how to shoot. I can drop a deer at thirty yards and I won't hesitate to shoot you!"

"What do you want?" His thoughts were whirling furiously. Why hadn't he foreseen this? No time for recriminations now. How could he get out of it? Was she planning to kill him?

"I don't think it's fair for a good man like Robert Kellman to go to prison for something I did. He saved my life when I had cancer. But you—I don't care what happens to you. You've become a problem, the way you've been snooping around about the murder." She waved the shotgun. "Sit down. Get some paper."

"Why? What do you want?" His mouth was so dry he was finding it difficult to speak.

"You're going to write a letter confessing to the murder of Alicia. Then you're going to kill yourself with this." She held up the plastic parcel she had brought. "Look! It's the knife I used to kill Alicia. So everyone will believe your confession and they'll release your father."

Travis took deep breaths, trying to control the rapid beating of his heart. His mind raced through the possibilities. If he did as she asked, at least his father would be free. If he refused, he knew Denise would shoot him anyway.

But if he wrote out a confession, everyone would believe he killed Alicia. His son would grow up thinking his father had been a murderer.

Even JayBee might believe it.

"I won't do it. And if you shoot me, people will realize there's a murderer on the loose. So what good will that do?"

"You will write out the confession. I sent Bradley Morrow over to JayBee's house to kidnap your son. If you write the confession, Bradley will release him. If not, he'll take that boy away and no one around here will ever see him again."

Denise looked intently at him, then grinned at his reaction. "Oh, you were so concerned the other day," she said mockingly. "You thought I was some poor, deluded middle-aged woman in love with Bradley, didn't you? No! I just thought he might be of use to me."

"Why did you kill Alicia?" Travis asked, unable to deny the question he'd been thinking about all evening.

"She was having an affair with my husband. I wanted to teach them both a lesson."

Travis frowned, wondering what was she talking about. Was it true? Had both Katie and Alicia been sleeping with Austin? "How did you find that out?"

"Ever since Austin had another affair, a few years ago, I've had my ways of checking up on him. I got into his e-mail and saw the messages he and 'a-k-kellman' were sending to each other."

A-k-kellman! So she didn't know that was Katie's e-mail, not Alicia's.

Travis did not correct her.

"Denise, I can't believe you're doing this!"

"You'll believe it when Bradley gets over here with your son," she told him, her eyes boring into his. "Maybe you'll be willing to write that confession when I hold the gun to your boy's head."

* * * * *

"Put your hands behind your back, Juliet. No tricks, now."

He slid the barrel of the gun up the side of her face, so that she could see it out of the corner of her eye. It was a nine millimeter, the kind the cops in town carried.

She put her hands behind her back. He was going to tie her hands. Could she do something while he fumbled with the rope?

In an instant, he had snapped handcuffs over her wrists. "Walk ahead of me. We're going inside."

"No, Bradley. Please! Do whatever you want to me, but don't hurt Angel!"

He chuckled, a grotesque sound in the otherwise quiet night. "Would I hurt my own pretty little wife? Don't be silly, Juliet." He poked her in the back with the gun. "Move!"

Angel came to the door, asking, "Who hit the Corolla?" just as the two of them came up the steps. When she saw Bradley, she gasped and backed away.

"It was me, dear. I had to get one of you outside somehow."

Angel clutched the kitchen table. All the color had drained from her face.

Bradley herded them into the living room. "Kneel on the floor!" he told JayBee. When she hesitated, he narrowed his eyes. "Better do what I say or I'll shoot one of you right now."

Slowly she knelt, disgusted with her own helplessness.

Bradley smirked at her. "You certainly look good in that position, Juliet. If I had time, I'd make you give me a blowjob." He smirked. "Maybe another time, sweetie."

Just try it. Watch me bite it off.

She turned her face away, hating to remember that they had been lovers once.

"I brought you a lovely piece of jewelry," Bradley said to Angel. He produced another pair of handcuffs. Fastening one end to her right wrist, he attached the other around one of the wooden posts of the railings that led upstairs.

Bradley turned back to JayBee. "Get up, Juliet. I'm not going to leave you downstairs to get into mischief." He motioned her to get in front of him.

"How did you find out where we live?" she demanded.

"I have friends in high places," he answered.

Denise! thought JayBee. Was she involved in this somehow?

JayBee stood and went slowly up the stairs, feeling the barrel of the gun poking her back. If she could only get the drop on him—startle him somehow—do something to fight back…

"What do you want upstairs?" she asked.

"Well, Juliet," he said, in a chillingly conversational tone, "you and your sister must be punished for the way you treated me. I figure that nothing I can do to you or Angel would bother you as much as hurting that child. So I think I'll take him with me." They were at the top of the stairs now. He grabbed her arm, turning her and bringing his face menacingly close to hers. "And you two can spend the rest of your lives wondering what I've done with him. Maybe I've killed him…or maybe I've sold him to some people who really, really love children…if you know what I mean." He shook his head, mock-sadly. "You meet some unsavory people in prison, unfortunately."

One thing she knew, she wasn't going to let him leave the house with T.J. No matter what.

T.J.'s door was closed.

"Go ahead!" Bradley ordered, waving the gun.

"I can't open the door with my hands behind my back!"

He found the hall light switch and turned it on. "All right, I'm going to open the door," he said. "Stand back. If you try anything, I'll put a bullet through that kid's head, right in front of your eyes."

JayBee bit her lip. She was behind him now. Could she karate kick him in the balls? But he had the gun raised, all ready to shoot. T.J. was asleep, defenseless. She couldn't do anything that would risk the boy's life.

Slowly and noiselessly, Bradley turned the doorknob. Once the door was ajar, he kicked it hard. It opened with a bang. T.J. cried out, struggling to sit up, his hands going to his frightened face.

Queenie sprang off the bed, leaping at Bradley with a snarl.

Now! JayBee swiftly swung her leg up in a high kick, getting Bradley squarely in the testicles. He doubled over, still clutching the gun.

"T.J.! Run downstairs!" JayBee screamed. She kicked at Bradley's hand but missed and fell, off-balance because of the handcuffs.

Queenie danced around Bradley, barking furiously. He hit at her and she darted forward, snapping at him.

T.J. ran out of the room. JayBee waited, hoping to hear his steps on the stairs. She kicked at Bradley from the floor, trying to bring him down. He took aim and fired at the dog, but the shot went wild, hitting the wall.

Raising up on her knees, JayBee head-butted Bradley in the back of the legs. He staggered and fell as she struggled to her feet. She kicked his hand. This time her aim was true. With a yell of pain, he released the gun, which clattered to the floor. JayBee lunged at it, moving it out of Bradley's reach with her foot.

Queenie went for Bradley's throat. He punched her in the muzzle. Yelping with pain, she came back for more.

T.J. appeared in the doorway with the phone in his hand. "I called 9-1-1! I said there's a bad man here with a gun!"

Bradley made a grab for the boy, but T.J. slid by him and ran to another room.

"You haven't seen the last of me, you bitch!" Bradley snarled at JayBee. Turning, he ran down the stairs, Queenie in hot pursuit.

"T.J.!" JayBee called frantically. "Bring me the phone!"

"I'm scared!" His voice sounded muffled. Was he hiding in the closet again?

"T.J., please!" Was Bradley working with Denise? Was something going on at Travis' house?

* * * * *

Please, God. Save my boy. Save JayBee. Please!

Somehow Travis felt a thin thread of hope. JayBee was strong and clever. He remembered how she'd helped him when he fought Ray. Maybe, somehow, she would save herself and his boy.

Denise checked her watch. "Damn it, Bradley was supposed to be here by now!" She looked at the laptop on Travis' desk. "Maybe I should just shoot you and then type your confession myself," she mused. "I could make it look like a suicide."

"The police will see through that," Travis scoffed.

"Oh, I know exactly what to do to make it convincing," she answered. "I'm not a cop's wife for nothing." She raised the shotgun.

A knocking came from the kitchen. Denise froze. Travis held his breath.

"Bradley?" Denise called.

"Travis?" Louisa's voice came from the kitchen. Denise half-turned. Travis threw himself forward in a long dive across the floor.

Whirling around, Denise fired at him.

"Louisa, run!" Travis shouted, as his shoulder exploded with pain.

Denise looked frantically from Travis to Louisa, who was standing in the dining room doorway. She raised the shotgun, then hesitated as Louisa ran back into the kitchen. Backing away, Denise turned and fled through the kitchen.

Travis staggered to his feet, clutching his left shoulder with his right hand. Blood poured down his arm. A siren wailed louder and louder in the dark.

"What's going on?" Louisa demanded, coming to him. "My goodness, Travis, you're bleeding!"

"Louisa!" Travis panted, "Call 9-1-1! Send them to five-twelve Forest Avenue! Tell them it's urgent!" Grabbing a kitchen towel, he pressed it to his shoulder to stanch the bleeding.

He staggered outside. Denise was fumbling with her car keys, but raised her head as the police cruiser pulled up the driveway. She dropped her keys, glanced around frantically, then began running toward the barn.

The cruiser stopped with a jerk and Austin MacReedy stepped out. "Denise?" His voice rang with disbelief. "What's going on?"

"You bastard!" she screamed at him. "I tried to teach you a lesson! I tried!"

Officer Ming got out of the passenger side of the cruiser and dropped to her knees, taking up a firing stance.

"Hold your fire, it's my wife!" MacReedy ordered her.

"She's got a gun, sir!" Officer Ming protested.

"She's got my shotgun," MacReedy answered, in a tone of mild correction. "What's going on here? Denise, what are you doing?" He stepped toward his wife and she backed away.

"She shot me!" Travis shouted. "She killed Alicia because she thought you were having an affair with her!"

"That's right!" Denise screamed. "I killed her to teach you a lesson, you cheating bastard!"

"But Denise, I never went out with Alicia," MacReedy said, his tone reproving.

"I saw the e-mail!"

"It was Katie!" he admitted.

As though her name had conjured her presence, Katie's door opened. She stood still, a perfect silhouette in the lit doorway. "What's going on?" she called out.

Denise whirled around at this new interruption.

"Katie!" Travis shouted frantically. He tried to run toward Denise, but his steps were shaky. "Go back in! Now!"

Denise raised the shotgun.

"Denise! No!" MacReedy screamed.

Officer Ming pulled her trigger.

* * * * *

Travis had lost a lot of blood by the time the ambulance arrived. He couldn't see very well...everything had turned gray. He fought to stay conscious. "Is T.J. all right?" he kept asking. "What about JayBee? Where's Katie?" But no one answered him.

Finally, he smelled the chief's spearmint gum breath near his face. "I can't understand what you're mumbling, Trav,"

MacReedy told him. The chief's voice sounded thick. Did he have a cold? Travis wondered dreamily. "Your boy's fine. His foster mother and her sister are fine. Everyone's fine…except my poor Denise."

Chapter Twenty-One

Travis sat at the kitchen table, Blackie in his lap. The yellow gladiolas that JayBee had brought him in the hospital brightened the room and filled it with fragrance. He watched out the window for JayBee's damaged Corolla. Dinner was going to be served at seven o'clock, Katie had planned, but Travis had told JayBee to come at five because he wanted some time alone with her and T.J.

He had spent a day in the hospital after the shotgun pellets were removed. An unusually subdued JayBee had visited, sitting beside him and holding his hand. Not that he had had much to say either, dazed on pain medication.

He hoped that today she would have recovered some of her gaiety and spunk.

Hearing the car, he set Blackie down gently and went outside. He wanted JayBee to see him on his feet, looking relatively healthy.

Stepping out of the car, JayBee was a lovely sight in a dark-green velveteen dress, a simple gold locket around her slim neck. T.J. was dressed up too, wearing new oatmeal-colored jeans and a dark-blue shirt with buttons down the front.

"It's so good to see you up and about!" She ran to him and flung her arms around his waist. After kissing him, she drew back, gazing into his eyes. "You're so pale!"

"I'm doing fine. You two look great, all dressed up like that."

"I wanted us to make a good impression on your family."

T.J. was watching them with curious eyes. "We're going to stay overnight!" he told Travis.

"I know." Travis bent and took his son in his arms, giving him a hug for the first time. The child stood unresisting as JayBee watched them with a smile.

"Why did you do that?" the boy asked.

"Because I'm your daddy and I love you."

T.J. seemed to be thinking about that. Travis waited, wondering what would come out of the child's mouth next.

"Did you know a bad man came to our house?" he asked Travis. "He had a gun!"

"I heard. And you were a brave boy."

T.J. nodded. "I called 9-1-1, just like Angel showed me."

Queenie was busy sniffing the yard for a good spot to urinate. When she finished, Travis called her over. "You're a very good dog, Queenie." She wagged her tail, watching with interest as Travis pulled a Milkbone out of his pocket and gave it to her.

"I'll say," JayBee seconded Travis' opinion. "I cooked her a T-bone steak yesterday. I thought she deserved a reward for what she did."

Travis bent to stroke Queenie's head, trying to control his trembling mouth. Damn, he had been emotional all day.

It had to be the pain medication.

Straightening, he kissed JayBee's cheek, wishing he could stand there for a few hours, just holding her and his son. And Queenie as well. Keeping them all safe.

"I went out this morning and got you a present," Travis said to T.J. as they went inside.

"Oh, boy! What is it? Can I have it now?"

JayBee frowned. "Weren't you supposed to stay quiet today?" she asked Travis.

"I wanted him to have something to play with while he was here," Travis answered, handing the boy a bag from the local drugstore.

T.J. excitedly ripped the bag open, grinning when he found a jigsaw puzzle of a shiny Harley-Davidson motorcycle.

"What do you say?" JayBee prompted him.

"Thank you, Daddy! Can I put it together right now?"

JayBee's mouth twitched and she murmured to Travis, "That's a little advanced for a kid his age."

"We can help him with it." Travis pulled out a chair for T.J. at the dining room table. "Can you stay in here quietly while I talk to JayBee for a few minutes?" he asked. T.J. nodded, already absorbed in the puzzle.

Travis and JayBee went into the parlor and sat on the couch. She stroked the soft velvet surface with a bemused smile. "Old furniture is so nice. I wonder how many people have sat on this antique couch?"

Travis didn't want to talk about the furniture. "How's Angel doing?" JayBee had told him yesterday that Angel had gone to Dayton to stay with their father.

JayBee looked down, shaking her head. "I talked to her today. She's still very…I don't know what word to use."

"Upset?"

"Worse than upset. Disturbed." She sighed. "I was so glad when the police caught Bradley, but even that didn't seem to help Angel. She keeps saying, 'He'll just get out again.'"

"Hopefully not soon. Attempted kidnapping is a lot more serious than what he did before."

"That's what I keep telling Angel, but nothing seems to get through." She looked up at him. "How's Katie?"

"It's been tough on her. She keeps blaming herself for getting involved with Austin in the first place. 'Blame Denise,' I told her, but she won't listen." He frowned, remembering his sister's distraught, tear-stained face. "I thought it would be too much for her to do this dinner, but she insisted. She says we need a special dinner for Dad getting out of jail."

"We need a special dinner because we're all still alive," JayBee murmured.

Travis reached out and took both her hands, wincing a little as he moved his shoulder. "JayBee…" He squeezed her hands, uncertain of how to express what he felt. "I've never met a woman I admire so much. I think you're the bravest person I know."

She raised her eyebrows. "Thanks, but I didn't feel brave at the time. I just felt mad."

He gazed into those big brown eyes. "I could court you for a long time. I want to learn everything about you…but I already know I love you. I want to devote the rest of our lives to finding out about each other." He took a deep breath. "JayBee, will you marry me?"

She looked back at him, her eyes filling with tears. "Yes," she said, her voice huskier than he'd ever heard it, "as long as you understand…it can't be right away."

"Why not?"

Her expression seemed to beg him to understand. "Because of Angel. I'd love to get married immediately and come live here with you…and T.J…but I can't just leave Angel in the lurch. She's going to need me to be with her while she's getting over this." Her mouth crooked up in a half-smile. "I know she's the older sister…but it seems like I've always taken care of her."

"All right, honey. I guess I understand." He reached into his pocket, bringing out a small velvet box. "If you'd rather have something different, just tell me. But I thought—I hoped—that maybe you'd wear this engagement ring." He opened the box and lifted the ring out. The diamond flashed in the late afternoon sunlight.

"It's beautiful!" Then she hesitated. "Did Georgia ever wear it?"

He shook his head. "She didn't want something 'used'." He took a deep breath. "This ring—and her china—are the only things I have left from my real mother."

JayBee smiled and held out her hand. He slid it on her finger and turned her hand, watching the ring catch the light. He had never tried to give it to Beth. Georgia hadn't wanted it.

Now finally, the right person had it.

She leaned forward, putting her hand on his unwounded shoulder and they shared a tender kiss. "I can't wait for tonight," she whispered, looking deeply into his eyes.

He knew exactly how she felt.

Travis called T.J. into the room. JayBee leaned toward him, eyes bright, lips softly smiling. "T.J., how would you like to have me for your mom?"

"My foster mom? Instead of Angel?"

"Not exactly. I'm going to marry your Daddy, so then I'll be your mom."

The boy smiled. "Goody!" he exclaimed. JayBee laughed and hugged him.

"I have to work on my puzzle." T.J. slid away from JayBee's embrace.

"I wonder how much of this he'll remember when he's older," JayBee said, looking after the boy fondly. "He'll probably forget all about his poor grandmother."

Travis nodded. He was so happy tonight, he could even think of Alicia with nothing more than regret.

The opportunity had been there. If either he or his stepmother had been slightly different people, perhaps she could have taken his real mother's place, the way JayBee would take Beth's place for his little son.

But that had never happened and now it never would.

May she rest in peace.

A knock sounded. "I'll bet that's my dad," Travis said, getting up. JayBee rose too, nervously smoothing the front of her dress and pushing her hair back.

Robert stood at the front door, immaculate in a light gray suit. The two men were silent for a long moment. How often had Travis endured his father's searching eyes, always aware that the older man found him lacking, a poor second to his brilliant older brother.

Gazing at Travis as though seeing him for the first time, Robert smiled, a look of wonder and pride coming into his eyes. Travis smiled too and opened the screen door, his heart too full to speak.

Why an electronic book?

We live in the Information Age—an exciting time in the history of human civilization, in which technology rules supreme and continues to progress in leaps and bounds every minute of every day. For a multitude of reasons, more and more avid literary fans are opting to purchase e-books instead of paper books. The question from those not yet initiated into the world of electronic reading is simply: *Why?*

1. ***Price.*** An electronic title at Ellora's Cave Publishing and Cerridwen Press runs anywhere from 40% to 75% less than the cover price of the exact same title in paperback format. Why? Basic mathematics and cost. It is less expensive to publish an e-book (no paper and printing, no warehousing and shipping) than it is to publish a paperback, so the savings are passed along to the consumer.
2. ***Space.*** Running out of room in your house for your books? That is one worry you will never have with electronic books. For a low one-time cost, you can purchase a handheld device specifically designed for e-reading. Many e-readers have large, convenient screens for viewing. Better yet, hundreds of titles can be stored within your new library—on a single microchip. There are a variety of e-readers from different manufacturers. You can also read e-books on your PC or laptop computer. (Please note that

Ellora's Cave does not endorse any specific brands. You can check our websites at www.ellorascave.com or www.cerridwenpress.com for information we make available to new consumers.)

3. ***Mobility.*** Because your new e-library consists of only a microchip within a small, easily transportable e-reader, your entire cache of books can be taken with you wherever you go.
4. ***Personal Viewing Preferences.*** Are the words you are currently reading too small? Too large? Too... ANNOYING? Paperback books cannot be modified according to personal preferences, but e-books can.
5. ***Instant Gratification.*** Is it the middle of the night and all the bookstores near you are closed? Are you tired of waiting days, sometimes weeks, for bookstores to ship the novels you bought? Ellora's Cave Publishing sells instantaneous downloads twenty-four hours a day, seven days a week, every day of the year. Our webstore is never closed. Our e-book delivery system is 100% automated, meaning your order is filled as soon as you pay for it.

Those are a few of the top reasons why electronic books are replacing paperbacks for many avid readers.

As always, Ellora's Cave and Cerridwen Press welcome your questions and comments. We invite you to email us at Comments@ellorascave.com or write to us directly at Ellora's Cave Publishing Inc., 1056 Home Avenue, Akron, OH 44310-3502.